EVIL FOR GOOD

ELI COLT BOOK THREE

WILL MARLER

JOIN LEGACY READERS CLUB

Will Marler's Legacy Readers Club members get free books and unique items to accompany the novels.

Members are always the first to hear about Will's new book launches and publications.

At the end of the book there is more information on how you can sign up and receive a free gift.

PROLOGUE

Thursday, May 23

Kiara Johnson ripped her arm free from her twin sister's grip. Her heart pounded beneath the red glow of the *Teen Vibe Karaoke* sign. Overhead, the neon pulsed like an unheeded warning light. Aaliyah's eyes sparkled with a familiar fire—the kind that always spelled trouble. The kind that burned bright and wild, that dragged Kiara to a chaos she never wanted and rarely escaped.

Aaliyah rolled her eyes skyward. "Come on, Ki. We didn't ride all this way to chicken out now."

Catching their reflection in the darkened window of the karaoke studio, Kiara sighed. Two sixteen-year-old faces carved from the same mold rippled in the glass. Mama's high cheekbones, warm brown skin, and eyes like amber caught in candle light. Even their wrinkled St. Catherine's uniforms matched—white blouses half-tucked into blue skirts from the long bus ride. Kiara narrowed her eyes as she glanced at her phone's screen—7:26 PM—four hours before Mama's night shift ended. Four hours to ace her geometry study. Four hours to get Aaliyah home before their lie unraveled. One slip—one failed final—and her Auburn scholarship dream would disappear.

"I don't know, Aaliyah. Maybe we shouldn't—" But Aaliyah had already yanked the door open, releasing a wave of Taylor Swift and excited chatter. Wafts of burgers and fries and nachos hit Kiara's nostrils as they stepped inside. Momentarily dazzled by the swirling lights and glittering disco ball, she blinked. Boys and girls crowded around a stage where a girl belted an off-key rendition of "Shake It Off." The cheering crowd did little to ease the knot building in Kiara's chest.

"This is it, Sis," Aaliyah said over the din, her eyes shining. "We're in for a great night. You'll see."

Through the throng of cheering kids, dark thoughts spiraled in Kiara's mind. At a place like this, keeping Aaliyah out of trouble could prove impossible. The thumping beat matched Kiara's quickening pulse, amplifying the sinking feeling that sneaking out to karaoke could become the least of her worries.

"Come on, we're signing up," Aaliyah demanded, pulling Kiara to the song list. "Relax. Jasmine's got our backs. Don't think she didn't lie to Mama when she was our age? Now, what song?"

Kiara's gaze darted around the room, taking in the pulsing lights and rowdy teens. "I don't want to find a song. I want to go home," she yelled over the music. Aaliyah spun to face her, eyes flashing with a familiar fire. "Seriously? We came all this way and you want to go home now?"

"I'm trying to be responsible. Unlike some people."

"Oh, here we go," Aaliyah groaned. "Lady Ki strikes again."

"At least I'm thinking about our future," Kiara shot back.

"Are you serious?" Aaliyah laughed, but there was an

edge to it. "Our future isn't in some dusty textbook, Kiara. Or in those books written by people who've been dead for a hundred years. It's out here, in the real world."

"Teaching is the real world," Kiara countered. "It's the foundation for—"

"For what?" Aaliyah's voice rose enough to draw curious glances from nearby teens. "A life stuck in Prichard, working for slave wages at the same boring school we attend?"

"For college, Aaliyah," Kiara said as she leaned in. "For a chance at a real career."

"A real career?" Aaliyah's eyes flashed. "You think teaching snot-nosed kids is more real than becoming a star?"

"I think it's more likely," Kiara shot back.

Aaliyah recoiled as if slapped. "Wow. Thanks for the vote of confidence, Sis."

Guilt twisted in Kiara's stomach. "Aaliyah, I didn't mean—"

"Forget it," Aaliyah snapped while snatching the song list and scrawling her name next to a title. "I'm going to prove you wrong one of these days. Maybe tonight."

Aaliyah rushed to the stage. Tension coiled inside Kiara's chest. Between the harsh words and constant pressure, everything had gone too far. Now Aaliyah was angry and determined—a dangerous combination. The cool vinyl pressed against Kiara's calves as she slid into a booth, subconsciously pulling out a copy of *Pride and Prejudice*. Instead of being safe at home, she was here, watching her sister seek a spotlight that might swallow her whole. And the worst part? A tiny voice in Kiara's head whispered maybe, just maybe, Aaliyah was right. Maybe there was more to life than the safe path Kiara had mapped out. But if it was true, what did it mean for her carefully constructed future?

The opening chords of "Dreamgirl" blasted through the speakers as Aaliyah took center stage. Cringing, Kiara sank lower in her booth, opening her book to the marked page. Her sister's voice, more enthusiasm than talent, warbled through the first verse. Kiara couldn't help but scan the room to gauge reactions—a few polite smiles and several winces poorly disguised as coughs. One boy near the front looked like he was suffering from a sudden onset of indigestion.

"Your sister has quite the unique voice." The silky comment from behind startled Kiara. At her shoulder stood a woman who hadn't been there a moment ago. An aura of elegance settled around her like a perfumed cloud. Her dark hair was swept into a stylish updo, her deep brown eyes sparkling with hidden amusement. She wore a sleek black blazer draped over an emerald blouse cut dangerously low. Beneath perfectly tailored slacks, blood-red stilettos caught the swirling lights. Everything about this woman screamed wealth.

"I'm sorry?" Kiara said, her voice barely audible over Aaliyah's attempt at a high note.

The woman revealed perfect white teeth as she slid into the booth. "Your sister has a very distinctive sound. Quite memorable."

Was this woman tone-deaf? Or just polite? "Um, thank you?"

"I couldn't help but notice—you two are twins?" The woman leaned forward, her eyes sparkling with interest. A whiff of something floral and exotic drifted across the table. Unease crawled along Kiara's spine. "Yes, we are."

"Fascinating," the woman said. "Have you ever considered modeling? There's quite a market for twin models, you know, especially with you and your sister's striking appearance."

Striking? Alarm bells rang in Kiara's head. This woman, with her fancy clothes and smooth talk, was the exact kind of person Mama had warned about.

"We're not really interested in modeling—" Kiara started, but Aaliyah's song ended with a flourish, cutting her off. The smattering of applause energized her sister, who bounced off the stage with a megawatt smile. Aaliyah approached their table. The woman's gaze shifted, a predatory gleam entering her eyes. Her smile, all teeth and no warmth, was like Mrs. Danvers in "Rebecca." Whatever this was, Kiara had to stop it before it started. But a flushed Aaliyah was already at the table, oblivious to the danger Kiara sensed.

"Did you see me up there? I totally killed it."

The woman's red lips curved into a Cheshire cat grin. "Oh, darling," she purred, "you were absolutely unforgettable."

The woman pulled a card from her purse. "My dear, have you ever considered modeling? With that face and your unique talent, you could go far. I told your sister I need twins—for a designer clothing line."

Aaliyah's eyes widened, her mouth forming a perfect 'O'. "M-modeling? Me...uh? Us?"

"Oh, absolutely," the woman said. "In fact, I'm in town lining up candidates for a photo shoot tomorrow." She presented the card to Aaliyah like a golden ticket. "I'm Vivian. Perhaps we could discuss it in the morning?"

Time seemed to slow as Aaliyah reached for it with shaky fingers. "I'm Aaliyah, and this is my sister Kiara."

A war raged inside Kiara. She should snatch and tear

Vivian's card in two to protect Aaliyah from this too-good-to-be-true offer. But the hope shining in her sister's eyes made her hesitate. That would only make her sister more determined.

"Wow, thank you," Aaliyah gushed, handling the card like a valuable treasure. "This is... this is amazing."

Vivian stood, smoothing her blazer. "Well, girls, it's been a pleasure. But I really must be going. Perhaps we'll speak again soon?"

"Yes," Aaliyah practically shouted.

"Wonderful," the woman said, her eyes lingering on Kiara momentarily. "Do take care, now." As Vivian glided to the exit, Aaliyah tugged on Kiara's arm. "Come on, let's see what kind of car she drives."

Before Kiara could protest, Aaliyah pulled her through the crowd and into the warm evening. The woman approached a metallic-green Jaguar. A uniformed driver, white and probably in his mid-thirties, but with a face weathered beyond his years, held her door open. His posture was ramrod straight beneath his black suit, shoulders back. Sharp brown eyes scanned the surroundings as if searching for some unseen threat. Vivian slipped inside with the grace of Princess Lúthien, alighting upon a forest glade. As the car pulled away, its taillights fading into the distance, a chill settled over Kiara, despite the warm night.

Aaliyah hugged the business card to her chest, her eyes surely ablaze with visions of catwalks and glossy magazine spreads. But Kiara saw only the White Witch's sleigh, gliding away with Turkish Delight and broken promises—a memory from the C.S. Lewis story she'd read in grade school that now felt all too real.

Friday, *May 24*

Click. Click. Click.

The sound of fingernails tapping glass scraped against Kiara's consciousness, tugging her from restless sleep. Her eyelids fluttered open. The faint gray of dawn painted their shared bedroom in pale streaks. The tapping had stopped. The stillness was heavier somehow. Who was Aaliyah texting at this hour? Kiara studied her twin in the other bed. Aaliyah's eyes were wide open with excitement. But beneath it all was that familiar, reckless smile—the one that always danced on the edge of trouble.

"Who are you texting this early?" The words scratched her dry throat.

Aaliyah's fingers froze mid-tap. A car horn blared outside their window. Despite her startled jump, guilt lingered clearly on her face as she set the phone in her lap. "Just a friend."

The garbage truck's weekly rumble masked Kiara's frustrated sigh. Under her weight, the springs of her worn mattress protested as she pushed up on her elbows. "Aaliyah, please tell me you're not texting that woman from last night."

Aaliyah's defiant silence filled their cramped room. The faded brown curtains stirred in the breeze from their ancient window unit, carrying the sweet undertone from the magnolias next door. "Her name is Vivian Delacroix." Aaliyah lifted her chin. "And she's meeting us in an hour to discuss our modeling career."

"Our modeling career?" Heat crept up Kiara's neck as she kicked free of her tangled sheets. "We can't meet her. Our geometry final—the one you need to pass to graduate —is today."

"So what." Aaliyah slid off her bed, bare feet silent on

the scuffed hardwood. Their shared closet door creaked as she yanked it open, fishing out a sparkly top. "This could be our big break, Ki. Our ticket out of this two-bed prison."

The morning traffic beyond their window seemed to mock Kiara's racing thoughts—the steady stream of people heading to real jobs, not fantasy careers built on a strange woman's promise. "Or it could be dangerous." She crossed the narrow space between their beds. "Did you even Google this woman? Or her company?"

"I did." Aaliyah's eye roll reflected in their cloudy dresser mirror. "Her Instagram has thousands of followers. Real models, Ki. Girls like us who made it."

Aaliyah yanked the sparkly top over her head. "Not everyone is out to get us. Some people want to help."

"And some people prey on naive girls with big dreams." Kiara grabbed her sister's arm, the sparkly sequins rough against her fingers. "Think about it. What kind of woman approaches two teenagers in a karaoke studio, offering fame and fortune? It's textbook stranger danger."

Aaliyah yanked free, sending a perfume bottle wobbling on their dresser. "You're just jealous because, for once, I might be the successful one."

Guilt twisted Kiara's stomach. The old wound—deep as the crack running down the corner wall. Her, the bright brain. Aaliyah, the bright smile. "Successful at what?" Kiara asked. "We're just in high school."

"Yeah, where you're the honor student, and I'm just getting by." Aaliyah stepped into her jeans, the fabric swishing against the worn rug.

"Listen. Mom's at work. Jasmine's busy with baby Aiden. If something happens—"

"Nothing will happen except me finally having a shot at something bigger." Aaliyah adjusted her top in their mirror, the glitter catching morning rays like desperate stars. "And I'm not letting you hold me back."

"Hold you back?" The ancient floorboard creaked under Kiara's feet. "I'm trying to protect you!"

"I don't need your protection." Aaliyah's said as she dug through their shoe pile. "I need you to believe in me for once."

Nails bit deep into her palms as Kiara clenched her hands. "Fine. Go meet your strange woman. But don't expect me to watch you do it."

Aaliyah paused, fingers tight around her canvas sneakers. There was uncertainty in her eyes. After a long breath, she steadied herself. "I'm going, Ki. With or without you."

Across the room, Kiara's geometry textbook sat on the nightstand. The test she'd studied for all week waited, but so did whatever danger Vivian represented. The garbage truck's fading rumble matched her internal struggle.

"Aaliyah, please," she pleaded. "You don't know what you're walking into."

Aaliyah shouldered past, their mother's early shift absence heavy in the quiet house. The door hinges whined —a sound as familiar as her sister's stubbornness. "I'm sorry, Ki. But I'm doing this."

Kiara blinked at their shared space—two beds, two dreams, one choice. Protect her future, or protect her sister? The answer whispered like the magnolia-scented breeze— there was no choice at all.

TEN MINUTES past the start of Kiara's first class, the morning sun glinted off the metallic-green Jaguar parked in the loading zone outside Bama Brew. The black-suited driver puffed on a cigarette while scrolling his phone as he leaned against the car's front fender. Aaliyah's grip tightened around Kiara's biceps as they approached the café's glass doors.

"There's her car," she said, her eyes brimming with excitement. "I told you she was legit."

A wave of espresso-scented air washed over Kiara as they pushed open the door. The café buzzed with the early morning crowd—students hunched over their phones, laborers, and secretaries grabbing to-go orders.

Vivian Delacroix sat at a corner table, white manicured nails wrapped around a steaming black mug. Her casual elegance stood out amid this working-class mix of customers—white linen pants and a coral silk blouse that complemented her golden tan. A delicate gold necklace swung gently as she turned, spotting the twins. "Aaliyah, Kiara!" she said over the hum of conversation and the whirr of coffee grinders. Standing, she flashed a smile that crinkled the corners of her eyes. "I'm so glad you made it."

Aaliyah practically bounced as she approached the table, her sparkly top reflecting the cafe's lighting. Measuring her steps, Kiara followed, taking in every detail of the woman who promised fame and fortune.

What am I doing here?

Kiara suppressed a shiver despite the café's warmth.

Vivian gestured to the empty chairs at her table. "Please, sit. I've ordered you both caramel macchiatos—I hope that's alright?"

"That's perfect," Aaliyah said as she slid into her seat." Thank you."

Drumming her fingers on the thighs, Kiara hesitated before sitting, "Actually...I don't drink coffee."

"Oh, it's just a treat," Vivian said, waving a dismissive

hand. "You both deserve it after making the effort to meet me so early."

A barista draped in a white apron approached with two tall glasses of layered coffee and milk and swirls of caramel, setting them down with a smile and a wink at Aaliyah, who giggled in response.

"Now," Vivian leaned forward, her voice lowering conspiratorially, "let's talk about your future in modeling. I have some exciting opportunities lined up."

Aaliyah's eyes widened. "Really? Already?"

Kiara's gaze darted between her sister and Vivian. "But we don't even have portfolios or—"

"Darling," Vivian said, placing a hand on Kiara's arm, "in this business, it's all about the first impression. And you two?" She paused, her eyes sweeping over both girls. "You're exactly what I've been looking for."

The touch of Vivian's hand sent a shiver through Kiara. Pulling back slightly, she tried to catch Aaliyah's attention, but her sister was wide-eyed, hanging on Vivian's every syllable.

Vivian pulled out an iPad from her designer handbag. "Let me show you what I have in mind," she said, pulling up a collection of glossy photos. "This is from a shoot I coordinated last month in Paris."

Gasping, Aaliyah leaned closer. "Paris? Oh my, Ki, look at those dresses!"

Kiara lowered her brow to peer at the screen. The models were young—too young. Their poses seemed awkward, forced. Something about their eyes...

"And here," Vivian swiped to another image, "is the cover of *Teen Fashion* from last spring. My discovery, of course."

The model looked familiar." Wait," Kiara interjected. "Is

that Melissa Hartley? The girl who went missing last year in Pensacola?"

Vivian's smile faltered for a moment before returning to a wide grin. "Oh, you must be mistaken, dear. Why this is Angelique, who's French. Quite well-known in Europe."

Aaliyah shot Kiara a warning glance. "Ki, don't be rude."

"I'm not being rude, I'm just—"

"Girls, girls," Vivian interrupted—again. "Let's focus on the exciting part, shall we? I have a photographer lined up this afternoon for your first shoot. Nothing too revealing, of course. Just some casual wear to start building your portfolio."

Aaliyah bounced in her seat. "This afternoon? Really?"

Kiara's stomach twisted. "But we have school, and Mom—"

"Your mother wants what's best for you, doesn't she?" Vivian's voice was honey-sweet. "This could be your ticket to a better life. For all of you."

On the kitchen counter, mounting bills told the story of their mother's constant struggle.

"Now," Vivian said, closing her tablet with a decisive click. "Shall we head to my studio? My driver can take us."

Without containing her excitement, Aaliyah practically vibrated as she stood. Remaining seated, Kiara's gaze darted between Vivian's expectant face and Aaliyah's pleading eyes. Her throat tightened. Her untouched macchiato was a cold reminder of her unease. "I... I don't know if we should—"

"Ki, please," Aaliyah blurted. "This could change everything for us. For Mom."

Vivian's smile never wavered. "Your sister's right, Kiara. This is a once-in-a-lifetime opportunity. But it has to be now. I'm a very busy woman."

The implication was clear—come now, or lose the

chance forever. If Kiara refused, Aaliyah might go alone. If she went, she could keep an eye on her sister and hopefully be back at school before her Geometry test.

"We should at least call Mom first," she said, reaching for her phone.

Vivian's hand shot out, covering Kiara's. "Oh, darling, there's no need to bother her at work. We'll be back before she even knows you're gone. Trust me."

Trust me. The words sounded like a challenge. Meeting Vivian's gaze, Kiara searched for what? Reassurance? Honesty? If the girl's name in Teen Vogue was really Angelique or Melissa Hartley?"

"Kiara?" Vivian's voice was gentle, but her eyes were sharp. "Are you coming?"

———

"Wait, what?" Kiara sat straight in the back seat beside Aaliyah. "Where are we going?"

The Jaguar had failed to get off I-65 at any Mobile exit. Instead, the clicking sound of the car's blinker sounded at the I-10 West/New Orleans overpass.

Vivian turned from the front passenger seat, her smile unchanged from the coffee shop. "To my studio in Louisiana, of course. Didn't I mention that?"

Sitting bright-eyed beside Kiara, Aaliyah shrugged. "It's not that far, Ki. Relax."

But Kiara's couldn't relax. "It's more than two hours." The car was suddenly too small, too confining. "And no, you didn't mention that, Vivian. Take us back. Now."

Vivian's voice was honey-sweet, but her eyes went cold. "Are you girls comfortable? I'm a little warm. Turn up the A/C Remy.

"I could care less about the air-conditioning," Kiara said in a panic. "Take us back now."

Remy's brown eyes met Kiara's in the rearview mirror, the fan blowing cooler air through the console vent. He glanced at Vivian. Something unspoken passed between them. "I'm afraid that's not possible, dear," Vivian said. "We have an appointment to keep. And as they say—'Time is money.'"

Aaliyah giggled nervously. "See, Ki? It's just business."

Deep in Kiara's gut, dread pooled like ice water. On her phone's dark screen, the "no service" message mocked her attempt at calling her mother. Panic rose in her throat as the Jaguar accelerated west, carrying them further from home by the second.

"This isn't right," Kiara insisted, her voice rising. "We need to call our mom. She doesn't know where we are!"

Vivian waved a dismissive hand. "Oh, don't worry about that. We'll call her when we arrive. This is how the industry works, darling. You need to be flexible, ready to go at a moment's notice."

Vivian turned to pass Aaliyah her iPad, its screen glowing with a gallery of glossy headshots. "So, sweetheart, which look speaks to you? The natural light outdoors, or inside with the studio lighting?"

Aaliyah leaned in, her gaze drawn to the images as if they held the promise of a new self. Meanwhile, the driver's cold eyes found Kiara in the rearview mirror. "It's easier when girls don't fight what they can't change." His voice curled like a quiet threat. "Most figure that out."

PART I

S *aturday, July 27*

The dream burned in sixteen-year-old Gabriel Mendoza's veins as he raced down the sun-bleached dock at Mangrove Bight, the salt-worn planks groaning beneath his sandals. His brothers needed to hear this one. They had to see it—believe it. He would be the one to lead them to prosperity and he couldn't wait to tell them.

The family's battered trawler rocked ahead, Oscar and Ernesto's silhouettes sharp against the morning glare. Gabriel's heart slammed in his chest. The salty Caribbean air caught in his throat as their shoulders tensed, their hands froze mid-task among the fishing nets, and their eyes bore into him. "Here comes the dreamer," Oscar said as he turned away.

Gabriel fingers traced the intricate embroidery on his new guayabera shirt, a gift from his father for being the first of his family to be accepted to university. The crisp linen marked him as different—special.

"Listen, brothers," Gabriel pressed on, unable to contain

himself, "I stood at the helm of a gleaming white yacht. A terrible storm raged, but I guided everyone to safety and prosperity. You were there, working alongside me."

The thud of heavy boots on the dock snapped Gabriel's head around. Rafael, the second eldest brother, approached, his broad shoulders hunched with exhaustion or resentment—maybe both. "Oye, Gabriel," Rafael's voice grated like sandpaper. "Are you going to stand there all day like a statue, or are you going to help? Or is fixing engines the only thing you're good for?"

Standing straighter, Gabriel put a smile on his lips. "I was trying to share an amazing dream I had last night with Oscar and Ernesto. You were in it as—"

"Save it." Rafael's face grew darker than his tanned olive skin. "We don't have time for another one of your fantasies. Some of us have real work to do, not just tinkering with engines when Papa asks." He shoved a crate into Gabriel's arms. The rough wood bit into his calloused hands and the stench of yesterday's catch assaulted his nostrils.

He set the crate down, and doubt crossed his mind. Maybe he shouldn't have mentioned the vision he knew God gave him. But his excitement bubbled up again, and he couldn't help himself. "But Rafael, you don't understand. In the dream, I led us through this terrible storm. I saved everyone."

From the boat's bow, Oscar, two years older than Gabriel, twisted his face into a sneer, his brown eyes narrowing as they flicked at Gabriel's guayabera. "Look at *el mecánico mágico* in his fancy new shirt, dreaming of being our savior. Wouldn't want to get engine grease on it, would we? Or is that the only thing keeping you useful around here?"

Anger burned in Gabriel's cheeks, but he pressed on. "Papa was so proud—"

"Basta," Ernesto bellowed from the starboard, the eldest brother's face clenched beneath his salt-and-pepper stubble. His knuckles whitened as he gripped the railing to contain his frustration.

A blur caught Gabriel's eye as Nico, the youngest brother, came bounding down the dock, weaving between crates and coils of rope. "Gabriel. *Vas a pescar hoy*?"

Like a warm embrace, the familiar scent of tobacco and Bay Rum aftershave drifted through the air. From behind, a weathered hand settled on his shoulder. "Not today, *mijo*. Gabriel has more important things to do."

Pride swelled in Papa's voice when speaking about Gabriel. The same voice that barked orders at his brothers all morning. His siblings' faces dropped, just like they always did when Papa showed his preference. Rafael's jaw clenched so tight a muscle jumped beneath his stubbled cheek.

"From now on, Gabriel will work with me in the office to learn operations," Papa said. "One day, he'll take over the business. The only one of my sons with a head for numbers and a heart for people."

Papa's approval pressed against Gabriel's shoulders like a heavy coat—warm and suffocating all at once. Nodding eagerly, he tried to ignore Oscar's muttered curse, and Ernesto's hard stare, soaking in his father's praise like a sponge. Papa's faith in Gabriel was a blessing and a curse, widening the gulf between him and his brothers every day. Gabriel pushed aside this unease with eager ambition. "Just like in my dream, Papa. I saw myself leading the most beautiful boat into the calmest of seas."

The fishing vessel sailed out into the Caribbean. Papa steered Gabriel toward their small office with Nico tagging behind. "Just wait, Papa." Gabriel's voice carried through the entire village. "Everyone will rave about the ship I own. And our family will be so much happier working for me."

Papa's calloused fingers clamped down on Gabriel's ear. "Enough," he said firmly. He guided Gabriel around the corner out of his brother's sight. "Dreams are for sleeping, mijo. You speak of owning when you haven't earned. Or leading when you haven't followed." Releasing his hold, he turned Gabriel by his shoulders. "You won't earn your brothers' respect by boasting about some lofty dream. You must show them the wisdom God will give you." His eyes softened a fraction. "That wisdom comes from learning every part of this business, starting with the books. Now let's get started."

The office was stuffy with the smells of old paper and ink competing with the salt air. Papa spread out ledgers and contracts on the scarred desk, his excitement not contained by the confined space.

Nodding mechanically at his father's recited plans, Gabriel's attention drifted to the cloudy window. The family boat had disappeared as if making way for a new vision—a new future. A thin figure stepped onto the dock—an American. Despite the early hour, the stranger looked like he'd just rolled out of bed after a long night of *pachanga*. His skin was flushed and slightly sweaty, his movements restless and jittery. He squinted against the glare of the water, revealing bright teeth that contrasted with his rugged appearance. Gabriel felt a sudden curiosity about this gringo. He couldn't shake the feeling that there was more to this man than met the eye.

The dream flashed again—stark white hull contrasting

dark waters, his hands steady on familiar teak, his family in the ship with him as they tried to outpace a powerful storm.

"Are you listening, Gabriel?" Papa's voice snapped him out of his reverie.

"*Sí, Papá. Lo siento,*" Gabriel said, his mind still reeling from the collision of God's vision and this world's reality. "I was just thinking... Do you really think I'm destined for greatness?"

Papá chuckled, patting his son's shoulder. "Of course, mijo. You're special. That's why I'm preparing for you to take over."

Straightening in his chair, Gabriel lifted his chin. The yacht, the respect, the success—it would all come true. Yet his stomach clenched at the memory of Rafael's darkened face, Oscar's sneer, Ernesto's white-knuckled grip on the railing. No matter. They'd understand once he proved himself.

The sudden appearance of the American outside the office window snuffed out Gabriel's visions of his gleaming yacht and personal triumph, twisting his excitement into a dark knot of dread, a shadow now standing between him and his God-ordained destiny.

―――

THE SETTING SUN painted the sea in bruised purples and angry reds as the family boat limped back to dock with empty nets in its wake. Gabriel shifted his weight on the weathered planks, his crisp guayabera bone dry against his skin. All those hours studying ledgers and statements in Papá's air-conditioned office, and what did he have to show for it? Nothing that would matter to his brothers' sweat-stained shirts and defeated expressions.

After a full day at sea, they had nothing to show for their efforts. Gabriel grabbed the mooring line before Rafael could reach it. The rough fibers bit into his softening palms, but he welcomed the pain. Let them see he wasn't afraid of real work, that his dreams of commanding their future went well beyond his father's office.

Rafael was the first to disembark, his boots striking the weathered planks with staccato fury. "Another day wasted," he spat, glaring at Gabriel. "Did you enjoy the air-conditioning, university boy?"

Gabriel opened his mouth, but his words died on his tongue. What could he say? That he'd spent the day in shady air-conditioning, while they labored at sea?

Oscar shouldered past him. "I hope you learned something useful up there because we sure didn't catch anything down here."

The accusation stung like being snagged by a fisherman's hook. Grabbing a rope, the rough fibers biting into his palms, Gabriel helped secure the boat. The gesture, was small—pathetically inadequate.

Papá's voice boomed across the dock. "What happened out there?"

Rafael's laugh was harsh. "What happened? Your golden boy wasn't there, that's what happened." He jerked his thumb towards Gabriel. "While we were breaking our backs, he was playing businessman with you in the office."

Gabriel's cheeks burned, wanting to explain about the ledgers, the contracts, the plans Papá had shown him. But would any of that matter in the face of mounting costs and empty nets?

"Watch your tone, mijo," Papá said, his eyes narrowing. "Gabriel's work is just as important as—"

"Important?" Oscar's voice dripped with disdain. "Tell

that to our zero haul, Papá. Tell that to the bills piling up on your desk."

Gabriel's gaze darted between his brothers and father, the dream of his gleaming yacht seeming farther away with every word.

Papá's face contorted into an angry glare. "You think I don't know about our debts? About the competition from the big companies?" He jabbed a finger at Gabriel. "That's why we need his intelligence, his education. He is our future."

"Future?" Rafael exploded, kicking over a stack of crates. "We might not have a future if things keep going like this. The bank's threatening to take the trawler, and you want to spend money we don't have on university?"

The conflict pressed in on Gabriel from all sides. Turning to Nico in search of an ally, Gabriel found his little brother frozen in place—his eyes darting, as if desperate to end this argument.

"Papá, please," Tomás, usually the quiet one, stepped forward. "We're drowning here. We need Gabriel on the boat, not in some classroom miles away."

Gabriel's pulse quickened. Just like his dream—but where was the gleaming yacht? The sure-footed captain's stance? God had purposed him to guide his family through a storm, hadn't He? Or had pride twisted his vision into a selfish fantasy? Gabriel clenched his fists, but his hands still trembled. His brothers were waiting, expecting answers. Some leader he was, standing here useless while his family's future crumbled around him.

Suddenly, a commotion from the fish market turned everyone's head. Through the gathering twilight, Gabriel spotted the American tourist from that morning—all wide-eyed and manic energy—squaring off with old Manuelo.

"—cheating me, you old fraud!" the gringo slurred, his words thick with something harder than alcohol.

Manuelo's weathered face was set in stubborn lines. "No cheat. Fair price. No more money gringo. We had a deal."

The American swayed, his bloodshot eyes wild. "I'll show you fair, you son of a—" The American's hand shot out, grabbing Manuelo's shirt. Metal glinted in the fading light—a gun.

Gabriel's heart slammed against his ribs. Run. Hide. Do something. But his feet were rooted to the dock, useless as driftwood.

"The deal," The gringo laughed, a sound like breaking glass. "The deal has changed. You pay, or I'll feed your dead carcass to the sharks."

Shouts erupted around them. The market crowd swelled, anger rising like a tide. The American's head snapped up, bloodshot eyes darting from face to face. His grip on Manuelo loosened.

"This isn't over," he snarled, backing away. "You'll pay, one way or another." In a blink, he was gone, swallowed by a mass of stalls and gathering shadows. Manuelo sagged against a nearby crate, his bravado crumbling.

Gabriel's legs finally remembered how to move, and he stumbled forward, each step sending a fresh churn through his uneasy stomach. This was no dream of heroic captaining. This was real—brutal and messy and terrifying.

As he glanced back at his brothers and father, their argument forgotten in the face of this new threat, a chill ran through him, colder than any ocean breeze. All his dreams of yachts and success and prosperity for his family were hollow now. What good was ambition in a world where men like that American existed? Where violence lurked just beneath the surface of where people worked?

The crowd's angry murmurs faded to a dull roar. Something about the gringo's swagger, the casual way he'd pulled that gun—this wasn't his first time threatening bloodshed. And from the way his bloodshot eyes had lingered on Manuelo before leaving, this surely wouldn't be the stranger's last visit.

2

Wednesday, July 31

Eli Colt maneuvered his Jeep through a maze of potholes and broken concrete. Prichard, Alabama, was a different world from the leafy suburbs of Mobile, where he and his partner, Dakota Sutcliffe, had finished lunch a half-hour earlier. The windows of many homes were boarded or shattered. Graffiti covered abandoned houses, crude tags marking territory in a place where hope seemed scarce. Nearby sirens didn't faze the people lounging on rickety lawn chairs under sprawling oaks, or the children cooling their dark bodies from an open hydrant. Like most neighborhoods plagued with poverty, every corner told a desperate story.

Dakota scanned the area. "You sure about this?" His tone was tinged with skepticism. "It's been two months."

Eli studied the street signs. "Time doesn't make the girls any less missing or their mother any less worried." He slid his hand from the steering wheel to the Johnson file wedged between his calf and the armrest. At the intersection of

Wilson Avenue and Martin Luther King Jr. Boulevard, he eased on the brake and then turned into the neighborhood.

"What happened with the local police?" Dakota asked.

"According to the mother," Eli said. "The girls' case wasn't given much attention. The Prichard Police believed they ran away."

Dakota shook his head. "What about the county sheriff?"

"He retired last month and moved to Florida. Lindsey is waiting for him to return her call."

Five minutes later, Eli parked in the empty driveway. The door above the sagging porch opened as Eli shut down the engine. Monica Johnson stood there with hollow eyes and deep lines etched across her forehead. They hadn't even reached the steps, and already Eli sensed a mother's despair.

He approached the front porch with Dakota trailing him. Monica Johnson's frame was gaunt and thin, her shoulders slumped as if weighted down with hopelessness.

"Mrs. Johnson, I'm Eli Colt. This is Dakota Sutcliffe," he said, his voice crisp yet gentle. "We're investigators with Redemption Rescue."

Monica offered a slow nod and stepped aside.

"A lady called and said you'd be coming," she said, weariness in her tone. "Might as well come on in."

The house enveloped them in faint light and the smell of lavender. The carpet underfoot was faded and worn through in places. A soap opera played on a small flat screen not far from an old armchair with frayed fabric and a matching footstool. Knitting lay abandoned on a nearby end table, the needles mid-stitch in a half-finished scarf. She led them to the sitting room, her steps slow and deliberate. "Coffee?"

"Yes, please," Eli said as he and Dakota sat on a shoddy sofa.

Within moments, Monica reappeared from the adjoining kitchen, her delicate hands balancing a tray with three steaming cups. The nutty, roasted aroma filled the room, weaving through the faded curtains and dust-free shelves. She settled into the armchair, cradling her cup as if it were a lifeline.

"My wife, Lindsey, learned about your daughters from an article on Al.com," Eli said softly, easing into the conversation. "Our organization is always on the lookout for lost children."

Monica's grip on her mug tightened. "I've been praying someone would take interest," she said, her voice tinged with frustration. "The police, they didn't seem to care. Like my girls don't matter."

Dakota shifted uncomfortably. "What did they say when you first reported them missing?"

Monica sighed deeply. "They say I was overreacting. Said teenagers run off all the time. But this wasn't like them, not my babies." She stared into her coffee with sad eyes. "Kiara was studying hard to go to Auburn. Aaliyah wanted to be a singer," she chuckled, "but couldn't carry a note in a bucket." Her eyes glossed over. "I was working double shifts when they disappeared. Didn't know they were gone until their school called."

"And the police?" Dakota asked, his tone more probing. "Did they have any leads? Talk to witnesses?"

Monica's eyes flared with a mild sense of anger. "Barely. The case was closed not long after it started. Said they probably just ran away. My oldest daughter, Jasmine, has been fightin' tooth and nail to keep the search going."

"We're here to help, Mrs. Johnson," Eli said. "I promise

you we'll dig deeper. Look at every detail and follow every lead."

Monica's eyes welled, her years of grief showing through. "I appreciate that. Jasmine raised over $5,000 on GoFundMe to pay as a reward."

Dakota nodded resolutely. "We're well funded, so we're not doing it for the money. But if it can shake someone's memory about your daughters, we will use it."

For a moment, a flicker of hope crossed Monica's worn features. "Thank you. I just... I just need to know what happened to my babies. I just need to know."

Leaning over, Eli rested his hand on Monica's. "We promise to do everything we can to find them. Your girls deserve it, and so do you."

Ten minutes later, Eli stood on the cracked sidewalk outside the Johnson home, his pulse echoing the anguish that undoubtedly gripped Monica inside. Two months ago, her daughters had gone missing, followed by two months of police indifference.

"Poor woman's been to hell and back," Dakota said.

Monica's quiet despair cut so deep it had Eli grinding his teeth. Maybe because Lindsey had flagged this case. Or maybe because he was sick of watching cops write off kids in poor neighborhoods as runaways. "Let's head to Prichard PD," he said, his voice sharp as steel. "I want to know why two sixteen-year-old girls who were reported missing weren't worth more time and effort."

———

THE UNIFORMED DESK officer at Prichard PD barely glanced up when Eli mentioned the Johnson twins and his meeting with Missing Persons. With a bored nod toward a dimly lit hallway, the officer said, "Detective Barnes will meet you in the break room."

Eli and Dakota ambled through the cluttered corridor that seemed to get tighter with every step. Flickering fluorescent bulbs buzzed softly, casting shaky shadows on plaster walls. A phone rang from somewhere. Murmured conversations were muted, almost swallowed by the oppressive air. It was as if the building was trying to hide something.

They finally found the small, neglected room, its door creaking in objection as Eli opened it. Inside, a metal table marred with countless scratches and dented edges stood in the center. Four mismatched chairs surrounded it, their cushions frayed and stuffing peeking through. They took a seat and waited for the arrival of Detective Avery Barnes.

An older man with graying hair and tired eyes shuffled into the room. His shoulders sagged slightly in a defensive posture. "I'm Barnes," he said with a flat and lifeless tone.

Eli offered his hand. "We appreciate your time, Detective Barnes. I'm Eli Colt, and this is Dakota Sutcliffe."

Barnes nodded briefly and shook Eli's hand before glancing at Dakota. Dakota remained seated, his arms crossed tightly over his chest, his eyes narrowed with suspicion. He wasn't here to make friends.

"Let's get this over with," Barnes said, settling into a chair. His voice was clipped, as if he'd rather be anywhere but here.

Easing back into his seat, Eli maintained steady eye contact. His calm, deliberate movements contrasted with Dakota's rigid posture. The distinction was clear—Eli would talk. Dakota would press their seriousness.

"Detective Barnes, as I said on the phone, we'd like to learn what you know about the Johnson twins' disappearance," Eli said in a polite but measured tone. "Anything you can tell us would be of great help."

Barnes's eyes flashed mild irritation. "Well, as I remember, we followed standard procedures." His words came out monotone. "We talked to their classmates and teachers. They seemed to think the girls might've run away."

Dakota arched an eyebrow and shook his head slowly.

"Given their ages, did that seem conclusive to you?" Eli asked.

Barnes looked up at the water-stained ceiling. "Conclusive enough. We've got a ton of cases and don't have time to search for every teenager who runs away from home."

Dakota uncrossed his arms, leaning forward slightly. "Detective, with all due respect, how do you know they ran away?"

Barnes's jaw tightened. "Because these girls fit the profile of runaways."

"So, you followed this assumption?" Eli said with diplomacy. "Even if it meant missing something important?"

Barnes forced a tight smile but said nothing. The subtext was clear—he'd hastily closed the case, and everyone in the room knew it.

Eli bore his eyes into Barnes. "Detective, it seems unusual for missing minors to be dismissed so quickly. One of the girls was well on her way to earning a scholarship to Auburn."

"And one dreamed of being the next Beyonce." Barnes's expression hardened. "Look. We have statements from their teachers and classmates that state that Aaliyah Johnson always talked about getting out of Prichard. With the strain of balancing multiple cases with limited manpower, I decided to classify these girls as runaways."

"So," Dakota said with an icy chill, "you labeled them as

runaways to clear your workload, not because the evidence supported it."

Lifting his shoulders, Barnes bristled in his chair. "I don't appreciate the insinuation. I acted within department procedure and the resources available to me. This was not a cherry-picked decision."

"Perhaps." Eli leaned for emphasis. "But it certainly appears to be a hasty one."

Pressing his lips into a hard line, Barnes stood and paced. "We pursued what evidence we had. Budget constraints don't allow us to prioritize runaway cases."

Dakota's voice dipped into a growl. "Prioritize? We're talking about two missing girls here. What could possibly take precedence over that?"

"Look," Barnes said. "We did everything we could with what we had. I won't have you implying otherwise."

Locking eyes with Barnes, Eli decided to use honey instead of vinegar. "Detective Barnes, budget constraints aside, do you remember anything that didn't quite fit the runaway narrative? Perhaps something that stood out but wasn't followed up on?"

Stopping his pacing, Barnes turned with a defensive expression. "Nothing."

"You sure," Dakota pressed, "nothing that would have raised some alarms?"

Raising his eyes to the flickering light above, Barnes sighed. "Nothing."

"Then you won't mind if we see the file?" Dakota said, his tone a touch lighter.

Barnes returned to his seat and thrummed the table with his fingers. The light continued to flutter. "We've just upgraded our case management software. Sorry, those files were lost."

Misfiled. Right. The excuse was too convenient, too rehearsed. Either Barnes was hiding something, or someone above him was. Best to get what he could and call it a day with this heartless idiot. "Can you at least give us a list of everyone interviewed during the initial investigation?"

"I'll see what I can find," Barnes said, nodding slowly.

Two minutes later, humidity hit Eli like an invisible wall as he and Dakota exited the building. They strolled to the Jeep, disappointed in the police effort and their lack of solid clues.

Dakota sank into the passenger seat. "What now?"

"We'll check into the hotel and review what we have." Eli fired up the engine, anxious to get the air conditioning blowing. Barnes's dismissive attitude wasn't new—he'd seen it too many times before. Every time law enforcement wrote off missing kids as runaways, traffickers got bolder. And somewhere out there, Kiara and Aaliyah Johnson were paying the price for that indifference.

His phone buzzed with a text—Lindsey. "Just got a call from the sheriff. Looks like he may have some information about the twins' disappearance."

3

Thursday, August 1

That evening at home, Gabriel's eyes swept the scarred wooden table in the dining room, his heart pounding as if trying to warn him. Papa sat at the head, his face hard and unreadable, his silence louder than words. To his right, Nico fidgeted with a piece of bread, shooting nervous glances at Gabriel, as if sensing the same storm gathering. Shifting uncomfortably in his chair, Gabriel tried to steady his breathing. Across from him, Oscar, Rafael, and Ernesto were quiet, their sun-baked arms crossed, muscles still tense from pulling nets and lifting crates all day.

The ground felt like it was moving beneath him, but he knew it wasn't—it was what no one wanted to say. Saltwater and sweat clung to the air, mixing with the heavy scent of anticipation. Gabriel gripped the table. He had the sudden, terrifying feeling that whatever happened next would change everything. And no one was ready for it.

The silence made it hard to breathe. This was Gabriel's home, his sanctuary, yet tonight, dinner seemed like a prelude to battle. Rafael stabbed at his pork, teeth grinding. Oscar's gaze drifted to Ernesto, exchanging a slight nod. Their hardened expressions warned of an inevitable showdown with their father. Rafael dropped his fork with a clang. "We need to talk about Gabriel."

Papa's jaw tightened, but he didn't look up from his plate. "There's nothing to discuss. He goes to university next semester. It's settled."

"Settled?" Rafael's voice rose. "We're drowning here, Papa. The business is failing. We must have all hands on deck, not some far-off dream of education."

Oscar nodded vigorously. "Rafael's right. Let Gabriel return to the boat, not play with numbers in some useless classroom."

Their words sounded distant to Gabriel. Nico's eyes were wide and unsettled. Should Gabriel speak up? Agree with his brothers? The thought sent a bitter sting across his tongue. Papa remained firm and unyielding. "I've made my decision. I don't want to hear anything more on the subject."

Oscar's fists clenched on the table. "And what about the rest of us? You're willing to throw a lifeline only to Gabriel?"

Papa said nothing, and the room fell silent.

A minute or two later, Rafael spoke up. "What about Manuelo on the pier today?" he said, changing the subject. "The gringo who attacked him, demanding more money. Rumor has it Manuelo provides him people for caravans that go north to America."

Gabriel's stomach lurched. He'd heard whispers about Manuelo's dealings, but this... This was beyond anything he'd imagined. Papa's face darkened. "That's Manuelo's business, not ours."

"It became our business when that drunk waved a gun around our market!" Oscar slammed his fist on the table.

"What if he comes back? We need to protect our community."

"Is it true?" Gabriel asked in a trembling voice. "Is Manuelo really trafficking people?"

Papa's eyes met Gabriel's with sadness and resignation. "When times are hard, mijo, people do desperate things."

"But Papa," Gabriel protested, "that's—"

"Enough!" Papa cut him off. "We don't speak of this again. Understand?" Shame flooded Gabriel's insides. What had life come to in their fishing village? The business was struggling. Maybe he should offer to stay, to help—fight against the American if he returns.

But his dream—it was too real. "What if..." Gabriel struggled to speak. "What if I waited a year before going to university? Until we get caught up with the bills?"

Rage stormed in Papa's eyes. "No," he said, his voice low but firm. "You go next semester. It's non-negotiable."

The words hung over the table, heavy and final. Disappointment seared through him, leaving an unsettling knot in the pit of his stomach. He'd offered a compromise, yet Papa shut him down.

Rafael jumped up from his chair, sending it crashing against the wall. "This is madness," he yelled. "You're willing to risk the future of this family on your precious Gabriel. I won't stand for it."

Papa's face reddened as he slowly lifted himself from his seat. "You want to leave and start your own business? Go ahead. See who will loan you the money to buy a boat, nets, and navigation equipment."

"What makes you think we can't?" Oscar challenged.

"Because I've borrowed from every bank in Mangrove Bight," Papa growled. "They don't loan to upstart fishermen with no collateral."

Oscar's chair tipped to the floor as he stood to join Rafael. "You're choosing him over the rest of us," he shouted, jabbing a finger at Gabriel.

Papa leaned in, his fists pressed against the table. "I'm deciding what's best for this family."

"What future?" Oscar slammed his palm on the scarred wood. Plates rattled. "There won't be a business left by the time he finishes school."

"You think I don't know the risks?" Papa boomed. "But education is—"

"Education won't put food on the table now!" Oscar cut in.

"I could go on the boat!" Nico said, trying to be heard, but was ignored.

Gabriel's head spun. Education or no education, he believed his dream was from God—to ease his family's struggles, which they'd endured since his mother died. His brothers' expectations, their disappointment, their anger, the American waving a gun, the whispers of Manuelo's unforgivable sin—crashed down on Gabriel all at once. "Enough!" he finally screamed. "I can't... I can't do this right now."

He ran to the door and stormed out of the house, ignoring his father's calls. His feet carried him toward the docks that would be abandoned at this hour. Tears stung his eyes against the cool night air, the battle with his brothers still raging in his mind. He was torn between his father's faith in him and the life his brothers insisted he live. And the ugly reality of Manuelo's actions. What was happening to this island community?

As the sound of lapping waves grew closer, Gabriel knew one thing for certain—he needed to confirm where God truly wanted him.

———

Gabriel's sandals smacked in a steady rhythm on the wooden pier, each step propelling him forward. The sunscorched planks, scarred by years of salt and sea, felt too much like his soul—scraped raw by his impatience with God fulfilling His plan. A pungent mix of brine and fish rushed into his lungs with every breath, yet it couldn't quiet the tempest. He needed answers. He needed to think. He needed to hear from God.

Above the gentle lapping of waves against idle fishing hulls, the family argument still echoed. Across the deepening twilight, his eyes squinted as muted purples and grays painted the western sky. On the horizon, ominous clouds hovered, their edges catching the faint glow of Roatán's distant lights.

With sudden force, a gust of wind tousled his hair. Brushing his skin, the air felt cool and damp, raising goosebumps along his arms. In his haste to leave the house, he had forgotten a jacket.

The sounds of the town faded, giving way to the creaking of wood and the soft clinking of rigging and masts. Shadows stretched long and deep between the stalls. Moths fluttered frantically around buzzing lamps like restless spirits.

He paused, letting his eyes adjust to the increasing darkness. The familiar daytime bustle of fishermen and dock workers had given way to an unsettling quiet, broken only by the mournful cry of a gull. Gabriel's eyes caught a faint ripple—a shadow shifting near Manuelo's stall, followed by voices growing louder.

Ducking behind stacked fish crates, his breathing became jagged and shallow. There, in the dim light from a single bulb above Manuelo's stall, stood the American from earlier. A frigid wave slowed Gabriel's pulse to a crawl. The American's movements were jerky and unpredictable, his hands flailing wildly as he spoke urgently. "I need more *niños*," he snarled. "There's more demand in America."

"Niños?" So it was true. Manuel was supplying this gringo with children. The same children who waved to Gabriel on their way to school, their backpacks swaying with each step. The same children who trusted adults to protect them. And here he was, crouched behind a stack of empty crates, breath shallow, just like everyone else who suspected but did nothing.

He should intervene. Run home and get his father and brothers. Run. But his feet stayed rooted to the splintered dock.

His father's voice echoed in his mind—firm and resolute, the voice of a man who had seen desperate times. "Times are hard. People do desperate things."

Gabriel's hands trembled at his sides. Could he really turn his back on this? And if he did, what would happen to those niños? Could he live with himself, knowing he had walked away? But if he acted... What might happen to him?

The American's voice rose to a howl. "You promised a steady supply."

"*No más*," Manuelo said, a tremor of fear evident even from where Gabriel hid. "I can't... I won't do this anymore. My conscience... it won't let me sleep. These are children, for God's sake."

Although his legs were cramped, Gabriel didn't dare shift position. Each time the American screamed, Gabriel clenched his fists.

Manuelo was trying to back out, to do the right thing. But the menace in American's stance told Gabriel this wasn't going to end well. He had to do something, and fast. But what could he, a teenage boy, possibly do against this American trafficker?

Gabriel's heart thudded as the confrontation unfolded. The American took a threatening step toward Manuelo, his hand disappearing beneath his jacket and pulled out his gun.

"You don't get to back out," the American said, his every word laced with quiet intensity. "Not when I need you the most."

A loose board creaked under Gabriel's foot. The American's head snapped toward him. Gabriel held his breath, his pulse thumping in his ears.

"Do what you will," Manuelo stood taller, unfazed. "I've reconciled with my God."

Time slowed. The American's finger tightened on the trigger. Every part of Gabriel screamed to move, to shout, to do something—anything. But he remained frozen. A coward behind his crates.

The crack of the gunshot shattered the night. A scream caught in Gabriel's throat as Manuelo crumpled to the ground. The American hovered over the fallen body, his gun still raised, smoke curling from its barrel. Through narrowed vision, Manuelo's body lay motionless on the weathered planks. Gabriel choked, desperately needing to vomit.

The sound of hurried footfalls signaled the American's retreat. Gabriel remained frozen, afraid to move, afraid to breathe. His inaction felt like acid burning his insides. He had to see if Manuelo was alive or dead.

Gabriel hurried to Manuelo, a silent apology on his lips for doing nothing. Running as fast as his legs allowed, he found the old man's lifeless form as thunder rumbled in the distance.

With a slight push, Manuelo's body rolled to one side. Into the void, unblinking eyes stared past Gabriel. In a few short moments, safety had won over action, fear over courage. From this moment forward, everything would change. His father's demand he go to university, take over the family business in time. But could Gabriel do it? This night maybe proved his father picked the wrong son.

Footsteps crunched on the sand in the darkness from the same direction the American had fled. Had the gringo come back to kill again?

4

Eli leaned against the window frame of his Holiday Inn Express room in Mobile, Alabama, fixing his gaze on the parking lot below. The air conditioning purred, its cool breath fighting the humid evening. From the bathroom, the muffled hiss of the shower made it plain that Dakota was washing away the day's sweat and frustration. On the glass, Eli's breath clouded briefly, then disappeared, leaving the window as clear—and as empty— as the lot below.

Outside, a young family piled into their minivan. The children's laughter forged a bittersweet ache in his chest—a future he hoped for with his wife, Lindsey. But was having children wise, given the grim reality of his current case and those before it? He pushed the thought aside, removed his phone from his pocket, and punched in Lindsey's number.

"Hey, babe," Lindsey's slightly breathless voice floated through the receiver. Eli's shoulders eased a fraction.

"Hey yourself," he said. "You sound winded. Chasing down leads or just the mailman?"

Lindsey's laughter was light and tinkling. "Very funny,

Detective Colt. I'll have you know I just finished a five-mile run."

Eli surrendered to a full-blown smile, picturing her flushed face and tousled auburn hair. "Well, that explains your energy." He found himself relaxing as some of the day's tension melted away. "How's your day been?"

"It's been quite a day, actually," Lindsey said, her tone changing. "I went shopping with Tara and Julia in the French Quarter. We went to upgrade Tara's wardrobe for her first year at LSU."

Tara Colt was Eli's 17-year-old niece and daughter of his deceased brother. Two years ago, Eli and Dakota had saved her from a crazed cult leader named Commodore, spurring Redemption Rescue into existence.

"That sounds nice," Eli said. "How'd it go?"

"The shopping was great, but..." Lindsey paused, then lowered her voice. "Something happened in Jackson Square that you should know about."

Eli straightened, his interest piqued. "Go on."

"Tara thought she saw Andre Badeau," Lindsey said. "She only caught a glimpse before he disappeared around the corner near the Cabildo, so she wasn't entirely sure. But it shook her up pretty badly."

Andre Badeau was a pimp who had lured Tara from her home in New Orleans, eventually selling her to Commodore before escaping to who knows where.

Eli curled his free hand into a fist. "Badeau? Are you certain?"

"Like I said, Tara isn't positive," Lindsey repeated. "But given everything that's happened, I thought you should know."

"I'll look into it when we get back. How's she doing now?"

"She's okay," Lindsey assured him. "We made sure she felt safe before heading home. But maybe give her a call when you can?"

"I will," Eli promised, his mind already racing with the implications. He forced himself to refocus on the present. "So, aside from that, how was your day?"

As Lindsey launched into a recap of her afternoon, Eli's gaze drifted back to the parking lot. The family's minivan was pulling away, leaving an empty space that seemed to yawn like a chasm. His smile disappeared, replaced by a steely determination. He suddenly remembered that she had contacted the sheriff. "You talked to Thornton," Eli shifted his tone from casual to focused.

"I did." She sighed heavily. "He was pretty disgusted with how Prichard PD handled Kiara and Aaliyah's disappearance."

"Dakota and I feel the same way."

"Bad enough that he used the word 'negligent,'" Lindsey said. "According to Hank, Detective Barnes barely scratched the surface, only taking a few statements from the twins' classmates and teachers."

"Hank?" Eli furrowed his brow, a twinge of something—jealousy?—pricking at him. How old was this sheriff, Hank, anyway?

"Oh, sorry," Lindsey said with a slightly embarrassed tone. "The sheriff's name is Hank Thornton. Anyway, according to, uh... Sheriff Thornton, the girls' disappearance was less than 24 hours old when Barnes classified them as runaways."

"What else?" Eli asked, unsure about Lindsey calling the sheriff "Hank."

Lindsey's voice dropped. "It gets worse. The sheriff

thinks Barnes jumped to conclusions without doing any real investigating. He said he seemed... 'disinterested.'"

Eli nodded to himself. "Yeah, I got the same impression."

"But wait till you hear this. Barnes visited Monica right before Sheriff Thornton retired. He said that since they were so close to the girls' 17th birthday, it would be pointless to find them because the girls would be considered adults."

"So he just... gave up?"

"Seems like it..." Lindsey said, then added softly, "The sheriff thinks there might have been some bias involved. The Johnsons live in a low-income neighborhood."

"That they do," Eli said. "Anything else?"

"One more thing," Lindsey said, her tone grim. "When Monica first reported the twins missing, Barnes told her he couldn't open a file for forty-eight hours."

Eli's blood ran hotter than Chinese mustard. "This is... this is beyond incompetence. It's negligence, like the sheriff said."

"I know, sweetheart," Lindsey's voice was soft and comforting. "What are you going to do?"

Eli's gaze drifted back to the window, his reflection staring back at him with an unyielding intensity. "Simple. We're going to find out what happened to those girls."

The sound of running water ceased, leaving a noticeable silence in its wake. "I'll call Sheriff Thornton first thing in the morning," Eli said. "I want to talk with him face-to-face."

The bathroom door opened, releasing a billowing cloud of steam. Dakota emerged, his tight frame wrapped in a white towel from waist to knees. Droplets of water traced paths down his bare chest. A toothbrush protruded from the corner of his mouth, foam gathering between his lips as he worked it back and forth.

"About that," Lindsey said, her voice tinged with hesitation. "The sheriff's leaving for a fishing trip tomorrow morning. It's some annual thing with old buddies."

"Can you text me his number?" The digital clock on the nightstand glowed 5:47 PM in red.

"Who's on the phone?" Dakota mumbled between strokes.

"Lindsey," Eli said.

Lindsey broke in. "You tell him he better call Karina. She's worried sick. This is the first time he's left town since she and her family arrived in Madisonville."

Karina Castillo was a Latina woman from Juarez City, just south of El Paso, Texas. Eli and Dakota met her when they worked with her brother Emilio to take down the trafficking cartel, Los Diablos.

He ended the call with Lindsey, and a text soon followed. Sheriff Thornton's number was at his fingertips.

"Call your girlfriend. Then get dressed," Eli said. "We might be having dinner in Pensacola."

Dakota spread a layer of shaving gel across his cheeks and chin. "Girlfriend? You talking about Karina?"

Eli pocketed his phone. "Yeah, Lindsey says she's worried. First time you've left town since she moved to Madisonville, right?"

Dakota's expression softened. "It sure is." He side-eyed Eli in the mirror's reflection. "Our relationship is at a place where we're still figuring things out."

Eli raised an eyebrow. "You two seemed pretty close in Juarez. What happened?"

Dakota sighed, dragging his razor above his upper lip. "Nothing. That's just it. We had this intense connection when we were rescuing her family from Diablos, but now..."

"Now reality's setting in?"

"Yeah," Dakota nodded. "She's still adjusting to

Louisiana. Her family's trying to build a new life. And what you and I do doesn't leave much room to build a relationship."

"Are the feelings still there?"

"Definitely," Dakota admitted, wiping his clean-shaven face with a fluffy towel. "Every time I see her, it's like we're back in Juarez. That spark, that bond. It's all still there."

"So what's holding you back?"

Dakota shrugged. "Fear, maybe? What if it doesn't work out? What if I'm not what she needs now?"

Eli nodded sympathetically. "Look, man. Our job. It's tough. But don't let it keep you from something good. Give her a call on our ride over to Pensacola."

"Yeah, you're right. I may do that."

The streetlights spilled their artificial glow across the empty parking lot. Traffic hummed along I-65, indifferent to the two girls waiting somewhere beyond the reach of headlights—waiting to be saved. Eli's mission was simple— bring them home, no matter the cost.

He dialed the number Lindsey had given him for Sheriff Hank Thornton, knowing he had only hours to catch him before his fishing trip—and after that, any hope of finding the twins quickly would slip away with the tide.

———

Eli eased his Jeep Wrangler onto Lola Drive, a quiet suburban street in Pensacola lined with lush green lawns and swaying palm trees. The sun had just dipped below the flat horizon, bathing the neighborhood in a golden hue. Dakota scrolled through his phone and glanced up at the row of similar-looking houses. "That one," he said, nodding toward 221, a blue house with a welcoming porch that stood out from its neighbors. It had a distinct charm that felt at odds with the macho demeanor Eli had expected from "Hank."

"He's got good taste," Dakota added as Eli slowed to pull into the driveway. "I guess so," Eli replied, cutting the engine. They climbed out of the Jeep, the scent of blooming jasmine wafting through the warm evening air. Before they could knock, the front door opened, revealing Hank Thornton.

Standing about six feet tall, the older man was imposing despite his sixty-plus years. His weathered face, framed by a head of silver hair, broke into a broad smile. Warmth twinkled in his green eyes, but an underlying quiet intensity remained. "Evening, gentlemen," Hank greeted, his voice a deep, resonant baritone. He stepped forward, his hand already extended. "You must be Eli and Dakota."

"That's us," Eli confirmed, shaking his hand.

Hank's grip was firm—reassuring. "Call me Hank," he said. "Come on in. My wife made some lemon bars if you're interested."

Wife? A flicker of relief softened Eli's nerves. He chuckled lightly.

"We wouldn't mind at all." The inside of Hank's house matched its exterior in charm. The walls were lined with framed photos, many capturing a younger Hank in various stages of his law enforcement career. Others depicted fishing trips and family gatherings. Eli glanced at a group photo of smiling kids holding freshly caught fish and felt a pang of envy for the man behind the badge.

"Make yourselves at home," Hank said, motioning toward the living room. "Can I get you something to drink? Water, coffee... maybe iced tea?"

"We're good, thanks," Eli said, settling onto a well-worn

leather couch. He noticed fishing rods stacked neatly in the corner, a testament to Hank's retirement life. As Dakota settled in beside him, Eli couldn't shake the mix of gratitude and apprehension.

Hank lowered himself into an armchair, his casual warmth giving way to measured seriousness. His hands rested on the chair's arms, fingers drumming lightly. "Before we dive in, I want you both to know... This case—it stuck with me. I've been hoping someone would take a fresh look at it."

Eli leaned forward, catching the weight of Hank's words in his steady gaze. "We appreciate you taking the time to meet with us, especially on such short notice." Hank nodded, his expression tightening with quiet resolve. "Let's get to it, then. What do you want to know about the Johnson twins?"

Dakota straightened in his seat. "Anything and everything you can tell us."

Hank exhaled sharply. "It's a shame, really, how that case was mishandled." He leaned forward, resting his forearms on his knees. "Let me tell you what I know. First off, there's this fella named Joseph Patrick Washington." Hank's forehead creased as if the name left a bitter taste in his mouth. "Nasty piece of work, that one. He was active in Prichard around the time the girls vanished."

Hank's expression darkened. "Washington lived and worked near areas the twins frequented. A pattern emerged with young Black women, especially teenagers." His voice dropped as if weighed down by anger and regret. "He was known for abducting, shooting, and raping his victims. He got seventeen consecutive life sentences right before I retired."

Dakota's jaw clenched. "What happened to him?"

"Died last week," Hank said flatly. "Heart failure, just before he could stand trial for two more murders."

Relief mingled with frustration in Eli's chest. If Washington was their guy, he was no longer a threat. But his death meant they might never have concrete answers.

Hank's gaze became distant. "Then there's Leo Johnson, the twins' father. He's got a checkered past—assault, attempted murder..."

Eli's chest tightened. "Go on."

Hank leaned back, running a hand through his silver hair. "There were claims of a drug party at his house the day the girls disappeared. He acted mighty suspicious right afterward."

Dakota's eyebrows shot up. "Where can we find him?"

"Can't," Hank said. "He passed away last month. But here's the kicker." He raised his right hand for effect. "Leo allegedly told his doctor he thought the twins were dead."

"Great," Dakota muttered under his breath, shaking his head.

"What do you think of Leo as a person of interest?" Eli asked in a careful tone.

Hank shrugged. "I don't see it. Monica—his wife—always said he loved the girls. But because of his record, he became a person of interest."

Dakota shot Eli a questioning glance. "Any ideas on how we can eliminate him from our list?"

Hank shook his head. "Not really. But here's something else." He rubbed his forehead as if trying to pull a memory from deep within. "The older sister, Jasmine, admitted to me that she'd covered for the girls the night before they disappeared. They went to this karaoke studio downtown."

Eli straightened, the hairs on the back of his neck prickling. "Did you follow up on that?"

"Sure did." Hank's gaze sharpened. "I interviewed a bunch of kids who were there that night. Several mentioned seeing the twins sitting with a woman—mid-thirties to forty, well-dressed. Said she was talking to them for quite a while."

"A woman that age at a teen karaoke spot?" Dakota asked, frowning.

"Exactly," Hank nodded. "The DJ confirmed it was unusual. Said she stuck out. Some of the other kids said she claimed to be a talent scout for a teen fashion magazine."

Eli exchanged a glance with Dakota. "Did anyone get her name?"

"No solid ID." Hank's lips pressed into a thin line. "But it's interesting, isn't it? A mysterious woman shows up at a teen hangout the night before two girls go missing?"

"You think she's a viable suspect?" Eli asked.

"I'd definitely follow up if I were still in office. But I saved my favorite POI for last," Hank added, his voice dropping. "A white van was seen outside the karaoke studio that night. Jasmine swore she saw a similar van in their neighborhood the day the girls went missing."

"Any leads on who was in it?" Eli asked.

Hank's eyes hardened. "None. My term as sheriff ended before I could dig further. But I made copies of the case file." He stood and moved to a bureau on the rear wall, leaving Eli and Dakota in tense silence.

When Hank returned with the folders, Eli felt a glimmer of hope. "Thank you, Sheriff. This... this means a lot."

Hank's eyes softened. "Just doing what's right, son." But as Eli and Dakota stood to leave, Hank's expression turned somber. "One more thing, boys."

They paused.

Hank's voice was a low growl. "Watch yourselves. This

case... It's never sat right with me. Feels like someone's been pulling strings behind the scenes." Eli frowned.

"What do you mean?" Hank shook his head, his jaw tightening. "Can't put my finger on it, just a gut instinct. Just be careful whom you trust."

As they walked back to the Jeep, Hank's warning lingered in the humid night air. Eli glanced at Dakota and saw his own unease reflected in his partner's eyes. Whatever they were about to uncover, it was clear they had stepped into something far more mysterious than they had anticipated.

5

Eli blinked at the folders spread across both beds in his and Dakota's hotel room. His back ached from hunching over for hours. He rubbed his temples, trying to massage away the headache building behind his eyes.

Dakota hunched over his own pile of documents in the corner. "So what's our play?" Dakota tossed a folder onto the hotel bed. "Two solid leads, two months cold, and we're running out of time."

Eli leaned back in his chair. "Let's break it down. What do we know about the woman at the studio?"

Dakota consulted the notes. "Well-dressed, thirties to forties. Spent time talking to the twins. Several witnesses confirmed seeing her."

"And the van?"

"White, seen outside the studio that night. Then again in the neighborhood the next morning when the girls disappeared." Dakota looked up. "Jasmine—their sister—told Hank that she saw it, but Barnes told us nothing about a white van."

"The woman's our closest connection to the girls," Eli said. "The twins interacted with her."

"Yeah, but after two months?" Dakota shook his head. "Studio employees have probably turned over. Security footage is long gone. And 'a well-dressed woman' isn't much to go on."

"Could canvas the neighborhood around the studio. Someone might remember a woman matching that description."

"In Mobile, Alabama? That's a lot of ground to cover." Dakota started pacing. "The van, though—we've got multiple sightings, same vehicle, same time frame."

"And Jasmine never gave a formal statement about it to Prichard PD that we know of." Eli straightened. "Barnes dropped the ball there."

"But which one gets us closer to the girls?" Dakota stopped pacing. "The woman had direct contact. The van's just circumstantial."

"Unless they're connected." Eli stood up. "Think about it —a woman shows up at a teen karaoke spot, the van appears outside. The next morning, the same van's in their neighborhood?"

"You think she was working with whoever was in the van?"

"Makes sense, doesn't it? She makes contact while her partner watches from outside." Dakota ran a hand through his hair. "So which thread do we pull first?"

Eli drummed his fingers on the desk. "The van. Jasmine's our only witness who saw it. She might remember something Barnes never thought to ask about."

"And if she doesn't?"

"Then we hit the studio. But right now..." Eli reached for

his phone. "Let's see what Monica says about us talking to Jasmine."

"You sure about this?" Dakota asked. "The woman feels stronger."

"It does," Eli admitted. "But my gut says the van's our best shot. Two confirmed sightings, one witness we can actually talk to. That's more than we had yesterday."

Dakota nodded slowly. "Alright. Let's see what Jasmine knows."

One hour later, the steering wheel was slick under Eli's palms as he guided the Jeep down Martin Luther King Jr. Boulevard in Prichard. The humidity was still thick even as dusk approached. His gut churned at the thought of opening past traumas. What nightmares had the sisters' disappearance left with Jasmine?

"You're mumbling," Dakota said, breaking into Eli's thoughts.

"Just considering how to handle the interview."

"Any concerns?" Dakota asked, his voice lacking its usual confidence.

"Yep," Eli said, drumming his fingers on the wheel. Dakota's grim face glowed in the dashboard light. "So what's the play?"

"We go in soft. No pressure. Let her set the pace."

"Agreed," Dakota said. "Start with questions about the twins before they disappeared. Build a rapport, then we dive into the heavy stuff."

"Good call. But I can't help thinking about Jasmine. She sort of reminds me of dealing with Julia when I first met with her after Tara went missing. Digging into people's pain during their darkest moments is the worst part of this job."

Dakota said nothing, just nodded. His typical bravado

had faded, replaced by a somber determination that matched Eli's mood.

Jasmine opened the front door, one finger pressed to her lips. She stood there, shoulders hunched beneath an over-sized t-shirt, her gangly limbs at odds with the weary lines around her eyes. A baby's soft breathing drifted from a hooded bassinet in the corner of the living room.

"Hi, Jasmine," Eli whispered, careful not to wake the infant. "I'm Eli Colt, and this is my partner, Dakota Sutcliffe. Your mom said it was okay for us to talk to you about Aaliyah and Kiara."

With a dip of her chin, she stepped back to let them in, carefully closing the door to avoid any noise. She slumped onto her living room couch, positioning herself where she could see both her visitors and the bassinet. Eli sat across from her, giving her space.

"Your mom asked us to find out what happened to your sisters," he said, studying her eyes for any flicker of emotion. "Anything you remember, even if it seems small, could help."

Jasmine's eyes darted to a photo on the mantel—three girls laughing at the beach. "I saw them that morning. Before..." her words drifted.

"Take your time. Just tell me about that day, if you can," Eli said.

She closed her eyes as if rewinding her mind. "It was hot. Aaliyah was excited about something. Kiara, not so much." A ghost of a smile touched her lips, then vanished. "Mom had already left for work and the girls were late for school, so..." her voice cracked, "we didn't talk much."

"It's okay," Eli said. "Take your time."

Jasmine took a shuddering breath. "When they left, there was a white van parked across the street. It started up as soon as Aaliyah and Kiara ran for the bus stop. Then it drove off real slow-like."

"Did you see who was driving?" Eli asked.

She nodded, eyes still closed. "A man. Black. He had a scar, here." Her finger traced a line from the corner of her eye to her jaw. "Did you recognize him?"

Jasmine's eyes snapped open as if waking from a bad dream. "No, but... he smiled at me. It wasn't a nice smile."

A chill crawled across Eli's skin, raising goosebumps in its wake. He slowed his breathing. "You're doing great, Jasmine. Is there anything else you remember about the van? Any writing on it, or dents, or something unusual?"

She frowned. "There was... a picture. On the side. Like a mouse or a rat. It had pointy ears and a long nose."

"A logo?" Eli asked. "That's intriguing, Jasmine. Can you draw what it looks like?"

"I already have," she said. "For the police. But that detective didn't seem too interested." She rose and strolled into the next room, returning almost immediately. "There's something else." She shuffled through the pages. "I saw the van again. After. Near the old warehouse on Elm."

A jolt of electricity shuddered through Eli's system. Could this be the lead they'd been looking for? Eli wanted to push, but Jasmine's sad expression signaled she'd reached her limit.

"You've been so brave," Eli said as he folded the paper Jasmine handed him. "What you've shared will help us find out what happened to your sisters."

Inside the Jeep, Eli stared at Jasmine's sketch, the gears in his head churning. The image was too specific, too intentional. A company logo, no doubt about it. The elongated snout, the alert ears, the mousy eyes. This wasn't just a friendly family pet. No. This creature was a feral rodent. It reminded him of... *Crap.* Of course. Pest control. That's why it looked so familiar. Eli had seen similar logos on exterminator vans throughout the Southeast. A rat perched on the vans of a regional pest control service.

He handed the paper to Dakota. "What do you see?"

Dakota studied the logo for less than ten seconds before handing it back and pulling out his phone. "Wild Guard Exterminators," Dakota said. "They have locations from Louisiana to Florida."

Every nerve from Eli's core to his fingers came alive. "A pest control van has access to homes, businesses, and... abandoned warehouses." Dakota's eyes lit up with a fierce gleam as he scrolled his phone's screen. "I'm searching for Wild Guard's nearest location."

———

WITHIN THE HOUR, pungent vapors stung Eli's nose as he and Dakota eased into the back lot of Wild Guard Exterminators. Workers scurried between vans, hauling equipment and sloshing chemical containers that gleamed under the mid-morning sun. Eli clutched the door handle, his stomach churning with restless tension. Were they finally closing in on the Johnson twins' kidnapper? They stepped into the warm air. Eli studied each face he encountered in search of a scar.

Inside, a young woman greeted them with a smile that didn't quite reach her eyes. "Can I help you?"

"We need to speak with the manager," Eli said, flashing his PI badge.

Her smile faltered. "Of course." She pushed a button on her phone. "Jerry. The police are here to see you."

Eli didn't correct her.

"His office is down the hall," she said. "Last door on the right."

As they walked down a narrow corridor, Eli scanned their surroundings, noticing a whiteboard with routes and schedules. The manager's door stood ajar. "Come in," someone said from inside.

A balding man in his fifties eyed them from behind a cluttered desk. "What can I do for you gentlemen?"

"We're looking for one of your employees," Eli said, disregarding any pleasantries. "Black male, late thirties to early forties," Eli traced his face like Jasmine did the night before. "With a distinctive scar from the corner of his eye to his jaw."

The manager's face drained of all color. "I'm not at liberty to discuss employee information. You'll have to call Human Resources at the corporate office."

Dakota stepped forward, his voice kind but urgent. "Sir, we're investigating the disappearance of two young girls. Every second counts."

The manager's eyes darted between them, and his Adam's apple bobbed as he swallowed hard.

Eli didn't relent. "The Johnson twins. Aaliyah and Kiara. They've been missing for two months. This man was seen following them in one of your vans. We can wait for a warrant if you want the news to report that you didn't cooperate."

A heavy silence fell. Contemplation seemed to grind behind the manager's furrowed brow. Finally, he slumped his shoulders and sighed. "His name is Charles Reddick. I can give you his address."

"Is he working today?" Dakota's words tumbled out faster than usual.

The manager pulled a file from a cabinet and scribbled

on a piece of paper. "I'm not sure. You can check with the dispatcher."

As they left the office, Eli marched to the whiteboard in the corridor. There, next to Charles Reddick in big letters, was the location for his morning schedule—Telegraph Road.

"Excuse me," Eli asked the girl at the front counter. "What type of businesses do you service on Telegraph Road?"

She looked up from a stack of invoices. "Well, that's a commercial area. Nothing but warehouses."

"Is it close to Elm Street?" Dakota asked.

The girl's head tilted slightly. "It runs right into it."

Eli's blood froze in his veins. The old warehouse on Elm —where Jasmine had seen the van again.

He and Dakota practically ran to the Jeep. As Eli gunned the engine, a wave of doubt washed over him. "We're operating on circumstantial evidence at best," he said. "Maybe we should call Barnes, get some backup."

Dakota's face was grim. "You think he'll leave his desk to solve a case?" He chuckled. "I don't."

A traffic light at the next corner flashed red. Eli's foot eased on the brake. But if they were wrong... No. Not worth the risk. "Man, I hate doing this."

"What?" Dakota asked.

Eli fumbled for his phone, punching in the number before he could change his mind. "I'm calling Barnes."

The line rang for several seconds. Eli accelerated as the light turned green.

"Barnes." The detective's voice was gruff and impatient.

"This is Eli Colt. My partner and I got a lead on the missing Johnson girls."

"That so?"

"Look," Eli jutted his jaw forward as he braced for a confrontation. No time for pleasantries. "Wild Guard Exterminators. Their van was spotted following the twins and later by an abandoned warehouse. I've got a person of interest who matches an eyewitness description."

Silence stretched for a beat. Then two.

"And?"

"And we're heading there now. Thought you might want to join us."

Another pause. Eli could almost hear Barnes' gears grinding in the receiver.

"Fine," Barnes grunted. "You better not be wasting my time."

The line went dead.

Eli pocketed his phone as warehouses rose up ahead. In an alley near Elm Street, the white van with the rat logo glinted in the sun. "There," Eli indicated, pulling to the curb. A figure emerged, moving with deliberate precision. Sunlight caught the jagged scar etched from eye to jaw. Cold, calculating eyes scanned the area, locking onto the Jeep.

Charles Reddick, unmistakable even from this distance.

6

Eli's boots crunched on loose gravel as he eased out of the Jeep. If they waited for Barnes, Riddick would vanish—along with any chance of finding the Johnson twins. At his side, Dakota kept pace, his hand hovering near his holster. Their eyes met briefly, a silent conversation of shared anxiety.

Dakota fell in step beside him, one hand resting near his holster. Their eyes met—no words were needed. No more dead ends. Their person of interest was here.

Riddick disappeared into the warehouse through a rusted side door.

"Wait for Barnes?" Dakota asked.

"No time," Eli said, shaking his head. They had to follow now or risk never seeing this man again. One step forward. Then another. A cold fist swelled inside his chest. Beyond the rusted side door, Riddick waited.

Eli's hand found the grip of his pistol. Sweat formed at his temples. Ten yards. Five. The stench of stale rainwater was overwhelming. Eli hesitated at the threshold, straining to hear any sound from inside. Nothing. He gave Dakota a slight nod, then entered.

It took a few seconds for Eli's eyes to adjust, shapes slowly emerging in the darkness.

Feeble light filtered through broken windows, casting eerie shadows across rusted machinery. Dakota's shallow breathing ghosted behind him.

Eli and Dakota froze at a metallic clang. Then a scrape, like something heavy being dragged. Eli nodded Dakota forward. The sounds grew louder as they ventured into the cavernous space. Eli's pulse thundered against his eardrums, threatening to drown out everything else. They reached a corner and rounded it. And there he was—Riddick.

He stood in a pool of sickly yellow light, his scarred face and raging eyes an angry display of malice. No one moved for ten seconds.

"Hands where we can see them," Eli said calmly, despite the adrenaline rush.

Riddick's lips curled into something between a sneer and a smile. "Took you long enough," he drawled, not moving an inch.

Eli's fingers brushed against his weapon. The air was thick with dust and humidity. Riddick's eyes darted like a cornered animal.

"We have a few questions," Dakota said, his usual calm fraying at the edges. "We just want to talk."

"Talk about what?" Riddick's hands inched toward his back, the movement setting off alarm bells.

"Gun!" Dakota shouted as he dove behind a pile of scrap metal.

A deafening crack. Sparks flew as the bullet ricocheted off Dakota's cover. Then Riddick ran into the darkness.

Eli's body moved on autopilot, adrenaline overriding reason. "I'm on him!" he yelled to Dakota. A voice in the back of his mind screamed to wait, but he had to catch Riddick.

The warehouse stretched into a maze bathed in slivers of dusty light. Eli's breathing accelerated as he weaved through an obstacle course of abandoned equipment.

A flash of movement to his left. He pivoted, nearly losing his footing on the slick concrete.

"Stop!" The word tore through his throat. He plunged into the confused darkness. Light grew scarcer, shadows thicker. He strained his ears for any sound. A crash echoed ahead. Eli surged forward. Any rational thought gave way to finding the Johnson twins. He turned into a forest of floor-to-ceiling shelving. "Dakota?" he called, suddenly aware of his isolation.

No answer.

Wait for Dakota or find Riddick? Each second of indecision risked the twins' fate. He delved into the maze. Just a little further. Just one more turn.

A shadow moved two aisles over. Eli's pulse hammered harder. He sprinted to the bend only to discover an endless aisle between massive shelving. His boots pounded against the concrete as he sprinted. The familiar static assaulted his head. His vision wavered. His vision blurred—doubling, then tripling the shelves ahead. Each footfall sent lightning through his temples—his TBI symptoms flaring to life.

Please God, not here. Not when I'm this close.

The world tilted sideways. Nausea rose to his throat. He blinked hard, trying to focus. The ringing crescendoed, drowning out his labored breathing.

Eli somehow maintained his pace. Every few seconds,

he'd lift his gaze, scanning for any sign of Riddick in a canyon of metal fading into inky blackness.

Eli raised his head. Something suddenly appeared. Before he could react, his forehead slammed into whatever jutted out from the shelving. The impact sent him heels overhead. Stars exploded in his vision as his back crashed into the concrete floor.

His head now raged with a deafening roar. Pain blasted behind his eyes. His consciousness fading as footfalls approached.

Hands grabbed him. Lifted him. Propped his back against a rough surface.

Riddick loomed over him, gun still in hand. "Why you come here?" His voice sliced through the ringing in Eli's ears. "What I do to you?"

Struggling to focus, Eli labored to sit up. "You were seen stalking them," he said. "Right before they disappeared."

Riddick laughed—a harsh, grating sound. "Who disappeared?"

"Aaliyah and Kiara Johnson."

"Them twins who went missing," he said, his confusion genuine. "That weren't me."

"Like I said, you were seen following them the day they vanished."

"That weren't me, I tell you. That were a lady in a fancy car."

"What are you talking about?" Eli forced the words out. But light faded to dark, and he heard nothing else.

ELI BLINKED. The warehouse ceiling blurred and doubled, a kaleidoscope of rush and shadow. Each wave of consciousness brought a fresh surge of pain. The world tilted violently as he tried to sit up.

Not again. Please, not again.

The familiar fog of concussion crept in at the edges of his mind. His stomach twisted with a nauseating mix of vertigo and dread. Memories flashed—Freddy Badeau and his aluminum bat, the deafening roar of an explosion, Eli's body slamming into an unforgiving building. Another head injury could set him back months, maybe years, inflaming the TBI he'd fought so hard to conquer.

Pushing back against the encroaching cloud of confusion, he tried to focus. *Riddick. Where was Riddick? Gone.* The monster had escaped while Eli lay helpless on the cold concrete. And Dakota... "Dakota?" he screamed, setting off a ringing in his ears.

But only silence answered.

Should he chase Riddick alone, pressing through the fog and risking everything he'd worked for? Or find Dakota, get help, and let the trail go cold? Let the twins and their mother down. He recalled Aaliyah and Kiera in their photos, as if their eyes pleaded with him to continue. But then, memories of his recovery after returning from Juarez —hospital rooms, concerned doctors, endless months of therapy, and frustration.

"You're no good to anyone if you can't function."

With a groan of pain and resignation, Eli rolled to his knees, engulfed by a heavy sense of defeat. Trailing his hand along rusted metal shelving, he moved deeper into the warehouse. Each step echoed, broadcasting his vulnerability. Water dripped somewhere in the darkness.

Someone moved in the shadows ahead.

His heart hammered. *Dakota or Riddick?*

Drawing his weapon, he fought to keep it steady. A figure darted between containers.

"Police!" The word tore from his raw throat. "Don't move!"

The figure froze, then slowly raised its hands. "Eli? That you?"

"Dakota?" he responded with relief.

Dakota stepped into view, lowering his pistol as he rushed to Eli. "What happened?"

With his adrenaline ebbing, Eli sagged against Dakota in exhaustion. "Riddick. He got away."

Dakota braced Eli's head with one hand and lifted his eyelid with the other. "Right now, I'm more worried about your head. We need to get you checked out." He retracted his hand from behind Eli's ear. "You're bleeding. Another blow to the head?"

"I noticed," Eli said with a slight slur.

"Can you walk?"

Eli nodded but immediately regretted the movement as pain followed. "Yeah. Let's get out of here."

As they made their way to the exit, Eli couldn't shake the feeling that, for now, the case was over.

They'd lost because Eli had been foolish. Tomorrow, he'd be back in Madisonville getting his head examined. His neurologist appointment might do what Riddick couldn't— end Eli's chance of finding the twins.

The metallic tang of blood filled Eli's mouth as Dakota half-carried him to the warehouse exit.

"Easy," Dakota said. "Almost there."

They pushed through the door that groaned on its hinges. Red and blue lights pierced Eli's eyelids like hot needles. He squeezed his eyes shut against the throbbing of a fresh migraine. Dakota's shoulder was the only thing steadying him in a world that wouldn't stop spinning.

Eli forced his eyes open. Images swam into focus, then blurred again. But through the murk, a familiar figure caught his attention—Riddick. Even in his confusion, the scar was unmistakable.

His assailant stood near a patrol car, hands behind his back as a uniformed officer cinched his wrists with handcuffs.

Relief flooded through Eli, quickly followed by a nagging doubt he couldn't quite place. Something felt... Off.

Movement drew his gaze. Detective Barnes, his face set in hard lines, strode toward them. Eli's stomach clenched at the glint in the detective's eyes.

"Well, well," Barnes sneered as he reached them. "If it isn't our dynamic duo."

Dakota tensed beside him. "We got him, didn't we?"

Barnes's laugh was cold. "No, we got him. You two bumbled around like amateurs. And by the looks of it, you nearly got yourselves killed."

Eli was too exhausted to rise to the bait. "Detective," he said, his voice raw. "When do you plan to interview Riddick?"

"Soon," Barnes replied, as if he knew where this conversation was headed.

"I'd like to be there," Eli blurted through his nausea.

"Well, you won't be." Barnes leaned in so close that his warm breath hit Eli's cheek. "You're done here. Both of you. Go home and leave the real detective work to the professionals."

"Oh, please," Dakota retorted with thick sarcasm. "You'd be hard-pressed to find water if you fell in a lake."

Barnes sneered, then turned away. Behind him, the

patrol officer lowered Riddick's head as he entered the police cruiser. Through Eli's concussed haze, Riddick disappeared into the back seat. The patrol car's engine roared to life and rolled away, taking their only lead to finding the Johnson twins with it.

Eli balled his hands in restrained anger. He couldn't let Barnes take control of this case. Somehow, someway, he had to interrogate Riddick.

7

Gabriel's ears perked at the crackling from the marine VHF radio.

"*Pan-Pan, Pan-Pan*," shrilled Rafael's voice through the speaker, "*Pan-Pan*. Come in, Costa Segura. This is Esperanza, registration HN2670. Come in, Costa Segura. We have engine failure and are stranded at coordinates 16°5'N, 86°5'W. That's coordinates 16°5'N, 86°5'W."

Rain hammered against the corrugated metal roof of his father's office as Gabriel straightened in his chair, homework forgotten. The earthy scent of wet soil drifted through the window, mingling with the phantom smell of gunpowder that had lingered since that night on the pier when the American had murdered Manuelo.

Papa's hand trembled as he held down the transmit button. "*Esperanza*, this is Costa Segura. Hold on, son. We hear you. What's the status of the crew?"

"We're fine, but the engine's dead, and the storm's getting worse." Static hissed through a long pause. "We're drifting."

"Rafael, listen carefully," Papa said, running his

calloused hand through his gray-flecked hair. "Check the fuel line and make sure it's not clogged. Try to restart the engine. If that doesn't work, secure the anchor. I'm coordinating help right now."

"Understood, Papa," Rafael said, his voice wavering. "Trying to restart the engine. Please hurry."

"Stay calm, son. I'll have help on the way soon. Costa Segura out."

Thunder boomed overhead as Papa paced the small office, his heavy footsteps matching Gabriel's accelerating heartbeat. The walls seemed to close in around them.

"*Ay, Dios mío*," Papa said. "Sounds like they need a new fuel pump." He turned to Gabriel. "Start making calls. I'll get a repair crew out there now."

Gabriel's mind raced as his father's shoulders sagged with each unanswered emergency call. The storm's fury intensified, rattling the windows.

With sudden determination, Gabriel shot up from his seat. "I'll take the pump to them, Papa, while you keep trying the radio."

Papa halted his pacing, eyes wide with shock and apprehension. "No, Gabriel. It's too dangerous with this storm. I'll figure something else out."

"They're my brothers," Gabriel insisted, planting his feet firmly on the wooden floor. "I love them. And if I'm to run this business, I need to earn their respect."

Lightning flashed, illuminating Papa's conflicted expression. The shutters rattled against the building. "Please, Papa. Trust me," Gabriel's voice broke slightly.

Papa sighed deeply, his resistance fading. Finally, he nodded and pulled Gabriel into a tight embrace. "*Mi hijo,*" he said as he handed over the keys to the small dinghy. "I'll get the pump from storage."

With a last look at his Papa's troubled eyes, Gabriel turned and dashed into the storm that swallowed him in a torrent of rain. The roaring wind whipped at his clothes, and the thunder boomed so loudly it felt like the skies were about to tear apart. He shivered as the droplets soaked through his thin shirt when he stepped onto the dock. The steps were slippery and unsteady, but he finally reached the small skiff that would carry him to his brothers.

The memory of Rafael's rebuke that morning hit him like a spray of salt water. "Your books? Your dreams? You'll never be one of us."

Gabriel clambered aboard the snub-nosed dinghy, each movement sending icy rain sluicing down his back. With fingers numb from the cold, he clutched the wrapped fuel pump as if it were a king's treasure. The boat rocked precariously under the onslaught of relentless waves, and he struggled to secure the vital part in a waterproof compartment.

He fumbled with the GPS controls. "What if I'm not cut out for this?" He closed his eyes for a moment, allowing the tension to drain from his shoulders. With trembling fingers, he carefully entered the coordinates that Rafael had transmitted over the radio.

"C'mon, c'mon," Gabriel yelled in impatience, glancing nervously at the dark, frothing water that stretched endlessly in all directions. Finally, the device pinged with confirmation, a small but fervent victory amid the frenzy.

As the dinghy lurched forward, Gabriel braced himself against the jerking vessel, gripping the wheel with white-knuckled resolve. The storm raged around him, each gust of wind seeming sentient, determined to push him off course.

Salt spray stung his eyes, cutting his visibility. Out of the gloom, a swell reared up only yards ahead, sending his heart racing. He steered the craft to the side just in time to escape being capsized. The wave crashed down behind him.

Gabriel's lungs burned with every labored breath. "Focus, just focus," he urged himself, his eyes scanning the horizon for another boat.

Minutes, then a half-hour, slipped by in a punishing blur. The dinghy bobbed and weaved through the turmoil, each moment a battle against the ferocious sea. A sudden gust of wind caught him off guard, slamming his vessel hard to port. Gabriel's body slammed against the side, pain shooting through his ribs. Gritting his teeth, he strained his burning limbs to right the course.

Careful to stay on track, he stole glances at the GPS, reassured by the blinking dot guiding his path. But just as hope began to steady his nerves, a new threat emerged. A jagged reef loomed out of the tempest, its dark, razor-like edges barely visible until the last second. Gabriel's muscles screamed in protest as he yanked the wheel, the dinghy responding sluggishly, scraping perilously close to the deadly rocks.

Exhaustion clawed at Gabriel, but the sight of the coordinates ticking closer renewed his determination. For an hour, he fought the remnants of the storm, its rage finally beginning to wane. The rain lessened. The wind's shriek softened. The sea, though still choppy, began to calm.

With his body shivering from cold and exertion, he wiped his face with an oily rag and squinted against the gray horizon. Then, just as weariness threatened to overtake him, a shape materialized through the dissipating mist. Hope ignited in his chest. The silhouette of the trawler emerged, bobbing gently on the waves.

"There," he breathed, steering the dinghy toward the vessel. Relief crashed over him like a wave, lifting his fear and fatigue. The storm had tested him, but he'd endured. Now, the promise of his brothers' welcoming faces urged him forward.

His heart soared as the fishing vessel loomed into clearer view. But as he drew closer, his elation turned to confusion. The engine, which Rafael had claimed was broken, purred like a content kitten. Gabriel tied the dinghy's engine to the side of the larger vessel.

Climbing aboard, Gabriel was greeted with menacing glares. Rafael stood by the wheel, his knuckles white against the polished wood, just as he had gripped the dock post when he'd shoved Gabriel last week. Oscar and Ernesto lingered near the stern, Oscar's face twisted with familiar resentment, while Ernesto kept his eyes on the deck, shoulders hunched with shame.

"What's going on?" Gabriel asked, his voice rough from the salt air. "The engine, it's—it's fine. You lied. All that about being in danger—" His words caught in his throat as the truth began to dawn.

Rafael's lip curled in a sneer. "Always so quick to figure things out, aren't you, *hermano*? The smart one. The special one."

"The one Papa chose over us," Oscar said, taking a step forward. "While we worked with the nets, you worked with your books."

Ernesto remained silent, but his hands trembled at his sides.

Before Gabriel could press further, the sound of another engine diverted his attention. A fifty-foot vessel cut through the mist like a predator, its prow splitting the waves effortlessly. Dread pooled in Gabriel's stomach as he recognized the boat—the white yacht he'd been dreaming about for weeks. Was this some cruel joke? Was God laughing in heaven?

Fear sparked in Gabriel's chest as the face of the gringo—the man who'd gunned down Manuelo—became clearer. The same cold blue eyes, the same vicious smile. Beside him stood a rough-looking Honduran, his pitted face marred with tattoos.

"No," Gabriel said, backing away. "Brothers, please—you know what he did to Manuelo."

Rafael's face hardened. "Manuelo was weak and didn't understand business. We do."

The American leapt aboard their vessel with practiced ease. His boots hit the deck with a hollow thud. The Honduran followed, moving with the fluid grace of a cat hunting.

"What do you want?" Gabriel said, his voice betraying the terror he'd been fighting to contain.

The gringo's malicious smile widened. "I'm here to collect."

"What—what do you mean?" Through his stammered words, the truth revealed itself—in Ernesto's avoiding eyes, in Oscar's clenched fists, in Rafael's guilty shuffle.

"Your brother here," the gringo gestured to Rafael, "made a deal. And you, my friend, are it."

With his legs giving way, Gabriel's knees struck the deck hard enough to send shockwaves of pain through his body. He glanced at his brothers one last time, searching their faces for any trace of regret or compassion. "Rafael. Remember when we were kids? You taught me to swim, to tie knots. You protected me."

Rafael's jaw tightened. "This is protecting you," he said, but his voice wavered. "From your stupid dreams."

The gringo and the native stepped forward as one. There

was no escape. What his brothers had done was unforgivable—betrayed him to the man who had brought terror to their town.

The Honduran seized Gabriel's arm with a grip like iron. He twisted, trying to break free.

Rafael and Ernesto stood still with stony indifference.

Gabriel's eyes settled on each brother, one at a time. But the stares they returned were hardened.

Hurt and anger welled up in Gabriel's chest. "What do you think Papa would say if he knew?" He was searching for a love that once bound them together. But his words failed to penetrate their cold expressions.

Rafael stepped forward, his face a mask of resolve. "This is for the family, Gabriel. Papa doesn't know what's good for us."

The gringo drew closer with amusement in his eyes.

Then, without warning, Rafael ripped off Gabriel's guayabera shirt, tearing the fabric in two. The rain, though lessening, felt like needles against his bare skin. He was dragged to the gringo's boat, his feet scrabbling uselessly across the deck.

"Please," he gasped, the wind chilling his exposed flesh, "please."

Oscar turned away, unable or unwilling to meet Gabriel's eyes. Tomas stood motionless, his face a mask of silent acceptance.

As Gabriel was hauled onboard the fifty-foot yacht, Rafael's sneer was the last thing he saw before they shoved him into the hold and slammed the door shut with a final thud.

The betrayal was complete, but where would it take him? Where would the boat of his dreams take him?

8

Friday, August 2

Eli sat on the worn couch, his knee bouncing over the threadbare carpet, each silent tap marking another second Barnes could be closing the case on the wrong man. Lacing his fingers together, Eli fixed his gaze on Monica Johnson.

Across from him, Monica hunched her shoulders in a faded armchair as if bearing an unbearable weight. Jasmine, her eldest daughter, curled up in the corner of a matching loveseat. Dakota leaned back against the wall nearest the doorway, arms folded, eyes scanning the room.

The tick-tock of an old clock punctuated the heavy silence as if the time to solve the twins' disappearance slipped away. A family photo on the mantel caught the fading light. The twins' frozen grins haunted the room like ghosts of happier times.

"Monica," Eli said in an empathetic tone. "I know this might be hard to hear, but I don't believe Charles Reddick is responsible for Aaliyah and Kiera's disappearance."

"What?" Monica asked, her head snapping up. "But the police—they assured me he is the man."

"He drives the same van that followed my sisters the day they disappeared," Jasmine said. "They showed me a picture of it this morning."

"Look," Dakota interjected, pushing off from the wall and stepping forward. "We get it. But if we truly believed Reddick took your daughters, we'd pack our bags and go back to Louisiana."

Eli stood, running a hand through his hair as he began to pace the tattered carpet. "But we're not convinced," he said, pacing the room. "Did Aaliyah or Kiara ever mention talking to a woman who drove a fancy car?"

Monica and Jasmine gazed at one another, both wearing confused expressions. "No," Jasmine said, while Monica shook her head.

Stepping to the mantel, Eli stared at a photo of Kiara and Aaliyah beside a ticking antique clock. "We asked Detective Barnes if we could be present when he interviewed Reddick. He refused."

"Why would he do that?" Monica asked.

"Because he's looking to close this case as quickly as possible," Dakota said. "If he can charge Reddick for this crime, he can move on."

"Move on from what?" Jasmine asked. "That man never cared for my baby sisters. He moved on a long time ago."

"That's why we're here," Eli said. "We want you to demand Detective Barnes allows us to be there for that interrogation."

"We can demand all we want," Monica replied. "That doesn't mean he's going to listen to me."

Jasmine sprang from her seat, her eyes blazing with a sudden fire. "Mom, make the call," she blurted, her voice cracking with emotion. "We can't just sit here and do nothing. If Mr. Colt thinks there's more to this, we have to find out."

Monica recoiled as if struck, her shoulders curling inward. She raised a trembling hand to her mouth at her daughter's outburst.

Eli turned from the mantle, his expression relaxing as he took in Monica's distress. Crossing the room in a few quick strides, he crouched down to her eye level. "Monica," he said. "I know this is hard to hear. But we need to be in that room with Reddick. Some questions have to be answered, details we can't afford to ignore. If there's nothing there, then we can put this to bed, and you can grieve for your daughters."

The mantel clock's ticking seemed to grow louder in the tense silence.

Monica's gaze drifted to the twins' photo on the mantle, her eyes glistening with unshed tears. "Lord, my babies."

Eli's throat tightened. Monica squared her shoulders with newfound resolve. "What if that Detective Barnes says no?" she asked, her voice stronger now. "He hasn't been too keen on listening to anybody but himself."

Leaning in, Eli spoke softly but urgently. "Then you tell him you'll go to every news outlet in Mobile. Let them know how, from the beginning, the Prichard police didn't care about finding your daughters."

He exchanged a hopeful glance with Dakota, sensing a shift in Monica's demeanor.

Jasmine moved closer to her mother, placing a hand on her arm. "Mama, you gotta do this. For Aaliyah and Kiara. They can't forget about them girls."

Her mother nodded slowly, reaching for her phone on

the side table. "Alright then," she said, setting her jaw. "Let's see if Detective Barnes is ready to listen."

Eli caught Monica's eye and offered a reassuring nod. "You've got this, Monica," he said with confidence.

Monica's thumb hovered over the call button before she tapped the screen. She raised the phone to her ear and straightened her back as if preparing for battle. The room fell silent, save for the ticking clock.

Locking eyes with Dakota, Eli tilted his head toward the door. He'd just given Monica hope, but with it came the crushing responsibility to deliver.

At the threshold, Eli glanced back. Monica was speaking now, her voice low but determined, while Jasmine held her free hand. The scene hit too close to home—another mother fighting for her children, just like his sister-in-law Julia had fought for Tara. He vowed silently that this story would end the same way.

Time to make Barnes listen.

———

ELI STOOD rigid in the observation room, the air thick with old coffee and sweat. His faint reflection hovered in the two-way mirror, beyond which Reddick sat under harsh lights, his interrogation teetering on the edge of collapse. Dakota stood beside Eli, his breath fogging the glass.

Inside, three figures sat under the glare of a buzzing fluorescent light. Detective Barnes hunched over the battered metal table, his pear-shaped torso spilling against the rickety chair. Every line on his face seemed etched deeper by the harsh lighting, his thinning crown glinting faintly. The coffee stain on his wrinkled white shirt hadn't been fresh for hours.

Across from him, Charles Reddick sat with slumped shoulders, his eyes darting between Barnes and the young man to his left. The public defender, couldn't have been more than a year out of law school. His bargain-bin suit was still creased from the rack and his baby smooth face showed no hint of wear. Yet, despite his youth, the lawyer's voice cut through Barnes's gruff tone like a scalpel.

"You expect us to believe you just happened to be in the area?" Barnes's voice crackled through the speaker in the observation room.

Reddick's lawyer rested an elbow on the table, his tone smooth and unshaken. "Detective, my client has already provided a detailed account of his whereabouts. Unless you have evidence contradicting his statement, I suggest we move on."

"I'll decide what's relevant here, counselor," Barnes snapped, his face flushing an unhealthy red.

Dakota smirked. "Kid's got some teeth. He's making a meal out of poor Avery."

Eli's lips twitched, but his jaw stayed tight. " Barnes is losing control of the interrogation."

The young lawyer adjusted his tie. "Detective, if you're implying my client had prior knowledge of the crime, I must insist you present any evidence supporting that claim. Otherwise, this line of questioning is both irrelevant and potentially prejudicial."

Barnes scowled and shuffled through his notes, clearly thrown off balance. "I'm not implying anything. I have a witness, you young twit."

The lawyer raised a single eyebrow, like a professor correcting an unruly student. "Did your witness see my client take the girls?"

Barnes faltered, his lips parting in a moment of hesitation.

"And we've been more than cooperative," the lawyer added, smoothly taking advantage. "However, if you persist in this circular questioning without presenting new information, I'll have to advise my client to invoke his right to remain silent."

Eli's jaw clenched, his fingers tapping against the edge of the observation window. "He's getting played," he muttered under his breath. "Barnes can't keep up."

"I'd like to see you do better," Dakota said, though there was a hint of curiosity beneath the teasing tone.

Eli didn't rise to the bait, but his fingers stilled. "This isn't just a legal dance. He's digging Barnes's grave, and Barnes is handing him the shovel."

Barnes slammed a fist on the table. "That's it! We're done here!" His chair screeched against the floor as he shot to his feet.

Eli's gut twisted, a sharp pang of secondhand frustration. "Dear Lord," he muttered. "He's throwing away any chance of getting Reddick talking."

The lawyer didn't flinch, even as Barnes stormed toward the door. "Detective, this outburst will be noted at the arraignment," he called after him. "You can't bully my client into submission."

The observation room door banged open as Barnes stomped out, his face still flushed with anger. Eli stepped forward, planting himself in Barnes's path before the man could leave entirely.

"Save it, Colt," Barnes snapped, his glare sharp enough to pierce steel. "I know good and well you're the one who got Monica Johnson to threaten a media frenzy."

"You're right, I did." Eli met his glare head-on, his tone

even. "Because two months is a long time for a mother to wait for answers about her daughters. And you know it."

Barnes jabbed a finger at his chest, but the fire in his eyes had dimmed. "You're just a P.I.," he muttered, though there was no heat behind the insult.

"Former Army CID investigator. Over a dozen homicides cleared. Plus training in kinesics—reading body language and micro-expressions during interrogation." Eli softened his tone, sensing the man's defenses cracking. "Let me help you close this, Detective."

Barnes exhaled sharply, his shoulders slumping. The anger drained out of him as he rubbed a hand over his face, suddenly looking decades older. "Fine. But if this goes sideways, it's on you."

"Understood." Eli nodded, his calm hiding the thrill of victory. "How long do I have?"

"Fifteen minutes, Colt. After that, I'm arresting Reddick for kidnapping and suspicion of murder."

"And those girls stay missing forever," Eli replied flatly, brushing past Barnes and stepping into the interrogation room.

9

unday, August 4

Gabriel pressed his ear against the fiberglass wall, counting footsteps above the storage hold. Two days in this floating prison, and he still didn't know if they planned to sell him or kill him. The boat's gentle rocking mocked his churning insides, every sway whispering of home and the life he'd been taken from.

Sweat soaked his shirt as the morning heat seeped through the slick walls. If he was going to survive this, he needed to know where they were taking him.

Crawling methodically along the wall, Gabriel tested each section for the thinnest spots where voices carried best. So far, he had found three—one near the bow, another by the stairs, and this one closest to what must be the helm.

"Hey, pass me that line!" An American voice cut through the thrum of the engines.

"We're making good time," another voice said. "Should hit the Gulf Stream by nightfall."

The possibilities sent Gabriel's heart racing. Mexico meant cartel territory; Texas, human trafficking. More footsteps echoed above. He crawled to the spot where he could hear the clearest.

"...Cancun could be difficult," a voice drifted through. "Migration police are expensive..."

This was a piece of the puzzle, but it only confirmed Gabriel's fears. A harsh, mirthless laugh escaped his lips, echoing in the cramped space. What a businessman he was turning out to be—trapped, helpless—Gabriel Mendoza, the great disappointment.

The boat pitched suddenly, sending him sprawling. A heavy toolbox slid across the floor, missing his head by inches. The crash drew shouts from above. "Check the hold!" someone yelled. "Make sure our cargo's intact."

Gabriel scrambled back to his original position, his heart hammering. Not yet. He needed more information.

Lowering his head, he offered a prayer. *Father, I don't ask You to spare me. Just give me the wisdom to survive whatever comes. Show me how to use even this darkness for Your purpose.*

Boots scraped overhead, moving to the hold's entrance. Gabriel pressed his ear harder against the wall, desperate for one last clue before they arrived.

"...contact in Louisiana wants the delivery by Tuesday," a voice said. "Premium price."

Louisiana. Finally, a destination. But the knowledge brought no comfort, only dread. Two more days trapped in this floating coffin, and then...

A small spark of defiance flickered inside him. His dreams weren't wrong. It was this world that was cruel and unjust.

Footfalls thundered down the metal stairs. He jerked away from the wall. He had learned where they were headed. But what awaited him there?

A key scraped in the lock. He pressed himself against the

far wall. Maybe this was his chance to learn more, to understand what kind of hell he'd been sold into. The door creaked open, harsh sunlight spearing inside. A silhouette filled the doorway, backlit by the morning sun. He squinted after hours in darkness.

"Rise and shine, amigo." The voice was young, almost playful, but there was an edge to it that screeched against Gabriel's nerves, like fingernails on rusted metal. "Your new life begins now."

Gabriel tried to speak, but his parched throat produced only a dry rasp. His mind raced through the fragments he'd overheard—premium price, Tuesday delivery, Louisiana contact. Each piece was another nail in his coffin.

The figure chuckled, stepping into the hold. As Gabriel's vision cleared, he recognized the unpredictable gringo who had killed Manuelo. His wild eyes gleamed, and his grin twisted into an unsettling mix of menace and madness. "Name's Freddy," the American said, twirling a set of keys around his finger. "And you? You're my investment. My property."

Property. The word stripped away everything he'd ever been—son, brother, student, dreamer—leaving only this—human merchandise with a premium price tag. Papa's business lessons echoed in his mind with cruel irony—supply and demand from the wrong side of the equation.

"Welcome to the American dream." Freddy pulled out a syringe, its clear liquid catching the invading sunlight. "Time to put you on ice."

———

GABRIEL'S MUSCLES burned under the relentless grip of duct tape that pinned his body in place. Jammed into the cramped storage compartment beneath the guest stateroom, he shifted awkwardly, his mouth parched from the rag stuffed between his teeth.

After a brutal night and morning at sea from Mangrove Bight, the boat's once-rhythmic rocking had stilled in Cancun's harbor. Now, the midday heat radiated through the walls of his prison, turning the air into a suffocating blanket. His eyes snapped open, revealing pitch-black emptiness. A wave of panic surged through him as he thrashed against the sticky restraints. The gag cut into the back of his throat, choking him, while the tape sealing his lips left his tongue cracked and dry like used sandpaper.

What happened? Memories collided in his mind—Freddy's wild eyes, that twisted grin, the chilling words:"human merchandise." Each phrase—"premium price," "Tuesday delivery," "Louisiana contact"—was another nail puncturing his hope. He blinked hard, trying to focus. Where was this cramped, suffocating place? His dream had led him to research boats like this, studying every layout and hidden compartment—possible places where Freddy could stash a victim. Below deck, the stateroom floorboards concealed crawlspaces, chambers designed to remain out of sight.

The boat's rhythm changed, its gentle rocking giving way to jerks and bumps. Gabriel's heart raced; they were docking. Voices drifted from above—rapid Spanish mingled with broken English. This was it. His chance. He tensed, ready to kick, to scream through his gag—anything to draw attention. But Freddy's cold eyes flashed in his mind. "Make a sound, and I'll gut you like a fish," he had snarled while stuffing him into the compartment. "Your family too." Terror battled desperation, locking Gabriel's muscles in place.

A loud thud echoed through the hull—the gangplank dropping. Footsteps clattered. Gabriel's throat tightened. Do it now. But what if Freddy made good on his threat? The thought of Papa and Nico's lifeless bodies, their blood staining the deck of the family fishing vessel, froze Gabriel. He lay rigid and silent as voices approached. Please, dear God, let someone find me.

The sound of a hatch opening. Someone passed overhead. Gabriel stopped breathing. "Nice boat," a voice drifted down. Footfalls circled the room. "Very nice."

"Gracias," Freddy replied. "We work hard to keep her clean and efficient." The groaning of a drawer scraping open was followed by the thud of it slamming shut.

"I'm sure you do," the official said. "But you know, sometimes... things get overlooked."

Gabriel's heart hammered against his ribs. Say something. Ask about me!

"Overlooked?" Freddy responded, amusement in his tone. "I assure you, we're thorough." More footsteps. Shadows flickered through the floorboards. They were right above him now. Gabriel's muscles coiled, torn between causing a commotion and Freddy's threats.

"Ah, but thoroughness... it costs, no?" The official chuckled. "A thousand pesos might help me be less observant."

No! Gabriel's mind screamed. He thrashed against the unyielding tape. Look down here. I'm here.

"A thousand?" Freddy laughed. "Let's make it five thousand and call it a day."

"A man who understands business," the official said approvingly. "A pleasure, señor."

There was a pause, then the rustle of paper. "You know what?" Freddy's voice brightened. "Here's another five so I won't have to do this song and dance in Veracruz."

The official whistled. "Very generous, señor. I'll make

sure my colleagues in Veracruz know to expect you. Smooth sailing all the way."

"Much appreciated," Freddy said with satisfaction.

Shadows shifted. Footsteps faded. Gabriel's hope of rescue splintered like driftwood sinking. Minutes later, the boat's engine roared to life. Vibrations rattled Gabriel's bones as if mocking his helplessness. Cancun slipped away. He squeezed his eyes shut. Hot tears welled and seeped into the gag. They're leaving. The thought pounded relentlessly, like waves on a shore he might never see again. Silent sobs wracked his body.

Papa's weathered face—those once-proud eyes now filled with worry, maybe despair—came to mind. And Nico... little Nico. Who would protect him from his evil brothers? The engine roared to life, and the boat surged forward. Each shudder of the hull dragged him farther from home, deeper into the unknown. Trapped in darkness, Gabriel's world shrank, the vast ocean swallowing any hope of escape. His future, like the water beneath him, was endless—and terrifyingly uncertain. Where would they dock next—and would he survive long enough to find out?

———

GABRIEL TRACED the yacht's brass railing, memorizing details that might aid in his escape—three fishing boats to starboard, a container ship to port, all maddeningly out of reach. Muscles contracted painfully as waves of nausea struck. Still, he forced himself to stand tall, like his father had taught him, keeping his spirit free from the captivity surrounding him.

As the bustling docks came into view, Gabriel scanned the harbor, calculating his options. No uniformed officers paced the weathered piers, no police boats sliced through the choppy waters, and no flashing lights flashing above law enforcement vehicles—just the lingering proof of a bribe that had secured their smooth passage from Cancun to Veracruz. Help wasn't coming. Not here.

The yacht nudged gently into its berth, and Gabriel steadied himself, testing his legs. Could he run if it came to that? Freddy's hand clamped onto his shoulder, guiding him toward the gangplank. Gabriel's mind raced. The gap between the boat and dock was small—if he timed it right, a stumble might create just enough chaos to give him a chance. A few seconds. That's all he needed.

Then it appeared—the gun tucked in Freddy's belt. Gabriel's pulse faltered. Not yet.

On unsteady legs, the first step betrayed his days at sea and gnawing anxiety. Freddy's grip tightened as he steered Gabriel roughly across the sweltering pier. Diesel and salt wafted through the air. A rusted pickup waited in the parking lot.

Freddy shoved Gabriel into the cab, then slid in behind the wheel, cranking the engine. The truck lurched forward and pulled into the street, the sprawling city of Veracruz stretching ahead, hot and unfamiliar. As they drove into the maze of streets, Gabriel's mind churned with only one thought—how much longer should he wait before making his move?

Tropical vegetation and foliage passed outside the open window as they left Veracruz. The occasional cinderblock home, streaked with mildew and moss, appeared amid wild banana trees and lush palms. Gabriel's throat dried as the buildings grew scarcer, the spaces between them wider. Civilization was slipping away with each passing kilometer.

After twenty minutes, Freddy slowed the truck as they

entered a small town. The air changed, thick with the stench of stale beer and rotting fruit. Navigating sharp turns over broken concrete, he came to a stop at a run-down cantina. A pack of street dogs scattered upon their arrival, their ribs showing through mangy fur. No people were in sight—no one to help.

Weathered stucco sat beneath a rusted tin roof. Water stains ran down the walls like tear tracks. A hand-painted sign hung above the front door, its letters spelling out "El Rancho de Pando" in fading red and green paint.

Freddy pulled Gabriel from the truck, marching him to a man seated in an old metal chair shaded by tangled hibiscus and palms.

"Esteban," Freddy called out, pushing Gabriel forward. "Here's the package we discussed."

Esteban's face was lean and angular, with a prominent nose and deep-set eyes that seemed to bore into Gabriel. His thick, jet-black hair was swept back from his forehead, with a few rebellious strands across his temple. The sides were closely trimmed, creating a distinct border with the longer top. A neatly trimmed mustache, the same inky black as his hair, framed his upper lip, accentuating the stern line of his mouth.

Like puzzle pieces falling into place, each detail told its story—the slight favor of Esteban's right leg, the bulge of a weapon beneath his loose Panama shirt, and the watchful eyes scanning their surroundings. Gabriel was quickly learning that knowledge meant survival.

"So, this is your special export, yes?" Esteban's voice was soft, but it carried an undercurrent of danger.

Gabriel suppressed a shudder as Esteban's calloused hand gripped his chin, turning his face from side to side as if inspecting produce at a street market. The man's breath carried the heavy scent of coffee and cigarettes. "So tell me, why do you pay me the honor of transporting your prized product, and not your regular coyotes who travel through Juarez?" Esteban said, raising an eyebrow.

"There's a rush on this package," Freddy replied. "And this one very valuable."

Why the urgency? What made Gabriel different from other *packages*?

Freddy offered Esteban a thick envelope. "As agreed. The other half is in McAllen, Texas." Gabriel's throat tightened, as if the air had thickened into something he couldn't swallow—money was exchanged—again.

Freddy counted the bills—worn green notes sliding between tobacco-stained fingers—more money than his family earned in a year. His stomach twisted as Esteban thumbed through the stack. This wasn't just a temporary kidnapping. Men didn't invest so heavily in merchandise they planned to let escape.

The envelope disappeared into Esteban's pocket. "Time to go, *muchacho*."

Gabriel tensed as Esteban yanked him toward a yellow Nissan X-Trail, caked with mud that flowed up from its undercarriage. One sudden move might break the grip. Darting his attention from Freddy's gun to Esteban's bulging pocket, he decided against breaking away—maybe later, if the odds improved.

Esteban's hold tightened, as if sensing Gabriel's mental scheming. Their eyes met, and something flickered across Esteban's face—not just recognition, but uncertainty. For a heartbeat, the coyote's confident mask slipped, as if he were realizing he might have taken on more than he expected. Gabriel held that gaze, allowing Esteban to see beneath his submission. Let him think Gabriel was valuable. His value meant his safety.

"Watch this one closely," Freddy said. "He's worth every peso."

McAllen was in America—hundreds of miles farther from Papa and Nico. Could he find a chance to escape before crossing the border? And if that chance came, would he be ready? Not yet. He couldn't resist now. He needed to watch, to memorize every detail—times, places, faces. Knowledge was power, and power was his key to freedom.

10

Eli breathed in through clenched teeth. This was it —his chance to blow the case wide open or watch it slip through his fingers like dry sand.

He twisted the knob and stepped into the cramped interview room. The fluorescent bulb buzzed overhead. Reddick sat hunched at the table, his gaunt face marked with worry. His gaze darted between Eli and his young lawyer—rapid eye movement—a sign of stress, perhaps guilt.

The attorney exuded quiet confidence. He met Eli's gaze in a relaxed pose, a ghost of a smile playing at the corners of his lips. The kid adjusted his tie with a casual wrist flick. He'd just taken Barnes apart, and he knew it.

Lowering himself into the chair opposite Reddick, Eli mirrored Reddick's posture to establish rapport. Resting his elbows on the table, he fixed Reddick with a steady stare. The suspect's fingers stilled, and for a moment, the only sounds in the room were the whirr of the lights and the breathing of three men.

Leaning in, Eli softened his voice, aiming for a tone that was more confident than interrogator. "Charles, I know you've been through the wringer already. I'm not here to put you through that again. I just want to understand what you know about the twins. Can you walk me through that?"

A silence stretched between them. Reddick's gaze drifted past Eli, focusing on an invisible point behind him. Eli recognized this eye-blocking behavior—a subconscious attempt to hide from something uncomfortable.

The lawyer's hand settled on Reddick's forearm, a gentle touch that spoke volumes: Stay quiet. Don't engage. Let me handle this. Eli caught Reddick's subtle lean toward his lawyer—a sign he was seeking protection.

Clenching his fist under the table to maintain a calm facade, Eli took a deep breath, willing the tension from his shoulders. "Look, I'm not the enemy, Charles. I'm here because two young girls are missing, and that's all I care about right now. Do you have information that can help bring them home?" He lowered his head below Reddick's eye level to get his attention. "In the warehouse, you mentioned a well-dressed lady. Was that a deflection, or is she real?"

Reddick blinked. His Adam's apple bobbed as he swallowed hard—a telltale sign of tension.

"Mr. Colt, I appreciate your dilemma," the lawyer said. "But my client has already given his statement to Detective Barnes. Unless you have new questions, I don't see the point in rehashing—"

"I'm not asking him to rehash anything," Eli said, his tone gentle but edged with steel beneath it. "I just want his help." Leaning back slightly, he opened his posture to appear less threatening. "Charles, as a member of this community, you have an opportunity here to do the right thing. To make a difference."

The room fell silent once more. Eli waited, observing

Reddick's face for any signs of weakness, any hint that he might know something that would assist both Eli and himself. Reddick's slight head tilt and the way his eyes shifted left suggested he might be accessing memories rather than constructing a lie. "Charles, tell me about the well-dressed woman. What did you see?"

Reddick's eyes darted to his lawyer, then back to Eli. His shoulders tensed, but his feet uncrossed—a subtle sign of openness. "I... I saw her twice. At one of them singing places downtown, then the next morning in Prichard, at a coffee shop."

"Singing places?" Eli asked. "You mean a karaoke studio."

"Yeah. That's it—karaoke."

So far the story jives with Sheriff Hank Thornton's account. "When did you see them at the coffee shop?"

"The next morning. They was there to meet that fine looking lady." Riddick glanced at his lawyer.

"Go on," Eli said, maintaining an encouraging tone. Reddick's hands stopped fidgeting—signaling increased focus and truthfulness.

Reddick swallowed hard. "She was really put together. Expensive clothes. Stylish hair. Rode away in a silver Jag with a driver. That stands out around here."

Eli nodded in understanding. "Was this woman white, black, or Hispanic?"

"White woman," Reddick replied quickly. "Pretty, but much older than the girls. Between thirty and forty."

"Did you see her interact with Aaliyah and Kiara?"

"Yeah," Reddick said, his brow tightening as if recalling a memory. His eyes moved up and to the left—accessing visual memories rather than constructing a lie. "She talked to them at a table inside. Real friendly-like. But something felt… not right."

"How so?"

A muscle twitched along Reddick's jawline. "Just… the way she looked at them. Like they were… I don't know, something she wanted."

The lawyer suddenly held up his hand as if stopping traffic. "That's enough. My client, Mr. Colt, has been cooperative. Before he says another word, I want all charges dropped, and I want that in writing."

Eli's eyes never left Reddick. "I hear you, counselor. But let's finish this conversation first. Charles, if your information helps, I promise I'll go to bat for your release. What else can you tell me about this woman?"

Reddick inhaled and exhaled slowly. Decision made. "They got into that big silver Jag, and then they drove off."

Warmth blossomed in Eli's chest. "Tell me more about the Jag. Any details you remember?"

Reddick nodded slowly, his eyes focused as if seeing the scene again. "Yeah, it had Louisiana plates. And… there was a bumper sticker. It was for some politician."

"Do you remember a name?" Eli kept his voice calm despite his growing excitement.

The skin on Reddick's forehead bunched in concentration. "Beau something… Beau Bordelon. Yeah, that's it. It said, Beau Bordelon for Governor."

Reeling, Eli sat back and glanced at his watch—time was up. Had he gotten what he needed? It was something—but was it true?

"No more," said the young lawyer. "Not until we have a deal in writing."

The new information hit Eli like a runaway cement

truck. He had as strange feeling the Louisiana governor could be somehow connected to the twins' disappearance. If so, this case had just become a powder keg with a short fuse. The political implications alone could be devastating, potentially derailing a gubernatorial campaign and an entire state administration. He narrowed his eyes slightly. "Charles, are you certain about what you told me?"

With his gaze steady, Reddick's posture remained open. "Yeah, I'm sure. That woman. That car. That bumper sticker. They stuck out, you know?"

Reddick's face showed no sign of deception. The man's expression and movements were consistent with telling the truth. But what he said needed confirmation. Eli's mind raced to map out a plan. First, cross-reference Reddick's statement with video footage. Next, discreetly inquire about the governor's whereabouts without tipping off the wrong people. One misstep could send the whole case crashing downward—or worse, put the twins in greater danger.

———

An eerie stillness cloaked the Johnson home, as if the world itself held its breath. Eli flinched at the ping of Dakota's phone, shattering two hours of tense silence since leaving Bama Brew. This had to be it—the email that would finally push the case forward.

The neighborhood drowsed in the late hour, punctuated by the occasional bark of a dog or the rumble of a passing car. They'd verified Reddick's story about the "fine-looking woman" and her chauffeured green Jag with the help of a young barista at the coffee shop. But the security footage was gone, overwritten by the camera's loop. Another dead end.

Dark clouds churned on the horizon, heavy with restless energy. Something was coming—news that could finally break the standstill.

Rubbing his temples against the deep furrow forming between his brows, Eli leaned over, craning his neck to study the screen. Dakota's thumb tapped an email attachment. "It's from Blackwell," Dakota said, his voice rich with anticipation.

Blackwell had been instrumental in helping them bring down Los Diablos, the notorious Mexican human trafficking cartel, last year. They'd contacted the ex-FBI special agent to search for footage confirming Reddick's story. As the first frame appeared, the air in the Jeep seemed to grow warmer. Eli's eyes widened at the sight of Aaliyah and Kiara on the phone's screen. They stood beside a tall man in a black suit, pumping gas into a green Jaguar. "That's them," Eli breathed.

Dakota zoomed in on the Jaguar's bumper. A Louisiana plate and a bumper sticker featuring an American flag background came into focus. The text on the sticker read—"Re-elect Governor Beau Bordelon."

"Well, I'll be," Dakota said. "Reddick was telling the truth about the car."

Eli worked his jaw as if he were chewing tough meat. "The car, the Louisiana plates, the campaign sticker — it's all there."

A tall, slender woman with dark, shoulder-length hair and a model-like posture walked into the frame. She wore a coral silk blouse tucked into high-waisted white slacks, her look completed by a pair of designer sunglasses perched atop her head. She carried two plastic bags, probably filled with snacks and sodas, and motioned for the girls to get into the car.

"There she is," Eli said. "Just like Reddick described."

Dakota frowned. "What do you make of the bumper sticker?"

"Probably nothing. Half the cars in Louisiana have Beau Bordelon on their bumpers."

The phone chimed again, and Dakota swiped the screen, eyebrows shooting up as he read. "Blackwell sent the registration for the Jag's plate. You're not going to believe this."

"Believe what?" Eli leaned closer, his heart rate quickening.

"It's registered to Maxwell Kingsley."

Eli's breath escaped in a long, controlled exhale. His mind connected dots he'd rather leave unconnected. "Kingsley? The billionaire?"

Dakota's face paled slightly. "The very same. The governor's biggest financial supporter."

Eli ran a hand through his hair, tugging at the roots as he tried to comprehend what this meant. The case now threatened to be a tidal wave of the highest echelons of Louisiana politics, capable of drowning anyone who challenged it. A coppery taste filled his mouth as he bit the inside of his cheek. A cold realization crept through his veins.

Lord, give us wisdom.

As his gaze drifted back to the screen, he grappled with the implications.

"There's more," Dakota said, his voice dropping to a low rumble. "Remember those rumors about Kingsley? The ones about inappropriate parties with celebrities and—"

"Underage girls," Eli finished.

Dakota's shoulders slumped as his eyes remained on his phone. "This is worse than we thought."

"We do what we always do, Dakota. We follow the evidence, protect the innocent, and above all, trust God."

Nodding, Dakota smiled his typical brash smile. "So, what's our next move, Boss?"

Eli opened his door. "We tell Monica we're going back to Louisiana to find her daughters. Hope is the only thing we can give her right now."

11

M*onday, August 5*

Gabriel counted the curves in the mountain road, each bend taking him further from home and closer to whatever awaited at the border. Beside him, Esteban's patience was wearing as thin as the smoke curling from the cigarette butt between his lips.

A blur of emerald palms and vibrant banana plants rushed past on both sides of the X-Trail as the fiery orange sun dipped lower on the horizon. The sky was full of brilliant pink streaks offset by scattered gray clouds.

A rustle of movement caught Gabriel's attention. Esteban's hand darted toward him, causing Gabriel to flinch, only to realize Esteban was merely reaching for his cigarettes on the dashboard.

At that moment, Gabriel's stomach growled, reminding him of the meals he had missed since his brothers sold him in the Caribbean.

"Hungry, boy?" Esteban's voice was as rough as sandpaper. "Better get used to it. Where you're going, food's a luxury." Esteban lit another cigarette, the brief flare highlighting his cruel facial features. "Time to lay down some rules." His tone shifted from low to menacing. "If you ever get the urge to run, remember—I'll hunt you down, and you don't want that."

The X-Trail swerved suddenly. Gabriel's shoulder slammed into the door, pressing the seatbelt tight against his neck. Esteban leaned in close, his tobacco-laced breath hot on Gabriel's face. "*Escúchame bien, cabrón.* You try to escape, and I'll cut you up piece by piece. Leave you for the buzzards. *Entiendes*?" He barked as he straightened behind the wheel. "Don't think I give a crap about the rest of the money. What that *pendejo gringo* already paid me will keep me in Camarones and tequila for two years."

Terror clawed at Gabriel's insides, tightening his chest. He grasped for words that could steady him—Papa's reminder: Rejoice in hope, be patient in tribulation, be constant in prayer. The verse circled his thoughts, though it felt distant now.

Esteban's laugh was like gravel in a blender. "Good boy. You might just survive this trip after all." He cranked up ranchera music to a painful volume, drowning out any chance of conversation or clear thought.

The night seemed endless, a haze of headlights and dark silhouettes. The towns grew fewer and smaller, until only darkness stretched between them. Gabriel drifted in and out of sporadic sleep, jerking awake at every bump and turn.

His eyes burned with exhaustion, and his mouth felt as dry as cotton. The air conditioning had given way to the harsh stench of diesel filtering through partially opened windows. How long had they been driving? Hours blurred together, marked only by the gradual shift in the scenery outside.

As the inky blackness softened, the first hints of color

bled into the horizon. Slowly, almost imperceptibly, the world around Gabriel transformed. The suffocating darkness gave way to a vast, open landscape.

Farmlands and scrubland stretched to the skyline, bathed in the soft glow of dawn. The flat expanse seemed to go on forever, broken only by occasional clusters of buildings or solitary trees. Gabriel blinked to adjust his eyes to the changing light, transitioning from blue skies to a palette of blush and orange.

Industrial structures with sharp angles, softened by the morning haze, emerged on the outskirts. Next, residential neighborhoods came into view, with lights flickering on in house windows. Early risers walked their dogs along the silent streets. Rubbing his weary eyes, Gabriel yawned.

After more than ten grueling hours of travel, Esteban and Gabriel entered a large city. Gabriel couldn't shake the feeling that something irreversible had shifted. Was the morning's dawn not just the end of a long night but the beginning of his uncertain future?

After twenty minutes, the X-Trail slowed to a stop in front of a single-story house with vibrant yellow stucco walls and a blue metal roof. A black fence surrounded the property, topped with spirals of razor wire. A solid steel gate, freshly painted, stood at the entrance, with security cameras peering out from every corner.

Esteban cut the engine and grunted, "Out."

Gabriel's legs wobbled as he stepped onto the dusty street. The gate slid open with an electric whine. The house's red door opened, and a balding man emerged—thick build, grey-bearded. A San Antonio Spurs jersey stretched tight across his belly as he stalked down the stone walkway.

"Angel," Esteban said. "I got your package."

Angel's dark eyes dissected Gabriel piece by piece. "He looks scrawny," Angel chuckled, the sound cold. "You sure he can make the crossing?"

Gabriel's stomach fell at the word "*crossing*." He'd heard whispers back home—stories of boys who never made it, their bodies found weighted with bags in the Rio Grande or buried in shallow graves along its bank.

Esteban shrugged. "Not my problem." He held out an expectant hand.

Straightening his shoulders, Gabriel summoned the strength he'd built from hauling nets and repairing engines. If survival meant traversing the river, he'd find a way—just as his father had taught him about the sea—adapt or drown.

Angel pulled an envelope from his pocket and handed it to Esteban, who quickly thumbed through the contents before nodding in satisfaction.

"He's all yours," Esteban said, already turning back to his vehicle.

"Hey, Esteban." Angel stopped him. "What's the deal with these new gringos we're working for? I heard some crazy stuff."

Esteban hesitated, glancing at Gabriel. "Not here," he said. "Let's talk inside."

Angel grabbed Gabriel's arm, his fingers digging into muscle, and they moved to an oil-stained garage attached to the yellow house. The heavy door clanged shut behind them.

Through the wall, Gabriel could hear Esteban's muffled voice. "Andre Badeau paid double for this one. Says smart kids like this one are in high demand."

Gabriel glanced up to see an open window that was too far to reach on his own.

———

THE HIGH WINDOW was Gabriel's only hope. His eyes darted around the dim garage, searching for anything he could climb on while his weakened legs threatened to buckle beneath him. The sharp tang of marine diesel burned in his lungs. Near the rear of the garage, he spotted a thin gap between a door and the wall. Faint voices filtered through— Esteban's gruff bark and Angel's deeper murmur. They were just beyond the door, oblivious to the fact that Gabriel could hear them.

He crept to the gap and pressed his ear against it, slowing his breathing to catch every word.

"So, tell me about our new supplier," Angel said. "What makes them so special?"

"These gringos," Esteban whispered, as if afraid he might be overheard, "they're part of some big syndicate that supplies the Americans with young kids and cheap labor. The leader is a tough hombre called Andre Badeau. He took over the Diablos operation in Juarez."

Gabriel's breath hitched. Cheap labor. Young kids. The words sliced through him like cold steel. Where in America would they take him? Would he be buried in the vineyards of California, worked to the bone until his body gave out? Or was something even darker waiting for him? A cold dread coiled tighter, sinking deeper with every second.

"What's this Andre Badeau like?" Angel asked.

"All business. Cold. Doesn't mess around."

"And the nephew?" Angel grunted.

"Freddy." Esteban's voice dropped. "Violent. Out of control. Unpredictable."

Gabriel nodded to himself in agreement with Esteban's assessment.

"How bad?" Angel asked.

"He killed a man in Mangrove Bight. For nothing."

Gabriel's fingers dug into the concrete. Package. That's all he was to them.

A long pause followed. Gabriel held his breath, afraid they'd hear his thundering heart.

"I don't like it," Angel finally said. "New players. Crazy players. Sounds risky."

"Do what you want. I've been paid very well." Esteban answered with little emotion. "But if you want this kind of money to keep flowing, I'd suggest you get that kid to McAllen safe and sound."

His leg cramping slightly, Gabriel shifted from his awkward position. A small pebble skittered across the floor. The voices outside abruptly stopped. The silence lingered for five seconds.

"What was that?" Esteban asked.

"This old house is always making noises," Angel dismissed.

"When will you cross the river?"

"Tonight," Angel replied. "In a kayak. Quieter than a boat, harder for the Border Patrol's drones to detect."

"Smart," Esteban approved. "When will you leave?"

"After midnight. Less chance of patrols."

A knot grew in the pit of Gabriel's stomach. A kayak?

"Badeau will be waiting?" Esteban said. "Apparently, this boy is valuable merchandise for some American billionaire. You know where to bring him?"

"I got a text yesterday with the coordinates for the pickup. Shouldn't be too difficult."

Gabriel had only hours left before being handed over to the mysterious Andre Badeau. Should he try to escape? Perhaps wait for an opportunity tonight at the river?

"What if Border Patrol catches you?" Esteban said.

"They won't," Angel responded firmly. "But if they find us in the river, I'll throw the kid overboard. That will keep the agents busy long enough for me to make it to the southern bank."

Gabriel's pulse raced, and blood roared in his ears. He trembled against the concrete as memories of Papá teaching him to swim in the warm Caribbean washed over him. But this time would be different—dark water, a cold current, and his hands likely bound. If he fell into the river, he would sink like weights on fishing nets.

Should he try to run? Should he wait for the river crossing? His legs were weak, but adrenaline might carry him. The voices through the crack faded, leaving Gabriel alone with a choice—risk escape now or trust his fate to a higher power.

What would Papá do? Be patient like Joseph, or run like David? Time was slipping away, along with the chance for survival. Could he afford to wait, or would hesitating cost him everything?

———

GABRIEL STOOD beside Angel's Ford Bronco, its black paint barely visible in the late hour, except for the horizontal stripes of yellow, orange, and red that seemed to glow in the dark. The Rio Grande stretched fifty meters away like an black ribbon slicing through the midnight gloom. Overhead, stars pricked through the indigo sky, and a sliver of moon shaped like a clipped toenail offered little light.

"Hurry up," Angel hissed, gesturing impatiently at the plastic kayak latched atop the Bronco's roof. "Detach that side. We don't have all night."

With trembling fingers, Gabriel fumbled with the kayak's latch, catching his distorted reflection in the Bronco's window. In that warped image, he saw his former self slipping away, replaced by a desperate stranger about to cross a threshold from which there was no return.

Angel yanked the kayak free, its sudden weight nearly toppling Gabriel. The hull scraped gravel as Angel dragged it to the water's edge, leaving Gabriel to stumble after him. The river's surface, so deceptively calm, lapped at the shore with soft, sinister whispers. Gabriel's nostrils flared at the muddy earthy scent of the Rio Grande—foreign, like everything else in this nightmare.

"Get in," Angel ordered, steadying the small craft at the riverbank. "And stay low. Border Patrol's got night vision."

Gabriel's heart hammered as he lowered himself in. The plastic creaked beneath him, and the craft rocked precariously. Cold water seeped through his pants, shocking his skin. Angel shoved an oar into Gabriel's trembling hands.

"Remember, keep rowing," Angel growled, his eyes darting up and down the shoreline. "Quiet strokes. If you flip us, I'll leave you to drown."

With a powerful push, Angel launched them into the current. They lurched forward, and Gabriel's stomach clenched. The shore—American soil—loomed like a mirage, promising salvation or doom. Gabriel was at a loss to guess which it would be.

His arms burned as he paddled, each stroke a battle against the river's pull. The kayak sliced through the dark water, leaving a faint wake behind. Sweat trickled down his back despite the cool night air.

Halfway across, a mechanical hum froze Gabriel's blood. He squinted into the darkness as a pinprick of light appeared downriver, growing larger by the second.

"Border Patrol," Angel whispered harshly, producing a pistol from his elastic waistband. "Stop paddling. Now." Angel pointed the gun at Gabriel's head. His heart stopped mid-beat. Not a whisper of breath escaped his lips.

The current tugged at the kayak, pulling it toward the approaching beam as it grew brighter. With it came the unmistakable growl of an outboard motor. Searchlights swept the river, a blinding ray carving through the night. Gabriel hunched lower as his panic soared. Angel's hand clamped onto Gabriel's shoulder, grip vice-like and bruising —a silent warning. Don't move. Don't breathe.

The border patrol boat's engine idled nearby, so close Gabriel could smell gasoline fumes mingling with the river's musky odor. Voices carried across the water—clipped. Professional. English. Time stretched. Gabriel's lungs begged for air. As dark spots danced at the edges of his vision, the engine roared to life. The vessel surged away, its wake rocking the kayak nearly to the point of capsizing.

Angel's hold loosened. "Paddle," he said. "Now. Before they come back."

Gabriel's muscles burned as he dug the oars into the river. Each stroke propelled them toward the northern shore. The current fought against them, threatening to sweep them downstream. Sweat stung Gabriel's eyes, blurring his first glimpse of America.

"Faster," Angel said, paddling with brutal efficiency.

The distant bank morphed from a hazy outline to distinct shapes—scraggly bushes, a fallen tree, a steep embankment. A sharp crack pierced the night. Gabriel flinched, nearly losing his grip on the oar.

Angel cursed under his breath. "Don't stop," he jeered. "It's just a branch breaking. Keep moving!" The kayak lurched, almost capsizing as it thumped against something beneath them. Cold water sloshed over the sides, soaking Gabriel's pants. The shock stopped his breathing, but he kept paddling.

The hull scraped against the riverbed. Gabriel's unsteady legs stumbled onto the muddy bank, waterlogged shoes sinking into the drenched earth. Forward momentum sent his body sprawling, his fingers digging deep into the soil for stability.

"Move!" Angel barked, already dragging the kayak onto the land. "Into the brush. Now!"

Gabriel scrambled up the embankment, thorns and dry branches tearing at his clothes. His lungs burned, his breathing a ragged gasp. The earthy taste of muddy water lingered on his tongue.

They crouched beneath gnarled mesquite trees. Angel's eyes gleamed in the darkness, scanning the river and the sky. In the distance, the faint whir of a helicopter grew louder.

"We're not safe yet," Angel said, grabbing Gabriel's arm. "Two miles to the pickup point. You run ahead. You try to escape, and I'll shoot you in the back."

Gabriel ran. Each step carried him further from his past and into an uncertain future. The dream he'd had only a few days before seemed like a cruel joke as he fled like a hunted animal through the night. His lungs were on fire as he stumbled through the unfamiliar terrain, cacti spines catching on his pant legs.

Angel maintained a relentless pace, stopping only to study the stars for navigation. The distant whir of the helicopter faded. A strip of asphalt emerged from the darkness. "There." Angel pointed to a road branching off the highway.

They crouched in a drainage ditch hidden by scraggly bushes. Minutes crawled by like hours. Gabriel's shirt stuck to his back, soaked with sweat and river water. Every snapping twig or rustle of leaves sent his heart into his throat. Headlights appeared in the distance. Angel tensed beside him. "There's your ride," he muttered. "When I say run, you run. Understand?"

A black SUV with tinted windows slowed, turning onto the dirt road. As it drew closer, Gabriel could make out "Denali" in chrome letters that twinkled in the dim light on the driver's door.

"Now!" Angel shoved him forward.

Gabriel sprinted with leaden legs to the SUV, catching a glimpse of the rear bumper and its reflective tag. The passenger door swung open. A hand reached out, grabbing his arm and yanking him inside.

The door slammed shut, and the vehicle accelerated, carrying Gabriel deeper into a new chapter of his nightmare. As he collapsed into the leather seat, he whispered the words he saw in red letters on the license plate.

Louisiana.

12

Tuesday, August 6

Andre Badeau pressed the phone to his ear as he shifted in the Denali's front seat, the leather creaking beneath him. Hector, a former Diablos gang-banger, sat behind the wheel, his nervous eyes darting between the road and the dashboard. The boy—Gabriel—was unnervingly still in the backseat, his bound wrists resting in his lap. His eyes, though... too alert... too observant, taking in everything.

"Your nephew is becoming a problem." Rear Admiral Diego Bustillo's gravelly voice droned on. "A body was found on a pier in Mangrove Bight. Witnesses place Freddy in the area arguing with the man who turned up with a bullet in his brain."

The Denali's headlights cut through the predawn darkness, illuminating a green reflective sign— "BEN BOLT 23 ALICE 36 CORPUS CHRISTI 77"

Badeau pressed his fingers against his temples, trying to smooth the sharp ache that flared behind his eyes. Although he was dealing with the chief of the Honduran armed forces, the admiral still was a hired hand—nothing more, nothing less. "My monthly contribution to your retirement fund should cover any inconveniences, Admiral."

"The amount is generous, sí, but—"

"Then there's no problem." Badeau coated each word with frigid ice. "Unless you'd prefer I redirect those funds to someone more appreciative. Say, *el Presidente*?"

A heavy silence filled the line. "As you wish, Señor Badeau. But control your nephew, por favor."

After ending the call, a queasy lurch tugged at Badeau's stomach. Freddy's excuse fresh in his mind— "I had to do it. The man knew too much. He had to die." So cold. So detached. Like explaining a cockfight rather than explaining his crime.

Badeau rubbed his temples, trying to make sense of Freddy murdering the Honduran. This wasn't part of the plan. Freddy was becoming a liability, his actions too brutal, too risky. Where was he now? Probably high in some Roatan brothel running his mouth.

Hector offered more trouble. "We have a problem."

The battery warning light blinked on the dashboard. Great. This was the last thing he needed.

"Check out the engine," Badeau commanded.

Hector retrieved a flashlight from the emergency kit and popped the hood. Beams danced between the open hood's bottom and the console. "It's the alternator belt," he announced, his tight voice drifting through Badeau's window. "It's completely shredded."

Stranded in the middle of nowhere with a trafficked kid... this could be a big problem if a nosy state trooper stopped to help. Badeau glanced back at Gabriel, who remained still, focusing on the road ahead. With a light drizzle starting to patter against the windshield, Badeau's urgency to get moving grew.

"We need to call for a tow," Hector said, wiping rain from his brow.

Badeau shook his head vehemently. "Not with what we're transporting."

"What do you suggest?" Hector's voice rose with frustration. "We won't get five miles before the battery dies."

"I... I might be of some help," said the boy from the back seat.

Badeau turned to meet Gabriel's gaze. "How?"

"I've worked on my family boat engine many times."

Skepticism warred with desperation in Andre's mind. After determining he had no other choice, he nodded. "Fine. But I'll be watching over your shoulder." He signaled for Hector to let him out.

Gabriel examined the engine, his bound hands resting on the engine's housing. "If we had some strong cord, I could create a temporary belt."

"Where are we going to find cord way out here?" Hector scoffed.

"Your shoelaces," Gabriel said as his eyes fell on Hector's sneakers. "And duct tape, if you have any."

"My shoelaces," Hector squealed. "These are Off-White's. They cost over $500."

Badeau studied the boy. The rain was falling harder now. "Give him your laces," he said.

Gabriel set to work, his bound hands moving with surprising dexterity. Badeau's mind drifted to Freddy, imagining his nephew's likely response to this situation—probably a string of curses and demands to call for help, consequences be damned.

"Careful," Badeau found himself saying as Gabriel's

fingers slipped on the wet metal. The gentleness in his own voice surprised him. He couldn't remember the last time he'd shown such concern for... Well, for anyone.

Despite his bound hands, Gabriel worked swiftly and surely. His earlier fear seemed to vanish as he focused on the mechanical task at hand.

As the boy fitted the reinforced laces around multiple pulleys, Badeau had to pay the kid grudging respect. His resourcefulness was so unlike the ineptitude of many in Badeau's operation, including his nephew Freddy.

Hector turned the key. The engine coughed once, twice, then roared to life. "No warning lights," Hector said, his tone hovering between surprise and relief. "It worked."

With a spontaneous grin spreading across his lips, Badeau fixed his eyes on Gabriel. "Get in," he said gruffly, opening the rear door. As the boy climbed back into the back seat, a quiet pride gleamed in his eyes. Not another frightened kid calling for their mother. This one had shown ingenuity and calm under pressure. It was... Unsettling.

They pulled back onto the highway, the rhythmic swish of windshield wipers disrupting the silence. Freddy came to mind—his hair-trigger temper fueled by drugs and disregard. He was getting more and more out of control, creating problems faster than Badeau could solve them.

But this teenage boy, Gabriel—he'd saved them from potential disaster with quick thinking and skill.

As the lights of Ben Bolt appeared on the horizon, Badeau was struck with a troubling thought. Oh, how he could use this kid to shape into his successor.

"Good work back there," Badeau said softly, almost to himself. In the rearview mirror, he saw Gabriel's eyes widen slightly at the unexpected praise.

The rain tapered off as they entered the outskirts of Ben

Bolt. They'd made it, thanks to a makeshift alternator belt and their resourceful young captive. Did he really want to relinquish this good kid to Kingsley? For the first time since their business arrangement, Andre Badeau was thinking about crossing his main source of income.

PART II

13

Tuesday, August 6

Governor Beau Bordelon jolted awake, gasping for air. The silence of his suite in the Louisiana governor's mansion shattered as he sat up in the four-poster bed. Sweat-soaked pajamas clung to his trembling body as he blinked rapidly, struggling to orient himself in the familiar yet alien darkness of the room. His heart hammered like a hysterical animal trying to escape from its cage. He fumbled his hand across the antique nightstand until his fingers closed around the cool metal of his smartphone. The screen's glow vibrated in his hand as he frantically scrolled through notifications, searching for alerts that might explain the nameless dread clawing at his insides.

The clock on his phone read 4:57 AM, but Bordelon barely registered the time. Frantic notions cascaded through his mind, anticipating disaster bulletins that hadn't yet arrived. His body tensed for a crisis not yet born.

"Beau?" His wife's sleep-husky voice cut through his panic. "What's wrong?"

Bordelon's fingers tightened around the phone. His thumb panned over the emergency contacts. He opened his mouth to respond, but he couldn't speak through clenched teeth. How could he explain the vivid horror without sounding unhinged—Andrew Jackson sinking with an entire city into oblivion?

"Nothing," he said in a hoarse and unconvincing tone. "Just... just a dream."

He felt Sarah shift beside him, the mattress dipping as she propped herself on one elbow. Her hand, calm and steady, came to rest on his sweat-slicked back. "Must've been some dream," she murmured, concern evident in her tone. "You're soaked to the skin."

Bordelon swallowed hard as his eyes remained fixed on the screen of his phone. No alerts. No emergencies. Yet a suffocating premonition bore down on him, relentless and unyielding. He swung his legs over the side of the bed, his bare feet connecting with the cold hardwood floor. The shock of it grounded him, momentarily pushing back the lingering twists of his nightmare.

"I saw... I saw New Orleans drowning," he said. The words sounded ridiculous as they left his mouth, but once they started, he couldn't stop. "The statue in Jackson Square was spinning, Sarah—spinning like some demonic carnival ride. And then it just... sank. Took everything with it. The square, the buildings, the people..."

He ran a trembling hand through his damp hair. How unhinged he must sound. But the vivid images refused to fade. They were bound to his consciousness with terrifying tenacity, each detail etched in his mind's eye.

Sarah's hand moved to his shoulder, squeezing gently. "It was just a dream, honey. The city's fine. You're fine."

But Bordelon shook his head, unable to shake the

feeling of impending disaster. Standing abruptly, he shrugged off his wife's comforting touch and paced the room. "No, it's not. None of it. What if it's a warning? What if —" He cut himself off, realizing how his words must sound. The Governor of Louisiana, spooked by a bad dream. His political foes would have a field day with that one.

Drawn to the window, he yanked open the heavy curtains. The sprawling grounds of the Governor's Mansion lay shrouded in pre-dawn darkness, punctuated by the soft glow of security lights. Beyond them, the city of Baton Rouge slumbered, unaware of its leader's midnight crisis.

"Something's coming," he said, more to himself than to Sarah. A whirlwind of thoughts churned in his brain, the vivid images of his nightmare obscuring the peaceful scene outside. "I can feel it. It's like... the calm before a storm."

Sarah's reflection, her tangled blonde hair falling across her rounded shoulders, appeared in the window behind him, her brow tight with worry. "Beau, you're not making sense. It's the middle of the night. Whatever you're feeling can wait until morning."

But Bordelon barely heard her. The dream had awakened a primal fear of impending tragedy. "No, it can't wait. Don't you see? We're not ready. None of us."

He turned abruptly, striding to the desk in the corner of the room. "I need to call an emergency meeting. Get everyone together, all the department heads..."

"Before dawn? Based on a nightmare?" Sarah's voice rose, a mix of exasperation and concern. "Beau, listen to yourself. You're not thinking clearly."

He paused. Doubt crept in. Was he overreacting? But then the image of the sinking statue flashed in his mind again, and his resolve hardened. "I have to do something, Sarah. I have to be ready... for whatever's coming." Suddenly,

Sarah's hand was on his arm, her touch both startling and grounding. He looked up, meeting her worried gaze.

"Beau, honey, come back to bed," she said softly. "Let's talk about this dream of yours properly."

For a moment, he resisted, his body coiled with the need to do something, anything. But Sarah's steady presence slowly penetrated the fog of panic clouding his mind. He let out a shaky breath, allowing her to guide him beneath the covers, sinking onto the edge of his mattress, suddenly aware of how exhausted he felt.

Sarah's warm hand found his, her fingers intertwining with his own. "Now," she said, her voice low and soothing, "tell me about this dream. What exactly did you see?"

Bordelon closed his eyes. The vivid images rushed back with alarming clarity. He was there again—the balcony of the Patablo Building overlooking Jackson Square. Mardi Gras day. Streets packed with revelers from all over. It was as real as before. As real as the bed he sat on now. "Everything was normal at first," he said. "The crowds, the music, the excitement in the air. But then... Andrew Jackson's statue."

Sarah's hand tightened around his, a silent encouragement to continue.

"It started to spin right there in the center of the square," Bordelon went on, his words becoming more rapid. "Faster and faster, like some demented carousel. But nobody else noticed. They just kept celebrating, oblivious."

He opened his eyes, meeting Sarah's concerned gaze. The worry he saw there made his stomach clench. "I tried to point it out, to warn someone, anyone. But it was like I was invisible. And then..." he had to pause before continuing. "The statue started to sink into the ground, causing a spiraling wall of whites and grays churning with violent energy. And at its center, a dark void sucking everything into it. The buildings, the square, the streets, the people... all of it, just... disappearing into the earth."

A shudder ran through him, the memory of his nightmare still painfully fresh. "I watched helplessly as the entire city was swallowed up. And still, nobody but me seemed to notice or care."

Sarah's arms wrapped around his shoulders, pulling him close. The warmth of her body against his was comforting, but it couldn't completely dispel the chill that had settled in his bones.

"What do you think it means, Sarah?" he asked, hating how small and uncertain he sounded. "Why would I dream something like that?"

Sarah said nothing, but her silence spoke volumes. He could feel her tension, the unspoken worry radiating off her in waves. "I don't know, Beau," she finally said. "Dreams are often just our subconscious processing stress. You've been under a lot of pressure lately, especially with those horrid rumors about that despicable Maxwell Kingsley."

Bordelon pulled away slightly, frustration bubbling up inside him. "This wasn't just stress, Sarah. It felt... Prophetic. Like a warning." Standing up abruptly, he resumed his pacing. The first hints of dawn were starting to lighten the sky outside. "I can't just ignore this," he said, more to himself than to Sarah. "But I don't know what to do. How do you prepare for something you can't even define?"

Sarah sat on the edge of the bed, her hands clasped tightly in her lap. "Beau, you're scaring me," she said softly. "This isn't like you. Maybe we should call Dr. Winters to talk things through."

Bordelon whirled around, fixing her with a hard stare. "A psychiatrist? You think I'm losing it, don't you?"

"That's not what I—"

"I'm not crazy, Sarah," he interrupted, his voice rising. "Something's coming. I can feel it. And if I can't figure out what it is or how to stop it..."

The room settled into an uneasy silence, the ticking of the antique clock on the mantel being the only sound. Bordelon turned to the window, gazing out at the city stirring to life. Behind him, Sarah's uneven breathing betrayed her concern, her confusion thick in the air.

As the first rays of sunlight broke over the horizon, Beau Bordelon, Governor of Louisiana, remained motionless. He was caught between the cold logic of politics and the lingering grip of his nightmare. The day had begun, but the shadows of his dream clung to him, an unspoken warning of a storm gathering just beyond the horizon.

14

Eli Colt tightened his grip on the wheel, his thoughts circling the Kingsley connection as the Jeep rumbled down Redemption Rescue's driveway. A billionaire's silver Jaguar tied to a teenage girl's kidnapping would dominate headlines if they could prove it. But headlines wouldn't bring the Johnson twins home.

As they rounded the final curve framed by towering pines and sprawling live oaks, Dakota straightened in his seat, his expression sharpening with expectation. Ten acres of open green stretched ahead, dotted with bursts of yellow, pink, and lavender from Lindsey's meticulous gardens. Karina's blue Corolla sat parked beside his F-250 outside the modular office, while across the drive, Eli's silver Airstream glinted blindingly in the midday sun.

Eli parked next to Dakota's truck. "Home sweet home," he said, killing the engine.

"Yep," Dakota said, squinting against the brightness. "Let's hope they got the A/C cranking inside."

Eli and Dakota climbed out of the vehicle. The heat hit Eli hard as he took the three steps to the porch in a single bound. He paused at the glass entrance, breathed in, and stepped into the cool office, with Dakota following closely behind.

Julia Colt looked up from her desk with laugh lines around her brown eyes highlighted a warm smile. "Welcome back, boys," she said, raising her petite frame to greet them. "How'd it go in Alabama?"

Before Eli could answer, he found his wife. Lindsey hunched over a spread of purple and gold brochures with his niece Tara. She lifted her green eyes in an elated expression, framed by auburn-red hair cascading over her shoulders. "Eli," she breathed, quickly crossing the room to embrace him.

Karina stepped out of the small kitchenette, a steaming mug in hand. Her dark hair was swept back in a sleek ponytail, accentuating her high cheekbones and full lips. As her eyes met Dakota's, his face lit up with a broad, genuine smile. "Karina," he said in a voice softer than usual. "I didn't know you'd be here."

Karina's smile matched his. "Surprise," she said, setting down her cup and hurrying to him.

"Hey, Uncle Eli," Tara said, waving a pamphlet. "I think I've narrowed down my courses."

Eli, still holding Lindsey, glanced over at his niece. Her sharp eyes sparkled, framed by a face just losing its childhood softness. "Fantastic," he said, his tone warm with encouragement. "But I'm even more interested in hearing about what you noticed while shopping in the French Quarter."

It had been two years since her rescue, and she still carried herself with a wariness during an ongoing healing process. "Uncle Eli, I've been thinking more and more about what I saw." Her voice was steady. "I'm totally convinced it was Andre."

"Andre Badeau?" Dakota said. "Why am I only hearing about this now?"

"Nobody was sure, and we didn't want to get everybody worked up," Julia said.

Eli studied his niece, then nodded slowly. "Okay, Tara. Walk us through it again. Every detail that comes to mind."

"It's alright, honey," Julia said. "Take your time."

Tara's eyes revealed a glimmer of fear. "He was standing next to the Cabildo while we were walking past St. Louis Cathedral. I saw his face clearly. There's no doubt in my mind. It was him."

Karina frowned. "Who is this, Andre Badeau?"

"The man who lured Tara from our home in New Orleans two years ago," Julia said.

Dakota rubbed Karina's shoulder. "Remember I told you about it back in Juarez?"

"Well, if he's back from wherever he disappeared to, we need to figure out where he is," Eli said. "Dakota, contact our informants in New Orleans. See if they've seen or heard anything about Badeau being back in town."

Eli's eyes narrowed as he focused on his sister-in-law. "Julia, did you take a look at that security footage I sent you? The one with the woman and the Johnson twins?"

Julia raised her brow and exhaled slowly. "Tara, honey. Why don't you go pick us up some shrimp po-boys at Morton's? Grab some chips, too."

"I'll take an oyster loaf, sweetheart," Dakota chimed in. "Ketchup and hot sauce."

Eli handed her his credit card and walked her to the door. "Don't you worry, Andre Badeau is no threat to you now." He turned, focusing his attention on Julia. "What can you tell us about this woman?"

Julia pulled out a file from her desk. "Quite a bit, actually. Her name is Vivian Delacroix. She comes from old California money and has been a close associate of Maxwell Kingsley for years. They attended UC Berkeley together, where they were romantically involved."

"Maxwell Kingsley?" Karina asked, looking confused.

"Big-time investment banker who moved to Louisiana about ten years ago," Julia explained. "And this is where things get interesting. Kingsley was Beau Bordelon's biggest financial backer during his campaign for governor."

"That's a powerful connection," Eli said. "What else do we know about their relationship?"

Julia sighed. "It's complicated. Bordelon built his political career on integrity and family values. And from all indications, he's the real deal. Kingsley, on the other hand, has a reputation for being just the opposite. He throws lavish parties, often attended by influential men and women."

"And Delacroix?" Dakota prompted.

"She's always by Kingsley's side at these events," Julia said. "From what I've gathered, she plays a key role in entertaining guests. There have been rumors—nothing concrete —but whispers about young women, even minors, at their strange social gatherings."

A heavy silence fell over the room.

Karina held her hand to her mouth. "Those poor girls."

Lindsey's face hardened, and her eyes flashed with anger. "If there's even a chance those rumors are true, we have to do something."

"The dynamics between these three are intriguing," Julia said. "Bordelon seems to be trying to distance himself from Kingsley lately, probably to protect his political image. But

Kingsley still wields plenty of influence. And Delacroix? She appears to be Kingsley's right hand in many of his social ventures."

Eli nodded slowly, processing the information. "And now we have footage of Delacroix with the Johnson twins. This case just got more complicated."

"What's our next move?" Dakota asked, his expression grim.

Eli stood and paced the room. Each step matched a name, a face, and a ton of uncertainty. He was stymied and, because of the political angle, a little scared. "We need to be careful. Dig deeper without creating waves. These are powerful people we're dealing with."

The weight of it all settled heavily on his shoulders. Badeau back in play, a corrupt governor, trafficking networks reaching into the highest levels of power—and somewhere in the middle of it all, two teenage girls who needed help. He met Lindsey's worried gaze across the room. Two years ago, he'd nearly lost everything going after Badeau. This time, with a new wife and a growing team depending on him, the stakes were higher.

"Julia, keep researching. See if you can find any concrete links between Delacroix, Kingsley, and any suspicious activities." Eli scratched the crown of his head. "But before you do that, have our IT guy come out and strengthen our firewalls and VPN. And see what else we can do to ensure our internet searches remain private."

Dakota set his jaw. "I'll reach out to Marcus Blackwell. See if there have been any off-the-record investigations into Kingsley or Delacroix. Maybe someone's been building a case quietly."

Eli clasped his hands and straightened. "We've got two missing girls to find, and it appears we're up against some very powerful people. Let's be thorough but watch our steps. Finding these girls could be more dangerous than we initially thought."

His team dispersed to their tasks. The Johnson twins were here in Louisiana, buried in Kingsley's web of power and corruption. This time, stealth would matter more than force. One wrong move could bury them deeper—or worse —get them killed.

15

Governor Beau Bordelon slouched behind his enormous honey-hued desk fashioned from cypress in his massive state capitol office. Despite the warmth radiating through the tall windows, the cold grip of his nightmare remained. The Pelican Seal of Louisiana embossed on the carpet was a tangible reminder of his immense power. But this morning, weakness settled in, rendering him ineffective.

The intercom's buzz shattered his brooding. Bordelon flinched, knocking over a framed photo of Sarah and his two young children. He righted it with trembling hands as his secretary droned through the speaker, "Governor, Mr. Maxwell Kingsley is here for your ten o'clock." Bordelon's temples warmed as he glanced at his Rolex—10:15. Kingsley was late, a subtle power play. "Send him in, Patricia," he managed, his voice steadier than his nerves. He rose, straightening his tie and plastering on a politician's smile as the door opened.

Maxwell Kingsley strode in. His compact 5'8", barely 150-

pound frame fit into a tailored grey pinstripe, belying a persona as commanding as a lion tamer. At 42, his perfectly parted silver hair caught the overhead light like polished steel.

"Beau, my boy," Kingsley drawled through a shark-like grin, grasping Bordelon's hand in a grip that was a shade too firm. Cold as a glacier, his piercing blue eyes scanned the room before settling on Bordelon. "You're looking a bit peaky this fine Louisiana morning. Trouble sleeping?"

Bordelon withdrew his hand, suppressing a shudder. "Nothing a strong cup of coffee won't fix, Max," he said, gesturing to the leather chairs facing his desk. "Please, have a seat."

Kingsley lowered himself into a chair with casual grace, crossing one leg over the other. His eyes never left Bordelon's face. "I must say, I was surprised by your urgent request for a meeting. Thought we had everything squared away for the quarter." Bordelon settled back into his chair, trying to project an authority he didn't feel. He picked up a pen, a nervous habit, twirling it between his fingers. "Things change, Max. There are... rumors circulating. Disturbing ones."

"Oh?" Kingsley's eyebrow arched, his tone one of mild curiosity. "Do tell."

Bordelon shifted his weight, his voice dropping to a harsh whisper. "Parties, Max. With celebrities, political figures... and underage girls. It's hitting the media outlets. I can't be associated with this kind of scandal. Not now, not ever."

Kingsley's laugh was sharp. "My dear boy, since when did you develop such delicate sensibilities? As I recall, you didn't seem to mind much when you were in attendance at a similar soirée." He paused, his smile turning predatory. "Or when my money funded the PAC that got you elected."

The pen in Bordelon's hand snapped, the black ink spreading like the corruption creeping into his administration. His cheeks warmed with an anger that overrode his terror. He slammed his palm on the desk, scattering papers. "That was different, and you know it. I never—" He cut himself off, lowering his voice and leaning forward. "I never touched those girls. And I had no idea they were underage."

Kingsley leaned back, utterly unfazed by the outburst. His eyes glittered with amusement. "Of course you didn't, Beau. Plausible deniability is such a useful thing, isn't it? But I have videos, mind you. Footage that puts you in... Let's say, a compromising position." He smoothed an invisible wrinkle from his trousers. "But let's not quibble over the past. What matters is the present—and your political future."

Bordelon's face warmed as a flicker of defiance rushed beneath his skin. "You're forgetting, Maxwell, that I've already stuck my neck out for you. Pardoning Andre Badeau wasn't exactly a move that went unnoticed."

Kingsley's lips curled into a cold smile. "Ah yes, the pardon. A necessary step, wouldn't you agree? It allowed our mutual friend to return from his Caribbean 'vacation' and resume his... business activities. Activities that, need I remind you, fill my accounts and your campaign coffers with cash."

"That pardon could ruin me if it ever comes to light," Bordelon complained. "Then we best make sure it doesn't," Kingsley said smoothly. "Just as I'll ensure these charming videos of you remain our little secret. You see, Beau, we're in this together now. Your future is tied to mine, whether you like it or not."

The governor's shoulders sagged, the fight draining out of him. He slumped back in his chair, getting older by the minute. "What do you want, Max?"

Kingsley smiled, showing too many teeth. "It's not about what I want, my friend. It's about what you need to make this go away. You need my continued support if you want a shot at re-election." His voice dropped to a conspiratorial whisper. "And I need you to remember who your real friends are."

Bordelon swallowed against the noose of political favor tightening around his neck. He was caught between his ambitions and the devil sitting across from him. A muscle twitched on the side of his forehead. "And how exactly do you propose to 'make this go away,' Max? These aren't just whispers anymore. There are investigations, witnesses—"

Kingsley waved a dismissive hand. "Details, my boy. Mere details," he said with a voice low and silky. "You forget, I have friends in high places too. Friends who owe me favors. Friends who understand the importance of... discretion."

A bitterness filled Bordelon's mouth. He pushed back from his desk, standing abruptly. Pacing to the window, he stared out at the manicured grounds of the capitol, seeking a moment's respite from Kingsley's suffocating presence. "And what's the price for this discretion, Max?" Bordelon asked, his back still to Kingsley. "What do you want from me?"

The soft creak of leather declared Kingsley rising. The sound of footsteps announced his approach. "Nothing you haven't already given, Beau," Kingsley said as a heavy hand thumped Bordelon's shoulder. "Your loyalty. Your coopera-tion. And perhaps..." He paused, letting the silence stretch uncomfortably. "Perhaps a few small favors. Nothing that would trouble your conscience, I assure you."

Bordelon turned, finding Kingsley too close. "Small favors," he repeated, his voice hollow. "Like what?"

Kingsley's smile was all teeth. "Oh, just some minor adjustments to state regulations. A strategic appointment or two. Nothing you wouldn't do for any other significant campaign contributor."

The implication hung between them like humidity in the marsh. Bordelon's shoulders slumped, burdened by his willful ignorance. Each overlooked transgression felt like a stone added to an already crushing load. He opened his mouth to respond, but Kingsley held up a hand. "Don't answer now, my friend. Think it over. Discuss it with that lovely wife of yours if you must." Kingsley's eyes glinted with malice. "I'm sure Sarah would hate to see your bid for reelection torpedoed by some misunderstood footage on CNN."

Bordelon's hands clenched into fists. He watched, frozen, as Kingsley sauntered to the door, pausing with his hand on the knob. "I'll be in touch, Beau," Kingsley said, his voice drenched with false warmth. "Do try to get some rest. You look terrible."

The door clicked shut, leaving Bordelon alone in the suddenly cavernous office. For a moment, he stood motionless. Then, with a strangled cry, he swept his arm across his desk, sending papers, pens, and his family photo crashing to the floor. Bordelon collapsed into his chair, burying his face in his hands.

The ticking of the antique clock on the wall seemed to grow louder, each second another step toward an inevitable reckoning. Raising his head, his gaze fell on the shattered frame of his family photo amid the scattered debris.

With his fingers shaking uncontrollably, he reached for his phone. He hesitated, then dialed the three-digit extension. "Patricia," he said, releasing his emotion, "please let my wife know I'm coming home for lunch."

16

Beau Bordelon's palm left a damp imprint on the brass doorknob as he entered the Governor's Mansion. He loosened his tie, the silk suddenly constrictive against his throat.

The whiff of freshly baked bread from the kitchen did little to ease the sour taste in his mouth. Bordelon paused at the threshold, watching Sarah spread mustard on a slice of her famous sourdough recipe.

"Where is everyone?" he asked in a strained voice.

Sarah looked up, her typical warm expression tempered by her concern. "I gave the staff the afternoon off. Figured we could use some time alone." She set the knife down, wiping her hands on a dishcloth. "Since this is the first time you've come home for lunch as governor, I'm guessing it's serious."

A sharp pang shot through Bordelon's sternum. Of course, she'd sensed something was off. Twenty-five years of marriage had honed her intuition to a razor's edge. He swallowed hard, the sandwich fixings on the counter blurring as he struggled to maintain his composure.

"You're right," he managed, the words feeling like gravel in his mouth. "We need to talk."

Sarah nodded. Her calmness only heightened Bordelon's stress level. She gestured to the chair across from her. "Have a seat, dear. I'll serve."

As Bordelon sat, the weight of the moment—of the shame he was about to expose—pressed down so heavily it bent his shoulders. Sarah continued to slice a tomato. The routine of her actions only amplified the anomaly of what he was about to confess.

"Sarah," he started, his tone reduced to a strained murmur. "There's something I need to tell you about... about a party. One of Max's."

Sarah paused cutting, suspended inside the half-cut tomato. Her shoulders tensed as if bracing for impact. Slowly, she set the knife down and wiped her palms on her apron, leaving faint streaks of red on the yellow fabric. Her usually warm eyes were guarded now, twisting Bordelon's insides.

"Maxwell Kingsley," she said monotone. "I see."

A constriction clawed at Bordelon's throat. He reached for the glass of water Sarah had placed nearby, his fingers sliding against the condensation-slick surface. He managed a sip, the cold liquid barely registering as it slid down. "There were... girls there," he said, each word tumbling out like shards of broken glass. "Young girls. I didn't know, Sarah. I swear I didn't know until it was too late."

Sarah's expression didn't change, but the slight whitening of her knuckles around the counter's edge betrayed her tension. In the distance, the sharp buzz of a weed eater shattered the silence.

"Who'd want to do yard work on a day like this," she said, resuming her chore of slicing the tomato.

"I'm sorry, Sarah. I never want to do anything that might hurt you or the kids."

"And now?" Sarah asked, her voice low but sharp. "Why are you telling me this now?"

Bordelon closed his eyes, bracing himself for the worst part of his confession. When he opened them again, he found Sarah's intense stare, waiting.

"Because Kingsley has footage," his admission seemed to lay suspended between them. "And he's threatening to use it." His fingers clutched his chair's armrest as an anchor. "I swear to you, nothing happened. I left as soon as I understood—"

"Stop," Sarah said raising her hand, her wedding ring glimmered in the light streaming through the kitchen window. "I don't need the details. Not now." Her chest rose and fell slowly, visibly collecting herself. "What I need to know is what Kingsley wants. What's his endgame here?"

Bordelon released a breath he didn't realize he'd been holding. "He seeks influence and control over policy decisions, appointments, and contracts. He's been pushing for months, but I've been resisting. He believes this is his trump card and he's playing it."

Sarah's eyes narrowed, a familiar determination settling over her features. It was the look she wore when facing down challenges, the one that had seen them through countless political battles. "And if you don't play along?"

"Then the footage goes public," Bordelon said, the words leaving a bitter taste in his mouth. "My career, our reputation, the kids' futures—it all ends."

Sarah nodded as if processing. She moved around the island, closing the physical distance between them. Her hand came to rest on his shoulder, a gesture of support that nearly undid him. "We've weathered storms before, Beau. We'll weather this one too."

Bordelon looked up at her, hope warring with guilt inside his chest. "You believe me? That nothing happened?"

"I believe you," Sarah said, her voice firm. "But more importantly, I believe in you. I believe in us. Now, let's figure out how to outmaneuver that narcissistic leech."

Bordelon sagged in his chair and rubbed his temples. "Outmaneuver him? Sarah, I'm not sure we can."

For the first time all day, Bordelon had a sense of relief. He and Sarah were in this together, just as they'd been with every major issue in their lives. As Sarah pulled up a chair beside him, he knew that whatever came next, they'd face it as one.

"Sarah flashed her eyes with determination. Pacing the length of the kitchen island, she stood still for a moment, her fingers trailing along its marble surface before stopping at the far end. Turning to face him, she shifted her stance. "Tell me everything. Every detail about that party, about the footage, about Kingsley's demands. I need to know exactly what we're dealing with."

Bordelon's heart ached. He'd often pushed the images from the night to the side to avoid the guilt that always followed. "Alright, but it's not pretty."

Sarah's lips pressed into a thin line. "I didn't expect it to be. But I can't fight what I don't understand." She moved back to the table, pulling her chair closer to his. As she sat, her knee brushed against his, a small point of contact that steadied him. "Start from the beginning. And honey?" Her voice softened slightly. "Don't leave anything out. Not a single detail."

Bordelon breathed in the fresh bread aroma. He paused to gather his thoughts. "It was about six months before the election. Kingsley invited me to what he called a 'private fundraiser' at his hunting lodge in Jonesville."

Bordelon's words just sort of hung there for five, maybe ten heartbeats as Sarah's fingers tightened around her water glass. "Go on," she said with a steady tone.

"I arrived about eight. The place was plush, opulent, and neither word began to cover it. Crystal chandeliers, marble floors, waiters in tuxedos." Bordelon's mind became unfocused as he got lost in the memory. "Kingsley greeted me at the door, all smiles and handshakes. He introduced me to some big donors, poured me a drink."

Sarah nodded. Her expression was poker face unreadable. "Who else was there?"

"A mix. Business leaders, state senators, US congressmen, you name it." Bordelon paused, his throat working as he swallowed hard. "It wasn't until later, when we moved to the pool area, that I noticed the girls."

Sarah's breath caught, almost imperceptibly. "How young?"

Bordelon's eyes squeezed shut trying to picture them. "To be honest, I didn't pay much attention at first. The light was dim, the drinks were flowing, I was talking with Matt, the representative from Bossier City. Then I noticed."

"Noticed?"

"Some of the guys were getting handsy."

"And you?"

Bordelon's eyes snapped open. "I saw they were at least twenty years younger than me, and I got real uncomfortable. I made my excuses and tried to get out of there."

"But couldn't before Max got his footage," Sarah said to finish his story.

"The only thing he could have are pictures of girls

standing next to me with their arms around my waist. Just like I've taken a million times on the campaign trail."

Sarah was silent for a short minute, processing. When she spoke, her voice was carefully controlled. "Is that all, Beau. Be honest with me, or I can't help you."

Bordelon reached for his water. He took a sip, buying time, the cool liquid doing little to soothe his parched throat. "Nothing... explicit," he finally managed. "It's damning enough. Me at the party, talking with Kingsley, surrounded by those girls. There's a moment when one of them stumbles and spills her drink on me. I reach out to steady her, and it looks... well, it looks bad."

"How do you know?"

Bordelon pulled an envelope from his jacket pocket and handed it to Sarah. Sarah took it, flipped open the flap, and glanced at him. "I see," she said, her tone neither angry nor forgiving. "Any video?"

He shook his head. "None, thank God. But the photos alone... in the wrong hands, with the right spin..."

"Would be enough to sink us," Sarah narrowed her eyes and leaned back in her chair. "What are Max's demands?"

"Influence over key appointments. The head of Natural Resources, for starters. He's pushing for someone who'll be... friendly to his interests." Bordelon's voice dripped with disgust. "And he wants me to fast-track some environmental regulations that would benefit his alternative energy companies."

Sarah's expression hardened. "That will drive up fuel costs and affect the entire country."

Bordelon pressed his face into a tight grimace. "I've been stalling, trying to find a way out, but he's losing patience. He's given me until the end of the week to comply, or—"

"Or the footage goes public," Sarah concluded.

Suddenly, she stood up, the chair scraping against the floor. Moving to the window, she gazed out at the eight-acre estate. A silence stretched between them.

Finally, Sarah turned back to face him, her expression resolute, her fingers crumpling the photos' edges. She stared at them one last time before throwing them onto the counter. "You know what disgusts me more than these pictures?" Her voice trembled with barely contained rage. "That Maxwell Kingsley thinks he owns us now. That he believes with money and influence he can do anything he pleases."

Bordelon gripped his chair. "Sarah, our whole future—"

"Is worth nothing if we sell it to him." She planted both hands on the table, leaning forward until their faces were inches apart. "We fought too hard, sacrificed too much to let that parasite destroy what we believe in. I won't let him turn you into his puppet."

The certainty in her voice hit him like a physical force. "You understand what this means? The scandal, the media circus, the children—"

"Will know their father chose integrity over power." Sarah's eyes blazed. "We're not giving in to his demands. Not now, not ever. He can do his worst."

The weight Bordelon had carried alone lifted from his shoulders. He stood, taking Sarah's hands in his. "Together then?"

"Together. And God help Maxwell Kingsley when we're done with him."

17

W*ednesday, August 7*

The Louisiana mansion loomed into view as the Denali crested the hill, a pale monolith against the brilliance of the afternoon sky. Gabriel straightened in his seat, his chest tightening. His father's words stirred like embers in his mind—*count it all joy when you fall into trouble. Trials are God's way of producing patience.* Was this a test? If so, what would it demand of him? And could he endure it?

Royal palms lined the estate, their smooth, gray trunks rising skyward, indifferent to the churn of unease building inside him. Gabriel's eyes scanned the horizon, absorbing every detail. The mansion was immense, with columns so tall they seemed to support the sky itself. Yet even in its splendor, imperfections stood out—chipped paint on the far-left wing, a slanted shutter catching the light. They reminded him of the fishing nets back home, the ones Papa had him and his brother constantly mend. No matter how often you looked, there was always a tear somewhere.

"Big, huh?" Hector muttered, flexing tattooed arms as he

maneuvered the vehicle around a tight curve. The words Los Diablos and Ciudad Juarez scrawled across his skin as if they were alive. Gabriel didn't answer, keeping his focus on the mansion, its vastness both awe-inspiring and oppressive.

Badeau, sitting in the passenger seat, glanced back at him. His dark eyes carried a sharpness that seemed to pierce right through Gabriel's silence. "Don't look so impressed," Badeau said, his tone clipped. "You're not here for the view."

Gravel crunched under the tires as the Denali slowed, pulling into a driveway bordered by flawless hedges. Parked beside them was a metallic green Jaguar and a glossy black Escalade, their surfaces gleaming like crystal.

Hector killed the engine and stepped out. "Let's move." He opened Gabriel's door with a sharp motion, and the thick, humid air rushed in, clinging to Gabriel's skin like a second layer. The landscape was manicured gardens and and endlessly rolling lawn. Beautiful. And empty. Nowhere to hide, nowhere to run.

Badeau's voice broke the stillness. "Keep up." He was already heading toward the entrance, his stride confident and impatient. "Let's get this over with."

Gabriel's legs were unsteady as he stepped out, his shoes digging into the pristine pebbles. For a moment, he tilted his chin upward, drawing in a breath heavy with humidity.

The house loomed larger with each step, its facade blindingly white. As they reached the smaller building behind it, his gaze snagged on a thin crack on the bottom-right panel of the door. Barely visible. Almost hidden. But it was there. Even here, in this place that screamed perfection, flaws existed. Papa would've said there's no such thing as spotless—not in mansions, not in men.

The doorbell chimed, low and melodic, and a soft

mechanical hum signaled the security camera swiveling to life. Badeau pressed the bell a second time.

Footsteps approached, but they weren't from the house. A woman emerged from around the corner, leading a proud chestnut horse by its reins. Gabriel's breath caught. She wore a fitted black jacket and beige riding pants that hugged her long legs, her knee-high boots shining like polished mirrors. A leather crop dangled from one hand, tapping rhythmically against her thigh. Her gaze passed over Hector and Badeau before landing squarely on Gabriel.

Her lips curved into a smile. "What do we have here?" Her voice was smooth, like oil poured over glass, but there was something sharp beneath it—something that made the hair on Gabriel's neck stand on end.

The door to the building swung open. Cool air rushed out. A man stepped into the threshold, his shadow stretching across the driveway like a warning. He was broad-shouldered, with a complexion scarred from old acne and a nose bent from repeated breaks. His green overalls looked out of place against the pristine backdrop of the estate.

"This him?" the man asked, his voice gruff, his eyes narrowed as they raked over Gabriel. "The one from Honduras?"

Badeau nodded. "Sent special delivery."

With a gentle nudge, Hector urged Gabriel forward. Steadying himself, Gabriel recalled Papa's lessons about facing challenges with dignity. The man stepped closer, circling Gabriel with the slow, deliberate movements of a predator sizing up prey. Gabriel fought the urge to flinch, keeping his shoulders straight.

Honor God, even when it costs you.

The man stopped in front of him, his expression unreadable. "I'm Stone. I run things around here." He jerked his head toward the house. "What did you do back in Honduras?"

"His talents are limitless," Badeau said. "Has a brilliant mind, we've been told."

Gabriel swallowed against the tension gripping his chest. "I worked on my father's fishing boat. I studied too. I was accepted to university."

Stone's laugh was humorless. "University?" He spat the word as if it were a joke. "You're not here to read books, boy. You're here to work. Maintain the grounds. That's it. No slacking, no excuses." His tone dropped, turning cold enough to chill Gabriel despite the heat. "And if you screw up, you'll find out real fast what happens to failures around here. Understand?"

"Yes, sir," Gabriel said firmly.

"Good." Stone turned to Hector. "Take him to his quarters. He starts tomorrow."

Before Gabriel could move, the woman from outside entered the room with a deliberate stride, her presence commanding attention. "Well, what do we have here?" she asked, her voice smooth yet curious.

Stone's eyebrows lifted. "Ms. Delacroix, I didn't expect you to join us. This is a new grounds worker Badeau brought in from down south."

She stepped closer, her gaze locked on him as if she were examining something rare. He stood straighter, neither cowering nor challenging.

"Interesting," she said, appraising every inch of him. "Very interesting indeed. He's got a strong look," she mused, almost to herself. "He'd be perfect to work the gala this weekend. What do you think, Andre?"

"That would be up to Mr. Kingsley," Badeau said. "And you, of course."

"Oh, I'm sure Max wouldn't mind," she said as she turned to leave the room. "The boy's too beautiful not to show in public." With that, she walked away, leaving a strange feeling inside Gabriel.

As they walked to his quarters, the manicured grounds contrasted with the thorny reality of his situation. Yet he found peace in knowing that even here, in this elegant prison, God had a purpose for him. His task wasn't to escape but to remain faithful to his values and to be a light even in this darkness.

A modest two-story building came into view, contrasting sharply with the grand main house. This structure had a practical appearance, its white paint a shade duller than the mansion's gleaming exterior.

Hector entered a code on a panel, and the door clicked open. "Home sweet home," he said, his voice dripping with sarcasm.

The interior was sparse and dusty. A narrow staircase led to an upper floor, while a small kitchenette and living area occupied the ground level.

"Upstairs," Hector commanded, giving Gabriel a none-too-gentle shove up the steps.

The second floor held two bedrooms and a shared bathroom. Hector opened the door to the smaller room. "This is you. Don't get too comfortable. You start work tomorrow."

Gabriel took in his quarters—a twin bed, a dresser, and a desk. A single window offered a view of the back of the property.

He sat on the edge of the mattress. His fingers curled into the coarse fabric of the bedspread as a low ache settled in his chest. He dropped to his knees, pressing his hands together. "Lord, help me remember who I am. Empower me to stay true to your character." His prayer was but a whisper, but it carried every trial that had led him here. He prayed not for escape but for strength to endure.

A soft knock startled him. "Hello?" A girl's voice. Gentle. Innocent.

"Yes?"

"I... I brought you dinner," she said. "Can I come in?"

"The door's locked," he said.

The lock clicked open. A young woman with deep dark skin entered. Her eyes, when they met Gabriel's, were a mix of wariness and concealed fear.

"I'm Kiara," she said barely louder than a whisper. She stepped into the room, balancing a tray of food. Her eyes flitted toward the door, as if she expected someone to burst in at any moment. "Ms. Delacroix asked me to bring you this and... show you around."

Gabriel stayed where he was, watching her. Her movements were cautious, deliberate, like a bird skimming too close to a trap. She set the tray down on the small desk, her hands lingering on the edges as if anchoring herself.

"Listen," she said, glancing over her shoulder. Her shoulders were tense, her words rushed. "I know you just got here, and you're probably scared. Just..." Her voice dropped lower. "Be careful. This place—" She trailed off, shaking her head, as though finishing the sentence would summon something she couldn't face.

Gabriel studied her. She couldn't have been much older than him, yet her eyes carried a maturity not often seen in someone their age. Despite her warning, he didn't sense fear in her exactly—it was something quieter. Resignation.

He straightened. "Look. I'm okay. Because God put me here for a reason."

Kiara's head snapped up, her wide eyes locking onto his. "*God? Reason?* I hope for your sake that's so," she said, as though his faith might crumble under what she knew. "I hope that for myself, my sister, and every kid on this property, that's so. But I'm not sure you understand where you are."

"But I do," Gabriel said gently, holding her gaze. "Maybe not everything. But enough. My father always told me God doesn't waste trials." He forced a smile. "Even in places like this."

She stared at him, her expression softening, but her lips remained pressed into a thin line. "You're... different," she said at last, as if she didn't know what else to call him. "I'll give you that." She started to leave.

"Kiara?" Gabriel said softly as she moved to the door. "Thank you. For caring enough to warn me."

She paused, one hand resting lightly on the doorknob. Her face was unreadable, but the tension in her frame seemed to ease just slightly. "Don't thank me yet," she murmured. Then she stepped out, and the lock clicked into place behind her.

Gabriel sat for a moment, his thoughts circling like gulls over restless waters. He turned toward the tray with food. The aroma hit him hard—roasted meat, warm bread, something sweet. His stomach growled so loudly he almost laughed at himself. He hadn't realized how hungry he was until now.

But the food wasn't his biggest temptation. Ms. Delacroix's touch still lingered on his arm like a brand, the image of her sharp eyes and unreadable smile looping through his mind. She had looked at him the way a collector might look at a rare gem—something to display, to control.

Gabriel clenched his fists, willing the memory away.

Lead us not into temptation.

Papa had spoken to him often about moments like this.

The devil doesn't always come roaring like a lion, son. Sometimes his voice is beautiful as it whispers in your ear. Gabriel had always nodded, dutiful and trusting, but now he truly understood what his father meant.

Here, in this place that glimmered with wealth and power but reeked of something rotten beneath the surface, his faith had to be more than a comfort. It had to be his armor. If he allowed his guard to slip, even for a moment, he could lose himself in this place.

Gabriel slid to his knees, resting his elbows on the edge of the bed. The scent of the food pulled at him, but he focused instead on the silence and the steady beat of his heart.

"Lord, help me stay true," he prayed, his voice low but resolute. "Let me be a light, even here."

The hunger still gnawed at him. As he rose and turned to the tray, the question still swirled—could he survive this? One choice at a time?

18

Thursday, August 8

Thursday, August 8

The unfamiliar creak of the metal bed frame pierced the pre-dawn darkness as Gabriel stirred in his sparse quarters at Kingsley Estate. Yesterday's memories—his arrival, Stone's threats, Ms. Delacroix's tempting interest, and Kiara's whispered warning—whirled in his mind.

Beside him, separated by a thin wall, he could hear the soft, rhythmic breathing of the boy in the next room. Gabriel envied his ability to sleep so soundly in this strange place. Perhaps that came with time in captivity.

Swinging his legs over the edge of the bed, Gabriel sat up, his bare feet touching the cool wooden floor. Through the small window, he could see the first hints of dawn painting the sky in gold and orange. The sprawling grounds lay like a canvas of fear and danger.

As he dressed in the work clothes left on a worn chair in the corner—rough denim jeans and a lime-green t-shirt—Gabriel questioned how he would navigate this new world.

What tests awaited him beyond the locked door of these rooms? He bowed his head and offered a quiet prayer. "*Dios mío*, please guide me." Despite the uncertainty gnawing at his insides, a calm resolve settled over him. God was with him in his dreams in Honduras and here in his confinement.

He would work hard and impress those in charge. Perhaps, if he proved his worth, he could improve his situation—maybe even find a way back to his family somehow.

As the first rays of sunlight crept across the room, Gabriel stood ready to face whatever the day might bring. He could no longer be that boy who boasted of visions, but he could earn favor with the people who controlled his life.

A booming knock shocked Gabriel from his thoughts. "Time to work," a harsh voice came through the door. "Be outside in five minutes."

Gabriel's pulse pounded as he laced up his boots. He considered the empty dinner tray from the night before, wondering if he should take it with him. No, better to leave it.

He stepped into the hallway. The boy from the next room emerged, too. He was about Gabriel's age, his features indigenous and Latino. Though Gabriel couldn't place his origin, his high cheekbones and deep-set eyes suggested Central American. Like Gabriel, he wore rough denim jeans and a lime-green t-shirt that hung loosely on his thin frame.

The boy's eyes remained downcast, his movements carrying the resigned shuffle of someone who'd long ago accepted their fate.

Gabriel straightened with a determination to work harder than these people expected. As they descended the stairs, he caught sight of the vast lawn through a window that glistened with morning dew.

Outside, the humid air dampened his skin. A group of workers, mostly young men and boys, displaying the same resignation Gabriel had seen from the boy upstairs, huddled near a shed. Their wary eyes followed Gabriel as he approached.

"Listen up," Stone growled, his voice raspy. "We have a newbie here by the name of…" He stepped forward with a clipboard, wearing a blue denim shirt under green overalls. "Gabriel. He'll be with some of you today." With an intense glare, Stone nearly made Gabriel step back. "I can be your greatest ally or your worst nightmare. It depends on you. Those of you working with him, show him the ropes but don't get too friendly. You're here to work, not to make friends," he said, pointing a stern finger.

Assignments were barked out. "Miguel, Juan, you're on hedge trimming. Carlos, fertilizer duty." A piercing look landed on Gabriel. "Pete, take the newbie with you and teach him how to operate the mowers."

A lanky teenager with a mop of unruly red hair nodded sullenly. As the group dispersed, Pete gestured for Gabriel to follow him to a shed.

"Ever ride a zero-turn mower?" Pete asked Gabriel.

"No, but I learn quickly."

Pete's eyes darted nervously to Stone, who was berating another worker nearby. "Just don't mess up, okay? Stone doesn't like mistakes."

With callused hands, Pete demonstrated the mower's controls. A faded bruise appeared on his upper arm as he reached for a lever.

Taking to the mower with fierce determination, Gabriel pushed it in neat, straight lines across the vast lawn. Though the machine ran well, his experienced ear caught the telltale signs of poor maintenance—the irregular timing of the engine, the grinding of poorly lubricated belts, the slight hesitation when changing speeds. Back home, such neglect would have meant lost fishing days and empty nets.

Midway through the morning, a commotion near the stables captured Gabriel's attention. Stone was shouting at a worker who had apparently spilled a bucket of paint. The boy, no older than fourteen, cowered as Stone raised his clipboard before bringing it down on the boy's head.

Gabriel's muscles tensed. Is this what happens when someone makes a mistake? His face flushed with anger, and his nails dug into his palms. Then, as he shifted his eyes away from the scene, Ms. Delacroix, who was watching from the stable opening with an unreadable expression, glanced at Gabriel as if gauging his reaction.

Swallowing hard, Gabriel returned to mowing the grass. Impress these people and maybe, just maybe, he could change how things were done around here. But first, he had to understand the rules of this place—and find a way to bend them in his favor.

As the sun climbed higher, sweat dripped from Gabriel's chin and elbows. He'd nearly finished the property's north section when an odd structure near the tree line came into view. Beneath a canopy of towering pines, shrouded in the cool gloom of their shadow, the building stood out like a forgotten relic of another time. Its slanted roof sagged under warped shingles, many of which had slipped free. Rusted sheets of corrugated metal clung stubbornly to the rooftop, their ends curling like the brittle pages of an old book.

Questioning its purpose, he maneuvered the mower closer for a better look. The walls were a patchwork of rotting wood and peeling paint, once vibrant but now a ghostly gray-green that blended with the invasive weeds and thickets creeping up from the earth. A single window on one side, its glass long shattered, yawned open like an unblinking eye. Its jagged edges hinted at a violent past.

Gabriel eased off the mower's throttle, bringing it to a complete stop. Crouching down over the engine, he pulled the dipstick to check the oil while studying the building. A high fence crowned with razor wire surrounded the structure. From where he was, the strange building seemed to be trying to hide something sinister.

A towering man with dark hair tied back in a sleek ponytail stepped out of the building, the flick of his lighter igniting the tip of a cigarette. He fixed Gabriel with a suspicious stare, the black sleeveless t-shirt he wore revealing a sleeve of intricate tattoos that snaked from his right shoulder to his wrist.

Gabriel snapped back to his inspection. The oil on the dipstick was as black as tar and thick between his fingers—this mower hadn't seen proper maintenance in months.

"Hey! What's the holdup?" Stone's gruff voice blared over the lawn.

Gabriel straightened. "Sorry, sir. Just checking the oil. The engine was stuttering."

Stone's eyes narrowed as he strode over, clipboard tucked under his arm. Snatching the dipstick from Gabriel, he gave it a quick glance. "Your job is to cut grass, not fix engines." As Stone replaced it roughly, a slip of paper fell from his clipboard, catching beneath the mower's mulch discharge and the ground. Gabriel said nothing.

"Now get back to work," Stone scowled, oblivious to the lost paper. He stalked away but stopped to point at the strange building. "Remember this place, boy. Something tells me you'll be visiting it soon."

After Stone finally left, Gabriel retrieved the paper and shoved it in his pant pocket.

Pete sidled up on his mower. "You okay?" the redhead shouted over the engine. "Stone doesn't like people poking around."

Gabriel shot him a thumbs-up. "I'm fine. Just trying to learn the equipment."

Pete's eyes darted over his shoulder at Stone, who was fifty yards away and moving quickly. "That building... they call it The Shadows. Don't give them a reason to put you inside. Many have gone in, but few have come out." Speeding away, Pete's warning left Gabriel with a chill despite the August heat.

Spending the rest of the morning with his head down, Gabriel methodically mowed the remaining sections. Every pass sent him further from that building, but its presence remained in his periphery like a dark promise. He kept his eyes on his work, but his mind churned with questions about the structure, the dropped paper he'd placed in his pocket, and Pete's caution about kids disappearing.

That night, after a long, cold shower and feasting on stewed chicken and rice, Gabriel lay in his bed, exhausted. Then he remembered and pulled the slip of paper from his grungy pants. In the dim moonlight filtering through the window, he studied a series of columns and rows. *"The numbers never lie, mijo,"* he recalled his father's words as they pored over the family's ledgers.

These weren't random—they followed a pattern. Two columns, just like Papa's books. The first column listed quantities of supplies—fertilizer, horse feed, materials. The second listed associated prices. In the margin, someone wrote notes with larger numbers. Stone was inflating the costs, probably pocketing the difference from Kingsley.

Gabriel's pulse quickened. Knowledge is power—Papa

had taught him that too. But this knowledge could get him killed... or worse, sent to that place called The Shadows.

"Dios mío," he prayed, "give me wisdom to use this information wisely." His fingers twisted in the bedsheet as his mind raced. Knowing of Stone's crime could be a weapon or a death sentence. But what could a sixteen-year-old boy do with such dangerous information? Gabriel stared at the ceiling, sleep eluding him, as he considered which would be worse—acting on what he knew or keeping this secret buried until it consumed him.

———

MIDDAY HEAT BEAT down on Gabriel's neck as he steered the mower along the fence, Stone's potential corruption like poison in his mouth. Pete ran his thumb across his throat— a signal to kill the engine. Every instinct screamed to share what he'd learned last night with someone—anyone—but Pete's slouched shoulders warned him what happened to those who spoke up at Kingsley Estate.

Rattling machines sputtered to silence. Climbing off the tractor, Pete's movements appeared slow and stiff. He yanked a battered blue cooler from the back and dropped it onto the lawn without a word.

Lingering by the mulch pile, Gabriel flexed his fingers to work out the knots in his knuckles. The damp, loamy scent of cut grass rose around him. The news about Stone lodged like a rock in his throat that he couldn't swallow. He caught the slippery water bottle Pete tossed to him, nearly fumbling it. The cold liquid soothed his parched tongue.

Pete cracked open a can of soda with a sharp hiss, taking a slow gulp and shifting his eyes to land on Gabriel. "You look like you've seen a ghost," he said, wiping his mouth with the back of his hand. The words were casual, but his gaze lingered for a beat too long, as if waiting for something. Then he rummaged in the cooler, pulling out two foil-wrapped bundles and a couple of bruised apples, tossing one of each to Gabriel.

Inside the wrapping, Gabriel found a generous helping of chicken salad loaded between two slices of soggy white bread. The pungent smell of onions and relish hit his nostrils. After taking a big bite, he savored the tangy flavor of the sandwich. Pete crunched into the apple first, chewing in a slow, round motion.

Their silence continued for a few minutes, broken only by birds chirping and the distant rumble of an occasional vehicle speeding beyond the tree line. "So," Gabriel said, brushing the crumbs that had sprinkled across his damp t-shirt, "how long have you been here?"

Pete's tanned face creased into a frown. Then he took a pull from his water bottle before answering. "Going on two years now. Ain't much, but it's better than where I came from."

Gabriel nodded, encouraging Pete to continue.

"Grew up in Ville Platte," Pete said. "Pop was in jail most of the time when I was a kid. Mama tried her best working two jobs, but we never got ahead."

Gabriel widened his eyes in disbelief. This was America, where the streets were made of gold. How did Pete's childhood make Gabriel's struggles seem so trivial?

Pete snorted, misreading Gabriel's expression. "Don't go feeling sorry for me. I made my own choices too. Dropped out of school at sixteen, thought I knew everything. Ended up running with a bad crowd, doing whatever I could to make a quick buck."

"What happened?" Gabriel asked gently.

"Sold crank to a narc in my trailer park. Didn't hurt nobody, but that don't matter to the law. Done three years at juvie lockup in St. Martinsville." Pete's voice hardened. "When I got out, couldn't find work nowhere. Ex-con, no education—who's gonna take a chance on that?"

"How did you end up here?"

A wry smile twisted on Pete's lips. "Met this girl in group therapy after getting out. She did time turning tricks in the French Quarter. Introduced me to a pimp who brought me to Stone. Promised a job if I followed the rules and kept my mouth shut." A shrug accompanied the words. "Ain't no paradise, but it's a roof overhead and three meals a day. Could be worse."

Gabriel had always seen his dreams as a virtue, a gift from God showing him how he'd lift his family from poverty. But Pete's life was more about survival than striving. "I'm sorry you had to go through all that."

Pete waved him off. "Like I said, don't need no pity. Just keep your head down and do your work. And whatever you do, don't go snooping around." He shook his head slightly. "Nothing's worth getting caught poking your nose where it don't belong."

There was a flash of movement near the gate that opened to a back road. A gray van pulled up to meet Stone near a cluster of pine trees. A stuffed manila envelope poked out from inside the vehicle, and Stone grabbed it. He strode to the mansion, the envelope tucked under his arm. Gabriel's fingers tightened on his half-eaten sandwich.

Pete followed Gabriel's gaze of Stone near near the outbuildings."Like I said, nothing's worth getting caught poking your nose where it doesn't belong."

The grass pressed into Gabriel's palms as he pushed himself upright, his father's voice ringing — Choose God's way with your decisions. Integrity is a gift you shouldn't ignore.

Stone vanished into his office, but the weight of the moment remained—heavy, unrelenting, pulsing with the rhythm of Gabriel's thundering heart.

God help him, he couldn't look away.

Not here. Not now. Not ever.

19

F*riday, August 9*

Gabriel's eyes snapped open. Sweat trickled down his neck as the Louisiana heat pressed in through the dead-silent darkness. Something was wrong. The A/C should be running. The door creaked ajar, revealing Jorge, the boy from the next room. Jorge's eyes were alert despite the late hour. He put a finger to his lips and motioned for Gabriel to follow.

Curiosity overrode Gabriel's exhaustion. He slipped on his work boots and followed Jorge out into the muggy night air. The compound was eerily quiet, save for the chirping cicadas and the distant hum of the electric fence that surrounded the property.

As they moved across the freshly mowed fields, Gabriel walked over dead grass. Then, the sickly sweet stench of fertilizer burned his nostrils.

He trailed Jorge to the stables. Light flooded out from an open door. A horse whinnied and huffed. Four trucks were parked outside, their logos catching the moonlight—Bayou Landscaping Supplies, Cajun Feed & Seed, Thibodaux

Tractor & ATV, and Pelican Heat & Air Conditioning. Jorge led Gabriel to the window. Inside, Estate Manager Stone stood in the center of four people, each holding a thick envelope.

"Now, about those supplies," Stone said, pocketing an envelope from a man in blue jean overalls. "Can we get that price lower?"

"If you're willing to take a lower grade next shipment," the supplier replied.

A balding man wearing a pullover shirt with Bayou Landscaping Supplies emblazoned on the back nodded eagerly. "You're a gentleman, Mr. Stone. We'll make it worth your while on the new brand of fertilizer you ordered."

Stone turned to a heavyset woman in a Cajun Feed & Seed cap. "Marie, I trust the feed's protein content will be up to par this time?" he asked with a wink.

She passed over her envelope with a smile. "Well, you know how supply chains are these days…"

The man from Thibodaux Tractor stepped forward. "About those ATVs—"

"Ah yes," Stone said. "I'll inform Mr. Kingsley that we'll need to upgrade to keep up production."

"And their cost?" the man asked.

Stone patted the bulge in his front pocket. "Our little secret."

"The mansion's A/C—"

"Needs considerable maintenance in this heat," Stone finished the A/C contractor's sentence firmly. "But those in the outlying buildings must be checked."

The tech slid over his own envelope.

The pieces of the puzzle popped into place. Gabriel saw things crystal clear—the abandoned ATV, the dead grass, the shoddy maintenance on the lawn equipment. It all made sense now. He turned to Jorge, wanting to know how long this had been happening, but the boy had disappeared.

Confused, Gabriel spun back toward the stable to find Stone standing over him, his face contorted with rage. "What are you doing here?" He lifted a clipboard that appeared out of nowhere, raised it, and brought it down on Gabriel's head.

"No," Gabriel screamed, rising from his mattress. The sheets and his shirt were now dry, and the A/C hummed normally. The cool cotton beneath his fingers grounded him in reality. It had all been a dream. Gabriel steadied his breathing to slow his heartbeat. But as the adrenaline faded, the vivid images remained: the suppliers, the bribes, the evidence of neglect across the estate.

Dream or not, Gabriel understood what he had seen earlier that day. It was a message from above, echoing the vision that had uprooted him from Honduras. And he had to decide what to do with it. The revelation sat like a bad meal in his stomach. How could he, a boy from a distant land in a strange place, stand against the corruption that was now clear to him?

But how could he not?

———

It was lunchtime at Kingsley Estate—Gabriel's one chance to prove Stone's crimes. His work-hardened fingers trembled as he unfolded the misplaced invoice, the horses nickering in their stalls, oblivious to what their feed bills revealed.

Gabriel smoothed the paper against his thigh, studying the numbers he had memorized since retrieving it from under his tractor's tire last week—seventy bags at fifty dollars each. Jorge and Miguel had unloaded far fewer sacks from the delivery truck, but suspicion wasn't enough. He needed proof.

Recalling Stone's cruelty—the crack of the clipboard against Jorge's back—along with Stone's smile afterward, Gabriel pushed away from the stable wall. It was time to count inventory.

His adrenaline surged as he slipped into the storeroom. The musty scent of feed intensified. Every step he took felt like moving closer to a predator's den. One wrong move, one sound, and Stone could appear.

His hands shook as he started counting. Every burlap sack represented another piece of evidence—evidence that could either save him or destroy him. Footsteps echoed outside. Gabriel froze every muscle and stopped breathing. Images of Stone beating Jorge flashed through his mind. Would he be next? The steps faded. He let out a long exhale.

The numbers blurred as panic crept in. Fifty-three bags—seventeen missing, each worth forty-seven dollars. Stone wasn't skimming a little. He was stealing a fortune.

Gabriel's throat closed up as the magnitude of his discovery hit him. He had proof of Stone's corruption, and that could prove dangerous. In Honduras, men disappeared for knowing less. Here at Kingsley Estate, with no family and no friends, who would miss him if he vanished?

The stable door groaned open. Gabriel spun, crinkling the paper between his fingers. Stone stood in the doorway, blocking the exit, his narrow eyes suspiciously fixed on the invoice. As his gaze hardened, he reached for a riding crop hanging on the wall.

"What are you doing here, boy?" he said, cracking it hard as he stepped closer.

20

Gabriel stood frozen in the dimly lit storeroom. Stone filled the doorway. His lips peeled back in a snarl, bearing yellow teeth. "What are you doing here, boy?" he said in a low growl.

Gabriel's tongue went desert dry. He tried to speak, but the word evaporated on his tongue. The crumpled invoice in his fist was hot as a branding iron in his palm.

"I asked you a question." Stone rushed forward, cocking the crop behind his shoulders.

Gabriel lowered his body into a ball, protecting his head with his forearms, and waited.

"Stone! What on earth do you think you're doing?"

The sharp voice cut through Gabriel's fear. His eyes snapped open to see Vivian Delacroix standing in the doorway, hands on her hips, her crimson lips pressed into a thin line.

Stone lowered the crop, his face flushing. "Ms. Delacroix, I was just—"

"About to assault this poor boy?" Vivian's ice-cold gaze pinned Stone in place. She turned to Gabriel, her expression softening slightly. "Gabriel, right? Why was his brute about to strike you?"

Gabriel couldn't stop shaking from the adrenaline rush. He glanced at Stone, then back to Ms. Delacroix. His palm dampened against the crumpled invoice. Taking a deep breath, he held it out to her but said nothing.

She plucked the paper with manicured fingers, her eyes showing confusion as she read. She glanced up from the paper to Gabriel with a shrug.

Gabriel rolled his eyes over his shoulder at the stack of feed bags.

A flash of enlightenment hit Ms. Delacroix's features as she studied the invoice again.

Stone sputtered, "It's nothing, Ms. Delacroix. A simple misunderstanding—"

"Is it?" She cut him off, focused on the stack behind Gabriel. After her lips stopped moving from counting the bags and another glance at the invoice, the edge of her lips elevated in a broad, beaming smile.

Gabriel stood frozen, caught between relief and a new, unnamed fear. Stone's face had gone from red to pale, a sheen of sweat swept over his brow.

"Max will want to hear about this immediately," she said to Stone, keeping her eyes locked on Gabriel. You, come with me. Stone, you may want to start packing your bags."

As Vivian turned to lead him from the stable, Gabriel caught a glimpse of something in her demeanor—calculation, perhaps, or opportunity. Whatever it was, he sensed his life at Kingsley Estate was about to take an abrupt turn.

———

THREE HOURS LATER, Gabriel trudged behind Ms. Delacroix through the back door of the main house. They passed through a room filled with rubber boots, rain gear, and various shoes, into a huge kitchen with stainless steel surfaces and the aroma of roasting meat and herbs. Then, through a long hallway with pale-blue walls and gray-streaked marble flooring producing sharp, echoing clacks from their footsteps.

At the end of the hall, Ms. Delacroix paused before a massive black-varnished door. She turned its knob and pushed it open, revealing a room so grand it made Gabriel pause at the threshold.

Sunlight streamed through tall windows, gleaming across a polished wood floor. He remained frozen for several heartbeats, overwhelmed by the sheer size of the space— easily larger than his family home in Honduras.

Massive white columns, as thick as tree trunks, stretched to a ceiling so high Gabriel had to crane his neck to see it. Dark wooden bookshelves lined the walls, filled with more books than his school's library. The scent of polished wood mixed with something like roses, but richer, more exotic.

At the far end of the room, a man in a crisp white shirt and fitted blue blazer stood behind at a granite bar, his polished appearance making Gabriel more aware of his dirty work clothes. The man poured a rich brown liquid from an elegant bottle into a glass filled with ice, then glanced up as Ms. Delacroix and Gabriel entered the room.

Andre Badeau, the man who'd transported Gabriel from the border, lounged on a nearby sofa, its fabric shimmering in the light. As Gabriel entered, Badeau's sat up straighter, his eyebrows lifting slightly in surprise.

"Max," Ms. Delacroix said to the man behind the bar, shaking Gabriel from his wonderstruck daze. "This is the young hero who exposed Stone's larceny. Thought I'd bring him here to meet you properly."

Gabriel's mouth went dry. *Hero?* He wasn't a hero, was he? And Max. He must be Maxwell Kingsley, the man who owned this place. Kingsley's blue eyes fixed on Gabriel, and Gabriel fought the urge to shrink back.

"Well then," Kingsley said, his accent strange to Gabriel's ears, "let's have a look at the boy who's caused such a stir in my household."

Ms. Delacroix's lips curved into a smile as she rested a hand on Gabriel's shoulder. Gabriel felt warmth spread from where she touched him, unsure why her fingers seemed to linger. He wasn't used to such attention, especially from a woman like her.

"Indeed," Kingsley replied, swirling the brown liquid in his glass, his focus fixed on Gabriel. "My accountants have been busy since your boy's discovery. It seems our Mr. Stone has been quite the enterprising thief. Tens of thousands of dollars over the past year alone."

Gabriel's mouth fell open. That was more money than his family would see in a lifetime.

Ms. Delacroix's hand slid down Gabriel's arm, her touch light as a feather. "My, my. Quite the sum. Aren't we lucky we have our young, observant friend?" Her voice had a husky quality that touched the end of his every nerve.

Max turned to Badeau on the couch. "Badeau, refresh my memory. How'd we acquire this astute young man?"

Badeau leaned forward, resting his elbows on his knees. His gaze never left Gabriel, but there was a new intensity in his eyes. "My brother found him on the small Honduran island, Guanaja. All indications are, he is` a promising lad. We expedited his delivery through McAllen, Texas." A small smile played at the corners of Badeau's mouth.

Gabriel's stomach churned at the casual way they discussed his journey of cramped spaces and a confused river crossing, as if he were a shipped package. But he kept his face neutral, not wanting to show weakness.

"Well, Badeau," Kingsley said, a hint of amusement in his voice, "it seems your brother has quite the eye for talent. Our young friend here has already proved quite valuable."

Ms. Delacroix's fingers trailed along Gabriel's collarbone as she stepped away to the bar to make herself a drink. "Oh, I'm sure he'll prove even more valuable in time, won't you, Gabriel?"

Gabriel nodded, still not fully grasping the undercurrent of her touches. He only knew that somehow, in this room full of powerful people, he felt both important and terribly, terribly small.

Kingsley set his glass down on the polished bar with a soft clink. "Well, Gabriel my boy," he said, with a smooth edge that made Gabriel's skin prickle, "it seems you've got quite a knack for uncovering things."

Gabriel swallowed hard, unsure if he should speak. He settled for a small nod, his eyes darting between Kingsley and Ms. Delacroix who sauntered across the room taking her place once again, by Gabriel's side.

Her hand found its way to the small of his back, causing him to stiffen slightly. "You know, Max," she said, "I've been thinking about the upcoming gala."

Mr. Kingsley raised an eyebrow. "Oh? And what about it?"

"Well," Ms. Delacroix continued, her fingers tracing small circles on Gabriel's back. "Given Gabriel's keen eye for detail, wouldn't it be prudent to have him there? To ensure everything goes smoothly?"

Gabriel's heart raced. *A gala?* He'd never been to such a thing. The idea thrilled, yet terrified him.

Kingsley's eyes narrowed slightly. "At the gala? Vivian, darling, that's totally against all protocols for our... uh..." his gaze swept over Gabriel... "workers."

Badeau shifted in his seat, his jaw tightening momentarily before speaking. "Actually, Max," he said, his voice surprisingly calm, "I think Vivian might be onto something here."

**All eyes in the room turned to Badeau, including Gabriel's. Andre's face was a mask of composure, but Gabriel noticed a slight tension in his shoulders.

"Gabriel's already proven himself to be resourceful and observant," Badeau continued. "Having him at the gala can't hurt. He just might be useful where others aren't."

The alternator belt and the shoe laces seemed too have won Badeau's support.

"Well," Ms. Delacroix said with a wave of her hand. "If you trust my judgement in the people under your employ, I think you'll find his presence there useful. You know what disasters can happen with such a party."

Kingsley approached Gabriel, bringing with him the scent of cologne and whiskey. He studied Gabriel from head to scuffed work boots. "You'll have to find him something suitable to wear. Can't have him roaming the Audubon Tea Room like that."

"Leave that to me," she said with a confident tone. "He'll be the paragon of elegance." She squeezed Gabriel's shoulder. "What do you say, Gabriel? Would you like to attend our little party?"

All eyes in the room focused on Gabriel, pinning him in place. He knew this wasn't really a question he could refuse.

"Yes, Ms. Delacroix," he managed to say with a submissive nod. "Thank you for the opportunity."

Kingsley studied Gabriel for a another long moment, then nodded slowly. "Very well. But he'll need to be prepared, Vivian. We can't have him embarrassing us."

"Of course not, Max," Ms. Delacroix said with a widening smile. "I'll see to it personally."

As Gabriel stood there, caught between these powerful adults, he couldn't shake the feeling that he was stepping into something far bigger and more dangerous than he could imagine.

But what choice did he have?

21

Eli slapped the Johnson twins' folder onto the grill's side table outside the Airstream, nearly knocking over the barbecue sauce. Two months since the Johnson twins disappeared into Maxwell Kingsley's world, and they were no closer to getting them out.

The mouthwatering aroma of smoked ribs and grilled chicken wafted through the cool evening air, but Eli barely noticed. He was churning through scenarios to get inside Kingsley's organization somehow.

"You're burning the wings," Dakota said, nursing an iced tea in a nearby lawn chair. "What's eating you?"

Eli rescued the chicken, but his mind wasn't on the food. "The longer Kingsley has those girls, the more likely he sells them off. Once they're moved—"

He cut himself off as Lindsey, Karina, and Julia gathered around fold-out chairs and a picnic table carrying potato salad, coleslaw, and baked beans. This team dinner was supposed to be a break from the case, but each hour that passed felt like another step toward losing the twins forever.

Dakota rose to spread the paper plates and plastic utensils across the table. "Can't believe I'm saying this in August, but what a comfortable night."

Eli set the platter of smoked ribs on the table, its steam rising in wisps against the unusually crisp air. "Yeah, it feels more like October than the dog days of summer."

Karina laughed, setting down the last of the side dishes. "Well, don't get used to it. The weather channel says this cool snap is because of that tropical storm in the Gulf."

Lindsey wrapped her arms around herself, the fading sunlight highlighting the red in her hair. "Well, whatever the reason, it's a nice break from the nineties after sunset."

Julia's expression turned serious as she filled her Solo cup with lemonade. "Speaking of breaks, I've got some interesting news." She paused for everyone's attention. "Maxwell Kingsley is hosting a black-tie fundraiser for his nonprofit tomorrow night. The Kingsley Foundation for Children's Futures."

The atmosphere suddenly shifted. Eli's hand froze mid-reach for the barbecue sauce. "Where?"

"At The Audubon Tea Room," Julia said. "Every power player in Louisiana will be there. Including Governor Bordelon."

"Along with all the corrupt officials on Kingsley's payroll," Dakota added.

"Perfect cover for his real business," Eli cut in, his jaw tight. "We should go."

Lindsey touched Eli's arm. "Honey, they'll know who you are from the news coverage from Juarez last year—"

"What's the cost?" Eli glanced at Julia while heaping a mound of potato salad on his plate.

"Ten thousand per person."

"Ten grand?" Lindsey dropped her fork on her plate. "That's more money than we spent on transportation the last three quarters. Plus, these aren't just criminals, Eli. They're powerful people who make their problems disappear."

Dakota broke open a chicken wing. "Looks like we're one short tonight," he said, defusing the tension. "Where's Tara?"

Karina swallowed a bite of potato salad before answering. "Oh, she's with my mother and little sister. They're shopping for school supplies." She smiled, a gleam in her eyes. "It's Sofia's first year in an American school. She's so excited."

"I'm so glad you've decided to stay in Madisonville," Lindsey said. "You, your mother, and Sofia have become a welcome addition to our Redemption Rescue family."

"Hear, hear," Julia said, raising her glass. "You bring a new perspective to fighting the bad guys."

"A gala, huh?" Eli said in a low tone. "That's interesting, given what we suspect about Kingsley's extracurricular activities."

Dakota's eyes narrowed. "A lot could be learned in that setting."

"I'm sure it's all very above board," Lindsey said with disgust and sarcasm. "After all, it's for the children, right?"

A heavy silence fell over the group. The smoke from Eli's smoker, like the opportunity revealed by Julia's news, seemed to linger longer than usual.

Eli set down his rib, wiping his hands on a napkin. His eyes met Dakota's. Dakota winked. "So," Eli said in a neutral tone, "what do you think?"

"If there's even a chance the twins are there," Dakota said, his voice hard, "or any evidence of where they're being moved—"

"Eli?" Lindsey pressed her lips into a sardonic frown. "You're not seriously thinking of going, are you?"

Eli relaxed in his chair. "It's something we have to think about, sweetheart. It's a rare opportunity to get close to Kingsley and his circle."

"Two men showing up stag to a black-tie gala?" Karina said with an eyebrow raised. "I've hosted dozens of galas. You show up without a woman on your arm, and you'll look like a taco served at a Michelin restaurant."

A tense silence followed. The knocking of a distant woodpecker cut through the quiet.

"She's got a point, Eli," Dakota said. "We'd stick out like like sore thumbs."

Karina's eyes lit up, mischief crossing her face. "Unless... you don't go alone."

Dakota turned his head toward her and blinked. "What are you suggesting?"

"She's suggesting," Lindsey said with a playful grin, as if the danger of this event had suddenly become moot, "that you might need head-turning dates for your little under-cover operation."

Karina clapped her hands together, her eyes sparkling with excitement. "Oh! A chance to wear a formal gown! I haven't had an excuse to doll up since I left Juarez."

Lindsey's face fell slightly. "The most elegant thing I own is my outfit for psychology conventions."

Karina reached over, squeezing Lindsey's hand. "Don't worry, *amiga*. I have a dress that would look amazing on you." Her gaze focused on Lindsey as she lifted her hand to her chin. "We're about the same size, and with a few alter-ations..." She tapped her cheek with one finger. "Forget about dinner. Let's go check out my closet. We'll knock the socks off those socialites."

"Hold on," Dakota said. "The price for this little soirée just went up to forty grand."

Julia stood up, brushing off her hands, a sly smile spreading across her face. "Leave it to me," she said. "I think I have a way to get those tickets."

"I don't think we have that in petty cash," Eli said, rubbing his chin. "And dipping into our reserves may raise alarms with our donors."

Dakota shook his head. "There has to be a way to get into that gala. If for nothing else," he winked at Karina, "to save us from our women."

"What is your plan, Julia?" Lindsey asked.

Julia's smile widened. "Let me make a call. Sometimes the best way to crash a party is to walk right through the front door."

S *aturday, August 10*

Eli's chest burned where Aaliyah and Kiara's photos pressed against his heart, tucked securely inside the pocket of his rented tuxedo jacket. The hired Mercedes-Benz GLS limousine crept toward the Audubon Tea Room, its classical façade glowing under the brilliance of Kingsley's Charity Gala. The tall windows shimmered with light, casting sharp reflections into the humid night.

The dashboard blinked—91°F, 7:58 PM. So much for the promised cool front. Even with the air conditioning blasting, Eli's palms refused to stay dry. He wiped them against his trousers, the motion futile.

Ahead, a slow-moving parade of luxury vehicles—Bentleys, Rolls-Royces, and sleek limousines—crawled forward inch by inch, halting just shy of the grand entrance. At the drop-off, an elderly couple emerged, the woman gripping her chauffeur's arm as they ascended the steps with old-money grace.

Eli adjusted the tight collar of his tuxedo, the fabric pressing comfortably against his skin. The photos inside his jacket pocket felt heavier with each breath. Would he cross paths with the governor tonight? Or Kingsley himself?

He stole another glimpse of Lindsey—a vision in deep blue like twilight over open water, her gown hugging her slender form. Across from Eli and Lindsey, seated in two captain's chairs, Dakota straightened his bow tie, while Karina smoothed her blushing pink dress.

"It won't be but a minute, sir," said the middle-aged driver wearing a chauffeur's hat.

"Remind me how we ended up with invitations?" Dakota asked. "Your mother, right?"

"Yes, tell us," Lindsey turned, her diamond necklace and matching earrings catching the dim light. "We were in such a rush to get ready. You never explained how we got the tickets."

Eli tugged at his lapel. "I can't take any credit. Julia convinced my mother to convince my dad to ask the governor."

"Your father has that much clout?" Karina asked.

Eli shrugged. "Apparently. According to Julia, while I was in Afghanistan, years before Bordelon became governor, Dad's law firm handled a dispute on Gulf oil leases for Bordelon's drilling company."

The Mercedes stopped in front of the one-story building. All eyes outside seemed drawn to the vehicle's door as if to see which socialites would emerge next. The driver straightened his hat, stepped from behind the wheel, and opened the rear door. Stepping into the humid New Orleans air, Eli turned, offering his arm to Lindsey. As she exited the vehicle, the heels of her silver stilettos hit the red carpet, sending Eli a shock of remembrance of the signal Karina had used in Juarez.

Dakota and Karina followed, with Karina outwardly

enjoying the attention. "Quite a place," Dakota muttered, still tugging at his tie.

Eli nodded, his gaze drawn to open double doors. As they ascended the few steps to the entrance, the gleaming wood floors inside stretched out invitingly. The soaring ceilings seemed to reach impossibly high as Eli crossed the threshold with Lindsey on his arm. Lindsey patted Eli's hand. "You've got this."

He drew strength from her confidence. He handed their tickets to a man beside a red velvet rope. The scent of magnolias from the nearby gardens mingled with Karina's perfume.

"Show time," Dakota murmured, his gaze sweeping the room. "Let's act like we belong here."

"Easier said than done," Eli said with a frown.

A bright, toothy smile spread across Karina's face. "Just follow my lead." She nodded at a passing older couple. "Back in Juarez, I attended dozens of these events."

The air buzzed with upper-crust chatter, punctuated by the clink of champagne flutes and bursts of polite laughter of patrons adorned in pastel gowns and tailored tuxedos. As they made their way through the room, an expansive foyer adorned with high ceilings and elegant chandeliers greeted them. To their left, a bar served drinks, while to the right, tables were set with pristine white linens, filled with guests mingling and chatting.

Eli and Lindsey walked arm in arm, with Dakota and Karina close behind. The crowd flowed in well-defined channels, clusters of guests engaging in conversation. A string quartet played in a corner, the music blending with the hum of social chatter.

Moving deeper into the room, Eli scanned the area, noting the layout—an open space at the center allowed for mingling, while elevated platforms showcased floral arrangements. Karina turned heads in her pink dress, effortlessly blending into the vibrant atmosphere, while Dakota adjusted his bow tie, appearing slightly more reserved.

They passed elegant couples and clusters of guests, making their way toward the bar. Lindsey gripped Eli's arm tighter. "Three o'clock," she said, her lips barely moving. "Maxwell Kingsley."

Following her gaze, Eli's eyes locked onto Kingsley's steel-gray hair. The man exuded an air of casual elegance that belied his reputation. He stood amid a bustle of men and women, responding with nods and smiles to whatever Kingsley was saying.

"I see him," Eli said. "Let's not approach directly. We need to—"

"Excuse me," a voice interrupted. They turned to see a short man with an affable expression and a tablet tucked between his ribs and bicep. "Mr. Colt? Mrs. Colt? I'm Brian Sebastian," he said with a brief nod, "Governor Bordelon's chief of staff. Mrs. Bordelon asked me to find you. She'd like a word if you don't mind."

By the bar, a revealing emerald dress stood out and caught Eli's attention. The woman wearing it hung possessively on the arm of a young man who looked distinctly out of place. Eli's pulse quickened. This was the same woman with Aaliyah and Kiara in the photo tucked inside his jacket pocket.

23

Beau Bordelon's bourbon froze midway from the table to his lips. Across a sea of glitzily dressed patrons at the governor's table, Thomas Reeves—the man whose life Bordelon had helped to destroy—stood at the bar watching Maxwell Kingsley with dead eyes.

Three years ago, Bordelon had witnessed this good man's life crumble but said nothing. Now Reeves was present at Kingsley's gala, clutching a champagne flute like a weapon.

"Beau," Sarah, stunning in her black silk gown, murmured beside him. She nodded discreetly at a couple a few stools over from Reeves. "That woman is at it again."

Bordelon followed his wife's gaze to Vivian Delacroix, her long, sleek arm resting around the shoulders of a boy who looked still in his teens. "Good Lord," he said, shaking his head. "You'd think she'd show some restraint at an event like this."

"Apparently, that's too much to ask."

At the bar, Reeves' fingers drummed against his drink, out of sync with the quartet's rhythm. The liquid in his glass sloshed, tiny drops spattering his loose-fitting jacket. Kingsley's laughter boomed across the room. Reeves' jaw clenched.

The impulse to warn Kingsley warred with Bordelon's guilt. Let Reeves have his revenge. But if something happened and Bordelon stayed silent...

"Sarah," Bordelon leaned closer to his wife, focusing on a familiar face close to Vivian and her young companion. "Do you see the man behind Vivian? The one who looks like he's about to bolt?"

Sarah's eyes tracked until they stopped on Reeves. "He seems out of sorts. Who is he?"

Bordelon took a sip of his bourbon, buying time to collect his thoughts. "His name is Thomas Reeves. He used to be the CEO of Vermillion Offshore Explorations. You remember them, don't you? The natural gas company that was making waves in the energy market a few years back?"

"Of course," Sarah said. "They were all over the news. Didn't they suddenly go under?"

"That's right," Beau confirmed, his voice rising above the ambient chatter. "There was a scandal. Kingsley had significant interests in Vermillion Parish, and when things went south, he made sure Reeves took the fall for some questionable practices."

Sarah's eyes widened. "That's awful. How do you know all this?"

"Because I was there when it happened. I didn't have the courage to speak up because, well... you know."

Reeves wiped his brow with his forearm, his discomfort evident, even across the room. "Poor Thomas lost everything," Bordelon said. "His job, his reputation, his wife and kids. He'd be the last person I thought I'd see here. I can't imagine how he got in."

Sarah placed her hand gently on Beau's arm. "You seem troubled. Is there more to this story?"

"I'm not sure. But Reeves being here can't be a coincidence. He must have an agenda, and knowing what Kingsley did to him, I doubt it's a friendly one."

The opulent room was suddenly stifling, the chatter of guests a discordant buzz. Vivian Delacroix continued her sensual assault on the young man. Kingsley threw his head back in laughter, oblivious to the potential threat lurking mere yards away.

"Beau?" Sarah said, interrupting his spiraling thoughts. "You're a million miles away. What's wrong?"

"Nothing, sweetheart," he said, his fingers interlacing with hers as he met her concerned gaze. "Nothing to worry about," he insisted. "Just can't get over Thomas being here."

"Perhaps we should say hello," Sarah suggested, as if sensing her husband's conflict.

Bordelon flinched at the thought, then shook his head slightly. "I'm not sure that would be wise. Our history is not something easily addressed over champagne and canapés."

Reeves drained the last of his drink in a single swallow and signaled to the bartender for another. Whatever had brought him here tonight, Bordelon might not be able to stop it. Heck, given their history, maybe he didn't have the right.

But he had to try. Didn't he?

He slid back in his chair. His started to speak. One word from Bordelon could stop whatever was about to happen. But that word died as Reeves' dead eyes found his. In that moment of recognition, Bordelon saw his own cowardice reflected back at him.

"Governor?" Brian, armed with his tablet, materialized

over his shoulder. "Your wife asked me to inform y'all when Eli Colt had arrived."

The name caught Bordelon's attention. "Thomas Colt's son?"

"Yes," Sarah said, rising. "I've arranged for them to sit at our table. I hope Max doesn't mind."

Bordelon ignored his wife's sarcastic remark to refocus on Reeves.

What is that man doing here?

THE ALCOHOL FUMES stung Gabriel's nose, mixing with Vivian's jasmine perfume. Focus. Stay vigilant. But her fingers ran fire down his arm, each touch a reminder of his powerlessness in this glittering room.

"You should drink up, Gabriel." Her cheek brushed his. "The champagne is divine."

His throat worked against the knot of his black tie. This wasn't his world—chandeliers and champagne were as far from him as Venus from Pluto.

His gaze swept the room, searching for an escape when something strange caught his eye. The Governor of Louisiana sat rigid at his table, staring past Gabriel's shoulder like he'd seen death itself.

"Please drink, darling." Vivian tapped the top of his glass, her hand claiming his bicep. "You're so tense. Let me help you relax."

But Gabriel couldn't relax. Not with the Governor's face gone slack with recognition. Not with—there. A man in a loose-fitting suit stood mere feet away, radiating the same deadly focus his trafficker Freddy had shown before shooting Manuelo.

"Dance with me." Vivian said, her hand exploring his chest. Touches that should have thrilled him only heightened his sense of wrongness.

The stranger's hands clenched and unclenched at his sides. His gaze never left Kingsley, who was laughing with his admirers, oblivious to the threat.

This man means harm to Mr. Kingsley.

The voice from his dreams crystallized Gabriel's fears into certainty. But what could he do? Alert security? They'd never believe a servant. Warn Kingsley directly? Impossible with his wall of sycophants.

"Gabriel." Vivian's nails dug into his ribs. "You're being very rude."

The Governor slid back in his chair. Hope flared in Gabriel's chest. But a man with a tablet appeared, dragging an elegant couple into the Governor's orbit, stealing away Gabriel's last chance at intervention.

He was alone. A foreigner. A prisoner in expensive clothes. And the only person standing between Maxwell Kingsley and this potential killer.

24

Eli maneuvered around two young men in white shirts and black vests, serving flutes of champagne from gleaming silver trays. The chandelier above cast fractured light over a room filled with polished grins and meaningless pleasantries. Nearby, a stately woman in a black silk gown waited by the front center table, her posture regal, her gaze unwavering.

"Mr. Colt, I'm Sarah Bordelon," she said, her warm smile genuine. "I've been following Redemption Rescue since you and Mr. Sutcliffe rescued your niece from that horrible Commodore." Her admiration was unguarded. "And what you accomplished in Juarez was simply amazing."

The mention of Juarez scraped against raw nerves. There, he'd kicked down doors and pulled terrified kids from locked rooms. And now, here he was—trapped in a penguin suit, exchanging pleasantries while Aaliyah and Kiara... His stomach churned at the thought.

"Tom's boy has made quite a name for himself." The voice cut through the din like the snap of a whip. Governor

Beau Bordelon appeared over his wife's shoulder. "Different path than his old man's law practice."

"Please, join us," Sarah said, gesturing to empty chairs. "I'd love to hear more about your organization's approach to—"

"Now, now, Sarah." The interruption came smoothly, like a blade slipping between ribs. Maxwell Kingsley stepped through a couple standing near the table. They parted instinctively, like the Red Sea after a Moses's command. His sharp, ice-blue eyes locked on Eli as his lips curled into a smile that didn't quite reach them.

Kingsley extended a hand. "Maxwell Kingsley. I've read about your non-profit... fascinating. Tell me, what brings you to my little fundraiser? Seeking donors, perhaps?"

Eli caught Lindsey's glance—a flicker of excitement and apprehension. This wasn't planned, but it was an opening.

Before he could answer, Sarah leaned forward, either oblivious to or deliberately ignoring the thick tension. "I invited him. The work Redemption Rescue does with trafficking victims—"

"The governor's wife has a passion for charitable causes," Kingsley said, cutting her off as if it were of little concern. His smile remained intact, but the air seemed to chill. "Though sometimes I wonder if she truly understands the... complexities in such matters." The comment hit Sarah Bordelon's enthusiasm like a blunt instrument.

Governor Bordelon's face reddened, a flush creeping up his neck as his grip on the glass tightened. The ice rattled softly, betraying his hand's angry tremor.

Eli forced his breathing to stay even. "Some matters aren't complex at all, Mr. Kingsley," Eli said, the words escaping before he could stop them.

Lindsey's fingers dug into his knee beneath the table, a

silent warning, but he couldn't let it go. "Evil is evil. Simple as that."

Kingsley's smile widened—just a fraction, but enough. "Indeed? How refreshingly... idealistic." He turned to a passing boy in a crisp white apron. "More champagne for everyone. We should toast to idealism while it lasts."

A flush crept up Eli's neck. The crystal stem snapped under his enraged grip. A thin line of blood trickled down his palm. Lindsey smoothly slipped her napkin over the damage.

"Oh dear," she breathed, all Texan sweetness. "Darling, you've cut yourself. Mr. Kingsley, would you excuse us? The first aid station?"

Kingsley glanced at the crimson-spotted linen. "Of course. Though sometimes a little bloodshed is necessary to understand how complex our world truly is."

Eli let Lindsey guide him away, her grip iron-strong around his bicep. They both knew Kingsley's words weren't about the broken glass. They were a warning. Or a challenge.

Either way, Eli had just shown his hand. And Maxwell Kingsley had just dealt the cards for the next round.

———

GABRIEL'S FINGERS stilled on the bar as the stranger's hand disappeared beneath his jacket. The other guests continued their light chatter and laughter, glasses clinking, while the man's dead eyes fixed on Maxwell Kingsley.

"Loosen up, Gabriel," Vivian said with annoyance. "Enjoy yourself. I brought you here so the two of us could get to know each other."

He forced a smile but said nothing, keeping his eyes on

the stranger who looked ready to make his move. The man's eyes widened.

Gabriel shifted his attention to learn why. Maxwell Kingsley had separated himself from his circle of admirers, his booming laugh going silent as he swaggered to the governor, who stood talking with the attractive couple.

Five meters away, the man whose haunted eyes had kept Gabriel on edge earlier drained the last of his drink and set the empty glass on a passing waiter's tray. His gaze locked onto Kingsley, and he began moving as if pulled by an invisible thread.

The stranger weaved past Gabriel, his hand disappearing beneath his jacket, emerging a moment later with a pistol.

This was it—a moment to prove himself. Kingsley was in danger. Only Gabriel knew. His muscles coiled like dock lines under tension. His vision tunneled until all he could see was the weapon. Dark edges closed in like gathering storm clouds. He had to move. Now.

Gabriel lunged forward, shoving past Vivian. "Mr. Kingsley's in trouble," he muttered, eyes locked on the man with the gun. Three steps in, a portly man with blonde hair stepped away from a conversation. They collided like ships in rough waters. Champagne sloshed upward. A glass shattered on the wooden floor.

"*Lo siento, señor*," Gabriel gasped, trying to sidestep.

The assassin raised his pistol and outstretched his arm. A woman in red near him let out a piercing scream. Chaos erupted. Bodies surged away from the gunman—a human current Gabriel fought, like swimming against a rip tide.

He shouldered his way through the terrified crowd. A fleeing couple appeared from Gabriel's right and slammed into him. An elbow struck his ribs. He wheezed and stumbled, regaining his footing. Precious seconds disappeared.

Lord, give me strength.

The sea of people in the man's way split, opening a clear path to Kingsley. Gabriel was too far away. Just like with Manuelo.

Sprinting, he closed the distance. A wide-eyed waiter backed into Gabriel. A tray of champagne-filled glasses went flying. Gabriel slipped and crashed to one knee. He looked up. The assassin was almost to Kingsley. Time had run out.

Gabriel's knee throbbed, but adrenaline dulled the pain. The man was mere steps from Kingsley. No time to think.

He launched forward with the same practiced balance that had kept him upright on storm-tossed decks. Kingsley's laughter. The gunman's ragged breathing. Gabriel's thundering heartbeat.

Two more strides, then one. He leaped, arms outstretched, between the gunman and Kingsley. The assassin's face was a map of desperation—hollow cheeks, skin stretched tight over bone, eyes burning with rage.

"*Pare*," the word tore from Gabriel's throat, raw and primal. The dark muzzle and death pointing right at him. But he held still.

For one eternal heartbeat, he and the assassin were locked in their deadly tableau. Gabriel's prayer died on his lips as his mind screamed a single truth—he'd chosen to save the very man responsible for upending his life.

From the corner of Gabriel's eye, he glimpsed sudden movement. A man with sun-streaked hair and a bronze tan materialized beside the assailant. In one swift motion, he gripped the gunman's wrist and twisted it with a sharp snap. The assassin floundered to the floor, screaming.

The newcomer pinned the gunman with a foot to his chest, the pistol dangling loosely in his hand. "It's over," he said. "Stand down."

The assassin went limp. Defeated.

Gabriel's legs buckled, dropping him to the floor as the chaos around him blurred into a haze of voices, glass shards, and the tang of spilled champagne. His chest heaved, adrenaline ebbing away, leaving only the dull throb in his knee and the raw knowledge of what he had done.

He had saved Maxwell Kingsley.

The newcomer stood over the gunman, calm and composed despite the anxiety sweeping the room. He still held the pistol, its dark muzzle pointed at the floor.

Then, a heavy stamp of footfalls erupted. Kingsley's security team filtered through the crowd, weapons raised over panicked guests before locking onto Gabriel's rescuer "There!" someone shouted. "He's armed! Take him down!"

The man's eyes flicked toward them, his calm expression hardening. "You've got the wrong guy," he said evenly, his voice cool but firm.

"Drop the weapon! Hands behind your head!" one of the guards barked, his weapon trembling slightly.

The stranger didn't move. "That's not going to happen. This is your man here." He pointed beneath his foot.

A second guard advanced. "He's not complying! Take the shot!"

"No!" Gabriel shouted. He clawed at the floor, trying to rise, trying to scream louder, but his body refused to cooperate.

The stranger's gaze darted to Gabriel, then back to the pistols trained on him. His hands remained raised, his posture unthreatening, but his eyes burned with sharp defiance—as if daring them to pull the trigger.

"Stand down!" the security guard barked, but his command was swallowed by the chaos. Gabriel's vision swam as he struggled to rise, the guards barking over each other. The assassin groaned on the floor, ignored.

Time seemed to freeze. Would they fire? Would the man who had saved Kingsley's life fall under the crossfire of the very guards meant to protect him?

All Gabriel knew was that he couldn't save anyone this time. Not himself. And not the man who rescued him.

SATURDAY, *August 10*

"Drop the weapon!" The command thundered through the Audubon Tea Room, following a wave of chaos.

Eli tossed the bloodied linen onto the nurse's tray and shot Lindsey a glance. "Stay here," he muttered, already moving. His shoulders brushed against panicked guests as he pushed his way through the crowd—murmurs around him blending into an indistinct hum, rising and falling.

When he reached the source of the commotion, Eli froze. Dakota stood over a man sprawled on the marble floor, his foot pressing a man's chest flat. A Beretta .32 dangled from Dakota's finger, the barrel swaying gently as if to mock the tension in the room.

But it wasn't the disarmed gunman that made Eli's chest tighten—it was Kingsley's security guard. He stood a few paces away, his Glock trained squarely on Dakota, knuckles bone-white against the trigger.

Between them knelt the young man who had been with Vivian Delacroix earlier. He trembled, his hands limp at his sides, his eyes unfocused as if struggling to piece together the scene around him. A slow, shuddering breath escaped his lips, but he didn't move.

Eli's gaze swept the room. Guests clustered together in tight groups, whispers rippling between them. Others leaned over tables or craned their necks, eager for a better view. The clink of broken glass underfoot added to the strange, dissonant symphony of fear and morbid curiosity.

The air in the room had shifted, heavy now with unease. What had moments ago been an elegant fundraiser now buzzed with the sharp-edged tension of something far more dangerous. Suddenly, Kingsley's full detail pushed through a wall of people. They wore jackets modified to conceal weapons, their hair closely cropped, and their pupils dilated from adrenaline. Each guard opened his jacket, reaching inside. Eli tensed, sensing a volatile mix of fear and confusion. This situation could easily go wrong. He glanced between the guards and his partner, who was still restraining the would-be assassin and holding his weapon.

"Easy," Eli said in a steady voice despite his rapid breathing, raising his hands slowly, palms out in a placating gesture. "Threat is down. I repeat, the threat is down."

The security detail ignored Eli, advancing and steadying their weapons. Eli remained still, knowing any sudden movement could spark a disaster. Seconds seemed like minutes as Eli explored his options. He could try to disarm the guards, but that risked escalation. Or he could continue to reason with them, but they appeared unreceptive.

Sweat soaked his collar. He took a careful step, positioning himself between Dakota and the new threat. "Gentlemen," he said, his voice firm but non-threatening, "I need you to lower your weapons. The situation is under control."

The guards exchanged uncertain glances. Eli held his breath, hoping these men would show more competence.

Kingsley stormed to center stage. "Put those guns away, you idiots."

Confusion swept across the security team's faces as they shifted their focus to Kingsley.

Their employer marched his imposing frame to within five feet, his face a mask of fury. "Did you not hear me? I said holster your weapons." He gestured at Dakota and Eli. "These men just saved my life while you were off doing God knows what."

The guards hesitated, their weapons still raised, but their resolve was wavering. Eli remained still, aware that the slightest movement could still trigger a disaster. The onlookers had fallen silent, watching the confrontation and holding a collective breath.

"Sir," said the guard closest to Kingsley, "we thought—"

"You thought wrong," Kingsley snapped. He turned to Eli, his expression softening slightly. "I apologize for this incompetence. Please, lower your hands."

Eli lowered his arms, his movements slow and non-threatening. He could feel Dakota's tension and knew his partner was on high alert. The would-be assassin, still pinned beneath Dakota's foot, seemed oblivious to just how precarious the situation was.

"Now," Kingsley said, addressing his security team, "I want you to holster your weapons and step back. Then I want you to find your supervisor and tell him to come here immediately so I can fire him. Is that clear?"

The guards exchanged shocked glances before complying, their movements stiff with embarrassment. As they retreated, Eli allowed himself to relax slightly, though the adrenaline rush compelled him to remain watchful.

Kingsley turned back to Eli and Dakota, his expression somewhere between gratitude and lingering anger. "Gentlemen, I can't express how grateful I am for your quick thinking and bravery." He let out a long sigh, visibly easing as he regained his composure. "I insist you both join me for lunch Monday at my estate. A proper thank you is in order, especially to you." He nodded at Dakota, who still maintained his hold on the assailant.

The invitation prickled the back of Eli's neck. Something about Kingsley's sudden shift from rage to gracious host felt calculated.

More guests pressed closer, phones raised. A camera flash sparked from the crowd.

"Mr. Kingsley," Eli said, positioning himself to block the onlookers' view of the suspect, "we need to secure the detainee before reporters arrive. Is there a room—"

"There's a storage room in the kitchen that should work." Kingsley's voice carried an edge of command. He gestured to his remaining security detail. "Clear these people back." To Eli and Dakota, he said, "I'll have my driver pick you up Monday. We can discuss what happened here tonight and how I can reward your quick action."

"That's very generous of you, Mr. Kingsley," Eli said, his voice considerably calmer. "But Dakota and I should talk, and it will give us time to look at our calendar."

Kingsley nodded, placing his hands behind his back. "Of course, of course. We have more pressing matters at hand." His gaze shifted to Gabriel, who still sat nearby, looking shaken but determined.

"That young man showed incredible bravery," Dakota said. "Throwing himself between you and a gunman. I've seen agents in the field hesitate in similar situations."

Kingsley's expression softened slightly. "Yes, Gabriel has proven himself to be quite a valuable... uh... employee."

Eli caught Dakota's eye, who gave a slight nod while

keeping his foot pressed down on the suspect. "Let's get our friend secured before this turns into a circus." He turned to help Dakota with his prisoner, catching Lindsey's worried look across the room.

Her expression reflected the anxiety swirling in Eli's stomach. Between Gabriel's odd behavior and Kingsley's convenient invitation, something wasn't adding up. In less than five minutes, an assassin failed to kill a powerful man, his security team threatened his partner, and apparently, a teenage boy risked his life to save Kingsley.

Vivian Delacroix, the last woman seen with Aaliyah and Kiara, approached, her movements graceful despite the chaos around them. "Max," she said, her voice somewhat urgent, "we need to get Gabriel home. The press will be arriving any minute."

Kingsley nodded. "You're right, Vivian. Take him back to the estate. We'll deal with... everything else there."

As Vivian gently guided Gabriel away, Eli couldn't help but catch the boy's conflicted expression. There was clearly more to his story.

A spark of excitement burned through Eli as he and Dakota restrained the assailant. This wasn't just an assassination attempt—it was a door flung open. A visit to Kingsley's estate was next, and with it, the chance to bring him and Dakota one step closer to finding Kiara and Aaliyah.

25

In a windowless room above the Audubon Tea Room, Andre Badeau stood focused on the security monitors. "You'd better get out there," Badeau said to the two men beside him, his voice a low rumble of contained urgency.

Vivian's driver, Remy, and Kingsley's head of security exchanged a panicked glance. They ran from the room with explosive energy, slamming the door behind them. The hum of electronics took on a more ominous tone, like the growl of some unseen monster.

Leaning forward, Badeau's fingers hovered over the control panel. His typical calm demeanor was shaken. With deliberate slowness, he pressed the rewind button, his eyes glued to the center screen.

The footage played in reverse, showing figures moving in a disjointed dance. Badeau narrowed his eyes as he absorbed the chaos that had just unfolded on the monitor. Gabriel's movements were a blur of desperate courage as he threw himself between Kingsley and the gunman. "Foolish boy," Badeau muttered, "or maybe not so foolish after all." If

Gabriel could show this level of commitment to Kingsley after such a short time, how could that allegiance be redirected? Oh, what Badeau could do with that kind of loyalty.

His attention shifted to Dakota Sutcliffe, Colt's partner, who had helped take down Commodore and dismantle Cesar Garza's empire. He burst onto the scene with determined efficiency, disarming the assailant and securing the area. Badeau steepled his hands under his chin. Could they destroy Kingsley as well?

Now Kingsley, hands clasped together, eyes bright with surprise and appreciation, was talking with Colt and Sutcliffe. "What are you offering them, Max?" he murmured. "And how will that affect my operation?"

A blur on another screen showed Vivian leading Gabriel out of the ballroom. The little minx had her claws dug into the young lad. He paused the video, zooming in on the boy's face—a complex tapestry of emotions—fear, confusion, and something else. Something that made Badeau's stomach tighten with unease. Was it resolve? Determination? This game had suddenly become far more complicated.

Badeau paced the small room. Gabriel's unexpected heroism gnawed at him. The boy had shown a loyalty to Kingsley that Badeau wanted for himself. And then there was Colt. Watching his partner's effectiveness was both impressive and troubling. How could Badeau turn this disaster to his advantage?

He must operate in Colt's blind spot and remain hidden. However, Colt and his partner had repeatedly proven that they were formidable and dangerous. If Kingsley brought them in, Badeau's entire operation could be compromised. Yet, much like the destruction of the Diablos cartel, this situation could offer him an opportunity.

He stopped pacing and braced a hand against the

control panel. A determined reflection stared back from the darkened screens. An empire is built by anticipating threats and transforming them into advantages. Remaining in the shadows and adapting to circumstances is essential for finding ways to neutralize Colt, just as he had done with the Diablos cartel. But this was different. The stakes were higher than ever before. Badeau's enterprise was currently a house of cards; one wrong move or misplaced piece could bring it all crashing down. Years of hard work and billions of dollars hung in the balance. This was not a good time to worry about Freddy.

If Colt and Sutcliffe got too close, they could unravel everything. That would mean a shallow grave or a life sentence. There were dangerous people who would ensure that Badeau never lived to see the inside of a courtroom. "Time to adapt," Badeau said to the empty room. He needed a plan that would turn the changing situation to his advantage. Gabriel's loyalty to Kingsley should be tested, and he needed eyes on Colt and Sutcliffe. The real danger lay in the next shipment—a turning point that could redefine everything. If it landed successfully, Kingsley's empire would expand into untouchable territory, solidifying his reign at the top of the underworld.

Badeau's grip on the control panel tightened. Survival demanded action, and in this game, a single mistake could mean the end.

PART III

26

unday August 11

Gabriel's hands wouldn't stop trembling. He clasped them tightly behind his back, fighting to steady himself as the early morning breeze swept over the Kingsley estate's main house. The short walk from his quarters did little to calm him as the echoes of Saturday night's violence refused to fade. They replayed in his mind like a broken reel—the glint of the assassin's gun, the crush of bodies surging forward, his desperate lunge to save Kingsley. He'd saved a man's life—at least, that's what everyone kept saying. But would saving the man make the world a better place?

Doing the right thing always costs something. His father's words rang as clearly as if he stood beside him. So, what price was Gabriel here to pay now?

Before he could raise his hands to ring the bell, the entry door opened. Gabriel stepped back, his pulse spiking, only to meet the dark, sharp-eyed gaze of a boy about his age. His rich mahogany skin seemed to catch the sunlight, accentuating the clean angles of his jawline and cheekbones.

"They're waiting," the boy said, each syllable landing in perfect rhythm. He held the door open as if he'd been expecting Gabriel. "I'm Evens."

Evens stood still, watching him with a calm, unflinching expression. Gabriel hesitated, then moved forward, glancing back once. Somehow, the path from his quarters looked much longer than it had a moment ago. "Where are you from?" Gabriel asked him.

"Haiti," he said as they passed through the kitchen. "Been in America for some time now."

"How'd you end up here?"

"Vivian found me in a refugee camp when I was a child. " His tone suggested that the story was far from simple. "She took me here, and *voilà*. Collecting lost boys seems to be her thing, you know."

Lost boys? The term struck too close to Gabriel's own situation—plucked from his life, delivered to this strange world. But unlike Evens, Gabriel still had a family. Somewhere. They walked down the same marble hallway to Gabriel's first meeting with Kingsley and to the same dark panel door. Evens stopped abruptly and turned to Gabriel, his expression grave. "Listen carefully, *ti frè*. In this house, loyalty is oxygen. Breathe it, live it. And secrets?" He tapped his temple. "They're the currency that keeps you alive."

Gabriel nodded but had little understanding of what he'd just heard. How far had he strayed from his fishing village, from his dreams of bringing his family into prosperity? Now he was adrift in a sea of strangers, with different accents, different customs, and different ways of making a point.

Evens rapped his knuckles against the door. A muffled "enter" sounded from within.

"*Bon chans*," Evens said, pushing the door open to Kingsley's opulent office.

Maxwell Kingsley hunkered behind his massive desk, his gaze sharp and assessing. Vivian Delacroix perched cross-legged on the sofa, and Gabriel's skin prickled with her presence.

"Have a seat, Gabriel," Kingsley's voice held no emotion. "We have much to discuss."

As Gabriel stepped inside, the heavy door closed with a soft click. Trapped. Like a fish in a net.

Vivian stood and approached him. "Poor Gabriel, my sweet boy, how are you after Saturday night?" she said with dramatic concern, but her eyes were cat-like—wide, direct, chilling. "Did you sleep okay? It must have been difficult after such a terrible ordeal." She placed a hand on his shoulder and led him back to the sofa.

He fought the urge to shrug off her touch. Every instinct screamed to maintain distance, but survival meant playing along. Just like baiting a hook—sometimes you had to handle things that made your skin crawl.

Kingsley swiveled in his chair and cleared his throat. "Yes, about that. Your quick thinking was much appreciated."

"Appreciated?" Vivian said to Kingsley, but her focus remained on Gabriel. "More like lifesaving. Which is precisely why I think our brave friend deserves something more than just a pat on the back." She turned to face Kingsley.

Gabriel held still, like waiting for God's answer after his prayers.

Kingsley rubbed his jawline. "What do you have in mind?"

"Why, a promotion, of course," Vivian said. "After all,

he's proven his loyalty in the most measurable way possible. And with Stone gone, you're in the market for an estate manager."

Gabriel blinked. The word promotion was like a pebble in his shoe—uncomfortable yet impossible to ignore.

The lines on Kingsley's face etched deeper. "Estate manager? That's quite a leap from groundskeeper, especially for a young man so new to this world."

"Maybe that's exactly what you need," Vivian countered. "Stone had a flawless resume, and look where that got you. He fleeced us like sheep." Vivian glanced back at Gabriel, her full lips turning up slowly at the edges. "Besides, who better to run things than someone who risked his life to save yours?"

Gabriel shifted uncomfortably. It was as if the current of this conversation pulled him in deeper. Every word Vivian uttered was another fathom down.

"And what do you think about this, boy?" Kingsley said. "Do you think you're ready for such responsibility?"

"Of course he is," Vivian insisted before Gabriel could respond. "Aren't you, sweetheart?"

Gabriel swallowed hard. They want me to manage this place? "I... I would do my best, sir."

Kingsley scoffed. "Your best? This isn't some small-time operation. The annual budget for the estate runs into the millions."

"Exactly," Vivian emphasized. "Which is why we don't need someone tainted like that idiot Stone. Gabriel is a blank slate, Max. We can shape him to our needs." She rubbed his shoulder. "And whatever we desire."

Each word from Vivian's mouth was another brick in a wall between him and home.

Kingsley drummed his fingers on the desk. "And what about his experience, Vivian? This is a demanding position?"

Vivian chuckled. "Experience can be gained, Max. Loyalty, however..." She trailed off, letting the implication hang in the air.

Kingsley stood and moved to the sofa to tower over Gabriel. "Is that true, boy? Are you loyal to us now?"

Gabriel's heart grew heavy. His brothers' betrayal loomed in his mind. He looked up to meet Kingsley's gaze. "Yes, sir. This is my home now."

A tense silence followed. Vivian watched the exchange like a cat at a mouse hole. Kingsley remained silent, showing no emotion. Finally, he spoke in a measured tone. "Very well. We'll give it a trial run."

Gabriel nodded. "Yes, sir. Thank you, sir."

Vivian's smile bloomed slowly and dangerously.

Kingsley shook his head as if disappointed in his own decision. "And you, my dear, will be responsible for his training," he said almost as a whisper. "If he fails, it's on you."

"Of course, Max," Vivian purred, her eyes never leaving Gabriel. "I'll make sure he exceeds all your expectations."

Gabriel sat between Kingsley's scrutiny and Vivian's hungry stare. Was God still with him? How would running this estate affect his chances of seeing his father again?

———

GABRIEL'S NECK prickled at the sound of Vivian's heels clicking on the stone walkway behind him like exclamation marks. He hadn't walked this path since his arrival—not after he'd learned it led straight to Stone's office. Now, with Vivian at his back and his promotion dangling like a noose, he didn't have much choice. Kingsley had been indifferent. Vivian's expression bubbled like champagne. And him? Just a pawn for her enjoyment.

"Here we are," Vivian swept her hand across the doorway. "Your new domain."

No mahogany panels or crystal decanters here. The room had been stripped bare of Stone's grandeur. A scarred, utilitarian desk dominated the space, its worn surface hosting nothing but a laptop, a phone, and a printer. The high-backed chair behind it bore the same rugged wear—cracked leather and creases as deep as Stone's brooding had once been.

Two identical faces greeted them from opposite ends of the room. One twin lounged on a faded couch, dressed in a flowing summer dress that could've graced a magazine cover. The other—Kiara, he remembered from his first night —wore blue jeans, a plain T-shirt, and scuffed tennis shoes. Kiara's shoulders stiffened at their entrance, her wary eyes flicking between him and Vivian as if she were cornered.

"These are the twins, Aaliyah and Kiara," Vivian said with a dismissive wave. "Kiara's the shabby one. She'll help you sort out your duties." Glancing at her watch, Vivian pulled her phone from her purse and tapped the screen. "Hello, Rick? Yes, I'm on my way. I'll be there in thirty minutes."

Barely looking up from the glossy magazine in her hands, Aaliyah flicked through its pages with a listless air. Kiara scrubbed at the desk's surface with a cleaning rag, her movements sharp and purposeful.

"I'm off to New Orleans," Vivian announced, her voice now crisp and businesslike. "We'll continue your training this evening, Gabriel." Her lips curved into a smile that elevated her cheekbones. "At the main house—in my room."

Gabriel's stomach twisted. He forced himself to nod, keeping his expression neutral, though the churn inside threatened to bubble over. In her room?

"Don't look so worried, Gabriel," Vivian said, reaching to straighten his collar. "I'll make sure you're... thoroughly prepared for your new role."

She turned to the twins. "Girls, explain to Gabriel what Stone had you do when he worked here. And don't tell wild tales." Her heels clicked away down the stone pavers, leaving behind an uncomfortable silence.

Aaliyah stretched, flipping a page in her magazine. "Finally, the new Vogue. I've been dying to see the fall collections."

Kiara moved around the desk to a whiteboard with dates and tasks. "You'll need to check these inventory logs daily." Her voice carried the same wariness as her stance. "And update work schedules every Sunday night."

The mountain of ledgers and documents swam before Gabriel's eyes. How was he supposed to manage all this? And what game was Vivian playing?

"I should show you your quarters," Kiara said with a clipped tone. "This way."

"Have fun," Aaliyah said, not looking up from her magazine.

The room was small but private. A single bed pushed against one wall, a worn dresser opposite. Cigarette smoke seemed to seep from the wallpaper. Gabriel's gaze was drawn to the window, to the break in the tree line where he'd spotted the strange building on his first day. His fingers tightened on the windowsill.

"You've seen it?" Kiara asked, her voice tinged with fear. "The Shadows?"

Gabriel turned to see her lingering in the doorway, gripping the frame as if bracing herself.

"Vivian uses it to keep me in line," she said, wrapping her arms around her middle. "She threatens to send me there whenever I don't cooperate."

Gabriel nodded his understanding. "Stone threatened me with it. Never said what happens inside. Didn't need to."

"No one who goes in ever talks about it," Kiara said. "If they come back at all."

A chill swept over Gabriel. Sweat prickled at his temple. "This promotion—it feels like…"

"A trap?" she finished.

Gabriel turned back to the window, staring at the dark gap in the trees. *God always puts his faithful servants where he needs them.* Another lesson from his father. "Or maybe something else. What if there's a reason I'm here? A way to help?"

Kiara's eyes narrowed. "You actually believe that?"

"I have to." The strength in his voice surprised him. "Otherwise, what's the point of any of this?"

A long moment passed. Then Kiara's shoulders relaxed slightly. "Be careful what you say around Vivian. She likes to test new people to see how far she can push them." She looked back through the hallway. "I should get back before Aaliyah starts talking about Paris Fashion Week again."

She slipped out, leaving Gabriel alone with his thoughts and responsibility. Beyond the window, the Shadows crouched between the trees. God had placed him here to bring some light into this darkness.

His hands steadied on the windowsill. Vivian's "training"

waited. Stone's ledgers loomed. The twins' opposing paths revealed exactly what was at stake. The noose of his promotion had transformed into a test of faith. He had the sinking feeling, like at the gala dinner, lives depended on what he did next.

27

The Lord sees all that you do, Gabriel. Evil seeks to ensnare you; its cords will hold you down.

Papa's warning flooded Gabriel's mind as he buried himself in maintenance reports, trying to ignore the inevitable summons to Vivian's bedroom.

Maintain the discipline I teach you. Resist temptation, or it will lead you to destruction.

He'd been resisting temptation every time he came into Vivian's presence, but the lingering touches, the loaded glances—they made it clear. It wasn't *if* she would call him to sin, but *when.*

Scattered across the desk of his new office were pages of notes he'd scribbled on a legal pad—rotting support beams in the greenhouse, leaky pipes throughout the horse stables, faded paint on the main building. The volume of necessary repairs was staggering. Focusing on them helped strengthen his resolve for the test he knew was coming.

Gabriel framed an image in his mind of how he could restore the estate within a few weeks. The contrast between that vision and the reality he'd witnessed during his inspections had him shaking his head. How had Stone let things deteriorate so badly? And more importantly, would Kingsley allow Gabriel the budget to do the work?

He reached for a calculator, determined to prioritize the most critical repairs for the lowest cost. The ticking clock on the wall reminded him—he'd been working for more than ten hours.

A sharp knock cut through his concentration. Gabriel looked up as the door swung open, revealing Evens' lean silhouette.

"Ti frè," Evens said, his accent clipping each syllable. "Vivian wants to see you. In her room."

Gabriel's belly churned with thick apprehension. He'd been dreading this meeting all day.

"Now?" Gabriel asked, failing to keep his voice from shaking.

Evens chuckled. "With Vivian, there is only *now*."

As Evens turned to leave, his eyes snapped to the mass of papers on Gabriel's desk. For a moment, something like pity crossed his face. Then it was gone, replaced by his impassive expression.

Gabriel stood, his chair scraping against the floor. As he followed Evens out, he cast one last glance at the daunting task he'd left behind. Would he ever get the chance to prove his abilities as the estate manager after tonight?

He climbed the grand staircase, moved past a massive landing to a long hallway leading to Vivian's room. Each step felt like quicksand. His heart thundered and his pace slowed. Pausing at a set of glossy white double doors, he steadied himself before knocking softly.

"Come in, Gabriel," Vivian's sultry voice drifted into the hallway.

He pushed the door open. Its hinges groaned. Amber

light from scattered lamps suffused the room. Gabriel's gaze locked on Vivian, his eyes widening at the sight.

She reclined on a chaise lounge, her sleek, slender figure draped in a silk robe that hinted at hidden curves. Dark, shoulder-length hair framed her face in elegant waves, accentuating her sharp cheekbones. Vivian's expressive eyes, deep and alluring, met Gabriel's with an intensity that made him shiver.

"Close the door, dear," Vivian said, her lips curling into a knowing smile as she uncrossed her legs, the movement graceful and deliberate.

Gabriel's mouth was as dry as burnt toast. He stood rooted by the entrance, unsure where to look.

Vivian rose, her robe shifting as she moved toward him. "You've been working today, haven't you, sweetheart?" she said. "So hard that I prepared you a special reward."

Opulence dripped from every corner—heavy velvet drapes framed wide windows, a massive four-poster bed dominated one wall, its silken sheets gleaming in the low light. Crystal decanters winked from a bedside bar cart, promising liquid courage or oblivion.

The sweet, fruity scent of Vivian's perfume clouded his senses. Her fingertips grazed his forearm, sending a jolt through his nerves.

Evil seeks to ensnare you.

He froze as she invaded his personal space, her breath a warm caress brushing his earlobe. "You've been working so hard, sweetheart," she said. "Don't you deserve a reward?"

Vivian pressed against him. Her fingers stroked his jawline, stirring a war between restraint and desire. "Think carefully, Gabriel," she said softly. "Your future here could be very bright or very brief. The choice is yours."

Its cords will hold you down.

The truth of Papa's warning tightened around him like a noose as Vivian raked her long nails through his hair, her lips a hairsbreadth from his. "One kiss, Gabriel. That's all it takes to secure your place here. To prove you belong." Her other hand slid down his chest. "Or you can walk away and lose everything."

The promise of power, of belonging, of his dreams fulfilled—it was all right there. Papa's face flashed through his mind—his disappointment, his tears.

The Lord sees all that you do.

Gabriel's hands shot up, gripping Vivian's wrists. "No."

Fury blazed in Vivian's eyes. Her seductive mask crumbled, revealing something far more menacing. "You foolish boy," she hissed, nails digging into his scalp. "You have no idea what you're throwing away."

"I know exactly what I'm saving." He pried her hands away, even as she fought to maintain her grip. "My soul is worth more than any position you can offer."

Gabriel wrenched free and strode for the door, Vivian's rage rumbling behind him. "You'll regret this choice," she called after him. "In the morning, you'll beg for a second chance."

He didn't stop until he reached his quarters. Through his window, storm clouds gathered over the estate grounds he'd spent all day inspecting. Tomorrow he'd likely lose it all—the job, the dreams of restoration, and the opportunity to prove himself.

But as Gabriel touched the maintenance reports still spread across his desk.

The Lord sees all that you do.

Papa's words settled over him like armor. Let Vivian bring what she would.

28

Monday, August 12

Eli's TBI headache flared. He leaned against his desk for balance. The team had gravitated to their usual seats—Lindsey, Dakota, Karina, and Julia forming a tight circle in the communal office. The strong gusts outside swept across the office exterior, swaying the modular building on its foundation.

"You're not walking into Maxwell Kingsley's trap. Are you?" Lindsey's voice broke like a thunderclap, adding to the tension that had coiled around the room all morning.

Eli forced himself to concentrate. "If this weather gets any worse, discussing Kingsley's invitation may become irrelevant."

Julia's fingers flew across her tablet. "The Weather Channel says the storm in the Gulf hasn't budged. It has just settled in one place and is getting stronger."

"Let's focus," Eli said, drawing everyone's attention. "After Dakota disarmed Maxwell Kingsley's would-be assassin last night, he's invited the two of us to lunch at his estate today."

Lindsey's eyes narrowed to sullen slits, doubling down on her protest. "Wouldn't an operation put you at risk? I can tell you're struggling with your head injury." The pounding behind Eli's eyes roared louder. He pressed his fists against his desk, grounding himself as the room threatened to spin.

"I hear you, Lindsey," Dakota said, his pen twirling lazily between his fingers. "But dancing with this devil isn't storming his castle with an armed incursion. It's lunch, for goodness' sake."

The phrase sent a chill through Eli's spine. How many times had just a meeting turned into a disaster? His mind flashed to Prichard, to the warehouse, to Reddick.

Karina's voice trembled. "I danced with devils in Juarez, remember? And it got my brother killed."

The memory hit Eli like a hammer. He'd been there, providing cover while Dakota dragged Karina's brother from a firefight with Diablos. He pushed away from his desk, needing to move. "Look, we have an opportunity to understand the scope of Kingsley's operation firsthand. That's invaluable to our mission."

Julia tapped her tablet, each soft click echoing in Eli's throbbing head. "Let's break this down. First point—potential for finding the twins." She frowned at her screen. "But Kingsley's reach is extensive. With the governor in his pocket—"

"Is he though?" Lindsey said. "I watched Sarah Bordelon's face when Kingsley spoke last night. That woman despises him."

The memory surfaced through Eli's headache—the tight line of Sarah Bordelon's mouth, the flash in her eyes when Kingsley had dismissed her mid-sentence. "The governor too. You should have seen Bordelon's knuckles go white when Kingsley talked down to his wife."

"A crack in Kingsley's armor?" Dakota set his pen down. "The Bordelon's could make powerful allies."

"Or they could be too afraid to help," Karina countered. "If Kingsley has something on the governor—"

"Then maybe the governor wants him taken down as much as we do." Julia carried a note of hope.

"Our primary objective remains to find those twins." Eli pressed his palms against his desk. "Getting inside Kingsley's estate, even for a couple of hours—"

"Could get you killed." Lindsey's voice shook. "If Kingsley discovers why you're really there—"

"He won't just come after you two," Julia said. "He'll destroy everything we've built—our reputation and the work we do."

Dakota's pen stopped twirling. "Sometimes the biggest risk is not taking one."

"We've got two plays here." Eli pushed away from his desk. "While Dakota and I work inside the Kingsley estate, maybe you could reach out to the governor's wife?" he asked Lindsey.

Lindsey sat straighter, energy replacing worry. "Woman to woman. The way Sarah tensed when Kingsley spoke about trafficking victims as complexities and idealism tells me she's in play to help children. Besides, when Kingsley praised you and Dakota for saving his life," Lindsey pulled a card from her purse and waved it, "Sarah and I exchanged numbers."

Julia set down her tablet and rubbed her chin. "You told me she mentioned Tara at the gala. Knew her whole story. If I tell her Tara's ordeal from my perspective, about what these parents are going through..."

"That can't hurt," Lindsey said. "Speaking for other

mothers trying to get their children back. That could pull a heartstring."

"If Sarah Bordelon moves against Kingsley, the governor might follow." Dakota said.

"We work both angles," Eli had the first flicker of hope he'd felt in hours. "Dakota and I will go to lunch and gather intel. Lindsey and Julia will approach Sarah Bordelon with Tara's story and what we know about the Johnson twins." He met each team member's eyes. "We're not just going after Kingsley anymore. We're going to tear down his whole kingdom—starting tomorrow."

29

Governor Beau Bordelon stood at his office window in the Louisiana State Capitol, nursing a lukewarm cup of coffee. Heavy clouds hung over the sprawling lawn of the capitol grounds, casting an eerie gray pallor over the live oaks lining its edges. The air held an unnatural stillness, as if waiting for the heavens to exhale.

The barometer in the situation room had been dropping all morning, mirroring the sinking feeling in his gut. The events of Saturday night's gala still played in his mind like a frenzied disaster film—the glittering chandeliers, the soft clink of champagne glasses, the sudden eruption of Thomas Reeves trying to kill Maxwell Kingsley. And then, the swift, almost miraculous intervention of Eli Colt's partner.

Eli Colt appeared as a puzzle piece that didn't quite fit. Could this man be the key to finally freeing himself from Kingsley's insidious influence? Or would Colt prove to be yet another complication, ensnared by Kingsley like a spider does a fly? Bordelon's grip tightened on his cup as he tried to get ahead of these swiftly moving events.

The thought of Kingsley's manipulations led Bordelon's mind to wander to darker territories. And then there was his dream—occurring again last night—New Orleans sinking into oblivion, helpless against forces beyond human control. He shuddered, trying to shake off the lingering dread that clung to him like a second skin.

The intercom on his desk buzzed, startling him from his concerns. Patricia's crisp voice cut through the silence. "Governor, Dr. Clarisse Doucet from GOHSEP is here to see you. She's brought Dr. Evan Meadows from the National Weather Service with her."

Bordelon turned from the window. An unscheduled visit from the Director of Emergency Preparedness accompanied by a weather expert? A bitter taste coated his tongue. A cold weight settled over him as he prepared himself for bad news.

"Send them in, Patricia," he said, setting down his cup and adjusting his tie. As he moved to greet his visitors, he couldn't shake the feeling that his nightmare might be closer to reality than he dared imagine.

Bordelon straightened his posture and plastered on his practiced smile as the door opened. Clarisse strode in, her usual commanding presence slightly diminished by the deep creases on her forehead. Her copper-dyed hair, typically pulled back in a neat bun, had wisps escaping around her face. The crisp lines of her navy suit contrasted with the nervous energy radiating from her rigid persona.

Meadows trailed behind, fumbling with a stack of papers that threatened to spill from his grasp. He wore rumpled khakis and a flushed face, suggesting a man not familiar with attending high-level meetings. His receding hairline glistened with sweat above thick-rimmed glasses.

"Governor," Doucet said, her voice tight, a manila folder

clutched in her hands. "Thank you for seeing us on such short notice."

Bordelon gestured toward the chairs in front of his desk, his smile never wavering despite struggling to temper his nerves. "Of course, Clarisse. What brings you and the National Weather Service to my office?"

As they settled into their seats, Doucet's fingers fidgeted with the edges of the file she held. Meadows squirmed like a schoolboy called to see the principal. Whatever news they brought wouldn't ease the alarm brewing in his belly.

Leaning back in his chair, Bordelon adopted a relaxed posture. "So, what's on your mind?"

Dr. Doucet shifted, exchanging a quick glance with Meadows. "Governor, we're following concerning data about atmospheric conditions offshore."

Meadows nodded so hard his glasses slipped down to the edge of his nose. He pushed them back up with a trembling hand. "Yes, sir. The models we're seeing... well, they're unprecedented."

"Unprecedented how?" Bordelon asked firmly, his calm facade slipping.

Doucet opened the folder she'd been clutching, revealing a collection of colorized weather maps. "We're looking at what could potentially lead to a storm more powerful than anything we've seen before. More devastating than Hurricane Katrina."

The mention of Katrina hit Bordelon between the eyes. His nightmare. His state destroyed. He leaned forward. "How certain are you?"

"Certain enough to be here, sir," Doucet said with conviction.

Bordelon felt the blood drain from his face. "And our current preparedness?"

"If these projections hold, our protocols may need significant adjustment," Doucet said. "We should start preliminary mobilization soon."

The potential disaster weighed on him, but so did the political ramifications of crying wolf prematurely. A sudden exhaustion overwhelmed him. Evacuations, even preparations for them, would disrupt the daily life of every citizen. Economic impacts, public panic, backlash—too much to take in right now. "We can't jump the gun here. With no storm in the Gulf yet, we can't throw the state into chaos over a prediction, no matter how dire."

Doucet opened her mouth to protest, but Bordelon held up a hand. "However, we must be ready. Clarisse, I want you to quietly alert the coastal mayors and parish presidents. Get them in the loop, but stress discretion."

She nodded, jotting notes in her folder.

"And let's call an emergency meeting," Bordelon continued. "All relevant department heads. We'll start preemptive planning immediately. If this storm materializes, we'll be ready."

As Doucet and Meadows gathered their materials, Bordelon's gaze drifted back to the window. The grey sky mocked him, hinting at the potential catastrophe on the horizon. He couldn't shake the feeling that this was just the beginning of a natural disaster that could reshape more than just the coastline.

"One more thing," he added as they reached the door. "Let's keep this under wraps for now. We don't need a media frenzy over a hurricane that may or may not hit us."

Doucet and Meadows exchanged a glance at Bordelon's final instruction. Meadows fidgeted with his glasses. Doucet pressed her lips into an apprehensive frown. "Of course,

Governor," she said in a neutral tone. "We'll keep this confidential for now."

As the door closed behind them, Bordelon slumped into his chair. He reached for the phone on his desk, his mind fumbling through worst-case scenarios, each more catastrophic than the last.

Sarah. He needed Sarah. Their recent clash over Kingsley's blackmail attempt had revealed something he'd been too proud to see before—his wife possessed a clarity of thought, a way of cutting through the noise to find solutions he couldn't. The memory of her unwavering stance, her refusal to let him cave to the billionaire's demands, had proven her to be his most valuable advisor.

He pressed the intercom button. "Patricia, please rearrange my schedule. I'm going home early."

Let's hear what Sarah has to say about this.

———

A BATTERED blue Civic blocked his usual parking spot behind the Governor's mansion. Bordelon's foot tapped a rapid staccato as his driver circled to find another space.

Every minute counted. The forecast numbers from Drs. Doucet and Meadows burned in his mind—a Category 4 hurricane bearing down on their coast. He needed Sarah's steady hand on this. Needed her gift for cutting through chaos to determine the clearest path forward.

With his knees protesting, he hurried from the Suburban. The midday sun bore down, but the sweat dampening his collar came from imagining New Orleans underwater. Again.

Female voices floated from the east parlor, Sarah's measured alto blending with unfamiliar tones. *Crap.* She was entertaining. The storm brewing outside—and inside—wouldn't wait for idle conversation.

Pressing his back against the cool, polished paneling, he swallowed his impatience and focused. The door stood slightly ajar.

"We tracked them to a silver Jaguar," an unfamiliar voice said, low and firm. "Louisiana plates, registered to Maxwell Kingsley."

Bordelon's fingers curled into fists. Kingsley. As if one catastrophe wasn't enough.

"The girls got in willingly?" Sarah used that gentle probe she reserved for difficult conversations—the same tone he desperately needed focused on evacuation strategies, not Kingsley's mess.

"That's what an eyewitness in Prichard, Alabama, told my husband." The second voice he recognized—Lindsey Colt, Eli Colt's wife from the charity gala. "But Mrs. Bordelon, they're sixteen. Twins. Their mother trusted them to walk to school, not end up in Vivian Delacroix's car."

The vamp Vivian. Kingsley's worse half, always whispering in his ear like some discount Cruella de Vil. The image of her practically undressing that young boy at Kingsley's fundraiser turned Bordelon's stomach.

"And the police?" Sarah asked.

A bitter laugh from the unknown woman. "The detective called it a standard runaway case. Didn't even look at the footage until Eli and Dakota forced the issue."

"Two months," Lindsey Colt added, her voice carrying the same steel he'd heard at the gala. "These girls have been missing while Kingsley and Delacroix host fundraisers that deepen his pockets for his trafficking enterprise."

The forecast numbers flashed in Bordelon's brain. He straightened his tie and strode into the east parlor.

The women's conversation died. Sarah sat perched on the Queen Anne settee, her spine rigid. Lindsey Colt occupied one end of the sofa, and a woman he didn't recognize sat beside her, a manila folder flat in her lap.

"Ladies." He crossed to Sarah and kissed her cheek, breathing in her familiar lavender scent.

"Beau, you remember Lindsey from the gala, Eli Colt's wife."

"Why, of course," Bordelon extended his hand. "Nice to see you again."

"And this is Julia, Eli's sister-in-law," Sara moved to Julia's side. "She's Tara's mother, the niece Eli rescued from Commodore."

"A pleasure to meet you," Bordelon said. "I'm sorry I must cut your meeting short, but I need to speak with Sarah about an urgent matter."

"We understand, Governor." Lindsey rose, gathering her purse. "Thank you for your time, Sarah."

Julia Colt tucked the manila folder into her bag. "Yes, thank you."

"I heard mention of Maxwell Kingsley and Vivian Delacroix as I came in." Bordelon kept his tone neutral, gubernatorial. The air conditioning hummed.

"I'm sure your wife will explain our concerns," Lindsey said with a polite nod.

Sarah's hand found his arm as the Colt women made their exit. The parlor door clicked shut behind them.

"Beau, these ladies—"

"Want to take down Maxwell Kingsley," he said. "But we have a catastrophic hurricane aimed at our coast."

Sarah's brow pressed together. "Sit with me," she said, leading him to the settee. "Tell me about this storm."

Bordelon sank into the cushion. "It's Katrina all over

again. Tidal surge could top twenty feet in some areas." The numbers flashed through his mind again. "I have to decide on mandatory evacuations."

"When will it hit?"

"Can't say. It's just hovering over the Gulf, getting stronger every minute." He loosened his tie. "But this Kingsley thing has you worried."

"Those women showed me photos, Beau. Young girls. Children. They're disappearing, and Kingsley and that woman are behind it. Here. In our state."

"Sarah—"

"I know about the storm. I know what's at stake." She gripped his hand. "But families are being destroyed, and we attend their fundraisers."

Bordelon closed his eyes. "What are you asking me to do?"

"Let me work with Julia Colt. She has evidence—photos, financial records. While everyone's focused on evacuation plans, we can finally connect the dots." Sarah leaned forward. "These girls have families searching for them, Beau. Mothers who deserve answers."

The air conditioning hummed against the growing pressure outside. Two storms bearing down on Louisiana. One would ravage the coast and the other destroy lives from within. And here was Sarah, ready to fight the one that Bordelon couldn't.

30

Tuesday, *August 13*

"Quite the crib," Dakota murmured as a white-columned mansion emerged over the last hill. "Nicer than that tin trailer you hang your hat in."

Eli guided his Jeep between the tall pines and lush ligustrums of Belle Terre. This wasn't just a thank-you lunch— it was their best chance to find Kiara and Aaliyah Johnson. Beyond the long sweeping driveway, access to answers waited if he and Dakota played their cards right. Eli's eyes darted from the manicured lawns to the building's facade, cataloging security cameras and guard positions. "We need to stay alert. Somewhere in these thousand acres, those girls could be hidden."

They passed a meticulously sculpted garden where a young man with a clipboard roamed the mansion's exterior.

"Hey," Dakota said, "isn't that the kid who almost took a bullet for Kingsley at the gala?"

"Sure is," Eli said as he parked in the circular drive. "Something about that young man. He doesn't seem to fit with Kingsley's operation."

"Kingsley would probably disagree with you," Dakota said as he opened the passenger door. "Without him, he'd be dead."

"Remember," Eli said as he exited the vehicle, "we're just two ex-military guys who run a non-profit. Maybe looking for a donation from this creep billionaire."

A young man with dark skin and sharp features emerged from the front door. "Gentlemen," he said in something like a French accent. "Mr. Kingsley is waiting for you. Please follow me."

"Haitian," Dakota said under his breath. "And I'm sure the other kid is from South or Central America."

"Honduras is my guess," Eli said. "Just like those boys we rescued in Juarez."

The Haitian boy, who introduced himself as Evens, led them through a grand foyer with stained windows highlighting a crystal chandelier in rich red, green, and purple tones. Beneath the decorative fixture was an enormous staircase straight from a Hollywood movie set—polished wood banister, intricate balusters, and wood steps with scarlet carpet streaming up the center.

Instead of the dining room Eli expected, Evens strode past the stairs, through a marble hallway to a dark paneled door, and knocked once before swinging it open. "Mr. Colt and Mr. Sutcliffe for Mr. Kingsley," he announced.

Eli stepped into the immense office with Dakota on his right shoulder. Floor-to-ceiling windows framed a view of the estate's expansive grounds. Bookshelves lined with leather-bound volumes flanked a massive desk. Behind it was Maxwell Kingsley, raising himself from a high-back burgundy chair.

But it was the woman in the room that made Eli's pulse quicken. Vivian Delacroix, the woman in the video feed with the twins that Blackwell had sent them, stood astride Kingsley. She wore tight beige riding pants with glossy black riding boots and a black jacket. She held a crop in her right hand as if she were ready to whip them.

Stay calm, Eli. Stay focused.

Eli shared a loaded glance with Dakota. This meeting had just become far more interesting.

"Gentlemen," Kingsley said in a voice as smooth as aged bourbon. "I trust you don't mind if we have our lunch served here in my office. More... private."

Delacroix didn't move for a long second, then took a seat in a nearby loveseat. Eli and Dakota took the chairs Kingsley indicated across from his desk.

"Let me begin by thanking you again for your actions at my fundraiser," Kingsley said. "I'm not sure what would have happened if you hadn't intervened."

"That kid outside with the clipboard would have probably taken a bullet," Dakota said without hesitation.

"Yes," Kingsley said as his eyes mellowed, and he rubbed the crown of his head. "Gabriel is proving every day he's an invaluable associate to our operation." Kingsley picked up a manila folder in front of him and waved it briefly. "Which is why I've been particularly interested in learning more about Redemption Rescue."

"Not much to tell," Eli said, keeping his tone even. "We're just trying to make a difference."

In his periphery, Vivian Delacroix shifted on the sofa, but her gaze remained focused on him and Dakota.

Kingsley opened the file. "Impressive work you do, Mr. Colt. But I'm curious about something. How do you decide which children are worth saving?" The question carried an edge.

"I'm not sure I understand," Eli said.

"He wants to know if you're selective in the work you take on," Delacroix said. "Or if you only stick your nose in a case when parents come calling."

"Redemption Rescue is quite remarkable," Kingsley said, leafing through the file. "Particularly what you did in Juarez. Sixteen children rescued from a cartel operation? Impressive."

"We have good people," Eli said. "And solid intelligence."

"But limited resources, I imagine." Vivian's voice carried a note of sympathy that didn't sound completely sincere. "Non-profits always struggle with funding, especially with the scope of work you do."

Kingsley closed the folder. "Which is precisely why we asked you here today. Beyond expressing our gratitude, we'd like to discuss a substantial donation to your organization."

Eli shared a quick glance with Dakota. This wasn't what they'd expected.

"How substantial?" Dakota asked.

"Two million," Vivian said, studying her riding crop. "To start."

The air in the office thickened. Eli knew there had to be a catch.

"That kind of money could save a lot of kids," Kingsley said softly.

"And all we're asking in return is your... expertise with a delicate situation," Delacroix continued.

"What situation?" Eli asked.

Delacroix rose from the loveseat and strolled to the window. "We've recently discovered something disturbing about someone who used to work here. A man who we thought we could trust."

"This man was fired recently for stealing," Kingsley added. "We've recently learned he took documents from our discreet files—documents that could be damaging to many people's reputations."

"Including yours?" Dakota asked.

Vivian turned with an amused smirk. "Including certain business associates who'd prefer their privacy."

Eli felt the conversation shifting into dangerous territory. "And this person is...?"

"James Stone." Kingsley's voice hardened. "My former estate manager."

"What exactly has this James Stone done?" Eli asked carefully.

"Besides stealing from us?" Vivian's laugh was cold. "Let's just say his... appetites run toward the younger crowd. We've recently learned he's been involved in some truly deplorable activities."

Dakota leaned forward slightly. "What kind of activities?"

Kingsley opened a drawer and removed a thick manila folder. "The kind that would interest people in your line of work, Mr. Colt." He slid the file across his desk. "Take a look."

Eli pulled out several photographs and studied the troubling images—a middle-aged man with young girls—very young girls. "When were these taken?" Eli asked, fighting to keep his voice steady.

"Over the past year," Vivian said. "We had no idea, of course. Not until one of our security personnel discovered his private collection."

Dakota glanced at the images. "And the police?"

"I'd like this to remain quiet," Kingsley said. "My reputation, you see. Besides, I'd like to take that pound of flesh myself."

"Are these the originals?" Eli held up one of the photos.

"Those are just copies," Vivian said. "The originals, along with some rather disturbing video, are on this." She pulled a USB drive from her jacket pocket and placed it next to the envelope. "Everything you need to know about Mr. Stone is there."

"Including," Kingsley said, his voice dropping, "surveillance footage from one of his private sessions with a fourteen-year-old girl."

If these allegations were true, Stone wasn't just a potential witness—he was a predator.

"And the two million?" Dakota asked.

"Consider it a donation," Vivian smiled. "To help ensure other children don't suffer the same fate."

Eli studied Kingsley's face, searching for any signs of deception. "Why us? Why not handle this internally?"

"Because you have a reputation," Kingsley said, "for dealing with people who hurt underage boys and girls. And because your organization could do so much more with proper funding." He paused, letting the words sink in. "Think of it as justice that benefits the innocent."

"And if we decline?" Eli angled himself between Dakota and Vivian. The riding crop tapped against her boot in a steady rhythm, like a metronome counting down their time to decide.

Vivian's smile didn't change. "Then we find someone else to handle it. And Redemption Rescue will have to continue operating on a shoestring budget. Such a shame, really. All those children you could save..."

If what they said about Stone was true, he was exactly the kind of predator they hunted. But something about this was wrong. Too convenient.

"We'll do it," Dakota said suddenly.

All eyes in the room snapped to Dakota. He reached for the USB drive, his movements smooth and confident.

"My partner here," Dakota said, nodding towards Eli, "likes to consider all angles. But sometimes, you just need to handle things directly."

Eli's mind raced. This was spiraling out of control. But as he started to speak, he caught Dakota's eye. There was a warning there, a silent plea to trust him.

"Well then," Kingsley said, standing and moving to a crystal decanter, "shall we seal our arrangement with a drink?"

"I like brandy as much as the next man," Dakota nodded to Vivian, "or woman. But you might want to produce some working capital first."

Vivian laughed and strolled behind Kingsley's desk. She opened a drawer and tossed a thick envelope into Dakota's lap.

"Consider it a down payment," she purred. "The rest comes when the job is done."

"To new partnerships," Kingsley said, raising his glass.

The crystal caught the afternoon light, casting blood-red shadows across Kingsley's face. Eli lifted his own glass, hyperaware of Vivian's curious gaze. One wrong move, one slip in their performance, and they'd never save those girls.

"A final detail, gentlemen." She set her drink on Kingsley's desk, tapping her crop on its surface. She prowled toward Eli, each click of her boots against the floor making another heartbeat of tension.

"When you find Stone..." Her voice dropped to a whisper as she leaned close. The sweet scent of expensive perfume couldn't mask her cruel nature. "Make sure he understands the true cost of hurting children." Her dark eyes had the same coldness he'd witnessed in Blackwell's footage. "Some sins can only be paid for in blood."

Eli rubbed his thumb against his glass. He opened his mouth to respond, but Dakota cut in smoothly.

"We'll handle it," Dakota said, patting the envelope with confident casualness. "Quietly."

Vivian's lips curved into a satisfied smile. They weren't just making a deal anymore—they were allying with monsters to hurt a monster. And somewhere in this maze of corruption, the Johnson twins were waiting to be rescued.

As they walked back to the Jeep, Eli's mind churned. He waited until they were well down the driveway before speaking. "What was that back there?"

Dakota's face was grim. "That was us getting exactly what we came here for—access to Stone." He pulled out the flash drive. "And maybe enough evidence to bring down this whole operation."

"Or enough rope to hang ourselves," Eli said, but he knew Dakota was right. They were in now, whether he liked it or not. "You know they expect us to kill him."

"Of course. But the joke's on them. When we find him, we get him to tell us where the Johnson twins are. As the former estate manager, I'm sure he has an idea."

Eli opened his mouth to argue but shut it as he exited the property. He had to admit, Dakota came through. And somewhere on these hundreds of acres, Kiara and Aaliyah were waiting to be found. If that meant playing Kingsley's game—or even dealing with Stone—so be it.

Behind them, the estate's wrought-iron gates swung closed with the finality of a coffin lid.

31

Wednesday, August 14

Twenty-four hours to make Stone disappear. Two million dollars to do it. Twenty-four hours to learn where to find Kiara and Aaliyah before they vanished forever. The numbers tumbled through Eli's mind as he crossed the gravel lot from his Airstream to his office. His team wouldn't like this—he didn't like it. The morning sky hung as heavy as the decision weighing on his conscience.

Dakota would want to tell them straight. Karina would fight against violence of any kind. And Lindsey... last night's discussion had left a cold space between them. "There has to be another way," she'd whispered in the dark after they'd gone to bed. But where was that other way? The clock was ticking, and with every passing second, the twins slipped further from his reach.

Shaking off a chill that had nothing to do with the weather, Eli climbed the three steps up to the modular building. Above the entrance, the American flag snapped in the wind. A dull ache pulsed behind his eyes as he wrestled with the ethical minefield he'd address at the meeting.

Glancing at his watch, then the swirling sky, Eli tried to prepare. The clock was ticking, and there was no avoiding the storm—both outside and inside the office. The welcome smell of coffee greeted him as he pushed the door open. Dakota stood by the coffee maker, offering a mock salute as he poured.

From Dakota's workspace, Karina hunched over his computer. Julia's rapid typing punctuated the air as she scanned data on dual monitors. With her auburn hair pulled back in a casual style, Lindsey offered a quick nod from her desk. Eli caught her gaze and a flicker of reassurance. What had changed since last night?

Karina and Julia exchanged glances as Eli laid out Kingsley's demand. The silence that followed felt like a noose tightening.

"You can't be serious," Karina said. "We're talking about murder."

"Not murder," Dakota said with an edge Eli had rarely heard. "We're talking about making a problem go away. Sometimes that means getting our hands dirty."

"There's dirty, and there's damned." Julia pushed back from her computer. "We start down this road—"

A sharp knock at the door cut her off.

"Were we expecting anyone?" Julia asked, her hand hovering over her keyboard.

Eli moved to the door, gripped the doorknob, paused, then swung it open. Manny Mancuso's stocky frame filled the doorway.

"Morning, Eli," Manny said, his voice a rich blend of warmth and New Orleans cadence that instantly transported Eli back to their first encounter. "Lindsey told me you're in a bit of trouble with a case."

Stepping aside to let the retired New Orleans detective in, Eli's gratitude swelled for the man whose courage had once saved Lindsey from traffickers when she was just a teenager. That same unwavering resolve had helped Eli rescue Tara only two years earlier, forging a bond that felt as solid as family. His gaze swung to Lindsey, who met his eyes unflinchingly.

"I called him last night," she said, her chin lifting slightly. "I'm sure he's faced what you're facing a time or two." The unspoken truth hung between them—when it came to walking ethical tightropes to solve a case, no one had more experience than Manny, who'd become family to them both.

Dakota let out a low whistle. "Well, isn't this a cozy little surprise party?"

Manny's infectious grin beamed at Dakota. "Where you at, Dakota? Been a minute. Good to see ya."

Lindsey rose from her chair, gathering her purse and her briefcase. "Now that Manny's here, I'll head out to Safe Haven. I have a morning session in half an hour." She paused at the door, catching Eli's eye with a wink. "You've got this."

As the door closed behind her, warmth bloomed from his heart to his cheeks. Trust Lindsey to call the one person who was perfect to steer them through this ethical dilemma. From helping Eli in his fight against the NOPD while searching for Tara to mentoring him and Dakota in their early days of Redemption Rescue. Who better than Manny and his strong faith to show them how to navigate darkness without losing their souls?

"Alright then," Eli said. "Let's lay it all out for our new

team member. As I'm sure Lindsey has informed you, Kingsley wants us to eliminate a man named Stone."

Manny nodded, confirming he knew.

"And we've got twenty-four hours to make it happen," Dakota added.

Manny frowned but said nothing.

"Look," Dakota said, strolling to the coffee station. "I'm not saying we off the guy, but maybe get our hands a little dirty. Scare him so he'll want to disappear on his own."

Eli shook his head. "That's a slippery slope, Dakota. We start down that path; we might be forced to kill him."

"Then the problem's solved, right?" Dakota shot back. "We're not Boy Scouts here."

"We're not." Eli pushed off from the desk. "But if we dig up dirt on Stone to threaten him with exposure?"

"In twenty-four hours?" Dakota snorted. "Where are you gonna find that much dirt?"

"Then we're back to square one," Eli admitted, running a hand through his hair.

"Exactly," Dakota pressed. "We need to show we mean business. Get rough, then give him a choice—disappear or be fed to the gators."

"It's risky," Eli said, but he was not convinced. "If he doesn't bite, we're left with less time and potentially an angry Stone on our hands."

"But if it works," Dakota insisted, "we solve our problem, right?"

Manny cleared his throat. "Before you boys go off half-cocked," he said, "here's something you should know about your man Stone."

"He ain't just some run-of-the-mill thug," Manny continued. "He's got a rap sheet longer than the Mississippi. Multiple assault charges, illegal weapons possession, suspected ties to organized crime." He turned to Eli, his expression grim. "This guy's a powder keg waiting to blow."

"And..." Dakota said with impatience.

"And," Manny's eyes hardened. "If you decide to strong-arm this guy, you better be careful. Stone won't go down without a fight. Then you pull the police into the equation, and maybe a few charges of your own you'll have to contend with. That is if you survive."

Eli leaned back against his desk. "So we're screwed either way," he said.

"What if we approach this from a different angle?" Karina spoke up from behind her computer. "Instead of making Stone disappear, what if we make him want to leave on his own?"

"I have an idea," Julia said. "What if you just tell Stone the truth? That Kingsley hired you to kill him?"

"And risk him coming after us?" Dakota scoffed. "Or worse, going straight back to Kingsley?"

"Not necessarily," Eli said, straightening up. "If we frame it right, we could make Stone think his life is in danger if he stays in Louisiana. Not from us, but from Kingsley and his associates."

Manny nodded slowly. "That's good. You find a way to push Stone out without leaving your fingerprints on it."

"But how do we make that happen in twenty hours?" Dakota demanded.

Karina's eyes lit up. "Wait a minute. If the Johnson twins are on the estate, Stone would know about it. He'd know where they're being kept."

A charged silence fell over the room as the obvious sank in.

Eli pushed off from the desk, pacing the small space.

"You're right. Stone could be our key to finding Aaliyah and Kiara. But if we spook him, he runs."

"We lose our best lead," Dakota finished.

Manny ambled to the coffee station. "So, not only do you need Stone to disappear, you must get information from him, then convince him to vanish. All without tipping off Kingsley or getting yourselves killed in the process."

Julia swiveled in her chair. "It's risky, but I think if Stone thinks Kingsley's out to kill him, then he'll be primed to get out of town. And who knows, if you play your cards right, you may be able to set up a quid pro quo to help him leave."

Eli nodded, considering. "It could work. But we'd be putting all our cards on the table. If Stone doesn't bite..." Eli looked around at his team, then back to Manny. "Alright, let's break this down step by step. We need to cover all our bases and have contingencies for every scenario. Manny, where do we start?"

"According to my contact at Baton Rouge Major Crimes," Manny said with a grim expression, "Stone spends his afternoons at a biker bar in Denham Springs..." He flipped through his notepad. "The Gator Pit."

32

Eli saw three potential threats as he parked his jeep in the Gator Pit parking lot—loud Harley motorcycles arriving, their riders staring at him and Dakota too long. Two thugs sharing a joint in the back of a rusty pickup truck. A shadowy figure pacing beside a crammed dumpster.

"Let's see what's rumbling inside," Dakota said with easygoing confidence as he opened the passenger door.

They stepped out into gusting wind and horizontal drizzle. Muffled laughter and country blues spilled out as a leather-clad couple stumbled through the double doors. Eli straightened his Oxford shirt. Out of place. Exposed.

Eli and Dakota entered a haze of cigarette smoke, stale air, and dim light from flickering beer signs.

Crack! Billiard balls scattered as Eli and Dakota passed. Conversations hushed. Eyes followed. Hank Williams lamented a cheating heart from an ancient jukebox.

There, Stone sat at the bar, laughing with a burly bartender in a stained white tank top clinging to broad shoulders, tattooed arm extended, pouring from a quart bottle.

Eli led Dakota through the smoky bar. Stone's laughter faded, and his eyes narrowed as they approached. With Dakota beside him, Eli sported an easy grin that suggested he felt right at home. He slapped a few bills onto the sticky surface. "Two drafts, and whatever he's having," he said, nodding at Stone.

Stone drained his glass and pushed it to the bartender.

Lightning lit up the windows. A deafening boom followed. The storm was nearly there. The bartender filled Stone's glass before sliding two frothy mugs to Eli and Dakota. Eli leaned closer to Stone and said, "We need to talk. About Kingsley."

Stone's lips pressed close together. He motioned to the bartender for the bottle, then grunted and slid off his stool. "Five minutes," he growled, nodding to a dark booth in the corner. As they settled into the cracked vinyl seats, the jukebox switched from Hank Williams to Johnny Lee Hooker.

"So what's this about Kingsley?" Stone said, filling his glass.

"Word is, he wants you to disappear," Dakota said. "Permanently."

Stone barked out a laugh. "Kingsley? Please. That silk-suited coward wouldn't dare."

"You really think he'd dirty his own hands?" Eli said, tightening his fingers around his beer mug. "C'mon Stone, you know better than that."

"I can take care of myself, no matter who he sends." Stone glared at Dakota with contempt.

"Maybe you won't have to," Eli said with a tight throat. "Maybe we can make your problem go away."

"The hell you say," Stone laughed loudly and slammed his fist on the table.

Heads turned their way. The pool game paused. Even the bartender stopped wiping glasses.

Had Eli pushed too far, too fast? He'd always prided himself on his ability to read people and navigate tense situations. But now, watching Stone's face darken with anger, he second-guessed every word he'd said. He was walking a tightrope now. But if Stone knew something about the girls...

Stone filled his glass again. "Why are a couple of pretty boys like you taking an interest in all of this?"

Dakota's face flushed an angry crimson. "Look, man, Kingsley wants you dead. Don't you get that?"

"Kingsley's all talk," Stone scoffed, swirling his drink. "He wouldn't dare come after me."

Dakota took a long pull on his beer. "No? It took us all of ten seconds to learn you'd be here."

"So?" Stone's fingers curled into fists on the table. "Why don't you tell me what you want? Why are you so anxious to save my skin?"

"Because we think you may have something we need," Eli said, forcing his shoulders to relax.

"Oh yeah?" Stone's fist slammed the table with a thud. "And what makes you think I'd give you anything?"

"We're looking for two girls," Eli said. "Sixteen-year-old twins. Kiara and Aaliyah Johnson."

"Well," Stone said, pouring himself another drink. "Even if I knew where these black girls were, I wouldn't tell you. So why don't you hit the bricks and leave me alone?"

Dakota leaned forward. "Who said they were black?"

Stone's drink froze halfway to his mouth. His eyes darted to the bar where three men had stopped watching the game on TV.

"You just proved you know exactly where they are," Eli said, keeping his voice low. "And you're going to tell us. You know, Kingsley paid us to make sure you go away."

"You threatening me, boy?"

"Not at all." Eli matched Stone's stare. "Kingsley is. We're offering you a way out."

A pool cue clattered against the floor. Boot heels scraped across wooden planks. The jukebox died mid-song, leaving only the growl of thunder.

"Last chance," Dakota said, his hand disappearing under his jacket. "Talk to us now, or talk to Kingsley's cleanup crew later."

Stone's face twisted. He jerked his chin toward the bar. The three men peeled away from the counter. The bruisers from the parking lot filed through the front door, blocking the exit.

"The only talking that's gonna happen," Stone said, standing, "is my friends explaining why you two shouldn't stick your noses where they don't belong."

Eli's pulse hammered against his eardrums. One hand reached for his weapon, the other grabbed Dakota's arm. They were surrounded. The information they needed was right here, trapped behind Stone's stupidity.

They were out of time. Out of options. The storm outside roared, rattling the windows as if nature itself was sounding a warning. At that moment, Eli knew— their next move would determine whether they walked out of Gator's Pit under their own power... or not at all.

"Alright, Stone," Eli said, his voice eerily calm. "We're leaving. But when Kingsley comes after you, don't say we didn't warn you."

Dakota hesitated for a second, then nodded. They stood

slowly, hands visible. The approaching men paused, their eyes darting between Stone and the two outsiders.

Eli and Dakota eased to the exit with hostile gazes tracking their every step. Thunder growled outside. And there it was—just as they backed through the doorway— raw panic flashed across Stone's expression. Not bravado. Not anger. Just pure, naked fear.

As they slipped outside into the storm, Eli was sure he'd see Stone again.

33

*T*hursday, August 15

Kiara's sneakers scuffed against the marble floor as she approached Vivian's office, her twin sister Aaliyah practically floating beside her. Three weeks at Kingsley Estate had widened the gulf between them—Aaliyah embracing their situation while Kiara's heart ached for Mom.

"Can you believe it, Ki? A real party." Aaliyah twirled. The light caught the pink in her floral summer dress. "I bet there'll be celebrities and everything. Maybe even that photographer from New York."

The excitement in Aaliyah's voice twisted Kiara's stomach. How had street-smart Aaliyah fallen for all this fantasy so easily? Mom's warnings about hustlers and pimps played in her mind—gifts, isolation, promises of money and fame. Every alarm had sounded.

"Let's just see what Vivian has to say." Kiara tugged at her plain t-shirt, the soft cotton revolting against Vivian's endless attempts to remake her.

Vivian's driver's grip tightened on Kiara's arm as they

approached the glossy white double doors. His knuckles rapped twice like a judge's gavel on a Law and Order episode.

"Enter," Vivian said.

The office stole Kiara's breath, no matter how many times she saw it. Sunlight poured through towering windows, highlighting museum-like art and a butterfly-in-a-glass display that always drew her eye. Beautiful. Trapped. Dead.

Vivian sat behind her massive desk in a yellow blazer, her smile pained in place as she peered over an open file. "Come in, dears." Her mascaraed eyes never left the paperwork.

Kiara hung back while Aaliyah swept into the room like she belonged there, perching eagerly on one of the leather chairs. The jade pendant beneath Kiara's shirt pressed against her chest—Mom's graduation gift, a reminder of home. A reminder of who she really was.

"Ms. Delacroix, thank you so much for inviting us," Aaliyah gushed, smoothing her dress. "We're so excited!"

"Please, have a seat." Vivian finally looked up, her sharp gaze landing on Kiara. Irritation washed over her perfect features. "Must you continue to wear those rags? Look how lovely your sister looks."

A sudden warmth flushed Kiara's cheeks. The designer clothes they'd been given weren't gifts—they were chains, each one adding to a debt they'd never agreed to. She remained standing, arms crossed.

Vivian pushed the file aside with manicured fingers. "I've selected you both for a special event this weekend." Her smile widened. "It's quite the opportunity and a chance for some of you to get in my better graces."

"I knew it!" Aaliyah clapped her hands together. "Is it a fashion show? A photoshoot?"

The familiar spark in Aaliyah's eyes—the one that had gotten them into this mess—made Kiara's chest ache. For a fleeting second, the allure tugged at her too. "What kind of event?" Kiara said, trying to keep her voice steady.

Vivian's eyes glinted as they locked onto Kiara. "Why, it's your debut, of course. The chance to show everyone just how special you both are."

The words drifted to Kiara like irritating smoke. Aaliyah leaned forward, bubbling with excitement. Kiara's spine stiffened. Three weeks of overheard whispers, of seeing girls disappear after similar "opportunities," of watching her sister slip further into Vivian's web—it all crystallized into certainty. This wasn't an opportunity. It was a trap.

"This party will allow you to meet some very influential people," Vivian said, steepling her fingers. "Contacts who could help launch your careers."

"Really? Actual modeling agents?" Aaliyah's voice lifted like a child's on Christmas morning.

Kiara's skin burned angry hot. The way Vivian's lips curved reminded her of a snake, mesmerizing its prey in a nature documentary.

"And photographers," Vivian said. "People who can make you stars." She pulled out an iPad and scrolled through photos. "Look at these models from our last event. See how far they've come?"

Kiara's hands grew slick with sweat as she glimpsed the images. Beautiful girls in stunning outfits, but their eyes... empty. Hollow.

"Oh my god, Ki, look at those dresses!" Aaliyah gasped. "Is that Versace?"

"Indeed." Vivian's smile widened. "We spare no expense

for our models. Speaking of which..." Her gaze sliced toward Kiara. "We'll need to discuss your... wardrobe situation before Saturday."

Stay together. Protect her. The words pounded in Kiara's head.

"I'll do it!" Aaliyah bounced in her seat. "When do we start?"

"Excellent choice, dear." Vivian turned to Kiara, eyes hardening slightly. "And you?"

The silver cross pendant felt heavy against Kiara's chest. One of them had to be clear-headed. One of them had to be free, to fight, to find help, to reach Mom.

"I need time to think about it," Kiara said firmly.

Vivian's smile vanished. "Time? After everything I've done for you?" She stood, circling the desk like a shark. "Your sister understands gratitude. Why must you always be so... difficult?"

"Ki, don't ruin this." Aaliyah's words were more penetrating than Vivian's glare. "For once in your life, stop trying to take control."

Vivian's hands settled on Kiara's shoulders, heavy as chains. "Listen to Aaliyah, dear. You wouldn't want to jeopardize her opportunity, would you? To be... separated?"

The threat slithered to Kiara's ears. Her fingers found her cross, warming its silver. Mom's voice grew stronger—sometimes love means being the only one to say no.

"The car arrives at eight," Vivian said. "I assume you'll need help selecting something... appropriate?"

"Please, Ki." Aaliyah pleaded. "We could be famous. Together."

For a moment, Kiara's resolve wavered, a crack in the armor she had so carefully built. Then she drew a steady breath, squared her shoulders, and lifted her chin. "No."

The word was soft, but it carried the weight of unshakable determination.

Vivian's nails dug through Kiara's t-shirt. "What did you say?"

Kiara rolled her shoulder. "I said no. I won't be attending your party."

"You ungrateful little—" Vivian caught herself, smoothing her features. "Aaliyah, dear. Go wait outside while I speak with your sister."

"Fine by me." Aaliyah stood, shoulders stiff. "I'm tired of her ruining everything anyway."

The door clicked shut behind Aaliyah. Something shifted in Vivian's eyes—all pretense vanishing like smoke. "You think you're clever?" her voice dropped to a dangerous whisper. "You think refusing will save you?" She picked up the receiver on her desk phone. "You have no idea what you've just done."

Kiara lifted her chin, channeling every ounce of her mother's strength. "I know exactly what I'm doing."

The door opened. Before she could turn, rough hands gripped her arms.

"Take her to The Shadows," Vivian ordered. "Perhaps some time there will help her understand the opportunity she's throwing away."

As they dragged her toward the back door, Kiara's eyes caught on the butterfly trapped in its glass case one last time. But she wasn't like that fragile thing—she wouldn't be pinned, wouldn't be caged, and she surely wouldn't exist for someone else's pleasure.

As the door to "The Shadows" loomed, cold dread coiled around her heart—but determination burned hotter. She must remain true to her virtue.

34

Gabriel stuffed his few possessions into a pillowcase. Better to risk an escape than wait for Vivian's revenge. A sharp rap at his door froze him. He tensed. Had Vivian dispatched someone to fetch him? Approaching the door, he tread lightly on the creaky floorboards.

"Open up, Gabriel. It's Evens."

The Haitian's voice eased Gabriel's grip on the pillowcase. He unlatched the door to find Evens, arms crossed, clothes dark with dampness. Droplets gleamed in his hair like tiny diamonds. "May I come in?" he asked, glancing over Gabriel's shoulder.

Gabriel stepped aside, allowing Evens to brush past. The smell of wet earth and night air accompanied him, filling the room with a fresh, raw intensity.

"So," he said, turning to face Gabriel. "You stood your ground with Vivian."

Gabriel's jaw dropped. "How did you know?"

"I see more than most around here," Evens said. "And I've watched how she tests the new ones she brings in."

"I... I couldn't do what she wanted."

"You did good, ti frè. But..." He shook his head.

"But what?" Gabriel's voice snapped. Thunder rumbled outside as if punctuating his question.

"Vivian's game runs deeper than you know. She cultivates loyalty through different means."

"What do you mean? I stood up to her."

"I know, I know," Evens said, raising a hand. "And that's brave. But you're not the first to resist her advances."

"You sound like you know from experience."

Evens's expression softened for a moment. "There was a girl back in Haiti. Fabienne." His voice, usually so controlled, now carried an edge of raw pain. "We shared a tent in the refugee camp after the earthquake. She kept my spirits up, always singing those old Creole hymns her grandmother taught her." His fingers traced invisible patterns on the windowsill. "When Vivian found us, she promised us a good life in Louisiana. An education for us both."

Thunder rattled the windows. Evens continued. "The first few weeks here seemed like a dream. Clean clothes, real beds, hot meals. Fabienne and I worked the grounds together, still singing those hymns." His jaw tightened. "Then Kingsley hosted one of his special parties. Vivian dressed Fabienne up like a doll and drugged her with a glass of champagne. Three days later, they found her in a guest cabin. The official story was an overdose." Evens pulled a small silver cross from his pocket—tarnished, hanging on a frayed string. "This was all they let me keep. Her grandmother's cross." His fingers closed around it. "I tried to run afterward. Made it as far as Baton Rouge." He tucked the cross away. "I spent a month in The Shadows learning my lesson. That's when I understood—the only way to fight them is from the inside. Patient. Careful. Like catching crabs —slow steps. One at a time."

The chill from the rain seeped into Gabriel's bones. "The detention building?"

"The Shadows. You've heard about it?"

"I've saw it on my first day while mowing the back section." Gabriel straightened. "Why are you coming to me now?"

"Because you did something rare tonight. You showed courage." Evens tapped his temple. "But courage without wisdom? That's just another way to die here."

Thunder cracked, vibrating through the floorboards and up Gabriel's legs. "What exactly are you proposing?"

"A partnership. To save the ones who can't save themselves."

"The children you mentioned?" Eli asked.

"Yes." Evens moved to the window, keeping his voice low. "This estate, it's more than just Vivian's playground. It's a waypoint. Kids from Haiti, Honduras—" he glanced meaningfully at Gabriel "—even the locals. They come through here, disappearing into private planes and expensive cars."

"How do you know all this?"

"Three years watching. Learning. Understanding who answers to whom." Evens turned back to Gabriel. "You think Vivian's at the top? No, no... she's just another piece on the board."

"And Kingsley?"

"Higher than that. Politicians. Judges. People who can make problems vanish with a phone call."

"Then why risk telling me?" Gabriel studied Evens' face for any trace of deception. "How do you know I won't go straight to Vivian?"

A slight smile touched Evens' lips. "Because I've watched

you too, ti frè. The way you treat the grounds crew. How you question things others ignore. You still have a conscience. Like I used to."

"Used to?"

"Had to bury it. To survive. To learn their secrets." Evens stepped closer. "But tonight, seeing you stand up to Vivian… it reminded me of who I was. Who I need to be again."

"What exactly would this partnership involve?" Gabriel kept his voice even despite his racing heart.

"Your position as estate manager gives you access, freedom to move about without suspicion." Crossing his arms, Evens leaned against the wall. "I have the knowledge —schedules, contacts, where the evidence is hidden. Together we have a chance."

"What if we make a mistake?"

"We die." Evens' bluntness sent a chill through the room. "Or wish we had."

Lightning flashed, illuminating Evens' face. In that moment, Gabriel saw something he recognized—the same haunted look he'd seen in his father's eyes when discussing their family's future.

"We'd need to be patient," Evens said. "Plan every move, calculate every risk, and be careful moving forward." He straightened. "I won't blame you if you say no. But know this—whatever you decide, this conversation never happened."

Gabriel moved to the window, watching rain slash against the glass. The storm outside matched the turbulence in his mind. Every warning his father had given him about trust screamed for caution. Yet something in Evens' words rang true—a chance to fight back, to protect others from suffering.

"I need to know," Gabriel turned back to Evens. "Why

not attempt an escape? There must be some way out of here."

"You think I haven't tried?" Evens' eyes met his. "The security, the connections they have—there's no way. Not really. They'd find us." He shook his head. "But we can destroy what they've built. From the inside, where they least expect it."

Thunder rolled across the sky as Gabriel made his decision. "How?"

"We wait. Vivian is busy planning a party for Kingsley's political contacts. And then there's the weekly orgy near New Orleans."

"Orgy?"

"Where he drugs little girls and boys and puts them in the arms of powerful men and women." Evens moved to the door, then paused before leaving. "Don't do anything for now, ti fri. I'll come get you when there's an opportunity, which should be soon."

As he slipped out into the dark hallway, Gabriel turned to the half-packed pillowcase on his bed. Ten minutes ago, he'd planned an escape. Now he was preparing to go to war.

35

F*riday, August 16*

Tap, tap, tap. Gabriel pulled the pillow over his head to avoid the annoying sound in his bedroom.

Tap, tap, tap. The rapping at the door was faint at first, almost polite, but then grew into an insistent repetition.

Gabriel's eyes fluttered open, his mind still foggy with sleep.

Tap-tap-tap-tap-tap! The knocking crescendoed into a desperate demand. The digital clock's red numbers glared 2:12 AM on the nightstand.

Gabriel bolted upright. The rain that had lulled him to sleep earlier had finally stopped. He swung his legs over the bed's edge, bare feet meeting the cool wood floor. The floorboards creaked and groaned beneath him, as if sharing in his irritation.

"Gabriel!" An urgent whisper broke through the wooden door. "Gabriel, wake up!" It was Evens.

Gabriel's fingers fumbled with the lock before it yielded with a resolute click.

Standing in the doorway, Evens's eyes were wide and

wild. "Get dressed," he hissed like a gust of wind. "There's something you must see at The Shadows."

"Can't it wait until morning?" Gabriel yawned.

"Now, Gabriel. Now."

The recent rain's scent swirled into the room, bringing with it a sense of foreboding. Gabriel pulled on his rubber boots. What could be happening in these dark pre-dawn hours?

His boots sank into the sodden earth as he followed Evens beneath a gray sky. The night air clung to his bare arms like a damp towel. Crickets hushed as they passed, as if sensing some danger.

"Evens," Gabriel said, his voice just above the sucking sounds of their footsteps. "What's going on?"

Pressing a finger to his lips, Evens jerked his head toward the concrete building looming ahead. As they drew closer, Gabriel's feet froze in a puddle. Something was off. Wrong. Inexplicable. The Shadows, typically silent and still, now pulsed with an unsettling energy.

"We need to get closer," Evens whispered. "There's an opportunity here."

Get closer? Gabriel could turn back and retreat to the safety of his room. He could pretend this night never happened, living in blissful ignorance of whatever dark deeds were unfolding, and get about the work of being estate manager.

But what would stop Vivian from her seductions or worse? Then there was something deeper he couldn't shake —a sense of responsibility suddenly pulling him toward The Shadows.

Evens's grip tightened on his arm. "We need to move. We don't have much time."

The sounds from the stable grew louder—a muffled cry,

the slam of a car door. Gabriel filled his lungs with damp air and crept forward, low and hugging a line of lush shrubs.

A massive truck idled near The Shadows' entrance, its headlights cutting through the mist. Gabriel's throat ached at the sight of Freddy stumbling around the vehicle's rear, movements jerky and unpredictable. The man who'd purchased Gabriel from his brothers now looked more demon than human in the harsh security lights.

"Get down," Evens said softly, pulling Gabriel behind a row of ligustrums.

Andre Badeau emerged from the building, neat and pristine despite the hour. He grabbed Freddy's clipboard with barely contained disgust. "Get yourself together," Badeau snapped. "These are valuable assets, not your playground toys."

The back doors of the truck groaned open. Children spilled out—small, frightened faces that mirrored Gabriel's emotions from his first night on Freddy's boat. A boy, maybe twelve, stumbled down the ramp, blinking. Freddy shoved him forward.

"Careful!" Badeau's voice snapped like a whip as he motioned to two guards. "Get him away from those kids. I'll handle the processing."

Gabriel's nails bit into his palms. *Kid.* That's all he'd been when Freddy smuggled him out of Honduras. But not anymore. Being hauled over sea and land like a lifeless object had aged him far beyond his years. And now Freddy was here again—stealing children, shattering innocence.

At the end of the line, a tiny girl's voice broke through the chaos. "Mama!" she cried, her Honduran accent hitting Gabriel like a blunt instrument. His chest tightened. How many more children would be ripped from his homeland?

How many more parents would grieve, like his papa surely did?

"We have to save them." Gabriel started to rise, but Evens' grip turned to iron.

"They'll kill you," Evens hissed. "Then who will help set these kids free?"

Badeau directed the children into The Shadows, marking his list as they passed. Each check with his pen was another life cataloged, another soul processed into Kingsley's machinery of suffering.

"That's forty-three." Badeau's announcement carried over the wet grass. "Get them settled. Freddy, sober up. You're useless like this."

Freddy's high-pitched giggle cut off in a snarl. "Why don't you get off my back, Uncle Andre? You wouldn't have one kid going into that building if it weren't for me."

"Shut up." Badeau's face was a mask of rage. "Before I have to tell my sister you had a bad accident."

The last child was hauled into The Shadows. Gabriel's chest burned with helpless anger. He'd escaped whatever fate awaited these children, but at what cost? His position at the estate suddenly felt like thirty pieces of silver—comfort bought at the expense of others' suffering.

Oh God, what have I become part of?

Evens' hand clutched Gabriel's shoulder. "We need to move." His gaze surveyed the grounds behind them.

Gabriel watched the taillights of the tractor-trailer as it disappeared through the rear gate. "What can we do? We can't just—"

"Listen carefully," Evens cut him off urgently. "We're going to get that checklist from Kingsley's office. Then we're going to send it to the State Police."

"How are we going to get that list?" Gabriel asked.

"You're going to steal it."

———

TWENTY MINUTES LATER, as Gabriel eased himself into his chair, wincing at every creak while he worked off his muddy boots, Evens darted between the window and the door, shoulders tight with nervous energy. They couldn't risk even a lamp—not with the main building's floodlight washing the grounds in accusatory brightness.

Evens finally settled into the faded brown chair across from Gabriel. "Alright, here's my plan. Tomorrow night, Kingsley is throwing a party for influential political and business leaders across the state. He and Vivian will be busy for at least four or five hours. It would be a perfect time for you to get inside his office."

Gabriel tensed his shoulders as if bracing for an impact. "Why?"

Evens produced a device from his pant pocket. "To attach this USB extender to Kingsley's computer while everyone is distracted at the party."

"And this does what?" Gabriel reached for it.

"Gives me access."

"Access to what?"

Standing, Evens ambled to the door and pressed his ear to it. "To Kingsley's computer and everything that will link his organization to human trafficking."

"Don't you need a cell phone or another computer to capture the data?"

"I have one." Evens pointed to Gabriel's laptop on the desk.

"You can't access anything outside its hard drive. Believe me, I've tried."

"Yes, I know," Evens said, opening the notebook. "It has surf blocker software. I can get past that."

"How?"

"I'm a computer geek," Evens said, his lips twisting into a humorless grin. "Kingsley and his goons? They see a dumb Haitian kid. Makes it easier to fly under their radar."

Gabriel drummed his fingers on his knee. "So, how will I get into Kingsley's computer? He must have some complex security measures."

"You'd think," Evens chuckled. "All he has is a password, and here it is." He pulled a sticky note from his shirt pocket. "I've been here so long it's like I'm part of the furniture. I got this yesterday, but he changes it every Saturday. So if we're going to do this, we need to do it tomorrow night."

Gabriel's heart thudded, and his gaze drifted to the window, to that mysterious building he'd glimpsed on his first day. The image of children being unloaded earlier still burned in his brain.

"After the party goes into full swing, everyone will be focused on the festivities." Evens leaned forward, his voice hardening. "Look, we're running out of time. Kingsley's changing his passwords, and there's a new shipment coming."

The thought of more children brought bile up from Eli's gut. More children, like those he'd watched disappear into The Shadows.

"But what if I'm caught?" Gabriel's legs wouldn't stay still. His heart hammered so hard it hurt.

"You're the estate manager," Evens said, his tone maddeningly calm. "It's your job to ensure that pending work gets done on time."

"During a party?"

"You're dedicated. Eager to impress. Tell them you're

leaving a contract you've prepared for Kingsley to review. Simple."

Evens' calm tone grated against Gabriel's nerves. "Nothing's *simple* here. You won't be the one inside Kingsley's office." He choked on the words, remembering those small figures being herded into The Shadows. "Why aren't you doing this yourself?"

"Because I have to ensure the data is transferring. A lot can happen between the two points during the transfer. I need to be at the receiving end to troubleshoot any surprise problems."

Gabriel couldn't question Evens. He knew nothing about data points and transferring information. But his heart rate soared regardless, as if that mysterious shed were closing in around him. He squeezed his eyes shut, trying to block out the voices in his head. When he opened them again, Evens was standing, his gaze unwavering.

"You sure this will work?" Gabriel's voice was almost foreign to his ears.

Evens nodded once, slowly.

Gabriel rubbed the USB extender with his thumb. Such a small item to risk his freedom. But those children's faces— scared, confused, disappearing into The Shadows. He could walk away, keep his head down, and pretend he hadn't seen anything. But God had placed him here, given him this position, this opportunity. To refuse Evens now would be to turn his back on God's purpose. To ignore everything his father had taught him.

He closed his fist around the device. "Tell me exactly what I need to do."

36

Saturday, August 17

Wired on coffee, Eli squinted at his laptop in the shelter of his Airstream. Rain peppered the aluminum roof, a ceaseless barrage that matched the pounding in his temples. He blinked hard, trying to focus on Google's satellite images of Kingsley's compound. *Rats.* Something about the site nagged at him, a detail he couldn't quite pin down.

His eyes returned to a small structure set apart from the main buildings, partially obscured by trees. It didn't appear on any official property records he'd seen. What was Kingsley hiding there?

A gust of wind rocked the trailer. Metal groaned in protest. Eli's gaze snapped to the window. Night had swallowed everything beyond the glass, leaving only darkness and the relentless rain. His computer told him it was 11:37 PM.

"You planning on getting any sleep tonight?" Lindsey said, concern mixed with her gentle teasing.

Eli glanced back to the screen. "In a minute," he muttered, zooming in on the secondary structure. "I need to go over these images one more time."

The TV mumbled over the storm—a meteorologist's voice rose above the din—"...tropical storm Fiona has intensified. There's a possibility it could strengthen into a hurricane before making landfall in Galveston..."

She reached for the remote, turning up the volume slightly. "Looks like this weather isn't letting up anytime soon," she said.

He nodded absently, his focus locked on the mysterious building. *Could the twins be in there?* "The storm might work in our favor," he said, thinking aloud. "Keep people inside, fewer eyes on us." *Or it could complicate things. Bad weather has a way of throwing a wrench in the best-laid plans.*

Eli looked up, meeting his wife's gaze. The concern in her eyes was unmistakable, mirroring the unease churning in his gut. They'd been at this for days now, chasing leads from Mobile to Baton Rouge to New Orleans to Kingsley's estate. But something about this storm, these images, felt different. Were they on the cusp of a breakthrough?

Or a breakdown.

He suppressed a shiver that had nothing to do with the temperature. Whatever came next, he sensed it would change everything.

Rubbing his eyes to relieve the tension, Eli zoomed in on the hidden structure again. Dang it, Stone, if only you'd talked. "There's something off about this building, Lindsey. It's not on any permit requests or tax assessments."

Lindsey stepped to look over Eli's shoulder. "Could be nothing. Rich people love their secret wine cellars and panic rooms."

"Kingsley's not exactly the panicking type," Eli said humorlessly.

"No, he's not," she agreed somberly. "More likely to cause panic in others."

"If the twins are in there—"

"That's a big 'if,'" Lindsey said. "We can't afford to make assumptions with someone as powerful as Kingsley."

Swiveling his chair to face her, he noted the worry lines around her eyes. "What's your gut telling you?"

She ruffled her hair with her fingers. "My gut? It's screaming that we're in over our heads. Kingsley's not just some small-time crook. He's got powerful connections. If we're wrong about this?"

"And if we're right?" Eli countered. "If those girls are there, suffering, waiting to be found?"

"Then we do everything we can. But we must know they're there before we storm Kingsley's castle. Otherwise, it's an unnecessary risk."

"When have I ever taken unnecessary risks?"

Lindsey arched an eyebrow. "Do you want that list alphabetically or chronologically?"

Her humor alleviated the night's tension, but as it faded, the gravity of their situation settled back in. "I know you're worried," Eli said softly, reaching to take her hand. "But I can't get those girls out of my mind. If you had seen the look on their mother's face."

She squeezed his hand. "I'm not saying back down. But know what's in there before you go in. You can't help if you're caught... or worse."

The growl of a Harley engine cut through the storm's din, growing louder by the second. Instinctively, Eli opened his desk drawer and reached for his weapon.

"You expecting company?" Lindsey said as she peeked out the window.

Eli rose with his Glock and eased to the door. "Stay here."

Rain lashed at his face as he stepped outside, the wind threatening to tear the door from his grip. The Harley's headlight sliced through the darkness, the downpour slanting in sheets across its beam. Eli squinted against the glare, his shirt already soaked through.

The rider's face was obscured by a black helmet. He extended a gloved hand, protecting a folded piece of paper. Eli hesitated before taking it. Without a word, the rider gunned the engine and sped back into the storm.

He unfolded the paper with wet hands, but the message was blurry, close to unreadable. Cursing under his breath, he ducked inside.

"What is it?" Lindsey said breathlessly, waiting at the door.

Eli smoothed out the paper on the table. "It's from Stone." He read as the water dripped from his hair onto the message. "He wants to meet—tonight."

"Tonight?" Her brow arched in surprise. "In this weather? At this hour?"

"Says here there's an old boathouse off of Old Highway 22."

Lindsey set her jaw in restrained anger. "Why does he want a meeting now?" She paused, the muscles in her neck taut as bowstrings. "And how did he even know where to find you?"

"The press from the Mexican operation, maybe?" he said with little certainty. "We weren't exactly low profile."

"That was months ago," she countered. "And this isn't a listed address."

"And we're not a safe house for the CIA." But Eli felt the weakness of his argument.

"Or someone's been watching us," Lindsey said, crossing her arms. "Following us."

"All the more reason to meet Stone." Eli stepped inside the bedroom to put on rain gear. "Learn what he knows."

"Or walk right into whatever trap he's planned. Stone made it clear he wants nothing to do with you."

Eli paused as he searched for his car fob. "People change their minds."

"And sometimes they set up ambushes," Lindsey shot back.

"This could be a chance to discover what's in that building. Or better, where we can find Aaliyah and Kiara."

Lindsey's shoulders sagged a fraction. "And what if you end up at the bottom of the bayou?"

Eli grabbed his rucksack. "I'll be careful."

"You always say that," Lindsey said, not meeting his gaze.

Eli's hand dropped to his side. "I have to go," he said, straining his voice over the rain.

"At least call Dakota to go with you."

"Not enough time. He went to New Orleans with Karina and her family to shop for Sofia's school clothes and got caught in this storm. They're having to spend the night."

"I don't like it," Karina frowned. "You going alone."

"I know you don't," Eli said. "Just remember what we're risking here. Girl's lives."

Eli's hand hesitated on the cool doorknob before he twisted it open. Stepping outside, he was immediately hit by the storm's fury. The wind-driven rain pelted against his slicker and stung his face, but it was Lindsey's unspoken fear that hurt him even more. The door clicked shut behind him, echoing with the finality of a judge's gavel.

Eli squinted into the darkness, the path to his Jeep as murky as the choice he'd just made.

The storm raged harder. He cranked the engine. Stone made it clear in The Gator Pit that he didn't fear Kingsley.

So why did he want to talk now?

37

Sunday, August 18

Ten minutes past midnight, three motorcycles glistened in Eli's high beams as he pulled off the road where Stone said they'd meet. Rain poured over his windshield, the wipers struggling against the deluge. A flash of lightning lit up the Tchefuncte River, illuminating the old boathouse where his only lead to the Johnson twins waited.

He parked his Jeep behind a line of trees and killed the engine.

The structure's soaked weatherboards had a silver-gray tint, warped and cracked from years of exposure. A faint yellow glow leaked from a dirty window.

Eli stepped out of the truck, the weight of his Glock in the small of his back offering a slight sense of security. Rain tapped against his slicker. Mud squelched beneath his boots. His heart rate exploded as he approached the old camp.

This is it. No turning back now.

The door suddenly opened. Stone stood in the entrance with a thuggish man behind each shoulder.

"Get in here," Stone said, his eyes darting past Eli into the darkness. "Before someone sees you."

Eli stepped inside, hyper-aware of the two burly figures with Stone. The door shut with a dull thud, sealing him in to his fate. A solitary bulb swayed slightly from the ceiling, stretching long, uneven shadows across the room. The smells of wet leather and cigarette smoke dominated.

Eli clenched his hand, fighting the impulse to grab his weapon. Four against one—not the best odds if this meeting goes sideways.

"Alright, Stone. I'm here," Eli said with a level tone. "Why'd you call me out here at this hour? And just to be clear, my entire team knows where I am."

Stone's weathered face twisted into an indifferent grimace. He gestured to a rickety table in the corner. "Sit."

Eli cataloged his surroundings. Two exits—the door he'd entered and one in the back. Windows—too small to fit through quickly.

The three men spread out, effectively boxing him in.

Stone lit a cigarette as the two men sat, the flare of the match briefly illuminating his tense face. "So you want to know about these two girls—Aaliyah and Kiara?"

Eli leaned forward, his curiosity raging. "So you do know something? Why not just tell me at the bar?"

Stone narrowed his eyes. "Because speaking in public could get you killed. Kingsley has spies everywhere."

Eli leaned back, studying Stone's face. "So, where are they?"

"First, I want out," Stone said, stubbing out his cigarette. "I need guarantees for me and my brothers."

"If your information pans out, I can make that happen. What can you tell me?"

"Not yet," Stone said, shifting his gaze between his men and Eli. "First, you get me federal protection."

"You know I can't promise that."

"Can't you?" Stone said. "I read you're real chummy with the FBI after that stunt you pulled down in Juarez."

"That was a one-off operation," Eli said. "The agent I worked with is retired."

"Marcus Blackwell. I know," Stone said, flicking an ash on the bare wood floor. "He now runs an influential security firm, right? Serves government agencies, huge corporations, and very rich individuals—like Kingsley, yeah?"

"So," Eli shrugged. "What does that have to do with me?"

"It means you and your high-octane sidekick have allies in your fight for truth, justice, and the American way."

"I'm not sure I know where you're going with this," Eli said.

"Where I'm going is, I want you to get me immunity for all related crimes and relocate me to a remote island where my friends and I are sipping Mai Tais on a faraway beach. And identities that ensure Kingsley and his cohorts can't find us."

"Hold on," Eli said. "What makes you think I can pull that off? I'm not part of the government."

"You're not without resources either." Stone made a show of dropping his cigarette and grinding it into the floorboard with his boot. "That's my deal, take it or leave it."

Eli tilted back in his chair, lifting its front legs, weighing the risks. Promising Stone protection without official backing was dangerous, but the potential lead was too valuable to pass up. But could he persuade Blackwell to assist him with Stone's demands? "Alright," he said, scratching his cheek. "I'll go to Blackwell to see if he can get the FBI to relocate you. Now, what do you know?"

"The twins are at Kingsley's place. One dresses up to take pictures with influential people." Stone lit another cigarette, its smoke curling up to the ceiling. "The other's a bit of a problem child. She's confined to The Shadows."

"What is *The Shadows*?"

"A detention facility on the compound for those who don't do as they're told."

"Why is she there?"

Stone's expression soured, as if the question were stupid. "Because she won't dress up and rub up against Kingsley's influential minions."

Eli's heart pounded with anger and excitement—at least now, he had a solid lead. "And Kingsley?"

"Kingsley's the man with the money and power," Stone spat. "But it's that Delacroix broad you gotta watch. She's the real—"

A sudden sound of tires splashing through flooded potholes cut through the drumming rain. Headlights swept across the windows, briefly illuminating the room.

Stone cursed, stubbing his cigarette out on the table. His three companions tensed, hands moving inside their leather jackets. "You bring backup, Colt?"

"No," Eli said, fighting to remain calm. "You?"

With fear in his eyes, Stone shook his head. "Then we got trouble. Big trouble."

The room fell silent as footsteps sloshed outside. Eli realized he was trapped between Stone's crew and an unknown threat.

The footsteps grew louder, accompanied by determined voices. Stone and his men drew their weapons. All eyes were fixed on the door.

Stone's intel about Kingsley and Delacroix and the detention facility was helpful. But he needed more.

Stay or go?

The muffled sound of boots on the wooden porch decided for him.

The door handle jiggled. "Break it down," someone shouted from outside.

Eli bolted for the back door as heavy footsteps thundered behind him. The front door burst open with a deafening crash. He raced through the back door, the rain lashing against his face like icy needles. He plunged into the darkness, adrenaline surging through him as he fought to put distance between himself and the chaos inside.

Staccato gunfire raged behind him—automatic weapons mixed with Stone and his men's handguns. He dove behind a fallen oak, heart hammering against his ribs.

"Where's the guy from the Airstream?" a voice carried through the rain.

"He's not here," came the answer.

Eli dashed away from the chaos, the echo of gunfire mingling with the shouts of men caught in the firestorm. An ear-splitting explosion shattered the night. Flames erupted from the old boathouse, casting jagged shadows across the clearing and painting the sky in a fiery glow.

Stumbling, Eli shielded his eyes from the searing light as debris rained down. A shockwave knocked him sideways, and he clung to the rough bark of a fallen oak to steady himself. His breath came in ragged gasps, the acrid tang of smoke burning his throat.

Through the billowing smoke, a figure emerged from the wreckage. A blonde-haired operator staggered toward the row of Suburbans, his tactical uniform torn and bloodied. His left hand clutched his thigh, where blood seeped through the fabric, and his eyes held a hollow, haunted look. Heavy dread settled in Eli's stomach.

This wasn't over—not yet. Heart pounding, Eli slipped into his Jeep, started the engine, and sped toward home—toward his wife—driven by a a single concern. Get home to Lindsey.

38

Gabriel's fingers trembled on the doorknob to Kingsley's office. Drunken laughter echoed from the ballroom as his party raged on in the early morning hours.

No going back. No room for error. No second chances.

One wrong move, one creaking floorboard, and he could find himself confined in The Shadows.

He gently pushed the door open, slipped inside, and closed it behind him. Darkness surrounded him, pierced only by slivers of moonlight filtering through the tilted wooden shutters. The room smelled of cigars and brandy.

Time was slipping. Fear was mounting. His palms were sweating profusely. Fumbling in his pocket, he clutched the cold plastic of the USB extender. Each step was like a mile as he approached the massive desk.

Ten minutes to secure evidence. Ten minutes to save lives. Ten minutes to escape and get back to his quarters.

He opened the laptop. The Apple logo splashed across the monitor with a hum then disappeared, replaced by the login screen. Gabriel's fingers hovered, doubt creeping in.

What if Evens' information was wrong? Taking a deep breath, he typed in the password. A moment's pause. Then the desktop appeared. Bingo.

Reading each file name with his heart in his throat, he stopped at one titled "Bills of Lading." Next, down to yesterday's date and a receipt of livestock feed to the Kingsley Estate. Was this what he needed? He inserted the drive. The progress bar crawled.

Five percent. Ten percent. Fifteen.

The mouse felt slippery in his hand, sweat pooling in his palm as he clenched it tighter. The wood floors creaked outside in the hallway. Gabriel froze. The squeaking grew louder. Closer. Someone was coming. A shadow moved across the sliver of light beneath the door. The doorknob rattled.

Hide? Run? Explain?

A muffled voice spoke—Vivian's sultry tone, followed by a man's deep chuckle. The shadow disappeared. The footsteps receded. Gabriel released a shaky breath he didn't realize he'd been holding. He glanced back at the screen. Twenty percent. Twenty-five. Thirty.

The download crawled on, each second an eternity.

Outside, the party continued. But Gabriel's world had shrunk to this room, this moment, this desperate gamble to stop Kingsley's trafficking crimes. Suddenly, a pop-up window appeared on the monitor— "Critical system update required. Estimated time: 7 minutes."

Update now?

Another seven minutes? That would put him closer to twenty. Forcing the download could corrupt the files. But waiting meant risking discovery. Ignore the update? Finish the download? The progress bar crept across the screen— Thirty-five percent. Thirty-six. Thirty-seven.

Another pop-up—"Warning: System vulnerable. Update strongly recommended."

With his pulse thumping in his neck and his temples, Gabriel struggled to choose the quickest option—update or not.

Thirty-eight percent. Thirty-nine. Forty.

The progress bar slowed to a trickle. A burst of laughter from the party had him flinch. How long before someone came inside?

Sweat trickled down his forehead. He sifted his focus between the door and the computer, every second stretching unbearably.

Forty percent. Forty-one.

A new pop-up—"Update will begin automatically in 60 seconds."

Would that slow the process? Would stopping it slow it more?

Forty-two percent. Forty-three.

A countdown began—30 seconds. 20 seconds. 10 seconds.

His hand shook as he moved the mouse over the cancel button. The download had to finish first. It had to. Five seconds. Four. Three...

The progress bar inched forward. Forty-five percent. Forty-six. Voices from the hallway got louder and closer. "—can't believe you allowed it to happen here, on the property." Kingsley's voice was sharp with anger. Shadows emerged beneath the door.

"That was Ms. Delacroix, sir." A man's voice, unfamiliar and nervous.

Wiping his brow, Gabriel glanced at the computer screen. Forty-seven percent. Not even halfway.

"It better not," Kingsley growled. "If word gets out—"

Gabriel fought to steady his breathing. What was that conversation about?

He crept to the door, each step careful on the wooden floor. The voices became clearer.

"Three more shipments will be arriving next week, sir."

"I'll talk to Vivian," Kingsley said. "But make sure they don't come on this property."

Gabriel leaned closer, his ear brushing against the cool wood surface.

"And Stone?" Kingsley asked.

"Taken care of, sir. He won't be a problem anymore."

The computer dinged softly. Gabriel whirled around with elation. "Download complete," the screen flashed.

Thank goodness.

Gabriel stood to grab the file.

The doorknob clicked.

He froze. There was nowhere to hide, no chance to run. The door creaked open, and Vivian Delacroix stepped inside, her long red dress flowing like liquid silk, pooling elegantly around her heels. Her expression remained unreadable as her eyes landed on Gabriel, caught in the act of yanking the flash drive from Kingsley's computer.

For one endless heartbeat, the world seemed to hold its breath. Gabriel's hand hovered in the air, the drive clutched in his trembling fingers. Then, Vivian's crimson lips twisted into a slow, calculated smile—one that sent an icy dread plunging into the pit of his stomach.

Then Gabriel saw it. Around her neck. The silver necklace Evens had showed him when they'd planned this theft.

"Well, well," she blustered. "Looks like someone has his hand in the cookie jar."

"What do we have here?" Her driver's imposing figure darkened the doorway behind her. Before Gabriel could respond, Kingsley boomed down the hallway. "Vivian, what were you thinking by bringing product onto estate property? The risks are too—"

Kingsley went quiet the moment he entered the office, his eyes narrowed to tiny slits as if deciphering a complex code. Panic crawled up Gabriel's throat, parching his tongue into desert dryness. Say something. Excuses. Explanations. Something. Anything. But his voice failed him.

Vivian's smile didn't waver. "Our new manager seems to have stumbled upon some sensitive information."

Kingsley's gaze shifted between Vivian and Gabriel. His eyebrows inched upward as the pieces of the puzzle snapped into place. "You set this up?" he asked Vivian.

She shrugged with no remorse. "I had to be sure he was... trustworthy."

Kingsley's eyes blazed as he charged at Gabriel. "You're here to gather evidence against me after what I've done for you?"

Gabriel backed away, moving past Kingsley's desk until his back hit the wall.

"Remy," Kingsley barked, never taking his eyes off Gabriel. "Take him to The Shadows. I'll deal with him later, when I've had time to think."

Remy's massive hand clamped down on Gabriel's shoulder. As he was led from the room, Gabriel caught a glimpse of Vivian's triumphant smile over the silver necklace. Evens had lied to Gabriel—delivered him to Vivian so she could exact her revenge.

And now, The Shadows awaited.

ndre Badeau stood motionless as Vivian's driver dragged a terrified Gabriel out of Kingsley's office. Something cracked loose inside Badeau when the boy moved past him. He pressed himself behind an arch, across from a painting featuring Zeus, Athena, and Hercules —all glowering at him with dark, thunderous eyes. The upbeat music from down the hallway grated on his nerves.

Vivian stood off to the side, all sleek curves in her crimson evening gown. Her red lips twisted into a sneer, cold as winter frost. But it was her eyes that chilled him— empty and devoid of emotion, yet somehow triumphant.

Kingsley swept through the office doorway. Even now, a part of Badeau envied the man. His tailored suit was as pristine as polished armor, and his steel-gray hair caught the light from the wall sconces. His gaze burned through Badeau like acid, stripping him bare.

The air in the hallway grew thick with Vivian's perfume as she circled closer to Gabriel. "The Shadows is a special place," she said with satisfaction. "A place where screams don't carry."

Badeau's palms were slick with sweat. He had walked this path for years without a second thought, but now, every breath felt like a countdown to an uncertain outcome. He locked eyes with Gabriel, and the raw terror in the boy's gaze sent a sharp jolt through Badeau's body, nearly buckling him to his knees before he steadied himself.

What are you doing in here, kid? This isn't your fight.

But Gabriel had guts. He'd always had guts—fixing the alternator with shoelaces, saving Kingsley's life, and now this. Dumb, sure. But brave. The kind of bravery Badeau admired. But to save others? Why?

"Oh, Gabriel," Vivian said, her tone as quick as a snake strike. "Did you really think you could pull one over on us? Stupid boy."

Gabriel looked down at his shoes. He'd been wide-eyed when he first arrived at the estate, but now he was Vivian's lapdog. Badeau didn't have to think long to understand how she'd shaped him—breaking him down and bending him to her will.

Just like you've done with countless others, the voice whispered. His fingers twitched, itching for a cigarette, almost tasting the smoke and feeling the familiar burn in his lungs to dull the edge of guilt slicing through him.

Speak up. Save Gabriel.

What if he did? Best case? They'd laugh it off. Worst—his body dumped in the bayou, a meal for the gator. Everything he'd built would crumble—the power, the respect, the fear in kids' eyes when they saw him coming. He'd buried them for years, drowning them in ambition, booze, and drugs. But now they were back, rising like ghosts he couldn't escape—tear-filled, pleading, accusing. How many lives had he destroyed? How many families had he torn apart? Kingsley's fingers drummed against his jacket pocket, the same pocket that held his concealed weapon. He said something about "making an example," but the words faded in and out.

Do something, Andre. Do something. End this right now. Open your mouth—say the word—it'd be so easy. You can't let this happen. Not again. Not to this kid.

But even as he imagined speaking up for the boy, a different voice sneered in his head. *Do you think they'd give up the kid that easily? You know Max. You know Vivian. They'll murder you. No doubt about it. If you're lucky, a bullet to the head. If not... a torturous death.*

Why would he do it? Everything he'd scraped and clawed for would vanish. No more designer suits, no more respect. He'd be worse than nothing.

This is your chance, Andre. Your last shot at doing something right.

Gabriel's eyes met his—just for a second. In them, Badeau saw a reflection of himself, years ago, when he was a boy in Lafourche Parish.

Badeau's mouth went dry. He took a step forward, unsure of what he would do or say, but knowing he had to do something.

God help me.

His fingers stretched. He could feel the thin air between him and Gabriel. The music from the party swelled, drowning out the sound of his ragged breathing. This was it —the point of no return. Letting his hand fall to his side, he watched as Gabriel was led down the hallway.

Where can I find the courage to do what is right?

———

EACH BUMP of the ATV brought Gabriel closer to The Shadows—a fortress where Kingsley kept his merchandise, a prison where he sent his problems to disappear. Bushes and trees whipped in the stiff wind. Thunder cracked, and the sharp bite of ozone filled his nostrils—a warning from his coastal upbringing.

The storm was closing in. The ATV's headlights cut through the darkness, revealing stained cinder block walls that seemed to drink in the light and devour it. Live Oak branches reached down like gnarled fingers, as if ready to snatch anyone who dared approach.

A sudden screech of metal on metal pierced the night as a fence gate opened. The ATV stopped. Gabriel stumbled out with unsteady legs, bracing himself against its warm fender.

"Let's go," Remy barked, yanking Gabriel by the collar and dragging him toward the entrance. The rancid stench of unwashed bodies and human waste hit him like a wave, twisting his stomach with nausea as he stepped into the dimly lit corridor. From the shadows of an alcove, the hulking Samoan he'd spotted smoking on his first day emerged, his presence as massive and unyielding as the walls around them.

"Loto will show you around," Remy said. "Help you get situated."

A young boy's cry echoed deep within the building, causing his skin to crawl with cold terror.

Loto chuckled. "Don't worry. Just one of our guests getting acquainted with our accommodations. Speaking of which—" Loto slammed a fist into Gabriel's gut. Air exploded from his lungs. The world blurred. He gasped, then folded to the ground, desperate for a breath that wouldn't come.

"Rule number one..." Loto crouched over him. "Don't ask questions. Rule number two... Do as you're told. We clear?"

Gabriel nodded.

A guard with a left eye that twitched in an unnerving rhythm appeared out of nowhere to circle Gabriel. "New meat, huh?" The guard's boot caught Gabriel in the ribs. "Let's see how well you take your lessons."

As Gabriel looked up at his tormentor, his perception shifted. Behind the guard's twitching and cruel smile, he saw something else—darkness, yes, but also pain. Old pain. The kind that turned little boys into monsters.

"Your father beat you with his belt," Gabriel said, the words coming from somewhere beyond himself. "Every night after he drank."

The guard's twitching froze, and his face drained of color.

"You were seven the first time," Gabriel continued. "He used the buckle end."

The guard stumbled back a step. "How...how could you..."

"The cruelty in you," Gabriel said softly, "it's not yours. It's his. You carry it like a curse."

Raising his baton, Loto stepped forward, but the guard held up his hand. He stared at Gabriel with a mixture of fear and wonder. "Get him to his bunk," the guard said, then hurried away, his boots echoing down the corridor.

With his grip tighter than before, Loto yanked Gabriel up. "Clever trick, boy. But tricks won't save you here."

As they moved through the dim barracks, a familiar figure came into focus—Kiara, one of the twins. Her eyes locked on his, filled with unspoken questions. She had seen everything.

Gabriel lowered his eyes, accepting his place as just another prisoner. But inside, he held onto what he'd seen in the guard's soul. Everyone here carried darkness, but in darkness, the truth became clearer. And truth, he knew, was the first step to freedom.

"Yours." Loto shoved him onto the lower bed in the corner. "Sleep tight. Tomorrow's when the real fun begins."

Gabriel sank onto the thin mattress, every breath sending daggers through his ribs. Around him, other prisoners shifted in their bunks, their fear a palpable presence in the dark. A young boy whimpered somewhere to his left.

"Lights out in two minutes," Loto barked. "Anyone caught moving after that answers to me."

Through the gloom, Kiara watched him from her top bunk. Her eyes held something—recognition. She'd seen something in him, just as he'd seen something in the guard. The lights snapped off with a harsh buzz, plunging the room into darkness broken only by thin strips of lightning through the high windows. As his eyes adjusted, the shadows seemed to pulse with the collective prayers and pain of everyone trapped here.

It was too much. Too many souls crying out in the dark. But perhaps that was why he was here—not just to escape but to see. To understand.

Thunder cracked outside, closer now. The approaching storm mirrored the tempest building in his soul—a gathering of power he would have to learn to control. He caught Loto's silhouette in the doorway, watching him, waiting for him to make a mistake. But Loto couldn't see what Gabriel saw—flashes of the lives and sorrows surrounding him— the guard's childhood trauma, Kiara's fierce need to protect, Loto's buried shame.

Curling in his bunk, he clutched his ribs as thunder rolled overhead, shaking the walls. His body ached and his spirit was bruised, but beneath the pain and fear, something stirred—a presence. It wasn't loud or commanding. It wasn't a voice booming from the heavens. It was quiet, steady, and unshakable. Like a hand on his shoulder. Like a whisper in his ear.

I am with you.

He shut his eyes, and for the first time since arriving, the pressure in his chest began to lift. The storm could rage all it wanted; it couldn't reach him here—not where the Lord's hand rested on his heart.

As Gabriel drifted into a fitful sleep, the presence whispered through him again. Not just comfort now, but something more—a command, clear as lightning—*See their darkness. Know their pain. And I'll them free.*

40

Three men were dead, and Eli had watched them die. The strong scent of coffee cut through the Redemption Rescue office, grounding him as he prepared for the emergency team meeting. They had to know the truth—Kingsley had them in his crosshairs, and danger was no longer a distant threat; it was here, on their doorstep.

Through the window, dawn spilled gold and amber across the grounds, a cruel contrast to the storm churning in Eli's mind. Last night's clash with Stone, his men, and a shadowy government agency left Eli with more questions than answers. He wasn't sure if time—or trust—was on their side.

Eli tightened his grip on the mug, the ceramic warm against his palm, as he leaned back against his desk. Behind him, Lindsey sat in his chair, remaining quiet after their three-hour briefing earlier that morning. By the window, Dakota prowled like a caged predator, his restless gaze sweeping the driveway as if expecting trouble to arrive at any moment.

Karina hunched over her tablet, the faint blue glow accentuating the lines of concentration etched into her brow. Across the room, Julia's clacking keystrokes filled the heavy silence.

A tight knot of anxiety twisted in his insides. How could he explain the chaos of the previous night? How would they react? "Last night…" He kept his voice low and controlled. "I had a meeting with Stone."

Dakota turned from the window. Karina and Julia's typing stopped.

"He had two of his bikers with him—the same ones Dakota and I saw at the bar." Eli swallowed hard. "And he confirmed Aaliyah and Kiara Johnson are at the Kingsley Estate."

"You should have waited for me," Dakota said, crossing his arms.

Eli glanced back at Lindsey. "It was a now-or-never situation. I made the call to go alone."

Julia's eyes widened. "Any trouble?"

Lindsey's expression soured. "You could say that. Go on, Eli, tell them."

"While I was there, a couple of SUVs arrived with a tactical team," Eli said. "Then everything went to hell. I got out before they cut down Stone and his men."

Karina crossed to him, placing a gentle hand on his arm. "Are you okay?"

"I'm fine for now," Eli said. "But as I was leaving, I noticed something. The vehicles had government plates."

The room fell into a brief silence, then Dakota spoke. "Government involvement? That sounds a bit sinister."

"Are we equipped to handle something like this?" Julia asked. "I mean, we're just a small PI agency."

Eli nodded. "That's why I called this meeting. We need

to decide how to proceed, knowing the risks in this case have dramatically escalated."

"Kingsley may be protecting his empire," Dakota said, scratching his jawline. "Did the G-men spot you?"

"I don't think so," Eli said, shaking his head. "I bailed out the back as they came through the front door and managed to get to my Jeep hidden in the tree line unseen."

"So what did Stone say about the Johnson twins?" Julia asked. "Are they alive?"

"They're alive," Eli said. "One is being exploited into sexual servitude to bribe influential power brokers. The other is on the Kingsley estate in a building he calls The Shadows. I'm pretty sure I found it on Google Earth last night. It's tucked back on the property, and there's no record of its existence."

"The perfect place to hide something or someone," Lindsey said.

Eli shifted his attention from one team member to another. "So, what's our next step?"

Suddenly, blue lights flashed across the office walls. Dakota dipped his head to see out the window. "We've got company," he moaned, stepping back from the glass.

An unmarked sedan led two patrol cars up the driveway, lights on but sirens silent. The vehicles came to a stop in a practiced formation that made the hairs on the back of his neck stand on end.

"I have to say, this isn't surprising," Eli kept his voice controlled despite the adrenaline rush. "Plainclothes detective and four uniforms."

Lindsey was at his side in an instant, her hand reaching for his. "They're here about last night, aren't they?"

"Only one way to find out." Eli turned to face the team.

The worried expressions on their faces mirrored the fear of what he expected to happen. "I'm going to talk to them outside. Dakota, call Manny just in case. The rest of you say nothing about what we discussed this morning."

"Wait," Lindsey said, rushing to her husband. "I'm coming with you."

"It's okay," he assured her, trying to project confidence he didn't entirely feel. "No need for you to get in the middle of this. Watch from here."

As Eli stepped onto the porch, the low sun momentarily blinded him. Blinking to regain focus, he turned his attention to a stocky man in his late forties approaching with a serious expression.

Descending the steps, Eli met the detective halfway across the yard. A sense of awareness lingered from the office window, where he felt Lindsey's gaze. Cautiously, the detective approached, while the officers stood by their vehicles, hands resting on holstered weapons.

"Can I help you?" Eli asked, raising his hands openly.

The detective's gray eyes locked onto Eli's. "Eli Colt?" he asked, though it sounded more like a statement than a question.

Eli nodded, fighting to keep his face neutral. "That's right."

The detective opened his blue blazer to reveal the badge on his belt. "I'm here to inform you that we have a warrant for your arrest."

Eli stood his ground as the detective approached. "What's the charge?" he asked.

The detective's eyes narrowed slightly. "The murder of James Stone and Patrick Bellamy. We found their bodies in an old boathouse last night."

How could they possibly... "There's been some kind of mistake," he said, careful to keep his hands visible. "I'm not guilty of any crime."

"We have a witness who says otherwise," the detective countered, his hand moving to the small of his back. "Please turn around and place your hands behind your back."

A witness? Of course. The realization hit Eli like a bucket of ice water. The detective mentioned Stone and only one other as victims. The third must have survived and was now pinning the whole thing on him. But why? And how did they know to look for him specifically?

"Detective, I can explain—"

"Save it for the DA," the detective said forcefully. "Right now, I need you to do as I say. Turn around and place your hands behind your back."

Eli turned to find Dakota's face flushed with rage and Lindsey's drained of color—her hand up to her mouth.

Eli let out a huge sigh. "Alright," he said. "But I want to make it clear that I'm innocent of these charges."

As the cold metal clicked on his wrists, Eli's mind whirled with the implications. Someone was framing him, and they had the power to manipulate the police.

"Eli Colt," the detective's voice blared. "You have the right to remain silent..."

As the Miranda rights were read, Eli locked eyes with his team, their faces pressed against the office windows. Lindsey's tears confirmed his worst fears. If that government hit squad could eliminate Stone in a remote boathouse, what chance did he stand in a Baton Rouge jail cell?

He gave Dakota one last nod as the detective led him to the patrol car. *Stay calm. Protect the team. Find the girls.*

The door slammed shut, sealing him in, and Eli's world

shrank to the view through reinforced glass. Somewhere out there, evil was winning. And for the first time since founding Redemption Rescue, Eli feared he couldn't defeat it.

PART IV

onday, August 19

A nightmarish swirl of reds, oranges, and yellows blended on the largest screen in GOHSEP's situation room. Governor Beau Bordelon stared at the storm data, his recurring dream of New Orleans sinking beneath the waves suddenly feeling prophetic.

His staff, law enforcement officials, and meteorologists moved frantically through rows of computer stations and weather monitoring equipment.

"Governor," Brian Sebastian, Bordelon's chief of staff, called from across the room. "The Coast Guard reports that two helicopters are already grounded. High winds are making the evacuation of oil platforms impossible."

He recalled the news footage during Katrina—families trapped on rooftops, waiting for rescue that came too late. Not on his watch. But if he ordered an evacuation now and these storms shifted?

To his left, Dr. Evan Meadows adjusted his thick-rimmed glasses with shaky hands, his receding hairline glistening with sweat under the LED lighting. His rumpled khakis and askew black tie betrayed the long hours he had worked before Bordelon's arrival.

The room fell silent as The Weather Channel appeared on one of the smaller screens. A reporter in Grand Isle, wind whipping his hair, stood on an abandoned street with rain slanting sideways. Leaves and branches blew past him.

A stray lock had slipped free from Dr. Clarisse Doucet's typically neat bun, softly framing her face as she leaned over a console in the front row. Her fingers danced over the keyboard, summoning data sets that flickered across the monitor she intently studied.

The decisions he would make in the next few hours could mean life or death for countless Louisianians. His stomach churned as he pushed the thought aside. His recurring nightmare surged back—New Orleans sinking, displaced citizens screaming for help. Now, faced with the swirling chaos on the screens, his dream felt eerily prophetic.

Bordelon suppressed a shudder. The thought of being the governor who lost New Orleans was paralyzing, but he couldn't freeze now. Louisiana needed him to push past the fear and focus so that his horrifying dream wouldn't become a reality.

A wide-eyed Dr. Meadows gestured at a smaller screen. "Governor, I think you need to see this."

Bordelon stepped closer, squinting at the display. "What am I looking at, Evan?"

"This," Meadows pointed to a small swirl of clouds forming off the southeast of Cuba, "is a new low-pressure system that's just developed. It's following almost the exact path as our primary storm."

Bordelon's chest tightened. "Are you saying there are now two storms threatening us?"

Dr. Doucet joined them, her face grim. "It's worse than that, Governor. If this new system continues on its current trajectory and speed, it's likely to make landfall within thirty-six hours of the first storm."

"My Lord," Bordelon said. "What does that mean for us?"

Meadows swallowed hard. "It means we could be looking at two storms of unprecedented strength hitting us within a week's time. We can't predict the potential impact. We're in uncharted territory here."

Bordelon's heart pounded as the twin storms swirled on the screen, appearing unstoppable. His dream of New Orleans drowning beneath merciless flooding became more real. He gripped the console, struggling to steady himself. This was his nightmare coming to life, and he was powerless to stop it.

Dr. Doucet's frantic voice pierced his spiraling thoughts. "Governor, I've run the preliminary flood models." A new map appeared on the main monitor, displaying red and orange across the coastline. "With these two systems combined, we're looking at a potential storm surge of 20 to 25 feet in some areas. New Orleans's levees..." She paused briefly. "They aren't designed to handle this."

Before Bordelon could fully process this, an aide hurried over with a phone. "Sir, we have reports from the Coast Guard. Several offshore oil rigs are having trouble evacuating in strong winds and high seas. Flying helicopters over the Gulf right now is extremely dangerous."

Bordelon took the call, listening to the frantic voice on the other end. Hundreds of workers were still out there, trapped between the approaching storms and the unforgiving sea. He ended the call, his mind reeling with the growing list of potential casualties.

As if on cue, his cell phone buzzed. It was his State Coordinating Officer. "Governor, I just got off a call with FEMA. They're hesitant to commit significant resources at this time. They want to wait and see where the hurricane lands before deploying."

Bordelon's anger surged. "Wait and see? We don't have time to wait and see!" He forced himself to lower his tone. "What about the other Gulf states?"

"They're preparing for their own impacts, sir. No one's willing to spare much until they know what they're dealing with."

"Governor," Dr. Doucet said. "We need to make a decision about evacuation. Now."

Bordelon felt the blood rush from his face to his chest. He needed to sit, but that would be a sign of weakness. "Walk me through my options one more time."

Dr. Meadows fidgeted with his glasses. He hesitated, glancing at Doucet, as though waiting for her to deliver the hard truth. "If we evacuate now, we have a better chance of getting people out safely. But—"

"But we risk significant commercial impact," Doucet finished. "Shutting down businesses, ports, refineries—it could cost the state billions. And if the storms veer off or weaken, we'll be criticized for overreacting."

"And if we wait?" Beau asked, already knowing the answer but needing to hear it aloud.

"If we wait," Doucet said, her voice grim, "we get more data. We might avoid unnecessary economic disruption. But if these storms do what the models suggest they could..." She let the sentence hang.

Bordelon completed the thought in his mind. If they waited and the hurricanes struck as predicted, people could die—children, families. Faces he'd have to see in the news, in his dreams for years to come.

Expectant stares from all around bore into him. His political instincts screamed at him to wait, to avert any potential embarrassment and economic fallout. The federal government was waiting. Other states were waiting. Why not him?

But waiting could cost lives—lives he was responsible for, lives he had sworn to protect. Should he risk billions in economic losses or gamble with the welfare of his citizens? It was a no-win proposition.

Bordelon stared at the twin storms swirling on screen, each frame of radar data showing them growing stronger. It was time to decide. He squared his shoulders. "We're not waiting. Lives are worth more than any political hit we might take." He turned to Dr. Doucet. "Clarisse, initiate the coastal evacuation protocol. I want everyone from the shoreline to I-10 further inland within 48 hours."

Doucet nodded sharply, already reaching for her phone. "Yes, Governor."

"Evan," Bordelon addressed Dr. Meadows, "coordinate with the State Police and the National Guard. I want their assets mobilized to assist with the emergency response."

"Right away, sir," Meadows said, hurrying to his station.

Bordelon raised his voice to address the entire room. "Listen up. We're about to face one of the greatest challenges in our state's history. But we will face it head-on. Louisiana is counting on us. Let's get the job done."

The room erupted into action—phones ringing and orders being relayed. Bordelon had just risked his governorship—and possibly his political future—on this decision. Somehow, that seemed like the least important thing at stake. His cell phone buzzed in his pocket. He looked at the screen and stepped away from the noise.

"Sarah? Is everything okay?"

"Beau, I know you're dealing with this storm situation." Her voice came through a bit frantic. "But Tom Colt just called and says he needs to speak with you immediately. He wouldn't tell me what it was about, but he sounded... desperate."

Bordelon frowned. What could Tom Colt want at a time like this? And what could be so urgent? "Did he say anything else?"

"Just that it's a matter of life and death for several children. And that Maxwell Kingsley is involved. Beau, what's going on?"

He pinched the bridge of his nose with the advent of another crisis. "I don't know, Sarah. But don't worry. I'll give him a call."

Two storms bearing down on his state, and now Kingsley.

The devil himself couldn't have picked worse timing.

42

Kiara stood at the entrance of The Shadows' makeshift kitchen, willing her hands to stop shaking as she stirred the morning's grim offering—rubbery scrambled eggs clumped together in unsettling chunks. The party had been last night. Had they forced Aaliyah to attend? The thought of what might have happened turned the coffee in her stomach to acid.

Holding her breath, she scooped the eggs from the cast-iron skillet into two tin bowls, careful to avoid the charred bits stuck to the bottom of the pot and the occasional flecks of shell that hadn't been fished out. The blue Sterno flames flickered beneath the pan, casting a glow that made everything look sicker than it already was.

As she reached for the tray of stale bread, her eyes drifted to somber kids clustered near their bunks, a scene of lost innocence. Some sat on their mattresses, eating in silence, their bodies hunched and weary. A few younger ones whispered to one another, their eyes leveled at the entrance as if waiting for Loto's daily abuse.

Kiara's stomach twisted—not just from hunger but from

the worry gnawing at her. Where was Aaliyah now? What was being done to her? Last night had been the night of the party. Kiara tried to shake the images invading her mind—Aaliyah's body crumpled, her eyes pleading for whatever was happening to stop. She couldn't go there, not now.

Oh God, please protect her. Please.

Gathering a few pieces of stale bread, she balanced the bowls as she made her way to Gabriel's bunk.

"Hey," she said softly, forcing a smile as she settled next to him. "Breakfast is served, though I can't promise it's edible."

She set the food between them, her gaze taking in the hollow eyes and slumped shoulders of the other children—a painful reminder of their shared struggle. As she glanced at Gabriel, she sensed the importance of what she was about to reveal.

"Thanks," Gabriel said as he took his bowl and examined it with suspicion. "I wasn't sure what they'd feed us, if anything."

"Don't get your hopes up," Kiara replied with a chuckle. "Those eggs are part adventure and part torture."

Gabriel's lips curved, and his eyes crinkled at the corners, smiling with understanding. Kiara considered how different life had been just days earlier—before she'd been sent to this dank prison. And now Gabriel, once the estate manager, had somehow ended up here too.

"Why'd they put you in here?" Kiara asked.

"They caught me in Kingsley's office rifling through his files."

"Why would you do that?"

"Because Evens tricked me by bringing me to watch dozens of kids being loaded into vans from this building."

Kiara's eyes darted around the room, scanning for Loto.

"We're not supposed to talk about that," she said in a low tone. "That Evens is Vivian's lap dog. Let me guess. She came on to you, and you refused."

Gabriel nodded as his eyes surveyed the room. "So, what's with this place? And where's Aaliyah?"

"Well, this place is a hellhole, and Aaliyah decided to play ball with Vivian." She shook her head. "God, I'm so worried about her."

"Play ball? Does that have something to do with that party last night?"

"Everything." Kiara dropped her eyes. "I wouldn't go, and that's why they moved me in here."

"This place seems to be overcrowded," Gabriel said. "Are any of us going to be leaving soon?"

"I don't think so. Loto told me to prepare another bunk for an arrival."

"Just one?"

"Just one," she said. "And like you, someone special."

Gabriel's face fell, and Kiara felt a knot forming in her stomach. Then a ripple of commotion surged through the room, breaking the moment.

Loto appeared in the doorway. Behind him was a boy no older than thirteen. His skin was sallow, and his clothes hung off his gaunt frame. He shuffled into the room like an animal expecting the worst. The sharp angles of his face—the cheekbones, the jawline, the set of his mouth—stirred something faintly familiar.

Gabriel stood. The tin bowl slipped from his lap, its contents scattering across the floor. "Nico."

"Gabriel," Kiara said. "Is that your—?"

"He's my brother," he rasped, cutting her off. His eyes stayed on the boy as though, if he lost sight of him, Nico might vanish.

Loto shoved Nico into the room. "Find a spot and stay out of the way," he said before turning and slamming the door behind him.

Kiara's gaze lingered on the brothers' reunion, but a cold dread crept over her.

Where is my sister?

43

*T*uesday, *August 20*

Andre Badeau shielded his eyes from the plantation's floodlights. It was another Tuesday at Crescent Oaks. Another group of children was inside. Another parade of Mercedes and Porsches flowed onto the plantation grounds. Another Tuesday where wealthy men in thousand-dollar suits, hands already twitching for young flesh, gathered.

Hector collected invitations handed through the windows of approaching vehicles while checking names off his list. Security protocol. Guest verification. These were solid things. Manageable things. Things that didn't make Badeau's stomach churn. A Bentley eased to a stop.

Focus on the job. Check faces and monitor threats.

The tech billionaire from Forbes magazine smiled from the rear window, just like last week and the week before.

"Good evening, sir." Hector's voice carried across the drive. The tech billionaire's eyes never left Hector's flashlight beam as he handed over his cream-colored invitation.

Those same eyes had watched a fourteen-year-old boy stumble down the plantation's hall last month.

Badeau's collar tightened against his throat. Check faces. Monitor threats. But the faces blurred—faces, past and present, swimming behind his eyes. He forced his attention to the next car, a Range Rover with diplomatic plates.

A hint of Glenlivet wafted past his nose.

More names to check. More faces to monitor. Badeau's shoes crunched against wet gravel as he paced to the house. Crickets chirped, frogs croaked, their song a low, buzzing warning.

The river's stench hit him—thick, sour algae rising from the Mississippi. Just like the swamp behind his uncle's camp. *No. Focus on the job.*

He straightened his collar and pushed away the memory. Time to earn his living.

Inside the main house, the grand ballroom swallowed the first wave of guests—senators, tech moguls, energy executives in tailored suits and cocktail dresses. They glided across the polished floor, sipping champagne and exchanging easy smiles. Badeau tracked their movements, his gaze calculating. Who lingered by the bar, who hovered near the exits, who stood alone checking phones—waiting.

Kingsley's security team—men in black suits with eyes like polished stone—ushered the merchandise through a separate door. Eight boys. Eight girls. Some couldn't have been older than thirteen. Dressed like adults. Painted like dolls.

Some beamed with giddy excitement, unaware. Others moved with heads bowed, shoulders hunched. Already broken. Just like—

Get in the truck, boy. Your uncle is waiting.

Copper flooded his mouth. Twenty-three years gone,

and it still snuck up on him. His mother's expression—tight-lipped, swollen-eyed. His uncle's fingers digging into his shoulder as she drove away.

Badeau's chest tightened, breath coming in shallow pulls. He turned to the bar and swallowed a bourbon in one gulp. The alcohol burned, but the memory burned deeper.

A crystal champagne flute shattered somewhere. A judge passed by Badeau as he entertained two teenage boys—the same judge who had dismissed his kidnapping charges for taking Tara Colt two years ago. His fingers itched to grab those kids and take them far from here. Instead, he signaled a server to clean up the broken glass. This was his job. This was who he was now. A bitter taste rose from his belly. He pulled at his collar. Too tight. Everything was too tight.

The investment banker from last month's Economist cover leaned in, whispering to a blonde boy—fourteen at most—his hand brushing too casually over the boy's wrist. A few steps away, a powerful attorney—whose face populated billboards along the Interstate—hovered near two young girls, his wedding ring catching the chandelier light. The scene played out like a twisted courtship, veiled in designer suits and polite smiles.

And then he saw her.

The new girl. One of the black twins from Mobile. She stood by the grand piano wearing a white dress that was too tight and too adult. The fabric hugged her curves closely, and her eyes sparkled with something unexpected. Hope. A misplaced hope. The kind he had seen in too many girls he had groomed for prostitution.

I'll take you places, baby. Buy you expensive clothes and jewelry. Make you a star.

His fingers curled around his phone. One call. Just one

call, and this whole house of cards would collapse. But that call would put him in prison. And these guests, with their lawyers and influence, would walk free. They were politicians and judges who owned the cops. And now owned him.

"Andre." Vivian's sharp voice broke through his thoughts. "Be a dear and make sure our new friend gets another drink."

Badeau nodded, his mask in place, but every step he took felt heavier. Andre, at twelve, walked beside him, shadowing his every move.

A commotion near the library caught his attention. The tech billionaire, worth more than twenty billion, led a stumbling boy through the mahogany doors. The kid wobbled like a newborn colt, his eyes glazed and unfocused.

"Just drink it down, boy. Help you relax," his uncle's voice hissed from the past.

Bourbon burned in Badeau's mouth. His hand shook, spilling the drink onto his sleeve. The same drink he had handed to that boy an hour ago, except then, Vivian's special additive had swirled inside.

Get it together, Andre. This is business. Just like you've done so many times before.

The boy's shoe caught the doorframe. The billionaire gripped his shoulder, steadying him with ease. Badeau's shoulder burned in the same spot where his uncle's hand had held him years ago, guiding him to the same fate he couldn't escape.

"Everything alright, Andre?" Kingsley materialized beside him.

"It is. Just keeping an eye on things."

"Good man. That's why I keep you around." Kingsley's hand settled on Badeau's shoulder.

Kingsley's eyes slid toward the black twin, his lips

curling into a hungry grin. "Look at that one, would you? I might have to break the first rule of business tonight."

"Sir?"

"Forgo the profit and enjoy the product."

Vivian sidled up to the target of Kingsley's attention, producing a fresh cocktail—a slight cloudiness floating in the liquid, topped with a blood-red cherry. Her special recipe. She placed it in the girl's hand. "Sweetheart, you simply must try this," Vivian said with a nod.

Accepting the drink with a pageant-girl smile, the girl lifted the glass to her lips. Her throat worked the heavy liquid down, and her eyes grew foggy. His uncle's voice echoed in his ear.

Good boy, just relax now. You should be feeling good by now.

"Andre," Vivian's voice pierced through his haze again. "Why don't you make sure Max's favorite cabin is ready? The one by the oak grove?"

Ten seconds to the door. Twenty minutes to New Orleans. He could escape this lifestyle once and for all, but his feet felt rooted. Instead, he nodded, his mask cracking but still intact.

Through the French doors, Kingsley guided Aaliyah across the floodlit lawn. Her heels sank into the wet grass, causing her steps to falter. Kingsley's hand rested gently against her lower back, steering her to the cabin—the same gentle touch his uncle had used.

Just let me take care of you.

Badeau's legs wouldn't move. His body locked in place, paralyzed as it had been all those years ago. The creak of the screen door, the sour stench of Jack Daniel's, the sound of a zipper unzipping.

Do something.

The voice was clear, but Badeau's limbs remained frozen,

as if he were that twelve-year-old boy standing in that same shadow. The girl stumbled at the cabin door, and Kingsley caught her elbow, whispering something that made her giggle—a sound so delicate that something inside him shattered.

The cabin door closed. Another child abused. Another Tuesday.

From inside the main house, a burst of laughter. Music swelled. Glasses clinked. Guests danced and drank, not caring about the empty spaces that once held children.

I can't do this much longer.

44

N o charges. No bail. No explanation. Eli stepped through the doors of St. Tammany Parish Jail under coal-grey clouds, gripping Lindsey's hand like an anchor. Wind gusts pushed skittering leaves across the pavement in frenzied dances.

"I still can't believe they just... let you go," Lindsey said, her voice betraying her exhaustion.

He squeezed her hand. "Makes two of us. I was arrested for murder just hours ago, and now I'm a free man? It doesn't make sense."

"There's something I need to tell you." Lindsey bit her lip. "I... I called your father right after you were arrested."

Eli said nothing, unsure of how he felt about his father knowing. The fragile truce with his father, brokered by Julia for the Kingsley gala invitations, did little to erase the strain over his brother's death.

"I didn't know what else to do," she explained hurriedly. "I thought maybe he could help, use his connections..."

Her words faltered as a dark Suburban pulled to the curb in front of them. A tall, stout man in a black suit exited the driver's side, his close-cropped hair and fit build suggesting military training. The man's eyes locked onto Eli as he marched toward them.

"Mr. Colt," the man said, his voice as crisp as his shirt collar. "I'm from the Governor's office. Would you come with me, please?" It wasn't a request. A gust of wind whipped around them, carrying the scent of rain and an edge of something uncertain.

Eli turned to Lindsey. "Well, there's our answer. Contact Dakota. My parents can't ride this storm out in New Orleans. Have him bring them to Madisonville, and if need be, take the Airstream north."

She nodded with a furrowed brow. "Be careful."

He pressed his lips to hers, then followed the aide to the SUV.

Forty minutes later, they threaded through Baton Rouge's congested streets. Cars lined up at fuel pumps. People poured from convenience stores with water and supplies. The whine of power drills echoed as workers hung plywood over windows. Digital signs flashed evacuation routes outside the towering state capital.

The aide parked in a restricted area near the front steps. Eli stepped out as lightning split the sky, unsure which storm would prove more dangerous—the one in the Gulf or the one inside.

He followed the driver into the Capitol and then into a room that resembled a military command center. Governor Bordelon stood beneath a large monitor, his silhouette slouched, his head swiveling from one screen to another displaying storm patterns and coastal images.

"Mr. Colt," Bordelon said, not turning. "Thank you for coming. We have a situation that requires your unique skills."

By reflex, Eli almost stood at attention. "Sir."

Bordelon's eyes didn't leave the screens. "I freed you from jail and brought you here because your father called me to help you. Again."

A thump of emotion hit Eli's chest. After years of separation, had his father finally shown that he cared?

"Follow me." The governor led Eli out of the room, down a hallway, and into a large, spacious office, shutting the door behind them.

As they entered, a familiar figure framed by the stormy sky outside a window caught Eli's eye. She turned, and he immediately recognized the governor's wife from the dinner at the Audubon Tea Room.

"It was federal operators that raided the boathouse and murdered the man you were arrested for killing," the governor said. "What was his name? Stone?"

"Yes, sir," Eli replied.

"They were working in conjunction with the DNI." Bordelon's tone sharpened.

"The Director of National Intelligence?" Eli's mind raced. "That's federal. How are they involved?"

"Because Maxwell Kingsley controls the woman who runs it," Bordelon answered with a tight voice. He finally turned to face Eli. "The same way he tries to control me."

"Mr. Colt," Sarah Bordelon said, her voice steady despite the storm rattling the windows. "At the gala, I sensed you were someone who gets things done. Now that I've spoken with your father, I understand why. But what we're about to tell you is...sensitive. Can we trust you to be discreet?"

Eli nodded. How could he refuse the man who just sprung him from jail.

"Maxwell Kingsley," Bordelon said, his voice rough. "Tell me what you know about him."

"Rich," Eli said with no hesitation. "Connected. Suspected of trafficking, but untouchable. Why?"

"Because he owns people—important people." Bordelon said as he glanced at his wife. "Five years ago, before I was elected governor, he invited me to a dinner in D.C. Drinks followed. After I had one—only one cocktail—everything went dark." He dropped his gaze in shame. "A week later, he showed me photos of me with two underage girls. I don't remember anything after that drink, but the evidence... is damning."

Sarah moved to her husband's side as if for support. "Kingsley's been controlling Beau ever since. And he's not the only one. Federal judges, senators, cabinet secretaries—they're all under his thumb."

The governor's confession, especially in front of his wife, was gut-wrenching. "So Kingsley's blackmailing you."

"And others in high positions," Bordelon said. "But now, with this storm coming, we have a unique opportunity."

Glancing between them, the tension from the gala returned. "What exactly are you asking me to do?"

"There are two hurricanes approaching the area," Bordelon said. "With the storms hitting, Kingsley's estate will be vulnerable. His security will be compromised, and his attention divided. It's the perfect time to infiltrate and dismantle his operation."

Eli raised his brow. "You want me to go in?"

"You're our best shot, Eli," Sarah said. "Beau can't move against him. Kingsley would destroy him politically, and he's already got other officials doing his bidding. But if you could get in and find evidence, you could bring his whole operation down."

Eli crossed his arms. "I appreciate the vote of confidence,

but I can't lose sight of my mission. I'm here to find twin girls and bring them back to their mother."

"We know, Kiara and Aaliyah Johnson," Sarah said, her eyes brightening. "But don't you think there's a good possibility they'll be on his property?"

Eli inhaled deeply and weighed the odds. The chance to destroy Kingsley and rescue the twins was worth the risks. "When do I start?"

"Immediately." Bordelon's relief was visible. "We don't have much time before the storm hits. But... are you ready?"

Eli nodded, determination hardening his voice. "I'll need some things only you can get for me—military equipment."

"The National Guard's armory is at your disposal."

"And I'll need a governor's pardon if things go south and I survive."

"Already done. For you and your partner, Sutcliffe."

Eli shot a surprised glance at Bordelon.

"I figured you'd need some help." Thunder cracked overhead, closer now. "The storm hits in six hours. Whatever you're going to do, do it fast."

45

Kiara lifted her face to the sun's warmth and the freedom she'd forgotten existed. Endless flowers stretched to the horizon of the meadow, violet and crimson petals dancing in a breeze that shouldn't be there. Butterflies painted the air with orange and yellow wings, and the sweet fragrance of jasmine wrapped around her like her sister's lost laughter. Her body felt weightless and free. This wasn't The Shadows. There was no wall, no darkness, no Loto. Thank goodness.

She twirled, laughter bubbling up, bright and untethered. Another spin, and the last of her confinement fell away, peeling off like old skin. With every step, every turn, her heart lifted higher as if her pain crumbled behind her. Aaliyah. The thought of her sister was warm, like the sun on her skin. They used to laugh like this during those endless afternoons when nothing mattered but the shared joy of being alive.

A crystalline fountain, liquid starlight caught in mid-fall, shimmered at the garden's center, its water cascading over smooth stones. She knelt, fingertips brushing the cool surface. Light danced in the ripples. Cupping her hands, she caught water for her lips. Cool. Cleansing. A butterfly landed on her finger, its wings pulsing with life.

"Kiara!" Aaliyah's urgent voice cut through the garden's harmony. Kiara's heart jolted as she rose, scanning the meadow's edge where shadows gathered beneath branches twisting like bony fingers. The flowers dimmed at the border, as though they sensed what waited in the dark.

"Aaliyah?" Kiara called with a shallow voice. The bright petals lost their color past the thicket. The ancient trees loomed, shadows grew darker, spreading like oil. Aaliyah's voice faded, now filled with fear. "Aaliyah?" she screamed.

"Help me, Kiara!" The desperate cry pierced her heart. Her feet twitched forward—then stopped.

She couldn't move. The garden's beauty held her like invisible chains, whispering promises of safety, of peace. Stay. The fountain's soft music, the warm sunlight on flower petals—this was where she belonged. Not in the dark. Not where shadows devoured light and hope.

"Come to me!" The cry tore free from Kiara's throat. The fountain's soft music, the warm sunlight on flower petals. But Aaliyah's voice faded, swallowed by the darkness. Why couldn't Kiara move? Why couldn't she follow?

Kiara's eyes flew open, her breath catching in her throat. The rough mattress of her bunk pressed against her back, and the meadow was gone. She blinked, feeling disoriented as she tried to grasp the fading remnants of her dream—the joy, the weightlessness, the promise. But reality crashed in, cold and heavy.

Gabriel stood above her, smiling, the faint morning light casting soft shadows on his face. For a moment, he looked like the garden—golden, bright, unburdened. "Do you always smile when you sleep?" he asked, his voice gently teasing.

Smile? Did she? No one had ever told her that. Not Aaliyah. Not anyone. "I guess I was dreaming."

Her feet pressed against the cold concrete floor as she tried to hold onto the joy from her heavenly respite. But guilt soon crept in—that moment when she couldn't move to rescue Aaliyah. What kind of sister finds peace while leaving her other half in darkness?

"Dream?" Gabriel said. "I know dreams. Tell me about yours."

———

"The garden was real," Kiara insisted, watching Gabriel pace the concrete floor. "I could feel the sun, smell the flowers—" She glanced at Nico, who sat cross-legged in the corner, his dark eyes tracking Gabriel's movement like a tennis match.

Gabriel's fingers traced absent patterns on his thigh as he walked, piecing something together in his mind. The dull light cast shadows under his eyes, making him look older. Wiser.

Nico shifted against the wall. "My Papa said dreams were messages from God." His quiet voice drew their attention.

"The garden..." Gabriel stopped his pacing. "It's not just escape you're dreaming of. It's who you were before." Something in his expression made her chest tighten. "The person who could laugh without looking over her shoulder. Who could just be herself."

The truth of it stung. She looked away, studying the corridor opening.

"But Aaliyah..." He paused as if choosing his words carefully. "She's still in the darkness. And you couldn't—" He caught himself and rephrased. "You weren't ready to leave the light."

Her throat ached with sorrow. "I abandoned her."

Nico pulled his knees to his chest. "Sometimes staying behind means surviving. Like when Papa kept Gabriel from going fishing with our brothers."

"You didn't abandon Aaliyah," Gabriel said with intensity. "God is telling you something. The garden, the safety there—that's strength. You can't help Aaliyah if you're lost in the same darkness."

She clasped her shaking hands into a ball, resisting the urge to disagree. But hadn't she felt it? That moment by the fountain, the water that filled her with... what had it been? Not just peace.

"Strength," he said, softer now. "The dream showed you two paths. Rushing into darkness after her voice—that's what they want. What Vivian counts on. But finding your strength first, building that safe place inside..." He pointed a determined finger. "That's how you survive. How you fight back."

Lightning flashed outside, and Nico flinched at the thunder that followed. He muttered something in Spanish that sounded like a prayer.

She held onto the image of light on water and the butterfly's wings against her skin. It felt so... whole. And maybe that scared her the most. For a moment, she remembered who she was before coming to Louisiana, before fear became as natural as breathing. She stood, pacing where Gabriel had been moments before. "Dear God, make me stronger. Courageous. I must save my sister. I will save my sister."

Nico lifted his head at her prayer. Gabriel moved closer,

their shoulders nearly touching. The warmth of his presence anchored her as thunder rumbled overhead. Her prayer had changed something in the air—and within herself.

"Then we'll keep looking for her," Gabriel said. "But you have to stay whole to do that. The garden in your dream? Keep it. Build it stronger. Because that light you felt... that's what they can't take unless you let them."

She closed her eyes to recapture the warmth of sunlight on her skin, the weightless joy. It now seemed distant but not completely gone.

A flash of lightning illuminated The Shadows through the narrow window. Somewhere in Kingsley's world, Aaliyah waited. But now, Kiara would face the darkness differently—not as a victim, but as a warrior.

46

In the dimly lit corridor of The Shadows, Badeau stood astonished by Gabriel's insights regarding the Johnson girl's dream. This remarkable young man had seen right through it, speaking truth with a power that made Badeau's hollow authority seem insignificant. After decades of crushing young souls, he had never witnessed such light shed on his darkness.

His phone buzzed with an alert—the category 4 hurricane was following the deadly path of Katrina and was headed for the Louisiana coastline. Six hours until landfall. Six hours trapped in this compound with nearly fifty kids and a small crew while Freddy sank deeper into his darkness. The late afternoon sun struggled through the hurricane's outer bands, casting yellow-green shadows across the concrete floor. Pine trees thrashed outside as maintenance crews raced to secure loose equipment. Security cameras whirred as they tracked movement, red lights blinking like accusing eyes.

Inside, Gabriel sat on a metal bunk beside the Johnson girl. Outside, the workers he had once supervised boarded windows and hauled sandbags. The governor had ordered a mandatory evacuation for South Louisiana, but Kingsley had been clear—no one leaves the property.

A door slammed somewhere behind Badeau, the sound sharp against the rising howl of the wind. Footsteps. His hand moved to his hip and clutched his pistol before he recognized his nephew's swagger. Freddy. The kid was high again.

"Uncle Andre." Freddy's voice crackled like static. He stumbled and caught himself against the wall. "Checking your inventory?"

Badeau returned his hand to his weapon. After what Freddy had done with Nico, for the first time in years, he wasn't sure he could avoid pulling the trigger. "Why did you bring that kid here? I don't remember giving you that order."

"Getting squeamish?" Freddy stepped closer.

"What?"

"Squeamish," his nephew repeated, the smell of sweat and cologne invading Badeau's space. "Is the storm getting you squeamish?"

The lights flickered again. "What are you talking about?"

Freddy chuckled, as if savoring the confusion. "Want to see what the kids' father looked like when he realized he'd lost another son?"

"You recorded it?"

"The best part was..." Freddy's grin stretched wide, showing too many teeth. "Got two for one. Stupid family were so busy trying to save their business that they didn't even see it coming."

The wind screamed through the pine trees like lost souls. Six hours until landfall, and Freddy was higher than a satellite, unraveling faster than the leaves in the storm.

His exact opposite, Gabriel, showed quiet strength as he moved among the bunks, comforting nervous children. The boy who had once fixed an alternator with shoelaces now offered his blanket to a shivering child across the room. The Johnson girl helped, whispering something that made a small boy stop crying.

"Go back to my room," Badeau said to Freddy. The words came out harder than he intended. "I'll see you there in a few minutes."

Freddy swayed and pulled a small bag from his pocket filled with white powder. "Want some? It helps with the nerves." He sniffed and wiped his nose. "Oh wait. This stuff doesn't affect you, right, Uncle Andre?"

Lightning flashed, throwing Freddy's hollow face into sharp focus and giving him a ghastly, demonic appearance. It was as if he had stepped out of a nightmare—a dark creation from Badeau's own world.

"I said leave." Badeau grabbed Freddy by the collar and shoved him toward the door. "Now."

Freddy's nostrils flared slightly. "Don't you touch me," he said, his lips twitching at one corner. "I'm not a kid anymore."

"You want a beating, boy?" Badeau narrowed his eyes into angry slits.

"Like I said, I'm not a boy anymore." Freddy raised his fists to challenge Badeau's authority.

The lights went out. In the sudden darkness, Freddy's ragged breathing grew louder. The frightened whimpers from the bunks mingled with the howling wind. When the lights returned, Freddy stood inches from Badeau's face.

"You're getting weak." A sneer pulled at Freddy's mouth, his bloodshot eyes cold despite the drugs flooding his system. "I'm sure Kingsley notices these things. I know I do.

Matter of fact..." Freddy fumbled with his phone, his pupils dilating as he focused on the screen.

But before he could finish, Badeau grabbed him by the throat and slammed him against the wall. "Listen. Closely." His fingers dug into Freddy's windpipe. "I did teach you everything. Including this." He slammed Freddy harder against the wall, feeling his bones creak. For the first time, real fear flickered in his nephew's drug-glazed eyes. "But I never taught you when to stop."

Badeau let go of his throat and grabbed his arm instead. "We're going back to the house. Right now." Rain stung his face as he dragged Freddy to the waiting ATV. Its engine growled to life, tires spinning in the mud before finding purchase. As they sped to the main house, movement on the road outside the tree line caught Badeau's eye. A black Jeep crawled through the storm, its driver barely visible through rain-streaked windows. The Redemption Rescue logo burned like an accusation on its door.

Eli Colt, the man who had been hunting them for years, had arrived.

Six hours—time to choose between Freddy or the children he had helped destroy.

47

A sharp pain shot through Badeau's chest as Freddy thrashed beneath the sweat-soaked sheets in Badeau's bedroom. The bedside lamp illuminated his every twitch and tremor from the poison coursing through his veins. The mansion's generator hummed softly amidst the expensive furnishings, while wind-whipped branches scraped against the bedroom windows.

God, Freddy. Why do you do this to yourself?

Freddy whimpered, a sound Badeau hadn't heard since his nephew was twelve. Gone was the street-smart kid who could outfox any mark, the nephew who had built their operation into something that commanded respect. In his place lay this hollow-eyed stranger, twitching and broken, wearing Freddy's face like a cheap mask.

Rolling thunder rippled through the mansion's empty halls. Each rumble seemed to pull Freddy deeper into whatever terror had him by the throat. Badeau had steered them through storms before—long nights, dangerous runs—but this time? This time he couldn't guide them to safe harbor. Not from this.

The ceiling fan ticked off seconds. The signs had been there—Freddy shooting Eli Colt in the Rigolets, laughing while he did it. The growing violence against the kids they trafficked, now merely for pleasure. Little cruelties that should have screamed a warning. But Badeau had looked away and counted the money instead. Now the devil wanted payment in full.

But maybe… maybe there was still hope. Gabriel—he'd done something with Aaliyah's sister earlier. Reached her. Got through. Maybe he could do the same with Freddy.

Badeau's fingers drummed against the wall as he watched Freddy's eyes roll beneath his lids. He needs more than I can give him. More than all this wealth can buy. More than the poison that's killing him.

After bolting upright with his fingers scrabbling against the duvet like it might turn into quicksand, Freddy's chest heaved. His sweat-soaked t-shirt mapped the outline of every rib. Lord, when had this kid gotten so thin?

"Easy now." Badeau kept his voice steady, like calming a spooked horse. "You're safe."

Freddy's eyes found him, pupils blown wide. The tremors hit harder now—the addiction's hold tightening, fingers working the sheets into garrotes as if ready to fight.

"Uncle Andre?" his voice cracked, echoing the tone he used when he was ten—a young boy who would plead for stories about the bayou and his uncle's wild, untamed youth. "I saw… I was…"

Another foundation-shaking boom of thunder. Freddy curled into himself, sleeve riding up to reveal the track marks marching up his arm like the stations of his own dark cross.

"Tell me." Badeau moved to sit on the edge of the bed, giving Freddy space. "The dream. Tell me what you saw."

Freddy's face lost color, his expression reflecting sheer terror. With a rigid jaw, he shook his head, as if refusing to let the nightmare reveal itself.

"Come on," Badeau pleaded. "We need to figure this out."

Freddy stared at the outstretched hand as though it might catch fire. "Figure what out?" His voice hardened. "I'm fine. I just need—"

"You need to stop killing yourself." The words came out too sharply. Badeau forced a breath to steady himself. "That boy Gabriel, the one you brought from Honduras... He understands dreams."

Freddy scoffed, his mouth twisting into a bitter smirk. "What is he, some kind of clairvoyant?"

"He helped a girl earlier—she had a dream, too." Badeau's voice softened, testing the waters. "He understood what it meant."

Freddy's fingers danced nervously against his knee. The flicker of panic in his eyes revealed a fear of some unseen horror.

"Just come with me," Badeau said, rising and moving to the door. "What've you got to lose?"

Freddy's laugh came out hollow. "My soul? That's what this is about, right?" He tried to stand, but his legs betrayed him. "I don't need—" His words cut off as he doubled over, retching. "If your prophet boy can't help—" His threat died as another tremor hit. The lights flickered once, twice, then plunged them into darkness.

———

BADEAU RIPPED through puddles and wet grass, past the parking lot, outbuildings, and stables. Freddy's fingers clung to the ATV's seat like talons, betraying more than fear of the storm. As they passed through The Shadow's wire fence gate, lightning momentarily blinded Badeau. He cut the engine near the entrance, the ATV's headlights catching the glinting razor wire above the electrified fence.

Inside, they stepped into the common room, finding Gabriel crouched beside a trembling boy with dark ebony skin, the child pressing against him with each crash of thunder. Gabriel's voice rose and fell, calm and steady, telling a story about Jesus on a boat calming a storm for His disciples.

Badeau's throat tightened. This scene wasn't right. Why was Gabriel offering comfort here, in a place he should despise? Would he even help Freddy after everything Freddy had done—after purchasing him, after ruining his life?

"Gabriel," Badeau cleared his throat, breaking the moment. "Got a minute?"

The kindness in Gabriel's eyes succumbed to quiet tension. Freddy shifted behind Badeau, suddenly fascinated by the floor.

"You'll be fine now, yes?" Gabriel said to the boy. The kid nodded, a little braver now. Rising slowly, Gabriel kept his distance from Freddy as he stepped nearer. "What do you need?"

"My nephew..." Badeau gestured at Freddy. "He had a dream. A bad one. I saw you help that girl," he nodded at the twin, "understand hers."

Gabriel's face was a mask of neutrality, making it difficult to understand his true feelings.

"Please," Badeau said, "he needs help. Just listen to what he has to say."

Gabriel studied them for a long moment, his gaze fixed on Freddy before he gave a slight nod. "Go on."

Freddy swallowed, pacing the common room, hands shaking as he tried to find the words. "I was in a field," he started, his voice rough. "The field was dead. The vines—twisted, black, rotting. The fruit was on the ground, covered in crows. Just... birds, everywhere. Big, black ones, ripping things apart."

Badeau searched for Gabriel's reaction. He'd never been able to read the boy. That calm expression, that steady voice. But now, with Freddy standing there like a shattered vase, Badeau could see it in Gabriel's eyes—quiet, patient attention.

"The sky—it was wrong," Freddy said, pacing faster now. "Like a whirlpool of clouds, pulling everything into it. I tried to run, but these shadows—these things—kept grabbing at me, pulling me down." His hands waved in the air, growing frantic. "Everything was dead. Everything was... gone."

Thunder cracked again, and Freddy flinched, wrapping his arms around himself as if he could protect what little remained. "They weren't just shadows," he whispered, his voice shaking. "They were... different. Alive somehow. They were consuming everything. Even me."

Gabriel leaned forward slightly, his expression soft despite everything Freddy had done to him. "And then?"

"Then..." Freddy let out a hollow laugh. "Then the birds came for me. Picking at my flesh."

The tension in the air intensified. After taking a breath, Gabriel spoke, low but steady. "I understand your dream, Freddy," Gabriel said, frowning. "I know what it means." He paused, letting his words settle. "God is giving you a warning about your future. Would you like to hear?"

Badeau's jaw ached from grinding his teeth. He wanted help for Freddy, but now, watching Gabriel's face, he feared what that help might reveal.

————

"Your dream warns of judgment, Freddy." Gabriel's voice filled the cramped room inside The Shadows. He gripped the cold, metal arms of his chair tightly as he studied Freddy, who had brought him here. Thunder rumbled outside, reverberating through the thin walls like an omen of doom.

Andre Badeau shifted uncomfortably near the heavy, rusted door, his body tense with unspoken dread. He crossed his arms tightly against his chest, his eyes glistening with unshed tears, reflecting the flickering shadows that danced across the room. A loose shutter banged violently against the frame outside, each slam resonating like an echo of Gabriel's unsettling divine warning, amplifying the tension that coiled in the air around them.

"The field of decay represents your soul, Freddy." Gabriel kept his voice low, gentle even, though it strained against the urgency building inside him. "The rotting fruit? Those are the lives you've destroyed. Mine. The children you've trafficked. The families you've torn apart." The lump in his throat grew larger with every word. Bitterness threatened to spill over, but he had to control his anger.

Tension in Freddy's shoulders coiled like a cobra. His eyes darted downward as he paced the floor, refusing to look at Gabriel.

"The birds are indicators," Gabriel continued, his fingers curling tighter around the armrests. "Dark angels of justice. They're coming for you, Freddy. First for your flesh, then for your soul—unless you turn from this path of destruction."

Freddy's footsteps faltered—a flicker, a hesitation. For a moment, Gabriel thought he'd found a crack in Freddy's armor, but then Freddy's face hardened again, his defiance slipping back into place. He stopped pacing and glared at Gabriel, his lips twisting. "What do you know about it?"

"The darkness pulling you down is familiar." Tension stiffened Gabriel's knees as he stood, yet his purpose fueled him. "Your sins. Your addiction. Your cruelty."

Freddy flinched.

"This dream is God warning you," Gabriel said. "Change for the good, or the darkness will consume you completely."

Freddy's nostrils flared, his hands curled into fists, his breathing grew too shallow, too fast. His eyes flicked toward the window, where lightning illuminated the room. Fear washed across his face for just a second, but Gabriel caught it. Freddy resembled a man standing on the edge of an abyss, too scared to fall in but too proud to run. "You think you're some kind of prophet now?" Freddy spat, but the edge of mockery in his voice cracked. He spun toward the door.

"I know what's coming," Gabriel said with certainty. "The hurricane? It's not just a storm, Freddy. It's God's judgment, closing in. You can feel it, can't you? That's why you're here—shaking, seeking answers."

Freddy whirled around, his face contorting, but the bravado was slipping. His voice wavered. "Go to hell!" He lunged forward, spittle flying. His finger jabbed at Gabriel's chest. "You're nothing but property. My property!"

Gabriel stepped into Freddy's space. Lightning flashed through the window, casting their shadows large against the wall. "No, Freddy. I'm God's property. And He's coming for what belongs to Him soon."

"Freddy—" Andre reached for his nephew.

Freddy pushed past Andre and flung open the door as if fleeing from the prophetic word. His footsteps echoed down the corridor like judgment. Taking a step to follow his nephew, Badeau surprisingly stopped at the threshold. He turned to Gabriel. "Care for a cup of coffee?"

48

W*ednesday, August 21*
"There. Freeze it," Eli said, pointing. "Military-grade perimeter fence. Same stuff we used in Afghanistan." The drone's flight controller cast a green glow inside Eli's Jeep. Rain pelted the canvas roof in a steady drumbeat. The real-time feed revealed layers of security Eli hadn't seen since his Army days.

Dakota zoomed in, highlighting the chain link with a tap. "Yeah, and those sensors—see?" A row of blinking red dots appeared. "Motion and heat detection every twenty feet. Whoever set this up knew exactly what they were doing."

"Run it back to that building hidden in the tree line."

The footage shifted, revealing a rectangular structure tucked beneath thick vegetation. Live oaks cast long shadows over the roof, almost swallowing it from view. Razor wire bristled along the welded panel fence, encasing the building like a steel snare.

"Geez." Dakota's whistle was low and sharp. "That's not just keeping people out. It's keeping them in."

The words were sour in Eli's ears. Somewhere inside this compound, Kiara and Aaliyah Johnson were trapped, waiting for someone to save them. Or worse—no longer waiting at all.

Lightning flashed, briefly illuminating Dakota's hardened expression. He pulled up another angle on the building near the main gate.

"Eight guards, maybe more inside." He gestured at a cluster of figures huddling for cover. "Kingsley's men are slacking."

"Don't underestimate them. Even the best military contractors stay inside to avoid the weather." Eli remembered his own Army experiences during Afghan dust storms.

"Well, let's take advantage." Dakota scrubbed a hand across his face. "A piece of cake, right?"

Thunder rattled the van. Eli studied the footage to formulate a plan. "See that maintenance shed on the east side?"

"Yeah?"

"Any patrol pattern?"

"Sporadic," Dakota said. "Very sporadic."

"Bingo." Eli checked his watch. "Hurricane makes landfall in ten hours. Their patrols will thin out even more."

"Why don't they just lock everything down and leave?" Dakota asked.

"Kingsley probably has too many kids to move without drawing attention," Eli's tone was grim. "If they scatter, someone will notice."

Dakota swiveled in his seat, his voice dropping. "You sure we shouldn't wait it out and call for backup?"

"The governor's tied up with disaster prep. After the storm, the state's going to be neck-deep in wreckage. No one's coming." Eli bit his bottom lip. "Monica's been waiting three months for her daughters. We're not waiting any longer."

The drone's camera pixelated. Static crawled across the screen. Whispering a curse, Gabriel's fingers flew over the keyboard. "Signal's breaking up. Storm's getting worse."

"Pack it up. We move in thirty." Eli gave his gear one last check—body armor, tactical vest, night vision. The weight settled on his shoulders like an old companion.

"You know if this goes sideways..." Dakota said, his voice calmer now.

"It won't."

"But if it does—"

"Then it was worth trying," Eli said, meeting his partner's gaze. "You have burial insurance?"

"Funny." Dakota snorted, dismantling the surveillance equipment with quick, efficient movements. "If I get killed, who's going to keep you alive?"

Outside, the wind howled, rising to a feral scream. Soon it would cover their approach. Eli's hand drifted to the photo in his vest pocket—two teenage girls, arms around each other, with their whole lives ahead of them.

"Hang on," he said under his breath to the images. "We're coming."

———

THE COFFEE MAKER IN THE SHADOWS' kitchen sputtered like something dying—a fitting sound for the questions Andre Badeau wanted answered. Through the dim light, he watched Gabriel measure grounds with steady hands. The boy's movements were precise despite the rain hammering the building's walls. This kid remained so calm, while

Freddy was back in his room falling apart. The power surged. Darkness swept through, tightening Badeau's chest before light returned—flashes of clarity, like his conscience, swallowed by familiar shadows. He wasn't ready for what lay within that darkness. Not yet.

Gabriel didn't flinch. The boy—no, the man—moved with the same quiet determination he had shown since Badeau first met him at the Mexican border. He radiated hope and helped others. The thought burned worse than cheap bourbon, especially considering how Gabriel seemed to carry that hope as if it belonged to him. Another power surge occurred. This time, the darkness lingered. Lightning slashed through a narrow window, revealing its glass along with Badeau's reflection—haunted eyes, stubbled jaw. He was the man who had taught his nephew cruelty and shaped him in his own violent image.

The lights hummed back to life. Gabriel poured two cups of coffee. Steam rose between him and Badeau like an offering...or a bridge, maybe. A bridge Badeau wasn't sure he could cross.

Gabriel slid a cup across the rickety wooden table. "Something on your mind?"

Badeau's fingers curled around the warm cup. This boy —weeks ago a stranger—dared to speak to him like an equal. Yet it was this boy's gift for deciphering dreams that made Badeau's failures with Freddy sting harder. The mug burned against Badeau's palms, and he welcomed the pain —something real to focus on besides the chaos churning inside. He stared into the steam, trying to lose himself in its spiral. "Freddy...Freddy wasn't always like this."

"Neither were you."

The words hit like a hammer to the chest—so simple, so true, yet harder than any accusation. Badeau took a scalding sip of coffee, the heat burning away his instinct to argue. "I taught him everything he knows—every trick, every short-cut, every cruelty."

Lightning strobed through the window. In the brief flash, Gabriel's expression held neither judgment nor pity—just the same steady patience that had earned Badeau's respect weeks ago.

"My papa once told me that a tree is known by its fruit," Gabriel said, tracing the rim of his cup. "But even a poisoned tree can be healed at the root."

Badeau barked a harsh laugh. "Where'd he learn that?"

"The Bible," Gabriel replied quietly. "Where all truth is found. The problem is, most people don't want to dig up the roots that cause them trouble."

The power flickered again. In the brief darkness, Badeau saw Freddy at twelve—his eyes wide as Badeau beat a nagging whore for money owed. By thirteen, Freddy was dealing weed. By eighteen, he had become Badeau's right-hand man, craving more power than Badeau could wield.

"I created a monster," Badeau said. "How do I fix that?"

"You don't," Gabriel replied, sipping his coffee. "But you can show him there's another way. The same way I'm showing these children there's hope inside these walls."

Badeau gestured at the barred windows. "Hope? In this place? Look around, boy. There ain't no hope here, no matter the location."

"So why did you pick here to talk when you have a comfortable room in the main house?" Gabriel said matter-of-factly. "Something inside you wants what I have, no matter your location."

Thunder boomed overhead, rattling the table. Freddy's empty gaze burned in Badeau's brain. "He's too far gone.

The drugs, the work we do. You didn't see him earlier—the look in his eyes..."

"Tell me about that look," Gabriel said, steady as always.

Turning from the table, Badeau wanted to stop this conversation, but something supernatural held him where he stood. "Empty," he said. "Like staring into a grave. I did that. Made him think like me—like control over others was everything." He paused to compose himself. "He's who he is because of what I am."

"And now?"

Badeau turned back to face Gabriel. "Now I'm watching him destroy himself. And these kids—" His voice cracked. "These children we—" He slammed his fist against the wall, harder this time, the pain shooting up his arm. "I've destroyed the lives of many just like them."

"Then change, Mr. Badeau," Gabriel said. "You can choose to change."

"Change?" Badeau laughed, but it sounded more like a sob. "How do you propose I do that?"

"You ever hear of the Apostle Paul?" Gabriel asked, his eyes unnervingly calm.

"Don't play games with Bible trivia," Badeau replied, his impatience flaring. "What's this saint from the Bible got to do with me?"

"Paul wasn't always a saint. In fact, he wasn't always a Christian. He was a hateful man who lived to persecute the Church, hunting Christians down, throwing them in prison, and being responsible for many of their deaths. He even taught others to do the same." He paused. "Just like you taught Freddy."

"And?"

"And God literally knocked him off his high horse, striking him blind so he could finally see." Gabriel pushed away from the table. "A man of violence became a man of peace. That encounter with Jesus changed everything about him."

The power died again, plunging them into absolute darkness. Gabriel's silhouette was a shadow against the storm-lit window.

"I'm no Paul," Badeau's voice was rough and broken. "I'm the one doing the persecuting."

"Exactly." Lightning illuminated Gabriel's face. "And like Paul, you've got a choice—keep destroying lives or help save them."

The lights sputtered back on, reflecting Badeau's broken expression in the window glass. But somewhere in that darkness, a spark had ignited—a possibility he hadn't considered. "These children..." Badeau's throat tightened. "If I help them escape—"

"It's not their escape that's important right now—it's yours." Gabriel stepped closer. "Ask God for His forgiveness and show Freddy there's another way—the same way Paul showed others after his eyes were opened."

Thunder cracked overhead, reverberating in Badeau's bones. He thought of Freddy's hollow eyes, of children torn from their families, of every terrible choice that had led him to this moment. "Tell me how." The words came out soft and slow. "Tell me how to save myself and Freddy before this storm kills us all."

49

Eli pressed against the mud, studying the estate's western perimeter as lightning strobed across the security fence he and Dakota would soon scale. Two missing girls—probably more. Only hours until the hurricane hit. Rain hammered sideways, pelting Eli's rain gear like shotgun pellets, and the wind—gusting over sixty miles per hour—wreaked havoc on their depth perception and timing.

Through his night-vision monocular, Eli scanned the terrain. The outer fence stood eight feet high, crowned with spiraling razor wire that gleamed briefly in the flash of lightning. Motion sensors perched like vultures on the trees beyond the fence line, while infrared cameras swept from poles every hundred feet. A few small pine trees lay uprooted, their root systems torn from the saturated ground, creating potholes and ankle-breaking obstacles. The storm might take down the sensors and cameras—or trigger every last one of them. Either way, they were going over.

Dakota tapped Eli on the shoulder with a flat hand and pointed to an old building about forty yards ahead. Its roof rattled like machine gun fire. Through the gusts of rain and wind, Eli spotted a blind spot between two sensor arrays. It was the only gap in a million-dollar security system. If Kingsley had the girls anywhere on the property, it would be behind this protection. The time on Eli's tactical watch read 0207. They had less than four hours before the eye wall hit —less than four hours to get in and out.

Dakota unfolded the tactical blanket, fighting to control the rubber-backed ballistic material as the wind tried to rip it away. One tear, one loose corner, and they'd fry on the electrified fence—if the razor wire didn't shred them first. Eli secured his end while Dakota anchored the opposite corner with a climbing piton, their movements synchronized from two years of working together. But they'd never operated in hurricane-force winds.

Testing each hold against the storm's assault, Eli went up first. Three points of contact, just like in the manual— except the manual didn't account for sixty-mile-per-hour gusts. A slip on the rain-slicked metal sent adrenaline surging through him. One wrong move, one lost grip, and the fence would spark him brighter than the lightning flashing overhead. He swung a leg over the top, straddling the fence line. Below, Dakota was already moving, a shadow among shadows, following Eli's path up. No hesitation— that's why they were still alive.

Eli dropped inside the perimeter, rolling to absorb the impact. The cold, wet earth smeared his gear, and he quickly gathered the blanket. Landing beside him, Dakota crouched low, flashing an approving thumbs-up. So far, no alarms. But the compound's security system could light up at any second, and they were still exposed. Too exposed.

Light beams swept across the compound. Two guards trudged through the wind-driven rain, their flashlights jittering wildly. Eli grabbed Dakota's vest and yanked him behind a cluster of azalea bushes. As the guards drew closer, Eli's stomach knotted. The shorter one moved with a slight limp, favoring his right leg. Rain-matted blonde hair gleamed in the flashlight beam. *The same operator who caught shrapnel at the boathouse.*

Eli leaned close to Dakota's ear. "The blonde one with the limp—he was at Stone's takedown."

Dakota's grip tightened on his weapon. Government-trained killers working for Kingsley. That explained the tactical gear and professional movements. The limping guard's partner, tall and broad-shouldered, stumbled, catching himself on his companion's shoulder. "This is crazy, man," the guard shouted above the wind. "What are we doing out here?"

Eli pressed deeper into the bushes as the beam swept past. The patrol moved closer, their heads bent against the rain. They passed nearby, too close—so close that the sheen of water dripping off their chins and elbows was clearly visible. Eli held his breath, waiting for the flashlights to swing their way. But they didn't—not yet.

A loud bang boomed as the wind caught the shed's door and slammed it against its frame. Both guards spun, their flashlights snapping toward the sound.

"Check it out," the bigger guard shouted over the wind. The beam of his light cut through the rain that now fell in sheets, hitting the shed squarely.

"Didn't expect that," Dakota whispered near Eli's ear. "Those guys are as insane as we are."

As the patrol moved away, lightning illuminated a drainage culvert about twenty yards to the left, revealing Eli and Dakota's only option. Water rushed from its mouth, gushing into the sodden earth. Eli tapped Dakota's shoulder three times—a signal to wait.

The guards reached the shed. The smaller one tugged the door open wider, disappearing inside with his partner.

Eli and Dakota dropped to their stomachs, crawling through the ankle-deep mud and water toward the culvert. The wind-driven rain lashed against their backs, providing some cover for their movements. Ahead, the channel opened up, but they needed to reach it before the guards turned back.

A crack of thunder rumbled overhead as Dakota slid into the culvert first. Eli followed, struggling against the current that tugged at his legs. The cold water rushed around them, rising higher as they pressed themselves against the curved metal walls. Above them, the guards' boots squelched as they passed by, unaware of their presence.

"Command to all posts," a radio crackled from one of the guards. "Grid power's down. Switching to backup generators. Check all security fences."

The water in the culvert was rising rapidly, forcing Eli and Dakota to go deeper as the angle steepened. A metal grate blocked their path. Eli knelt down and ran his fingers over the rusted bolts. After a few swift twists with the multi-tool he'd retrieved from his cargo pocket, he managed to remove the barrier. They emerged into a ditch, its steep banks offering cover. But the wind hit harder here, roaring through the open space like a freight train. Ahead, barely visible through the torrent, the massive live oaks Eli had seen on Google Earth stood silhouetted against the storm-black sky.

A generator's low thrum rumbled through the air. The backup power system was cycling on. Floodlights flickered to life behind the trees, sweeping the grounds in broad arcs. Two minutes, maybe less, before the patrol returned.

Movement on the bank stopped Eli cold. A figure stood there, outlined against the floodlights, wearing black tactical gear. Not a regular guard—this was someone else.

A dislodged tree branch, massive and splintered, crashed into the canal twenty yards ahead, providing them with brief cover. They scrambled up the bank and pressed themselves flat into the mud as the guards' lights swept over the debris.

Through the gaps in the wind-whipped branches, Eli saw it: an old wooden structure surrounded by another fence. A fence that crackled with blue sparks where the rain hit it. Backup generators buzzed nearby, keeping the power flowing even with the main grid down.

A gate stood at the center of the fence, reinforced and clearly motorized. There was no chance they'd get through without triggering alarms. Eli scanned for alternatives and glanced at his watch, which ticked past 0230.

Floodlights blazed to life, and the age's motor groaned as it opened. Eli pulled Dakota down as three figures stepped through the opening. He caught his breath as the tallest figure approached—Andre Badeau—the New Orleans pimp who'd abducted Eli's niece, Tara, two years ago before he vanished. But there he was, his Cruel face illuminated by the harsh light.

Badeau led the way, the young man who'd saved Kingsley at the gala trailed behind him with a young girl trailing with slumped shoulders. Lightning flashed, illuminating the girl's face as she turned toward the trees where Eli and Dakota crouched. His stomach tightened at the sight of one of the Johnson twins.

The pistol in his hand felt like a toy, useless and insubstantial. He wanted to act—to leap out and end this—but a voice in his head, cold and commanding, held him back.

Not now. Not yet.

Rage surged—so intense it nearly overwhelmed his focus. Andre Badeau was here, directly connected to Maxwell Kingsley. Eli's heart raced as he felt the weight of his mission pressing down on him. The storm outside mirrored his internal tempest, each crack of thunder fueling his determination.

With a deep breath, Eli steadied his grip on the pistol. This was no longer just about rescuing the twins—it was a reckoning. The girl standing next to Badeau, her eyes filled with fear, ignited a fierce protectiveness within him.

"Not today," Eli whispered to himself. He would storm this compound like the hurricane raging above, tearing down every barrier, every threat, until he reclaimed not just Kiara and Aaliyah but every child trapped in Kingsley's web of darkness.

No more waiting. It was time to act.

———

WEDNESDAY, *August 21*

Every instinct screamed at Eli to rush the gate, take Badeau down, and end this. But the odds were brutal—two operators against an unknown number inside the building, likely the security team they'd spotted earlier. Plus, they hadn't put eyes on the other twin.

Dakota aimed his M4 at Badeau as he guided the girl to an ATV. Eli grabbed his partner's vest. "Don't."

Badeau, the girl, and the young man who'd saved Kingsley jumped in. Lightning illuminated the Johnson girl's face as she turned toward the trees where Eli and

Dakota hid. For a moment, he thought she might see them.

"Are we really letting them take her?" Dakota asked in disbelief.

Eli nodded. "We're following them to the other twin." The gate whined closed behind the ATV, and blue sparks danced along the tracks. "Let's hustle," Eli said, starting to double-time in a crouched position, using the rain and terrain as cover. The patrol was somewhere between them and the main building.

Dakota's hand tapped Eli's shoulder three times—movement ahead. Another patrol ran from the guard shack, heading toward the generators. The storm was forcing them to check equipment more frequently.

Lightning flashed. The security team paused, conferring over a radio. One pointed at the canal where Eli and Dakota had emerged.

"They're sweeping back this way." Dakota's voice held an edge.

The ATV's lights shut off near the mansion's back entrance, the same entrance they'd used with the Haitian boy. Eli considered scenarios, each worse than the last. Let one twin go, possibly losing her forever, or abandon the other to rescue the unknown. Yet there was something else to consider—Andre Badeau. Eli owed him.

Thunder cracked overhead like artillery fire. Rain pelted Eli's face like icy needles as he sprinted up the winding driveway, his boots slipping on the wet asphalt. Wind and rain roared around him, drowning out everything but the frantic pounding of his heart. He glanced back at Dakota, who was right on his heels, his curls plastered to his forehead. They didn't speak. They didn't need to. The storm wasn't just their cover; it was their shield.

The house loomed ahead, its warm, golden light spilling out over the portico. Badeau was already there, one arm on Kiara's shoulder as he steered her across the slick stone tiles. His steps were hurried, his head on a swivel. The younger man walked with unnerving calm, his movements slow and deliberate, as if he had all the time in the world. It set Eli on edge. The guy's eyes darted to the tree line, scanning it with that same eerie composure. What was he looking for?

Flashlight beams slashed through the darkness, arcing through the thick trees. Eli instinctively pulled Dakota closer, pressing his back against the rough portico column. Rain poured off the copper gutters above them, the steady drumming almost deafening. It was as if the storm itself wanted to keep them hidden. He tightened his grip on the handle of his knife.

Through the beveled glass of the back door, Eli caught a faint sound—Badeau's voice. That slow, cutting drawl he'd heard in the Rigolets two years ago. Eli's stomach twisted. Badeau had already pushed the girl inside, but there was hesitation in his stride, as if something was bothering him. Then the man pressed on, his movements quick and deliberate.

A gripping sensation clutched Eli's chest. Tara—his niece—had once been led down a similar dark hallway on Commodore's yacht, *Leviathan*. Eli pushed the memory away. No time for that now. He reached for the doorknob. Locked. But Dakota dropped to one knee, pulling his pickgun from his pocket, rain dripping from his sleeve. He made quick work of it; the metallic click of the lock was almost too loud against the storm. Dakota stood, gave Eli a nod, and pushed the door open.

The cold air hit Eli like a slap, raising goosebumps beneath his soaked jacket. He and Dakota slipped through the entrance—the howling wind and crashing tree limbs were now muted, replaced by the distant echo of Badeau's deep drawl.

Eli motioned to Dakota, and they moved together, clearing each corner like clockwork. The pulse in his temple and every nerve screamed to stay alert. The mansion felt suffocatingly large—too many places to hide, too many ways things could go wrong. Badeau's voice faded.

Eli froze, scanning the area. One second, the three had been visible. Now, there was nothing. Not a sound, not a shadow out of place. Just an eerie, empty stillness where they had been, as if the house had swallowed them whole. Eli's hand tightened on his weapon.

"Where are they?" whispered Dakota.

A door slammed upstairs. Footsteps pounded down the marble steps at the hall's end. A figure emerged from the shadows, raising a pistol—Freddy Badeau. The psychopath who, two years earlier in the Rigolets, had shot Eli in the head. His grazed scalp had healed, but the scar burned fresh.

"Well, lookie here," Freddy's eyes were wild, pupils blown. "How's that fine niece of yours?" His gun hand trembled. He was high on something. Unpredictable. Dangerous. "Guess we get to finish what we started at that camp."

The barrel tracked between Eli and Dakota, back and forth, his sweat-soaked polo clinging to his chest. A dark stain spread under his arms, matching the fevered gleam in his eyes.

"Drop it, Freddy." Eli kept his voice low and steady. "No reason anyone should die tonight."

A twisted smile split Freddy's face. "Why not?" He touched his temple with his free hand. "I'll aim two inches lower this time."

Lightning rippled across the mansion's windows. Thunder followed, rattling the chandelier overhead.

Dakota eased to the left, trying to flank. Freddy's gun snapped toward the movement. "Don't. Just don't." His laugh was sharp and broken, more sob than threat. "Uncle Andre says I'm losing it. Maybe he's right. Maybe I'll just shoot you both and then myself."

Eli's muscles coiled. Could he take Freddy out before a shot was fired? His mind clawed at the memory of Tara's scream, the graze of Freddy's bullet burning his scalp. He shoved it down. Focus. Freddy wouldn't rattle him—not now. "Your uncle can't protect you," Eli said. "And trust me, you don't want to die."

Freddy blinked rapidly, like he was trying to clear static from his brain. His gun hand trembled harder. "You don't know what I want or don't want." His voice cracked. "Uncle Andre's the only one—" He sucked in a ragged breath. "The only one who ever cared for me."

"Where's the girl?" Dakota demanded.

"Here." The Johnson girl stepped from the corridor shadows, the boy who'd saved Kingsley's life with her.

Andre Badeau emerged from behind them, his face hard, his eyes fixed on Freddy. He raised his pistol from his hip—not at Eli, not at Dakota, but at his nephew.

"Put it down, Freddy."

Freddy flinched. His shoulders stiffened. But he didn't lower the weapon. "Uncle Andre?"

"Now, Freddy." Badeau's tone was iron. "Put the pistol down."

"I can't." Freddy choked out. "They'll take everything from us."

Badeau moved closer, slow and deliberate, his footsteps

soft against the marble. Freddy's eyes darted between him and Eli, panic pooling in their wild depths.

The tension broke like a thunderclap. Badeau lunged, grabbing Freddy's wrist and wrenching the gun free. Freddy let out a strangled cry, his knees buckling as the weapon slipped from his grasp.

Without hesitation, Badeau hurled the gun, sending it clattering up the grand staircase. It spun once, twice, before coming to rest near the feet of a tall, slender figure who stepped from the shadows at the top of the stairs.

Vivian Delacroix.

She bent gracefully, her perfectly manicured fingers curling around the gun's handle like it had been waiting for her. Straightening, she smiled—a sharp, glacial smile that chilled the air.

"Well, well." Her voice dripping with amusement. "What do I have here?"

Thunder crashed again, closer now. The mansion's lights faltered, plunging them into darkness for three heartbeats. When they fluttered back on, Vivian Delacroix stood at the top of the stairs. She held Andre's pistol loosely, almost casually, in one perfectly manicured hand. Her smile was sharp and cold, the kind that turned stomachs. "My, my," she said, her voice dripping with amusement. "Isn't this cozy?"

The gun swept across them, settling on Kiara. "I'm afraid Aaliyah's... indisposed."

50

Pins and needles pricked Kiara's fingers. The damp air struck her nose, thick with the scent of gunpowder and fear.

Vivian descended the stairs like a flame igniting. Red silk whispered with each step. Red lips curved in anticipation of victory. Red-tipped fingers caressed Freddy's pistol, now aimed at Eli.

She pulled the trigger.

Click.

The hollow sound shattered her composure. With a hiss of frustration, Vivian hurled the useless gun aside just as her driver stepped in front of her, weapon drawn and ready.

A flash burst from his muzzle, lighting up the stairway. The statue beside Eli exploded, spraying marble shards like shrapnel. Kiara covered her head as the fragments pelted the cold floor around her.

"Such perfect timing," Vivian laughed over the crack of gunfire. "Your sister just left with Max. By the time you find her..." She let the threat dangle, heavy and sharp.

Rage boiled within Kiara. After two months of watching

girls vanish from this place, she didn't need the rest of the sentence. She knew exactly what Vivian meant.

Eli's partner fired his rifle. The rapid shots thundered through the hall, the brass casings dancing across the polished stone like tiny, gleaming bells.

The driver slumped against the ornate balustrade, his body sagging like a marionette with its strings severed. For a moment, he hung there, limp and lifeless. Then he pitched forward, hitting each step on the way down. His gun clattered across the floor, skidding to a stop near Kiara's shoulder.

At the base of the stairs, he lay crumpled, a dark pool spreading beneath him. Silence followed, broken only by the faint ringing in Kiara's ears.

Then came the whisper of silk.

Kiara's gaze snapped upward as Vivian stepped from the shadows, her pale hand curling around the banister like a spider claiming its web. Not a hair was out of place. Her expression remained calm, the same practiced smile she wore every time Kiara saw her—serene, composed, and lethal.

Vivian glided down three steps and stopped, standing above them like a queen addressing her court. Her robe shimmered in the dim light, the crimson fabric catching the glow like fresh-spilled blood.

"Mr. Colt," she said with mock reproach. "All this violence. It doesn't suit you." Her gaze drifted to her fallen driver, then back to Eli. "Though I see you're quite capable of it."

The gun lay beside Kiara's shoulder, warm and heavy. Her fingers curled around it, trembling at first but growing steadier with each breath. All the fear, all the rage, all the anguish of the past two months seemed to flow into the cold metal in her hands. She rose to her feet, the pistol concealed behind her back.

"Where's the girl?" Eli demanded, his voice razor-sharp. "Where's Kingsley?"

Vivian's lips curved into a sly smile, her confidence unshaken. "Killing an armed man is one thing," she scoffed. "But an unarmed woman? Please."

Eli stepped forward and seized her elbow, steering her down the final steps. The silk robe rippled around her like the cloak of a fallen angel. She stopped mere inches from Kiara, her gaze cool and unbothered.

Kiara raised the gun. "You taught me something, Vivian," she said, her voice steadier than she'd expected. "About doing whatever it takes to get what you want."

For the first time, Vivian's mask slipped. Fear flickered in her eyes, cracking the veneer of control. "You won't shoot me," she said, but her voice faltered, a tremor betraying her composure. "You don't have it in you, dear."

"Two months ago, I would've agreed." Kiara's finger brushed the trigger. "But you changed all that." Her voice wavered, but the gun didn't. Tears stung her eyes, blurring her vision, but she blinked them away. "Last chance, Vivian. Where's my sister?"

GOVERNOR BORDELON'S shoulders knotted as he tracked the hurricane's red mass creeping northeast on the radar display. The first storm had finally moved into Arkansas and Mississippi, but the second system could swing north and hammer his battered coast again. His state had already suffered billions in damages. How much more could it take?

He wiped his damp collar, the gesture automatic after eighteen hours in this cramped space.

Phones chirped and keyboards clacked. Behind him, his emergency response team scurried between monitoring stations like worker bees building a hive, their whispered updates competing with the electronic thrum of equipment. Fresh coffee beckoned from the break room. How many cups could he drink in one night?

The storm's remnants pulsed on the screen, less dangerous now. Louisianans had to be exhausted. Yet they were out in force, helping neighbors, according to reports.

Dr. Meadows shuffled beside him, thick-rimmed spectacles slipping down his nose as he pressed a tablet against his rumpled khakis. "Governor." His voice barely contained his excitement. "The second system has stalled. New data shows it's actually turning south." He pushed his glasses up as he glanced at the display. "Tracking toward the Yucatán Channel."

Thank God. The tension melted from Bordelon's shoulders. One disaster at a time was enough. "Show me the track."

Meadows's fingers traced along his tablet, splitting the screen between the departing storm and the retreating threat.

"Governor." A young aide rushed forward, satellite phone extended. "Priority call from Eli Colt."

Bordelon's chest tightened, anxious about the news Eli might bring. "Colt?"

"We've got dozens of kidnapped kids here at the Kingsley estate." Eli's voice crackled through static. "Most are under fourteen. They need immediate evacuation."

Bordelon froze, the coffee in his stomach turning to acid. He flexed his free hand twice, then curled it into a fist.

Kingsley. Trafficking children. Deep down, Bordelon knew. Children's lives hung in the balance. And those blasted photos could bring him down.

"And Kingsley's on the move," Eli said. "He's got one of my twins with him. Heading for a private airport in New Rhodes."

Bordelon bit down hard on his fist. That demon wasn't going to get away. Not with a child. Not today. "How many children are at the compound?"

"Almost fifty. Some need medical attention." Another burst of static. "Governor, if Kingsley makes it to that plane—"

"Hold on Eli." Bordelon turned to the National Guard commander across the room. "General, I need a Black Hawk. Now."

51

T *hursday, August 22*

Thunder rattled the windows of Senate Committee Room #12, a relentless drumbeat from the storm outside. Damp jeans clung to Kiara's thighs as she huddled in the curved mahogany chair, sneakers squeaking faintly against the polished marble. Her stomach churned—not from hunger, but from Vivian's chilling words about Aaliyah at gunpoint less than an hour ago—*"He's taking her somewhere far away. His own personal treasure."*

The weight of the gun lingered in her memory, her hands still trembling as if she hadn't let it go. Snatching it from the mansion's floor had been instinct; pointing it—unthinkable. Yet in that moment, everything had narrowed to the cold metal barrel. Vivian's smirk had finally cracked when Kiara pressed it against her chest, demanding answers about her sister.

Gabriel's arm draped over her shoulders now, his warmth the only refuge in the well-lit chamber, though tension rippled through him every time Freddy's handcuffs clinked behind them.

"You're shaking," she murmured.

Two rows ahead, Vivian slumped in her chair, her designer robe caked with mud, matted hair plastered to her scalp. Handcuffed wrists rested heavily in her lap, the metal against pale, bloodless skin. Despite her disheveled state, her mascara-smeared eyes kept darting back toward Kiara, retreating quickly when their gazes met. The once-commanding woman appeared smaller now, diminished—but that only made the back of Kiara's neck prickle. A cornered snake was always more dangerous.

"I keep seeing her face," Kiara said softly, leaning into Gabriel. "When Freddy's gun didn't fire... Vivian looked so... surprised."

"Thank God Andre unloaded it," Gabriel replied, his voice low. "Protecting Freddy from himself while the drugs had him."

"He ended up protecting us too, didn't he?" Kiara's gaze drifted to Andre Badeau, who was slouched near the window with Freddy pacing feverishly behind him. The thought lingered—how close Vivian had come to killing someone that night.

Somewhere beyond the storm-lashed windows of the Louisiana State Capitol, Kingsley had Aaliyah. Sweet, trusting Aaliyah, who probably didn't even realize she needed rescuing.

Her sister's face flashed in her memory—beaming under cheap karaoke spotlights, chasing Vivian's empty promises of stardom. Then, as if on cue, Vivian's earlier words cut through her recollection like shards of glass: *"Max has... particular tastes. Young. Innocent. Moldable."* Kiara had nearly buckled under those words. *"Your sister? She's perfect. So eager to please."*

The sharp creak of the door jolting open brought Kiara

back to the present. A woman in a blue blazer entered, balancing a tray of sandwiches and water bottles, her broad smile painfully out of place. The smell of bread and deli meat turned Kiara's stomach. No meal could soothe the ache writhing inside her—not while Eli Colt and his partner hunted Kingsley to New Rhodes Airport, and not while every second dragged the distance wider between her and Aaliyah.

By the door, two state troopers leaned over a crackling radio.

"The trailing storm," one said casually, "is turning south—"

Kiara's eyes perked up. Maybe that would ground Kingsley's plane.

"Yeah, missing us completely now."

"Honduras is gonna take it straight on, though."

Gabriel tensed. Nico stopped breathing.

"Better them than us, right?"

A barely audible exhale slipped from Nico, shattering the fragile stillness in the room. He pulled his knees to his chest, curling inward as if to shield himself. Across the aisle, Andre Badeau stood slowly, his gaze flicking from Freddy's restless pacing to Nico's hunched form. For an instant, the hardness in his expression wavered. Gabriel reached for Nico's hand. Badeau froze mid-step, his fingers flexing uselessly at his sides. "Please," he said, his voice hoarse as he addressed the troopers. "I need to make a phone call."

The troopers glanced up, their faces blank with surprise. Then they laughed, a sound that sliced through the tension like a cruel blade.

The door opened again, cutting the laughter short. A tall woman in a crisp pantsuit strode inside, her heels clicking against the marble floor. In her arms was a bundle of dry clothes. "Good morning," she said warmly. "I'm Sarah Bordelon, the governor's wife." She handed Kiara, Gabriel, and Nico each a bundle, her gaze kind but piercing. "I'm so sorry for what you've been through. We're working to find a hotel for you, somewhere safe." Her attention shifted to Vivian, and the softness vanished from her voice. "As for you…" Her words struck like steel. "Our jail is too good for you. Trafficking children? In my state? I pray you and that partner of yours rot in prison for the rest of your lives."

Badeau stepped forward, raising his manacled hands. "These boys are from Honduras. Their family's in danger," he said, urgency spilling through his usual control. "I have contacts there—people in power. They can evacuate them before the storm hits. I just need two minutes with my phone."

Sarah Bordelon's eyes narrowed, studying him as if weighing his soul. Static burst from the trooper's radio. One of them tilted his head, listening. "The Blackhawk's approaching New Rhodes Airport."

A cold weight coiled in Kiara's stomach. She gripped Gabriel's hand tighter. Everything—Aaliyah, Gabriel's family, stopping Kingsley—hinged on the next few minutes. Each passing second dragged them closer to the brink.

52

Nylon straps dug into Eli's shoulder as the Black Hawk banked hard, the harness the only thing preventing a collision with Dakota beside him. Rain hammered the helicopter's skin in relentless sheets. Lights from New Rhodes Airport blurred into smeared streaks through the open side door, swallowed by the cloudy sky. At the doorway, the crew chief swung his 7.62mm door gun toward the approaching airfield, somehow keeping his balance despite the violent motion.

"One minute to target," the pilot crackled through Eli's headset, her Boston accent tight with tension. "Got eyes on a Citation M2 at your two o'clock. Engines spooling."

Gripping his M4, Eli glanced out the window. The business jet emerged from the storm's gray veil, its wet fuselage glinting beneath the terminal's emergency lights. Twin engines mounted high on the tail whined louder with each passing second, each moment slipping away from Eli's chance to reach Aaliyah.

"Movement on the ground," the crew chief broke in over

comms. "Two Suburbans approaching the plane. Seven... no, eight targets deploying."

Kingsley's security team spread out around the Citation's forward stairs in precise formation, visible through the rain-streaked window. Tactical gear marked them as the same operators from the estate hours earlier. One rifle snapped up, locking onto the helicopter's approach.

The chopper dropped lower, the crosswind tossing it like a toy. "Taking fire!" The mini-gun roared, a deafening growl overpowering the rotor wash.

"LZ's too hot," the pilot called. "Setting down behind the hangar."

Eli checked his magazine. "Dakota, we breach from the east. Tangos are focused on the terminal side." The Citation's cabin lights flared, illuminating a fleeting image of Aaliyah Johnson sprinting alongside Kingsley from the lead Suburban. The sight clamped Eli's throat tight, suffocating him with memories of helplessness he thought he'd buried long ago.

"Copy that." Dakota's voice stayed calm but clipped. "If that jet starts rolling before we get there—"

"Not happening." Grinding his teeth, Eli forced his focus back to the mission. He wasn't losing her. Not again. Not today.

The Black Hawk slammed down hard, using the hangar for cover. Eli and Dakota burst out, their boots splashing through puddles as they rushed toward the corner. The mini-gun's thunder lit up the sky, forcing three operators to dive for cover behind a fuel truck.

"Tangos at your two and four," Dakota muttered, dropping to a knee. Two quick bursts from his M4 dropped one of the operators.

The Citation's engines screamed, their shrill whine

nearly drowning out the chaos. Kingsley shoved Aaliyah up the forward stairs, his silhouette flickering in the downpour.

Forty yards of slick tarmac stretched between Eli and the jet. His chest pounded against his vest. If they reached the cockpit, they would lose her. "Cover me!" The order snapped out without hesitation.

Dakota's M4 roared in a steady rhythm, pinning down five operators. Eli surged forward, boots splashing over rain-slick concrete. A round hissed past his ear; another sparked off the ground near his heels. He didn't falter.

An operator emerged from behind the jet's nose gear, rifle raised. Eli's sights locked on him first—two sharp shots dropped the man in a crimson mist.

The jet jolted forward, brakes screeching as it crept toward the runway. Eli sprinted to close the distance. Twenty feet to the stairs. Fifteen. Muzzle flashes exploded from the open cabin door, forcing him into a headlong dive behind the landing gear. Bullets shredded the space he had just occupied, hammering into the rain-soaked concrete.

"Eli!" Dakota's shout came over the comm.

A figure appeared from the midst of the storm—an operator rushing toward Eli's position, rifle raised. Before Eli could pivot, the Black Hawk's mini-gun shredded the attacker. Blood and water mixed beneath the stairs, pooling around the splintered concrete. The remaining tangos scattered as rounds stitched a line of devastation across the tarmac.

Eli pushed off the landing gear, sprinting to reach Aaliyah. Two steps. Three. The cabin door loomed ahead, rain blurring the interior. Kingsley appeared in the doorway, dragging Aaliyah by the arm.

Inside, the narrow cabin was suffocating. Kingsley's hand clamped around Aaliyah's throat, the nickel-plated .45

pressed hard against her temple. His suit sagged, wrinkled and damp, silver hair jutting out in disheveled tufts. "Please help me!" Aaliyah cried as tears streaked her cheeks. "He said he'll kill me!"

"Shut up!" Kingsley's snarl wavered as beads of sweat trickled down his face. He extended the pistol toward Eli. "Drop it, Colt. You think you've won? You haven't. I own half the judges in Louisiana!"

The Citation began to lurch forward. "The jet's starting its takeoff roll," the pilot warned, her voice crackling in his earpiece.

"Sir!" the pilot shouted from the cockpit. "The helicopter's blocking the runway! The gun's pointed right at us!"

The jet lurched again, sending Kingsley stumbling. Aaliyah cried out, clawing at his arm.

"It's over, Kingsley." Eli stepped forward, his aim steady. "The governor's already talking to the FBI."

"I own the governor!" Kingsley spat as his wild eyes darted between Eli and the gun aimed at him. "I own this whole state! You think—"

The Black Hawk opened fire. Rounds tore into the jet's engines, ripping through the fuselage with a metallic scream. The Citation buckled, its nose slamming into the tarmac. Kingsley staggered, his grip faltering just enough.

Aaliyah's eyes locked on Eli's, a silent plea.

He didn't hesitate. The shot struck Kingsley's frontal lobe, snapping his head back. The .45 fell as his body slumped into an unceremonious heap. Aaliyah bolted from the corner, throwing herself into Eli's arms.

The cabin shuddered with the aftershocks of the gunfire. "Hold fire, Major," Eli barked into his comm. "Kingsley's down. Repeat—Kingsley's down."

The roar of the mini-gun cut off. Silence fell, save for

Aaliyah's sobs. Rain streamed through the shattered windows, mingling with the blood on the floor.

"I've got you, sweetheart," Eli murmured, holding her close. Her tears soaked into his vest, but he didn't let go. "You're safe now. Kiara's waiting. We're taking you home."

Dakota's shadow filled the doorway. "Tarmac's clear. Five tangos down, three surrendered." His eyes flicked to Kingsley's crumpled body and then back to Eli. "Nice shot."

Through the cabin window, the sun broke over the horizon, painting the sky in warm shades of gold and crimson. Light streamed in, cutting through the lingering chill of the rain soaking his clothes. He held Aaliyah close, her trembling finally easing against him.

Her nightmare was over, but the aftershocks lingered. He inhaled the crisp dawn air, carrying with it a fragile hope—a hope that he'd seen the last of monsters like Maxwell Kingsley.

53

F*riday, August 23*

A gleam of silver caught Gabriel's squinting eyes as the fuselage shone brightly, the plane's tires kissing the Baton Rouge tarmac. Beside him, Nico shifted restlessly from his right foot to his left, while Governor Bordelon stood stoically near the black SUV, his hands clasped behind his back. A breeze carried the sharp tang of jet fuel, overpowering the salt-heavy air that spoke of home.

Just two months earlier, the dock had been his world, where he dreamed of a white yacht with him at the helm and his entire family serving as his crew. Now, as the Honduran military transport rolled to a stop in a foreign country, those dreams felt more like the naïve longings of a favored son.

A lazy breeze sent ripples through the guayabera shirt he had purchased that morning. The crisp cotton felt foreign against his skin—too clean, too new—like the one Papa had bought him a lifetime ago. Back then, he had imagined a gleaming white yacht and himself at the helm, steering his family toward prosperity. Would that vision ever come true?

The plane's engines slowed to a whisper. Gabriel's heart pounded in his chest. In moments, he would see his family again. Would they recognize him? More importantly, would they recognize the man he had become?

The aircraft door swung open with a hiss, revealing a familiar silhouette. Ernesto stood tall, shoulders squared as always, carrying the weight of the eldest son. His gaze swept across the tarmac until it landed on Gabriel, and for a moment, the two brothers stared at each other, unmoving, until the hardness in Ernesto's expression crumbled.

He descended the stairs in long, hurried strides, all pretense of control abandoned. Before Gabriel could steady himself, his brother's arms were around him, squeezing tight enough to drive the breath from his lungs. Ernesto's shoulders shook with silent sobs.

A rush of movement followed—Oscar and Rafael barreling down the stairs, shoving and jostling as they raced toward him. Laughter and shouts rang out as they crashed into the embrace, turning it into a tangle of limbs, tears, and laughter. The smells of home—fish scales, salt air, diesel fuel—clung to their clothes, pulling Gabriel back to those early mornings on the dock, to a time when everything was simpler.

Through the blur of tears, a figure remained in the plane's doorway, unmoving. The shape was unmistakable.

Papa stood with one hand gripping the rail. Silver streaked his hair, and the lines on his face seemed etched deeper than before, carved by months of uncertainty and grief. For a long moment, he didn't move. Then, the stern façade cracked.

"Papá," Gabriel whispered, the word barely crossing his lips.

The first step was slow, then another, each more unsteady than the last. Halfway down the stairs, Papa stopped, his legs trembling as though they might give way. This was the man who had braved storms, commanded the sea, and never once faltered. Yet now, his hands rose to cover his face, his shoulders shaking with sobs he could no longer suppress.

The brothers parted without a word, creating a path for Gabriel. He didn't hesitate. His legs carried him forward, faster than he intended, until he reached the base of the boarding stairs just as Papa's knees gave out. Arms shot out instinctively, catching the older man before he could fall.

Papa's arms came around him, clutching Gabriel with a strength that didn't match his trembling frame. The tears soaking through Gabriel's shirt didn't matter, nor did the murmured words of apology and relief spilling from his father's lips. For all the weight Gabriel had carried—dreams of leading his family to prosperity, of proving himself worthy—it suddenly felt so small.

"Mi hijo," Papa choked, his voice rough and broken. "Mi hijo precioso."

The words hit harder than the storm Gabriel had recently weathered. He held him close, his own tears falling freely. All those dreams—of proving himself worthy, of earning respect—seemed so small now. What mattered was here, in this moment. He wasn't just another son. He had pulled them all back from the edge, a rescue born from desperation and Señor Badeau's well-timed call to the chief of Honduras's military.

A throat cleared behind them. Gabriel looked up to find

Governor Bordelon standing nearby, his eyes glistening with unshed tears. Papa straightened, wiping his face with steady hands, though his dignity had already slipped away.

"Señor Mendoza," the Governor said, addressing Papa with respectful formality. "I hope you'll accept my apology for your son's ordeal while in our state. My office is working to expedite immigration status for your entire family." He pulled an envelope from inside his jacket and handed it to Gabriel. "And Andre Badeau insisted you should have this."

Gabriel blinked, his mind still swimming in the haze of emotion. He opened the envelope and read the papers inside. It took a moment for the words to register. The document was a title deed. A yacht. Fifty feet. And the photo clipped to the corner—he recognized it instantly. The same white vessel that had carried him from Honduras to Cancun. The same white vessel of his dream. His dream that once seemed impossible was now all too real. "What happened to Señor Badeau?" he managed to ask in a hoarse voice.

Bordelon shifted, scratching his head. "It seems the federal government has taken an interest in him. He'll be in witness protection soon—testifying against some high-profile people. He wanted you to have the boat. He said you'd make better use of it than he ever did."

Gabriel's gaze dropped to the document again, his fingers trembling as he turned the page. The dream that had once felt so distant, so unreachable, now sat in his hands. But it wasn't just his dream anymore. The yacht, once a symbol of escape, had become something greater—a way forward, together.

"*Gracias a Dios*," he murmured, his hand tightening on Papa's shoulder.

When their eyes met, the lines in his father's face eased. For the first time in months, Gabriel felt relief and trust.

The future stretched before them now, as vast and open as the sea itself. And this time, they would navigate it each day—together.

54

S *unday, August 25*

A soft breeze swept over the back deck of Steve's Seafood Restaurant in Long Beach, Mississippi, carrying much of the summer heat with it. Eli pressed two fingers to his right temple, where Charles Reddick's pistol had connected at the start of the mission. The headache had mostly faded, but occasional twinges reminded him how close he'd come—three concussions in two years. Maybe that was pushing it.

Lindsey's hand covered his across the weathered table. "Another migraine?"

"Just a twinge." He forced a smile, but her eyes searched his as if she could see more than he said.

The waves lapped against the rocks by the jetty, their rhythm soothing, almost hypnotic. A pelican glided by banking sharply toward a splash in the Gulf. Eli replayed Monica Johnson's face as her daughters had run into her arms that morning—Kiara's laughter, Aaliyah's tears. Worth every dodged bullet, every throb in his skull. Worth getting arrested. And yet, something felt different this time. The stakes had shifted.

"I keep thinking about Aaliyah and what she went through." The words slipped out before he could temper them. Lindsey's expression shifted, her grip tightening slightly around his hand.

"I know. It's going to be a long road for her. The trauma she faced… it's like a shadow that clings to you."

"Do you really think she can recover from this?" Eli asked, his voice quieter now.

Lindsey leaned closer. "It's possible, but it will take time. She'll have moments of light—days when she feels okay—but then there will be shadows that threaten to pull her back in."

Eli nodded. "I wish we could do more for her."

"I saw to it." Lindsey's eyes brightened. "I arranged weekly counseling with a colleague in Mobile—a psychologist specializing in trauma recovery for girls. It'll be a safe space for her, and my colleague is one of the best."

"I'm not sure Monica can afford it," Eli said with concern.

"Safe Haven will pick up most of the cost," Lindsey assured. "I talked with Julia. She says Redemption Rescue can handle the rest."

The savory scent of blackened redfish and gumbo wafted from a server's tray. His stomach growled in response —the first real appetite he'd had in days.

His fingers drifted back to the sore spot on his temple. Lindsey caught the motion and crinkled her forehead. The same look she'd given him when she'd met him at the hospital after he and Dakota had brought Kingsley down. He exhaled slowly, letting his hand fall to the table. "I've been thinking about changing things up at Redemption Rescue."

She lifted her brow but said nothing.

"Dakota's ready to lead missions. He has been for a while." He surprised himself with how steady his voice sounded. "Julia's intelligence network is one of the best around. Better than some federal agencies, honestly."

Her eyes softened, reddening at the edges. She knew where he was going, but she waited for him to say it.

"I think it's time I step back. Focus on the administrative side—coordinating with law enforcement and building partnerships. Let Dakota handle operations." He massaged his temple briefly, the lingering throb reminding him of why this had to happen. "As you keep telling me, I'm not invincible."

A breeze caught Lindsey's auburn hair, and something shifted in her expression. Relief? Hope? Her fingers squeezed his. "Why now?"

He smiled, a touch of wry humor pulling at his lips. "Three concussions are enough of a wake-up call, but it's more than that. Redemption Rescue—it's bigger than me. It's not about one person running things. It'll outlast both of us."

The server arrived, setting down their iced teas. Eli ordered grilled snapper and garlic. Lindsey asked for a Caesar salad and gumbo.

When the server left, Lindsey hesitated, then pulled an envelope from her purse and slid it across the table. The Woman's Hospital logo caught his eye. His heart fluttered, then raced.

"What's this?"

"Open it." Her voice wobbled, her eyes shimmering with emotion.

His fingers trembled as he removed the grainy black-and-white image. It took him a moment to process it, but once he did, all the air emptied from his lungs. His vision blurred as he took in the unmistakable shape.

"Eight weeks," she said, her smile unsteady. "Looks like you've picked the perfect time to come off active duty."

Eight weeks? Something inside him unraveled. His future, the one he'd only imagined, stared back at him in the tiny, shadowy form from the ultrasound.

Eli's throat tightened as he shifted his gaze from the picture to Lindsey, and for a long moment, he just looked at her. His new world had narrowed to this—her and the news of his son or daughter.

The headache he had suffered earlier was already a distant memory. "I didn't think it could get better than today," he said softly. "I was wrong."

She laughed through tears, squeezing his hand tighter. "So was I."

The waves kept lapping against the rocks, the pelican circled back over the gulf, and everything, for the first time since they'd started Redemption Rescue, felt like it was exactly as it should be.

PLEASE LEAVE A REVIEW

If you have enjoyed this book, it would be a tremendous help if your could leave a review.

Reviews help me gain visibility and bring my books to the attention of other readers who may enjoy them. You can leave a review on My Amazon Book Page.

GET EXCLUSIVE WILL MARLER MATERIAL

Building a relationship with my readers is the best thing about writing. Join my Legacy Readers Club for more information on new books and deals plus:

A free copy of Eli Colt's adventure in Helmand Province, Afghanistan—"The Silver Star."

You can get your content for free by signing up on my website at www.willmarler.com.

ABOUT THE AUTHOR

Will Marler is an author of Christian suspense thrillers. He grew up in New Orleans, Louisiana and now lives on the Gulf Coast of Mississippi with his wife, Wendie, and their 100-pound Rottweiler, Bear.

This is Will's third installment of the Eli Colt Series.

For more information:
www.willmarler.com
will@willmarler.com